PRAISE FOR *THE BEST HORROR OF THE YEAR*

"Datlow unfailingly presents notable scary tales and—since her choices come from an immense variety of sources—even avid readers are unlikely to have encountered them all. . . . This is a perennial must-read for anyone who enjoys dark fiction."

—Paula Guran, *Locus*

"Ellen Datlow has been called the 'venerable queen of horror anthologies' by the paper of record itself [*New York Times*], and the 22 stories within the twelfth volume of her annual Best Horror of the Year anthology cement her status as royalty in the genre."

—Tonia Ransom, *Nightfire*

PRAISE FOR *THE BEST HORROR OF THE YEAR* VOLUME ELEVEN:

"Even with the overall high quality of the latest of Datlow's anthology series, there are some remarkable highlights . . . this excellent anthology demonstrates that Datlow's reputation as one of the best editors in the field is more than well-deserved."

—*Booklist* (starred review)

"Datlow has drawn her selections from a wide variety of sources that even the most dedicated fans may have overlooked, and her comprehensive introductory overview of the year in horror will uncover still more venues for great scares. This is an indispensable volume for horror readers."

—*Publishers Weekly* (starred review)

PRAISE FOR ELLEN DATLOW AND
THE BEST HORROR OF THE YEAR SERIES:

"Edited by the venerable queen of horror anthologies, Ellen Datlow. . . . The stories in this collection feel both classic and innovative, while never losing the primary ingredient of great horror writing: fear."

—*The New York Times*

"A decade of celebrating the darkest gems of the genre as selected by Hugo-winning editor Ellen Datlow, whose name, by this point, is almost synonymous with quality frights . . . [and] contributed by a murderer's row of horror authors. . . . Essential."
—*B&N Sci-Fi and Fantasy Blog*, "Our Favorite Science Fiction & Fantasy Books of 2018"

"With the quality ranging from very good, to fantastic, to sublime, there just isn't the space to discuss them all. . . . If I need to make a pronouncement—based on Datlow's fantastic distillation of the genre—it's that horror is alive, well, and still getting under people's skin. If you have even a vague interest in dark fiction, then pick up this book."
—Ian Mond, *Locus*

"A survey of some of the best horror writing of the last decade . . . highly recommended for anyone interested in contemporary horror and dark fantasy, as well as anyone looking for a collection of some of the best and most horrifying short fiction currently available."
—*Booklist* (starred review), for *The Best of the Best Horror of the Year*

"A stunning and flawless collection that showcases the most terrifyingly beautiful writing of the genre. Datlow's palate for the fearful and the chilling knows no genre constraint, encompassing the undead, the supernatural, and the cruelty perpetrated by ordinary humans. Exciting, literary, and utterly scary, this anthology is nothing short of exceptional."
—*Publishers Weekly* (starred review), for *The Best of the Best Horror of the Year*

"Datlow's survey of the first decade of her Best Horror of the Year series is also an argument about the field's major talents and trends. Its contents make a compelling case for the robustness of the field, a condition Datlow herself has done much to nourish."
—*Locus*, "Horror in 2018" by John Langan

"Award-winning editor Ellen Datlow has assembled a tasty collection of twenty-one terrifying and unsettling treats. In addition to providing excellent fiction to read, this is the perfect book for discovering new authors and enriching your life through short fiction."
—*Kirkus Reviews*

Also Edited by Ellen Datlow

THE BEST **HORROR**
OF THE YEAR

VOLUME THIRTEEN

EDITED BY **ELLEN DATLOW**

NIGHT SHADE BOOKS

NEW YORK

The Best Horror of the Year Volume Thirteen © 2021 by Ellen Datlow
The Best Horror of the Year Volume Thirteen © 2021 by Night Shade Books,
an imprint of Skyhorse Publishing, Inc.

Night Shade books may be purchased in bulk at special discounts for sales
promotion, corporate gifts, fund-raising, or educational purposes. Special
editions can also be created to specifications. For details, contact the Special Sales
Department, Night Shade Books, 307 West 36th Street, 11th Floor, New York,
NY 10018 or info@skyhorsepublishing.com.

Night Shade Books™ is a trademark of Skyhorse Publishing, Inc. ®, a Delaware
corporation.

Visit our website at www.nightshadebooks.com.

10 9 8 7 6 5 4 3 2 1

Library of Congress Cataloging-in-Publication Data is available on file.

Cover art by Reiko Murakami
Cover design by Claudia Noble

Print ISBN: 978-1-949102-60-4

Printed in the United States of America

Thanks to Adam-Troy Castro, Alvaro Zinos-Amara, and
Karen Heuler for their recommendations.

Thanks to the magazine and book publishers who sent me material for
review in a timely manner.

Thank you to Theresa DeLucci, Ysabeau Wilce, and Molly McGhee who
helped with the reading.

And special thanks to Jason Katzman, my editor at Night Shade.

Table of Contents

SUMMATION 2020

H ere are 2020's numbers: There are twenty-four stories, novelettes, and one poem in this volume. The story lengths range from 3100 to 12,000 words. Fifteen stories and the poem are by men, nine by women. The contributors hail from the United States, United Kingdom, Thailand, Italy, and Canada. For some reason, the overwhelming number this year are from the United Kingdom. Ten of the contributors have never before appeared in any volume of my *Best of the Year* series. Six have been in multiple volumes.

Awards

The Horror Writers Association announced the 2019 Bram Stoker Awards® winners on a YouTube Live presentation April 18, 2020—after Stokercon, scheduled to take place in Scarborough, England, was postponed as a result of the outbreak of Covid-19. The UK convention changed its name to ChillerCon UK, and will be held in 2022. Stokercon 2021 was held virtually, from May 20–23, 2021.

Superior Achievement in a Novel: *Coyote Rage* by Owl Goingback (Independent Legions Publishing); Superior Achievement in a First Novel: *The Bone Weaver's Orchard* by Sarah Read (Trepidatio Publishing); Superior Achievement in a YA novel: *Oware Mosaic* by Nzondi (Omnium Gatherum); Superior Achievement in a Graphic Novel: *Neil Gaiman's Snow,*

Glass, Apples by Neil Gaiman and Colleen Doran (Dark Horse Books); Superior Achievement in Long Fiction: "Up from Slavery" by Victor LaValle (*Weird Tales Magazine* #363) (Weird Tales Inc.); Superior Achievement in Short Fiction: "The Eight People Who Murdered Me (Excerpt from Lucy Westenra's Diary)" by Gwendolyn Kiste (*Nightmare* Magazine Nov. 2019, Issue 86); Superior Achievement in a Fiction Collection: *Growing Things and Other Stories* by Paul Tremblay (William Morrow); Superior Achievement in Screenplay: *Us* by Jordan Peele (Monkeypaw Productions, Perfect World Pictures, Dentsu, Fuji Television Network, Universal Pictures); Superior Achievement in an Anthology: *Echoes: The Saga Anthology of Ghost Stories* by Ellen Datlow (Gallery Books/Saga Press); Superior Achievement in Non-Fiction: *Monster, She Wrote: The Women Who Pioneered Horror and Speculative Fiction* by Lisa Kröger and Melanie R. Anderson (Quirk Books); Superior Achievement in Short Non-Fiction: "Magic, Madness, and Women Who Creep: The Power of Individuality in the Work of Charlotte Perkins Gilman" by Gwendolyn Kiste (*Vastarien: A Literary Journal* Vol. 2, Issue 1); Superior Achievement in Poetry: *The Place of Broken Things* by Linda D. Addison and Alessandro Manzetti (Crystal Lake Publishing).

The Life Achievement Award: Owl Goingback and Thomas Ligotti

The Silver Hammer Award: Leslie S. Klinger

The Mentor of the Year Award: Lee Murray

The Richard Laymon President's Award: Rena Mason

The Specialty Press Award: Paul Fry, SST Publications

The 2019 Shirley Jackson Awards, usually awarded during Readercon in Quincy, Massachusetts, were instead awarded in a virtual production July 12, 2020. The Jurors were Chikodili Emelumadu, Michael Thomas Ford, Gabino Iglesias, Kate Murayama, and Lynda E. Rucker.

The winners were: Novel: *The Book of X*, Sarah Rose Etter (Two Dollar Radio); Novella: *Ormeshadow*, Priya Sharma (A Tor.com Book); Novelette: "Luminous Body," Brooke Warra (Dim Shores); Short Story: "Kali_Na," Indrapramit Das (*The Mythic Dream*); Single-Author Collection: *Song for the Unraveling of the World*, Brian Evenson (Coffee House Press); Edited Anthology: *The Twisted Book of Shadows*, edited by Christopher Golden & James A. Moore (Twisted Publishing).

The World Fantasy Awards were, because of the Covid-19 virus, presented at a Virtual Convention put on by Salt Lake City Sunday, November 1, 2020. The Judges were Gwenda Bond, Galen Dara, Michael Kelly, Victor LaValle, and Adam Roberts.

The Lifetime Achievement Awards: Rowena Morrell and Karen Joy Fowler

Novel: *Queen of the Conquered* by Kacen Callender (Orbit); Novella: "Silver in the Wood" by Emily Tesh (A Tor.com Book); Short Fiction: "Read After Burning" by Maria Dahvana Headley (*A People's Future of the United States*); Anthology: *New Suns: Original Speculative Fiction by People of Color* edited by Nisi Shawl (Solaris Books); Collection: *Song For the Unraveling of the World* by Brian Evenson (Coffee House Press); Artist: Kathleen Jennings; Special Award–Professional: Ebony Elizabeth Thomas for *The Dark Fantastic: Race and the Imagination from Harry Potter to The Hunger Games* (New York University Press); Special Award, Non-Professional: Bodhisattva Chattopadhyay, Laura E. Goodin, and Esko Suoranta, for Fafnir, *Nordic Journal of Science Fiction and Fantasy Research*.

NOTABLE NOVELS OF 2020

Worse Angels by Laird Barron (Putnam) is Barron's third novel featuring former mob enforcer turned private detective Isaiah Coleridge, and it's moved from the subtle hints of the weird in the first two books to full bore supernatural in this one. He's hired to investigate a suspicious death and encounters a cult of the rich, who welcome the end of this world, as Coleridge encounters strangeness that might be real or chemically induced.

The Deep by Alma Katsu (Putnam) is a supernatural historical novel about the *Titanic* and her sister ship, the *Britannic*. A young woman who is assigned as steward to a wealthy family in first class miraculously escapes a watery death, only to find herself several years later as a nurse on the *Britannic*, now used as a rehabilitation center for badly wounded soldiers.

Red Hood by Elana K. Arnold (Balzer + Bray) is a fiercely feminist coming-of-age story about a teenage girl's journey to self-discovery and power in a world inhabited by boys and men who literally become wolves. This is a great read, by turns horrific, joyous, moving, and ultimately satisfying.

The Ancestor by Danielle Trussoni (William Morrow) is a powerful modern gothic, beginning with an unexpected inheritance requiring a young woman to travel to her ancestral home in Italy to claim it. Once there, she discovers both shocking and marvelous truths about herself and her family.

Coincidentally, *Mexican Gothic* by Silvia Moreno-Garcia (Del Rey) covers some of the same ground as the Trussoni novel for the first two thirds—except that it takes place in Mexico. A vain, spoiled young woman is sent to a remote mountaintop gothic home to check on a newly wedded cousin who has sent a crazy-sounding note to her family. The final third, though, is more Lovecraftian in its secrets, and more horrific than the Trussoni.

Ballistic Kiss by Richard Kadrey (HarperVoyager) is the penultimate volume of the energetic, entertaining, dark fantasy Sandman Slim series. James Stark, the last Nephilim (half human/half angel), is tasked with ridding LA's Little Cairo neighborhood of violent ghosts and tracking down a missing angel, and stumbles onto a secret club running excursions virtually guaranteed to kill at least some of their members.

Survivor Song by Paul Tremblay (William Morrow) is a brilliant, tense, heartbreaking pandemic novel. Written before and published just as Covid-19 was becoming a household term and a worldwide epidemic, the book perfectly captures the confusion, misinformation, and government missteps in handling an outbreak of virulent rabies that has jumped from mammals to humans. A pregnant woman and her friend, a doctor, try to outrun the virus in Massachusetts. Their relationship is what really makes the story special. Highly recommended.

Tender Is the Flesh by Agustina Bazterrica, translated by Sarah Moss (Scribner), is a grotesque, beautifully written/translated, deeply disturbing Argentinian dystopian novel about the official promotion of the breeding and consumption of humans, when a virus makes all animals poisonous. I've read books and stories about cannibalism before, but none of them delve into the details of the slaughter, nor the degradation of emotion and empathy in those who partake (most people). Highly recommended.

Malorie by Josh Malerman (Del Rey) is the excellent sequel to Malerman's bestselling novel (and movie) *Bird Box*. Malorie is paranoid—but with good reason. In a world where what you see can drive you mad, she has survived for twelve years by enforcing strict rules of engagement for herself and her two children, after the events of the first novel. But now those children are teenagers, chafing at her rules—wanting to live, not merely to survive. It's easy to empathize with both views and agonize for all three characters. Highly recommended.

The Only Good Indians by Stephen Graham Jones (Saga Press) is a brilliant, heart-wrenching horror novel about the breaking of cultural taboos, guilt, and vengeance. Four young Blackfeet commit a violent trespass on ancient land and years later a spirit of that land seeks retribution against them. As much of the novel's power lies in the straightforward depiction of contemporary Native American life as it does in the supernatural entity hunting its nemeses. Highly recommended.

The Loop by Jeremy Robert Johnson (Saga Press) is an absorbing, terrifying sf/horror novel about a northwest United States tourist town that becomes a hellhole of craziness and bloody, graphic violence overnight. A government conspiracy and bad science are almost certainly to blame for a nightmare that comes to threaten the whole world. But it's also a poignant story of several alienated teenagers banding together to survive an impossible situation. Highly recommended.

The American by Jeffrey Thomas (JournalStone Publishing) is a powerful and violent, fast-paced supernatural crime novel about a disfigured Vietnam vet who is called back to that country, years later, by the son of a friend when the friend's daughter is brutally murdered. The protagonist lost much during the war, but in exchange he's gained a supernatural insight into the darkness surrounding us and with that ability becomes entangled with two other Americans, both marked by incredible evil.

A Private Cathedral by James Lee Burke (Simon & Schuster) has all the hallmarks of Burke's Dave Robicheaux novels, featuring the ex-detective haunted by his predilection for booze, his experiences in Vietnam, and the loss of loved ones. Over the years the series has had more and more of the supernatural laced throughout, and this novel might have the most yet.

Two teenagers dream of playing rock 'n' roll but their respective crime families have other, darker plans. When the girl is given as a sex slave to the known pervert head of the boy's crime family, Dave and his best friend Clete find themselves embroiled in hallucinogenic and real nightmares that may crush their souls.

The Invention of Sound by Chuck Palahniuk (Grand Central Publishing) is a fast-moving, gruesome (without graphic details), satirical horror novel told in two strands. One about a man obsessed with finding his daughter, abducted seventeen years before, and who he is convinced is still alive. The other about a Foley artist who creates screams for movies, following in her father's footsteps. Their stories come together perfectly (and horrifically).

The Book of Lamps and Banners by Elizabeth Hand (Mulholland Books) brings back Hand's memorable anti-hero Cass Neary, a middle-aged, self-destructive, and very damaged individual who can sense "damage" in others. This time, she becomes embroiled in the sale, theft, and search for an ancient book that might enable a young visionary tech genius to recalibrate human trauma.

Wonderland by Zoje Stage (Mulholland Books) is a dark, suspenseful, totally effective supernatural tale about a couple from Brooklyn who move with their two children to the Adirondacks. What they discover in this beautiful, wintry, haunting environment is inexplicable, terrible, and dangerous.

Also Noted

Beneath the Rising by Premee Mohamed (Solaris Books/Rebellion Publishing) is a dark fantasy about two friends—one a child prodigy—who, because she invents something marvelous, become targets for Lovecraftian ancient ones who want to slip into our world to rule humanity. *The Roo* by Alan Baxter (self-published) is a short, fast-moving novel about a killer kangaroo that wreaks havoc on a small, outback town in Australia. Pulpy, violent, and fun. *The Living Dead* by George Romero and Daniel Kraus (Tor) is an epic encompassing the entire history of the zombie plague envisioned by George Romero in his movies. Started, but incomplete when Romero died, Kraus uses extensive notes to finish this new novel. *Clown in a Cornfield* by Adam Cesare (HarperTeen) is a timely slasher pitting young vs. old and tradition vs. progress as several high schoolers are blamed by their elders for, well, basically everything bad that's ever happened in their small town. *The Butchers' Blessing* by Ruth Gilligan (Tin House) is about a group of eight men—known as Butchers—in rural Ireland, who annually travel from farm to farm, slaughtering and dressing cattle. Tradition and modern life clash violently. *The Boatman's Daughter* by Andy Davidson (MCD/FSG) is an imaginative, brutal southern Gothic that occasionally trips over its overly complicated plot but never fails to grip the reader. *The Fourth Whore* by EV Knight (Raw Dog Screaming Press) is about the accidental release of Lilith into the world, seeking revenge for herself and all women. *The Children of Red Peak* by Craig DiLouie (Hachette/Redhook) is about the adult survivors of a religious cult who are drawn back to the place they grew up. *The Dirty South* by John Connolly (Atria/Emily Bestler) is the eighteenth title in the Charlie Parker series of supernatural thrillers, this one going back to the beginning of the protagonist's career. *We Hear Voices* by Evie Green (Berkley) is about a child who, having recovered from a deadly disease, is haunted by an imaginary friend that influences him to become increasingly violent. *Lucifer and the Child* by Ethel Mannin (The Swan River Press) was originally published in 1945. The bestselling author, who died in 1984, published more than fifty novels and numerous collections of stories, autobiographical, political, and travel writing. It is the only full-length work of speculative fiction by Mannin. *The Return* by Rachel Harrison (Berkley) is about a woman who disappears for two years, then returns. Three of her close friends from college decide to meet up with her for a weekend at a remote inn, and find her very different from the person they knew. *Seeing Things* by Sonora Taylor (self-published) is about a thirteen-year-old girl who is the only one who sees blood in the hallway of her school and subsequently the ghost of a girl in a locker. *Pine* by Francine Toon (Doubleday) is a gothic debut taking place in the Scottish Highlands, where mysterious and deadly things happen. *One Who Was With Me* by Conrad Williams (Earthling Publications) is about a family that moves from London to a village in the south of France after a brutal home invasion, attempting to rebuild their lives. *Munky* by B. Catling (The Swan River Press) is a whimsical farce about a monk haunting a village in England between the two World Wars, and what happens when a ghost hunter is brought in. *The Hollow Ones* by Guillermo de Toro and Chuck Hogan (Grand Central Publishing) opens with an FBI agent forced to kill her partner, who has become inexplicably violent. *The Storm* by Paul Kane (PS Publishing) is about the monstrous creatures unleashed by a storm in England. *Dead Lies Dreaming* by Charles Stross (A Tor.com Book) is part of Stross's Laundry Files series and takes place in a UK ruled over by a revived Elder God Prime Minister and magical enforcers. A mixture of thriller, horror, and satire. *The Hollow Places* by T. Kingfisher (Saga Press) is a tense, very enjoyable novel inspired by Algernon Blackwood's novella *The Willows*. A thirty-four-year-old divorcee goes to live with a beloved uncle and help run his Glory to God Museum of Natural Wonders, Curiosities and Taxidermy. She discovers a portal to another world within his house and things get weird and dangerous.

MAGAZINES, JOURNALS, AND WEBZINES

I believe it's important to recognize the work of the talented artists working in the field of fantastic fiction, both dark and light. The following created dark art that I thought especially noteworthy in 2020: Daniele Serra, Sam Dawson, Paul Lowe, Richard Wagner, Ben Baldwin, John Coulthart, Reiko Murakami, Glenn Chadbourne, K. R. Teryna, Harry O. Morris, Victo Ngai, Vince Haig, Iris Compiet, Les Edwards, Wendy Saber Core, Liam Barr, Stephen Mackey, Marko Stamatovic, Andrey Kiselev, George Cotronis, Vincent Chong, Fintan Magee, Danielle Tunstall, Adrian Borda, Mike Davis, Dave McKean, Samuel Araya, and Sarah Kushwara.

Rue Morgue edited by Andrea Subissati is an entertaining Canadian non-fiction magazine for horror movie aficionados, with up-to-date information on most of the horror films being released. The magazine also includes interviews, articles, and gory movie stills, along with regular columns on books, horror music, and graphic novels.

BFS Journal edited by Sean Wilcock is a twice yearly non-fiction perk of membership in the British Fantasy Society. It has reviews, scholarly articles, and features about recent conventions. *BFS Horizons* edited by Shona Kinsella and Ian Hunter is the fiction companion to *BFS Journal*. There were notable dark stories and poetry by Jenni Coutts, Eric Ortlund, A. N. Myers, Ashley Stokes, Daniel Hinds, Patrick Creek, and Lorna Smithers.

The Green Book: Writings on Irish Gothic, Supernatural, and Fantastic Literature edited by Brian J. Showers is an excellent resource for discovering underappreciated Irish writers. Three issues were published in 2020.

The first Issue #14, is dated 2019 but came out the summer of 2020. It contains reminiscences and interviews with writers active in the nineteenth through mid-twentieth century by their contemporaries, plus first-hand accounts of ghostly occurrences. The second issue of 2020 is (unusually) an all-fiction issue of nine supernatural reprints by Irish-born writers, such as Rosa Mulholland, Dorothy Macardle, and Robert Cromie, among others. The third issue continues to serialize *The Guide to Irish Writers of Gothic, Supernatural and Fantastic Literature*, publishing ten new entries. Showers and Jim Rockhill co-edited the volume.

Wormwood edited by Mark Valentine is an excellent journal for a general audience. The one issue published in 2020 included six articles, and review columns by Reggie Oliver and John Howard.

Penumbra No. 1 edited by S. T. Joshi is a promising new annual journal of weird fiction and criticism. This issue presents nine pieces of new fiction plus six poems, and articles about the work of China Miéville, Simon Strantzas, Edith Wharton, John Collier, and others. There was notable fiction by Dylan Henderson, Mark Samuels, and Michael Parker.

Dead Reckonings: A Review of Horror and the Weird in the Arts edited by Alex Houstoun and Michael J. Abolafia published two excellent issues in 2020, both filled with reviews, commentaries, and essays. There's a particularly interesting piece by Darrell Schweitzer in the spring issue about an earlier, longer version of John W. Campbell's great novella *Who Goes There?* The story—with three opening chapters that were eventually cut from the version we know—was originally submitted as *Frozen Hell* to *Argosy* magazine, and was rejected. According to Schweitzer, the published version is the better for it.

Lovecraft Annual edited by S. T. Joshi is a must for those interested in Lovecraftian studies. The 2020 volume includes wide-ranging essays about the author's work, life, and philosophies.

Supernatural Tales edited by David Longhorn is as an excellent source of supernatural fiction. There were three issues in 2020, with notable stories by Steve Duffy, Tim Foley, Tom Johnstone, Sam Dawson, James Machin, Michael Kelly, Victoria Day, William Curnow, and Chloe N. Clark.

Not One of Us edited by John Benson is one of the longest running small press magazines. It's published twice a year and contains weird and dark fiction and poetry. In addition, Benson puts out an annual "one-off" on a specific theme. There were notable stories and poetry in 2020 by Dan Coxon, Mark A. Nobles, Steve Toase, Phoebe Low, Hudson Wilding, Mark Seneviratne, Jennifer Crow, Pam Bissonnette, Jonny Spinasanto, Gerry Leen, Alexandra Seidel, Cate Gardner, and Rob Francis.

Nightmare edited by John Joseph Adams is a monthly webzine of horror and dark fantasy. It publishes articles, interviews, book reviews, and an artists' showcase, along with two reprints and two original pieces of fiction per month. During 2020, it published notable horror by Benjamin Percy, Ben Peek, Angela Slatter, Adam-Troy Castro, G. V. Anderson, Carlie St. George, Adam R. Shannon, Vajra Chandrasekera, Ray Nayler, and Milly Ho.

Conjunctions 74: Grendel's Kin: The Monster Issue edited by Bradford Morrow is a long-running literary journal published by Bard College that often contains the literature of the fantastic and/or horror. This issue is full of horror and the strongest, darkest stories are by Brian Evenson, Elizabeth Hand, Joanna Ruocco, Sofia Samatar, Lucas Southworth, Jeffrey Ford, Julia Elliott, Joyce Carol Oates, Karen Heuler, Terese Svoboda, Justin Noga, and Quinton Ana Wikswo.

The New Gothic Review is an online magazine of gothic fiction published by Ian McMahon. It debuted with two issues that show promise, with notable stories by Rebecca Parfett, Holly Kybett Smith, Heather Parry, and Nadine Rodriguez.

Weird Horror edited by Michael Kelly is a new, promising semi-annual horror magazine featuring fiction, articles, and movie and book review columns. The first issue was published in October with non-fiction by Simon Strantzas and Orrin Grey, and with notable stories by Steve Toase, Steve Duffy, Shikhar Dixit, Naben Ruthnum, and John Langan.

Black Static edited by Andy Cox continues its long run as the best, most consistent venue for horror fiction. Alas, Cox has mentioned that he's planning on closing down the magazine once he runs all the current inventory. This will be an incalculable loss to the field. In addition to essays, interviews, and book and movie reviews there was notable fiction by Lucie McKnight Hardy, Tim Cooke, Gregory Norman Bossert, Ray Cluley, Maria Haskins, Ainslie Hogarth, Christopher Kenworthy, Philip Fracassi, Andrew Reichard, Danny Rhodes, Steve Rasnic Tem, Shaenon K. Garrity, Françoise Hardy,

David Martin, Keith Rosson, and Stephen Volk. The Haskins and Volk are reprinted herein.

Phantasmagoria edited by Trevor Kennedy is a bimonthly magazine of horror, science fiction, and fantasy—I'd never seen it before receiving #3, part of a Special Edition series featuring M. R. James. Included are articles about and by James, and a reprint of his famous "Oh, Whistle, and I'll Come to You, My Lad." Plus a bibliography by Stephen Jones and Jamesian fiction reprints and a few original stories and poetry. There was a notable new story by Dean M. Drinkel. The issue features excellent art and spot illustrations by Les Edwards, Jim Pitts, James McBryde, Allen Koszowski, Dave Carson, Peter Coleborn, Randy Broecker, Stephen Jones, and Gch Reilly.

The Horror Zine edited by Jeani Rector is a monthly webzine that has been publishing online for eleven years. It features fiction, poetry, art, news, and reviews. Each issue include reprints by well-known writers with new stories by newcomers.

LampLight: A Quarterly Magazine of Dark Fiction edited by Jacob Haddon published some excellent literary horror during 2020, including notable stories by Priya Sridhar, J. A. W. McCarthy, Julie Mandelbaum, A. J. Bermudez, Monte Lin, Emily Ruth Verona, and Brigitte N. McCray.

Midnight Echo is the magazine of the Australasian Horror Writers Association. It's published annually, and the 2020 issue was guest edited by Lee Murray. There were some very good dark stories and poems by Jay Caselberg, Melanie Harding-Shaw, Rebecca Fraser, Joanne Anderton, and J. A. Haigh.

Podcasts have become more popular for *everything*, and horror is no exception. These two have been around awhile: *Pseudopod* edited by Shawn Garrett and Alex Hofelich, and hosted by Alasdair Stewart, is a weekly show that's been broadcasting readings of original and reprinted stories since 2006. There were notable stories featured in 2020 by Christi Nogle, Johnny Compton, Jonathan Lewis Duckworth, Lyndsie Manusos, A. C. Wise, Wendy N. Wagner, and Christine Lucas. *Tales to Terrify* is another weekly. It's been broadcasting readings of originals and reprints since 2012, and is hosted and produced by Drew Sebesteny. There were notable stories in 2020 by Jenny Blackford and Lauren Mills.

Mixed-genre Magazines

Bourbon Penn edited by Erik Secker, already good, gets better with each issue, mixing, horror, sf, and weird fiction. It's supported by a Patreon and is well worth the investment. The best horror stories in the three 2020 issues are by Chip Houser, Corey Farrenkopf, Casey Forest, Mark Pantoja, Erin K. Wagner, Barton Aikman, Crystal Lynn Hilbert, E.C. Barrett, Josh Pearce, and Vincent H. O'Neil. *The Magazine of Fantasy and Science Fiction* edited by C. C. Finlay (recently taking over the helm is Sheree Renée Thomas) is one of the longest running sf/f/h magazines in existence. Although it mostly publishes science fiction and fantasy, it also publishes very good horror. The strongest horror stories of 2020 were by Albert E. Cowdrey, Julianna Baggott, Richard Bowes, Holly Messinger, Essa Hensen, Mel Kassel, Rebecca Zahabi, Stephanie Feldman, Amanda Hollander, R.S. Benedict, M. Rickert, Ashley Blooms, Sarina Dorie, and Melissa Marr. *Weird Fiction Review Number 10* is dated fall 2019, but didn't come out until 2020. It was edited by John Pelan and contains almost four hundred pages of weird fiction, articles, and illustrations. The strongest of the dark stories are by Gemma Files, Kaaron Warren, Orrin Grey, Gregory Bossert, and Richard Gavin. *Weirdbook* edited by Doug Draa published one issue in 2020. Although there's usually more dark fantasy than horror, there were notable darker pieces by Adrian Cole and Rivka Jacobs. *F(r)iction* edited by Dani Hedlund sometimes refers to itself as a "literary anthology," other times as a journal. It's published by the Brink Literacy Project and proceeds support their nonprofit mission to "foster a love of literature, increase literacy rates, and empower underserved communities through storytelling." The magazine rarely publishes horror, but the three issues published in 2020 presented some well-wrought darker fiction by Sachin Waikar, Stephen Graham Jones, and Benjamin Percy. *Vastarien: A Literary Journal* is an excellent magazine of the uncanny and weird, edited by Matt Cardin and Jon Padgett. Two issues were published in 2020, the second one over three hundred pages. Most of the work is fiction, but there is occasional nonfiction as well. Some of the stories are dark enough to be classified as horror. The notable dark stories are by Miguel Fliguer, Matthew M. Bartlett, Lora Gray, David Stevens, Ivy Grimes, Jessica Ann York, Eddie Generous, Alex Jennings, Sam Hicks, Christopher Ropes, Todd Keisling,

Sarah L. Johnson, M. Christine Benner Dixon, Avra Margariti, and Cody Goodfellow. The Hicks is reprinted herein. The Tor.com website publishes stories and novelettes almost weekly (although not in December). Several in-house and freelance editors acquire fiction, including myself. There's a mixture of science fiction, fantasy, dark fantasy, and horror. The notable horror stories published in 2020 were by Stephen Graham Jones, M. Rickert, Usman T. Malik, Melissa Marr, Claire Wrenwood, Brian Evenson, Zin E. Rocklyn, Ian Rogers, Matthew Pridham, Alex Sherman, and Sarah Pinsker, this last reprinted herein. *The Dark*, a monthly webzine edited by Silvia Moreno-Garcia and Sean Wallace, publishes more dark fantasy than horror but, in 2020, there were notable dark stories by Steve Rasnic Tem, Kristi DeMeester, Orrin Grey, Stephen Volk, Tobi Ogundiran, Clare Madrigano, Gabriela Santiago, Ebuka Prince Okoroafor, and Kali Napier. *Sirenia Digest* has been published by Caitlín R. Kiernan for several years as an early iteration of Patreon. Sponsors pay a set amount for a monthly, emailed digest of new dark and weird stories, vignettes, and other bits springing from the mind of this excellent writer. Simon Bestwick began publishing original short stories on his Patreon account in 2020, and several are quite good, including one reprinted herein. *Uncanny* edited by Lynne M. Thomas and Michael Damien Thomas is a monthly webzine publishing fantasy, speculative, weird fiction, and occasionally horror poetry; it also runs podcasts, interviews, essays, and art. In 2020, there were notable dark stories by Rae Carson, Kornher-Stace, Arkady Martine, and Natalie Theodoridou. *Weird Tales* has been resurrected once more—issue 364 was published mid-December. Edited by Jonathan Maberry and featuring thirteen stories, flash fiction, and poetry. It includes notable horror fiction and poetry by Gregory Frost, Rena Mason, Lee Murray, Alessandro Manzetti, and Linda D. Addison. *Asimov's Science Fiction* edited by Sheila Williams is primarily a science fiction magazine but sometimes publishes fantasy or horror. In 2020, there were notable dark stories by Michael Libling, Y.M. Pang, Jason Sanford, and Rich Larson. The Sanford is reprinted herein. *Lackington's* edited by Ranylt Richildis bills itself as speculative, but sometimes publishes horror. In 2020, there were notable dark stories by Mike Allen, Steve Toase, and A. Z. Louise.

Some other magazines/webzines, and websites that on occasion publish dark work are K-Zine, Kaleidotrope, On Spec, and Aurealis.

ANTHOLOGIES

Fighters of Fear edited by Mike Ashley (Telos Publishing) is an anthology of thirty-one reprints about occult detectives, ranging from stories by writers such as Sheridan Le Fanu, Arthur Machen, and Robert M. Chambers, to more recent works by Manly Wade Wellman, Jessica Amanda Salmonson, and Mark Valentine.

Midnight Under the Big Top: Tales of Murder, Mayhem, and Magic edited by Brian James Freeman (Cemetery Dance Publications) is about circuses, and contains thirty-eight stories and poems. Nine of the stories and fourteen of the poems are published for the first time. The best are by Kelley Armstrong, Lisa Morton, Josh Malerman, Alessandro Manzetti, and Stephanie Wytovich.

Cursed edited by Marie O'Regan and Paul Kane (Titan Books) is an anthology about all kinds of curses. Seven of the twenty stories and poems are reprints. The best of the originals are by Catriona Ward, M. R. Carey, Maura McHugh, Alison Littlewood, Tim Lebbon, Lilith Saintcrow, James Brogden, and Angela Slatter.

Miscreations: Gods, Monsters & Other Horrors edited by Doug Murano and Michael Bailey (Written Backwards) contains twenty-three stories and poems (two reprints). With a foreword by Alma Katsu. The strongest originals are by Linda D. Addison, Josh Malerman, Max Booth III, Ramsey Campbell, Laird Barron, Brian Hodge, and Joanna Parypinski.

Shadowy Natures edited by Rebecca Rowland (Dark Ink Books) contains twenty-one new stories of psychological horror. The most interesting are by Lee Rozelle, C. W. Blackwell, and Scott Milder.

Arterial Bloom edited by Mercedes M. Yardley (Crystal Lake Publishing) is a nicely varied, unthemed anthology of sixteen stories, two of them reprints. The strongest are by Carina Bissett, Jimmy Bernard, Grant Longstaff, Kelli Owen, Linda J. Marshall, John Boden, Naching T. Kassa, and Dino Parenti. With a foreword by Linda D. Addison.

The Alchemy Press Book of Horrors 2 edited by Peter Coleborn and Jan Edwards (The Alchemy Press) is an all original, unthemed anthology of seventeen horror stories. The most impressive are by Pauline E. Dungate, Samantha Lee, Garry Kilworth, Pete W. Sutton, Eygló Karlsdóttir, Thana

Niveau, Tim Jeffreys, Sharon Gosling, and Gail-Nina Anderson. The Sutton is reprinted herein.

The Horror Zine's Book of Ghost Stories edited by Jeani Rector and Dean H. Wild (Hellbound Books) has twenty-six original modern ghost stories—mostly by newcomers, with a few by well-known writers. The best are by Joe R. Lansdale and a collaboration by Graham Masterton and Dawn G. Harris. With a foreword by Lisa Morton.

The Ghosts and Scholars Book of Mazes edited by Rosemary Pardoe (Sarob Press) features fourteen supernatural stories about mazes, six of them new. The chilling originals are by Victoria Day, C. E. Ward, Christopher Harman, Helen Grant, Katherine Haynes, and John Howard. The Harman is reprinted herein.

The Fiends in the Furrows II: More Tales of Folk Horror edited by David T. Neal & Christine M. Scott (Nosetouch Press) is a worthy follow-up to the first volume of tales, from which I reprinted two stories in *The Best Horror of the Year Volume Eleven*. This time there are eleven new stories, with especially notable ones by Jack Lothian, Alys Hobbs, Elizabeth Twist, Neil McRobert, Hazel King, Kristi DeMeester, and Tim Major. The Lothian is reprinted herein.

It Came From the Multiplex edited by Joshua Viola (Hex Publishers) pays nostalgic homage to the horror movies of the '80s, with fourteen stories (one reprint). The strongest are by Stephen Graham Jones, Steve Rasnic Tem, and Orrin Grey.

Weird Women: Classic Supernatural Fiction by Groundbreaking Female Writers 1852-1923 edited by Lisa Morton and Leslie S. Klinger (Pegasus Books) contains a selection of twenty-one stories by prominent writers such as Ellen Glasgow, Frances Hodgson Burnett, Marjorie Bowen, Charlotte Perkins Gilman, and others.

The Valancourt Book of World Horror Stories Vol. 1 edited by James D. Jenkins and Ryan Cagle (Valancourt Books) showcases twenty horror stories from around the world, all published in English for the first time. It's a fascinating look at the differences and similarities in horrific concerns from a variety of cultures. There were notable stories by Benardo Esquinca, Michael Roch, Christien Boomsma, Anders Fager, Marco Hautala, and Lars Ahn.

Great British Horror 5: Midsummer Eve edited by Steve J. Shaw (Black Shuck Books) continues its excellent annual series of original anthologies showcasing ten British writers and one from outside Great Britain, this time loosely themed around folk horror. There were notable stories by Alisa Whiteley, Robert Shearman, Simon Clark, Kelly White, Stewart Hotson, and Jenn Ashworth.

Shadows and Tall Trees 8 edited by Michael Kelly (Undertow Publications) is a predictably excellent annual venue for weird, often dark short fiction. This year's volume includes eighteen stories. There were especially notable ones by Alison Littlewood, Carly Holmes, Brian Evenson, Charles Wilkinson, Rebecca Campbell, V. H. Leslie, Seán Padraic Birnie, and Neil Williamson.

Don't Turn Out the Lights edited by Jonathan Maberry (HarperCollins) is a tribute to Alvin Schwartz's children's horror anthology series *Scary Stories to Tell in the Dark*. The volume is presented by the Horror Writers Association and contains thirty-five brief tales intended for very young readers. The more effective ones are by Linda A. Addison, Kim Ventrella, Madeleine Roux, and Tananarive Due.

Places We Fear to Tread edited by Brhel & Sullivan (Cemetery Gates Media) is an original anthology of twenty-five stories and one poem about weird happenings in real places around the world. There are notable stories by Gwendolyn Kiste, Sonora Taylor, Andrew Cull, C. W. Briar, and Jessica Ann York.

After Sundown edited by Mark Morris (Flame Tree Publishing) is an excellent, all original, unthemed anthology of twenty stories. Most of the stories are very good, by both the newcomers and well-known writers. Here's hoping it's just the first of a series. The Catriona Ward, Elana Gomel, and Michael Marshall Smith stories are reprinted herein. One of the best horror anthologies of the year.

Footsteps in the Dark edited by Gillian Whittaker (Flame Tree Publishing) presents forty-five gothic tales from a wide range of writers, including twelve originals. The best of the new ones are by P. G. Galalis, Ali Habashi, Damien McKeating, Aeryn Rudel, D. A. Watson, and Nemma Wollenfang.

A Winter's Tale: Horror Stories for the Yuletide edited by Cliff Biggers, Charles R. Rutledge, and James R. Tuck (Pavane Press) is an original anthology of thirteen seasonal stories, with notable ones by Cliff Biggers,

Patrick Kealan Burke, William Meikle, Charles R. Rutledge, Jeff Strand, and John Linwood Grant.

Lovecraft Mythos New and Classic Collection edited by Gillian Whittaker (Flame Tree Publishing) features forty Lovecraftian stories—five by H. P. Lovecraft (and two others by him and collaborators) and seven new ones. All the new stories are good. They're by Thana Niveau, R. S. Stefoff, N. R. Lambert, John Possidente, Helen E. Davis, Hal Bodner, and Donald Tyson. The Niveau is reprinted herein.

Black Cranes: Tales of Unquiet Women edited by Lee Murray and Geneve Flynn (Omnium Gatherum) is an anthology of fourteen stories written by Southeast Asian women, and intends to provide a counterpoint to the stereotypical, submissive Asian woman as envisioned by Westerners. While doing this, many of the stories focus their spotlight on family, food, folklore, and female responsibility. Nine of the stories appear for the first time, and the strongest are by Elaine Cuyegkeng, Rena Mason, Lee Murray, and Geneve Flynn.

Black Dogs Black Tales edited by Tabitha Wood and Cassie Hart (A 'Things in the Well' Publications) is a charity anthology of seventeen stories and poems (five reprints) for the Mental Health Foundation of New Zealand.

Not All Monsters edited by Sarah Tantlinger (Strangehouse Books) is an all-original anthology of twenty-one stories by women, with notable contributions by Joanna Roye, Hailey Piper, Stacey Bell, and J. C. Raye.

Final Cuts: New Tales of Hollywood Horror and Other Spectacles edited by Ellen Datlow (Blumhouse Books/Anchor Books) contains eighteen new stories about movies and movie-making around the world. The stories by A. C. Wise, Nathan Ballingrud, and Stephen Graham Jones are reprinted herein.

Ghosts of the Chit-Chat edited by Robert Lloyd Parry (The Swan River Press) celebrates an 1893 meeting of Cambridge University's Chit-Chat Club, during which M. R. James read two of his ghost stories to the ten members. The volume includes these two stories plus stories, essays, and poems by the members of the club.

Local Haunts edited by R. Saint Claire (self-published) collects nineteen new stories by contributors to the Horror BookTube, an online community of readers who discuss books on YouTube. Each contributor has written a story taking place where they live. There are notable stories by Kevin David Anderson, Cameron Chaney, and Andrew Lyall.

Nightscript VI edited by C.M. Muller (Chthonic Matter) is a fine, annual anthology series that features unthemed weird, dark tales. This volume is no exception, with seventeen stories, including impressive ones by LC von Hessen, Tom Johnstone, Ralph Robert Moore, Dan Coxon, Alexander James, Francesco Corigliano, Charles Wilkinson, Selene dePackh, and Julia Rust. The Johnstone is reprinted herein.

Terror Tales of the Home Counties edited by Paul Finch (Telos Publishing) continues the excellent series of horror anthologies Finch has been editing for a decade, with fifteen stories (one reprint) and interstitial material by Finch. The strongest in this volume are by Steven J. Dines, Reggie Oliver, Steve Duffy, Helen Grant, and Tom Johnstone. The Duffy is reprinted herein.

Lullabies for Suffering: Tales of Addiction Horror edited by Mark Matthews (Wicked Run Press) brings together six stories centered on addiction. The strongest are by John F. D. Taff and Gabino Iglesias.

Stories We Tell After Midnight Volume Two edited by Rachel A. Brune (Crone Girls Press) is an unthemed anthology, with twenty-four stories, three of them reprints. Included is notable work by EJ Sidle, Jeff Samson, Larina Warnock, DeAnna Knippling, and T. M. Starnes.

Powers and Presences: An Appreciation of Charles Williams by John Howard and Mark Valentine (Sarob Press) collects a novella by John Howard and a novelette and a brief essay by Mark Valentine in a lovely package, with cover and interior art by Paul Lowe.

Borderlands 7 edited by Olivia F. Monteleone and Thomas F. Monteleone (Borderlands Press) has twenty-two new stories, one reprint. The best are by Meghan Arcuri, Cory Cone, and Roby Davies.

The Best of Cemetery Dance II edited by Richard Chizmar (Cemetery Dance Publications) does the minimum in producing this follow-up volume to the one published in 1998. Fifty stories reprinted from the magazine. No bios or introduction.

Oculus Sinister: An Anthology of Ocular Horror edited by C. M. Muller (Chthonic Matter) is a strong anthology with twenty new stories. There's especially notable work by Steve Rasnic Tem, John Langan, Timothy Granville, Shannon Scott, M. R. Cosby, and J. A. W. McCarthy. The McCarthy is reprinted herein.

Worst Laid Plans: An Anthology of Vacation Horror edited by Samantha Kolesnik (Grindhouse Press) is a strong, all-original anthology of fourteen stories. Especially notable are the entries by Greg Cisco, Hailey Piper, Malcolm Mills, Jeremy Herbert, Mark Wheaton, and Laura Keating.

Wicked Women: An Anthology of the New England Horror Writers edited by Trisha J. Wooldridge and Scott T. Goudsward (NEHW Press) features twenty new stories and one poem. There's notable work by Jane Yolen, Gillian Daniels, and Jennifer Williams.

A Sinister Quartet by Mike Allen, C. S. E. Cooney, Amanda J. McGee, and Jessica P. Wick (Mythic Delirium Press) contains three dark novellas and a short novel on dark themes.

Come Join Us By the Fire is the second volume in an audio-only series of horror anthologies produced by Tor's horror imprint, Nightfire. The audiobook has eighteen reprints and nine originals—the latter by Laird Barron, Brian Evenson, Indrapramit Das, Gabino Iglesias, Sunny Moraine, and others.

Slay: Stories of the Vampire Noire edited by Nicole Givens Kurtz (Mocha Memoirs Press) has twenty-eight new vampire stories in which Black protagonists take center stage as vampires and vampire hunters. There are notable stories by Steven Van Patten, Milton J. Davis, V. G. Harrison, John Linwood Grant, Valjeanne Jeffers, LH Moore, and Steve Van Samson.

The Year's Best Dark Fantasy and Horror Volume 1 edited by Paula Guran (Pyr) continues the Guran-edited series that was published by Prime Books for nine years. The new volume, covering 2019 fiction, includes twenty-five stories and novelettes, none overlapping with my own *Best Horror of the Year Volume Twelve*.

Best New Horror #30 edited by Stephen Jones (Drugstore Indian Press/PS Publishing) covers the year 2018. It includes twenty-three stories, none of which overlap with my own *Best Horror of the Year Volume Eleven*, although we sometimes used the same authors. His anthology did overlap with one story in Paula Guran's *Year's Best Dark Fantasy and Horror 2019*. Jones also includes an extensive summation of the year in horror and a Necrology.

MIXED-GENRE ANTHOLOGIES

Straight Outta Dodge City edited by David Boop (Baen Books) presents fourteen new weird western stories—some horror, some not. The best of the darker contributions are by Joe R. Lansdale, Ava Morgan, Harry Turtledove, and Jonathan Maberry. *Tiny Nightmares* edited by Lincoln Michel and Nadxieli Nieto (Counterpoint Press) has a few truly creepy short-shorts. Of the thirty-nine new stories (there are also three reprints), the best are by Samantha Hunt, Meg Elison, Chase Burke, Sam J. Miller, Rachel Heng, Jac Jemc, Jei D. Marcade, Vajra Chandrasekera, Brian Evenson, Lindsay King-Miller, Kevin Brockmeier, and Helen McCrory. *Devil's Ways* edited by Anna Kashina and J. M. Sidorova (Dragonwell Publishing) contains twelve stories about the devil, five of them new. The best of the originals are by Persephone D'Shaun and R. S. A. Garcia. *The Willows Complete Anthology* edited by Ben Thomas compiles ten issues of a magazine of the weird, published 2007-08, containing poetry, fiction, and reproductions of Victorian advertisements. In addition, there are five very good new stories by Gemma Files, Jesse Bullington, Nick Mamatas, Orrin Grey, and Brian Evenson. *Uncertainties Volume IV* edited by Timothy J. Jarvis (The Swan River Press) is an unthemed anthology of fourteen original stories of unease—not all horrific, but most of them exceedingly dark. There are notable stories by Claire Dean, D. P. Watt, Brian Evenson, Lucie McKnight Hardy, Rebecca Lloyd, and Charles Wilkinson. *Crooked Houses* edited by Mark Beech (Egaeus Press) contains seventeen new weird and/or horror stories about cursed or haunted dwellings. The book looks beautiful, with interior spot illustrations and end papers reproduced from etchings by the late artists Franz Schwimbeck and Herbert Railton. The strongest stories are by David Surface, Lynda E. Rucker, Timothy Granville, Rebecca Lloyd, James Doig, Mark Valentine, Carly Holmes, Richard Gavin, Colin Insole, Steve Duffy, Albert Power, and Reggie Oliver. The Surface is reprinted herein. *Dim Shores Presents* Vol. 1 edited by Sam Cowan and Justin Steele (Dim Shores) is an anthology of thirteen weird stories, some of them dark. The best of the dark ones are by Jess Landry and Eric Schaller. *Evil in Technicolor* edited by Joe M. McDermott (Vernacular Books) contains a mixed bag of ten stories inspired by Hammer movies. There are notable darker ones by A. C. Wise,

Craig Laurence Gidney, Nick Mamatas, and Haralambi Markov. *Apostles of the Weird* edited by S. T. Joshi (PS Publishing) is an unthemed anthology of eighteen stories, each covering different aspects of weird fiction, which often overlaps with horror. The more interesting darker stories are by George Edwards Murray, John Shirley, Lynda E. Rucker, Richard Gavin, Nancy Kilpatrick, Lynne Jamneck, Stephen Woodworth, and Gemma Files. The Files is reprinted herein. *Women's Weird 2: More Strange Stories by Women, 1891-1937* edited by Melissa Edmundson (Handheld Press) has thirteen stories of weird and supernatural fiction by writers, including Katherine Mansfield and Stella Gibbons. *British Weird: Selected Short Fiction, 1893-1937* edited by James Machin (Handheld Press) features nine stories plus the 1933 essay "Ghoulies and Ghosties: Use of the Supernatural in English Fiction" by Mary Butts. *Strange Tales: Tartarus Press at 30* edited by Rosalie Parker (Tartarus Press) is an excellent celebration of this British Press. The all new stories are weird, and . . . yes strange, and often very dark. All the stories are quite good, but the standouts among those that might be considered horror are by Inna Effress, J. M. Walsh, and John Linwood Grant. *Eurasian Monsters* edited by Margrét Helgadottir (Fox Spirit Books) is the seventh and final volume of the series showcasing monsters from around the world. There are seventeen stories within (reprints and originals), only some horror. The best of those are by Karina Shainyan and Haralambi Markov. *Monsters, Movies, and Mayhem* edited by Kevin J. Anderson (WordFire Press) was a class project for Anderson's graduate program in Creative Writing at Western Colorado University. The twenty-three new monster stories are by a mix of professional and new writers and include dark fantasy, humorous tales, and some horror. The notable darker stories are by Steve Rasnic Tem, Kevin Pettway, and Jonathan Maberry. *His Own Fantastic Creation* edited by S. T. Joshi (PS Publishing) features fifteen stories with H. P. Lovecraft as protagonist. It's entertaining, but strictly for fans of Lovecraft. Most of the stories are new. *The Nightside Codex* edited by Justin A. Burnett (Silent Motorist Media) contains eighteen weird and dark stories about various texts—real or otherwise. The best of the darker stories are by Stephen Graham Jones, Alistair Rey, C. E. Casey, and Nadia Bulkin. *Strange Lands Short Stories* edited by Gillian Whittaker (Flame Tree Publishing) has thirty-nine classic and new stories. Twelve are new, and of those there are notable dark stories by Christian Macklam, Victoria Dalpe, and Ed Burkle. *Strange Days: Midnight Street Anthology 4* edited by Trevor Denyer (Midnight Street Press) presents thirty-six new stories and a poem loosely related to the pandemic, ecological disaster, and other dystopian current events. *It Came From Miskatonic University* edited by Scott Gable and C. Dombrowski (Broken Eye Books) has fifteen new stories, though includes no horror. It's mentioned here, however, because of its Lovecraftian connection. *Bitter Distillations: An Anthology of Poisonous Tales* edited by Mark Beech (Egaeus Press) has eighteen all new stories centering around poison. Some of the stories are horror, more are dark fantasy or weird. The most interesting were by Carina Bissett, Alison Littlewood, Jason E. Rolfe, Yarrow Paisley, Lisa L. Hannett, Ron Weighell, Jonathan Wood, and Kathleen Jennings. *Slashertorte: An Anthology of Cake Horror* edited by Ben Walker (Sliced Up Press) is silly, but at times, entertaining. There are notable stories by Nicole M. Wolverton, Douglas Ford, and Sam Richard. *Dominion: An Anthology of Speculative Fiction From Africa and the African Diaspora Volume One* edited by Zelda Knight and Ekpeki Oghenechovwe Donald (Aurelia Leo) features thirteen new stories and poems of science fiction, fantasy, dark fantasy, and horror. With a foreword by Tananarive Due. *Tales of Dark Fantasy 3* edited by William Schafer (Subterranean Press) has ten strong stories (two reprints) of dark fantasy and horror. The strongest originals are by Richard Kadrey, Caitlín R. Kiernan, C. J. Tudor, Ian R. MacLeod, and Bentley Little.

COLLECTIONS

The Best of Michael Marshall Smith (Subterranean Press) celebrates thirty years of excellent writing. Smith is one of the most consistently best contemporary authors of horror, and this is a great overview of his work.

These Evil Things We Do by Mick Garris (Cinestate) is a collection of four novellas, three previously published as chapbooks, one new.

Halloween Season by Lucy A. Snyder (Raw Dog Screaming Press) features fifteen stories and poems centered around every horror aficionados' favorite holiday, reprinted from a variety of publications.

The Immeasurable Corpse of Nature by Christopher Slatsky (Grimscribe Press) is the strong second collection by Slatsky, with fifteen stories, a novella, and essays. Although occasionally overly oblique, Slatsky imparts a sense of dreadful beauty to what he writes, and is always worth reading. With an introduction by Kristine Ong Muslim.

Cardiff By the Sea: Four Novellas of Suspense by Joyce Carol Oates (Mysterious Press) presents this mix of supernatural and psychological horror stories. One of them was originally published in my recent ghost story anthology *Echoes: The Saga Anthology of Ghost Stories.*

If It Bleeds by Stephen King (Scribner) features four new pieces: a short novel related to King's novel *The Outsider,* a novella about a young boy's relationship with an elderly benefactor, one about writers block and the lengths an individual will go to unblock, and one about strange incidents told in reverse.

Monster Movies by David J. Schow (Cimarron Street Books) has thirteen reprints and a new afterword explaining the author's long addiction/love of horror movies (especially those with monsters).

Tuxedo Junction by Thom Carnell (Macabre Ink) is the author's third collection and has nineteen recent stories, almost half new.

Only the Broken Remain by Dan Coxon (Black Shuck Books) is a debut collection, with fourteen stories published between 2017 and 2020. Three stories are new.

The Black Shuck Shadows series brought out a number of mini collections in 2020: *The Watcher in the Woods* by Charlotte Bond has five dark fantasy tales, four of them published for the first time. Bond is very good at putting her own spin on classic fairy tales. *Voices* by Kit Power has eight stories, four of them new, each very different from the other. *The Adventures of Mr. Polkington* by Tina Rath has three stories (one a reprint) about a London salesman who becomes involved in the supernatural. *Green Fingers* by Dan Coxon features six tales about murderous flora, three of them new. *Three Mothers, One Father* by Sean Hogan is an episodic novella, with each element based on European horror films. *Uneasy Beginnings* by Simon Kurt Unsworth and Benjamin Kurt Unsworth is an impressive collaborative effort by the seasoned author and his son, with seven new tales (none identified by authorship). The introduction by Simon Kurt Unsworth explains how the project came about. *Fearsome Creatures* by Aliya Whiteley has five stories, two new, each about a type of monster. *Stages of Fear* by Reggie Oliver has six stories, one new, all relating to the theater. *En Vacances* by David A. Sutton has six stories about people on vacation, one new.

Jagged Edges & Moving Parts by Pete Mesling (Other Kingdoms Publishing) is a collection of twenty-seven stories, eleven previously published in his first collection, nine of them new.

Thin places by Kay Chronister (Undertow Publications) is the debut collection of this promising writer and has eleven stories, three published for the first time.

Bloody Britain by Anna Taborska (Shadow Publishing) is the third collection by the British author and filmmaker. Most of the fourteen stories are brutal and gory. Five of them appear for the first time. Robert Shearman provides the introduction, and there's an illustration by Reggie Oliver for each story.

Hippocampus Press has started a "Classics of Gothic Horror Series," created by S. T. Joshi, reprinting novels and collections of weird and gothic fiction from the past two centuries. In 2020, the press published *The Dead Knew: The Weird Fiction of Mary Sinclair* edited by S. T. Joshi. This volume includes thirteen stories, a biographical introduction by Joshi, and a bibliography. *Back There in the Grass: The Horror Tales of Irwin S. Cobb and Gouverneur Morris* edited by S. T. Joshi. The two writers, both prominent in the early twentieth century, are each represented by several weird tales. It's the first time their work has been collected. Included is a biography and bibliography for each writer.

Dark Black by Sam Weller (Hat & Beard Press) is a debut with twenty stories of horror, dark fantasy, and weird fiction, eight of them new. With black and white illustrations by Dan Grzeca.

Read Me & Other Ghost Stories by Keith Minnion (Macabre Ink) is a collection of nine stories and the title novella. The novella and two of the stories are new.

Some Bruising May Occur by Gary McMahon (JournalStone Publishing) is a strong new collection with seventeen stories, five of them new. One is reprinted herein. With an introduction by Alison Littlewood.

Dead Trouble & Other Ghost Stories by Aidan Chambers (PS Publishing). Chambers, in addition to being an award-winning children's author, edited several ghost story anthologies between the 1970s through '90s. The eighteen stories in the book are some of his favorites. Illustrated by Randy Broecker and with a foreword by Stephen Jones and an introduction by the author.

Velocities by Kathe Koja (Meerkat Press) is the long-awaited second collection of thirteen dark stories (two new) by a stylish master of compression.

The Language of Beasts by Jonathan Oliver (Black Shuck Books) is the author's debut collection—and the seventeen (four of them new) varied stories demonstrate his talent as a writer. Oliver is better known as a book editor and as an anthologist of several award-winning anthologies. He needs to write more.

New Gods, Old Monsters by Bill Davidson (Dark Lane Books) is the debut collection of eighteen stories (four new) by a relatively new writer whose work has only been published since 2017. One of the stories was reprinted in *The Best Horror of the Year Volume Eleven*.

Ill Met by Darkness by Paul Finch (Sarob Press) presents four chilling new supernatural tales of folk horror. Finch also published *The Christmas You Deserve: Five Festive Terror Tales* (Brentwood Press), one of them new.

A Carnival of Chimaeras by Stephen Woodworth (Hippocampus Press) is a debut collection of eighteen stories, three of them new.

Borderlands Press continued their "little book series" with *A Little Magenta Book of Malevolence* by Sarah Pinborough, featuring uncollected fiction and essays, plus *A Little Amber Book of Wicked Shots* by Robert McCammon, featuring four stories involving alcoholic drinks, plus a cocktail recipe.

Children of the Fang and Other Genealogies by John Langan (Word Horde) is the author's fourth collection of short fiction and, as always, these twenty-one stories, novelettes, and novellas brilliantly showcase what he's published during the past eight years. One new story is included, along with story notes for each story, about its literary and cinematic influences. This is one of the year's best horror collections.

The Cuckoo Girls by Patricia Lillie (Trepidatio Publishing) is a strong debut collection, with sixteen stories, nine of them new.

A Season of Loathsome Miracles by Max D. Stanton (Trepidatio Publishing) is an impressive debut, with thirteen stories, three published for the first time.

Other Sandboxes by F. Paul Wilson and Divers Hands (Gauntlet Press/ Borderlands Press) is a collection of pastiches written in the style of Mary

Shelley, Ray Bradbury, Edgar Rice Burroughs, Sax Rohmer, and others. With a foreword by Joe R. Lansdale.

Murder Ballads and Other Horrific Tales by John Hornor Jacobs (JournalStone Publishing) is a strong collection of ten horror and dark crime stories two of which appear for the first time (and one of which is a novella).

Wyrd and Other Derelictions by Adam L. G. Nevill (Ritual Limited) is a short, powerful collection of seven stories told by an omniscient narrator about richly imagined derelict ships, campgrounds, holy sites—all of which have become scenes of alien infestation, strange ritual, and obscene slaughter-by persons-or things-unknown. All but one are new. The one reprint, "Hippocampus," was in *The Best Horror of the Year Volume Eight*.

The Skeleton Melodies by Clint Smith (Hippocampus Press) is an excellent second collection. While Smith sometimes uses pulp tropes, his writing is so good that the stories aren't pulpy at all. A real achievement. Thirteen stories, two of them new. With an introduction by Adam Golaski.

Dark Blood Comes From the Feet by Emma J. Gibbon (Trepidatio Publishing) has sixteen stories, most published for the first time.

The Halloween Store & Other Tales of All Hallow Eve by Ronald Kelly (Macabre Ink) has seven stories (two reprints) and two nonfiction pieces.

Her Infernal Name & Other Nightmares by Robert P. Ottone (Spooky House Press) collects seventeen stories and one novella; all the stories but one are new.

Catharsis by Tish Jackson (The Jackson Press) is a debut collection of eight stories, two of them reprints.

Aftermath of an Industrial Accident by Mike Allen (Mythic Delirium Press) is the author's third collection, with twenty-three stories and poems, three of the stories published for the first time. With an introduction by Jeffrey Thomas.

Grotesquerie by Richard Gavin (Undertow Publications) is the author's sixth collection of horror and the weird, and has sixteen stories—three published for the first time in 2020, one of those original to the volume, which is reprinted herein.

The Companion & Other Phantasmagorical Stories by Ramsey Campbell is one of two volumes of stories chosen by the author from those published during his sixty-year career. It has thirty-four stories plus an introduction, including a story written when Campbell was twelve years old. Cover art and interiors by James Hannah. *The Retrospective & Other Phantasmagorical Stories* by Ramsey Campbell is the second volume, with thirty-three stories, cover and interior art by Glenn Chadbourne. Both were published by PS Publishing.

Warts and All by Mark Morris (PS Publishing) presents thirty stories, one original, one in collaboration with Rio Youers. Introduction by Nicholas Royle.

As Summer's Mask Slips and Other Disruptions by Gordon B. White (Trepidatio Publishing) is this author's debut collection, with fifteen weird, often dark and creepy, horror stories, one reprinted in an earlier volume of *The Best Horror of the Year Volume Twelve,* and two of them new.

The Death Spancel and Others by Katharine Tynan (The Swan River Press) brings together, for the first time, twenty of the author's supernatural tales. Although a prolific and highly regarded author in the late nineteenth and twentieth century, she was not known for her ghostly stories. Hopefully, this collection remedies that. With a biographical introduction by Peter Bell.

Terrible Things by David Surface (Black Shuck Books) is the author's first collection and includes thirteen stories, two of them new. With an introduction by Lynda E. Rucker.

Red New Day and Other Microfictions by Angela Slatter brings together eighteen dark tales originally published in 2008 and 2009 on The Daily Cabal website. It's part of the chapbook series from Brain Jar Press. In the same series is *Travelogues: Vignettes from Trains in Motion* by Kathleen Jennings, an utterly charming chapbook of vignettes written over three years during which the author/artist traveled along the east coast of the US (not horror).

Ten Minute Warning by Em Dehaney (Brave Boy Books) is the author's second collection, featuring ten stories, three of them new.

What's Coming For You by Joshua Rex (Rotary Press) is a debut collection with ten stories, six of them new.

Dark Was the Night by Angel Leigh McCoy (Wily Writers) is a debut collection with eight stories, two of which are new, and one excerpt from a forthcoming novel.

Taiping Tales of Terror by Julya Oui (Penguin Random House) is a Malaysian collection that begins with a bunch of young boys sitting around a campfire telling ghost stories. By the end of the night, they realize there is one more of them than they started with.

MIXED-GENRE COLLECTIONS

Killer Come Back to Me by Ray Bradbury (Hard Case Crime) is a large reprint collection containing twenty of the author's crime stories—although many are better known for their science fiction or horror elements than crime. *The Ghost Variations* by Kevin Brockmeier (Pantheon) features one hundred very short stories, some of which are weird and/or dark. *The Best of Jeffrey Ford* (PS Publishing) showcases, in a beautiful package, twenty-seven science fiction, fantasy, and horror stories by Ford, with a note for each story and fabulous spot illustrations and cover art by Ford's son, Derek. One story is new. One of the best collections of the year. *The Dark Nest* by Sue Harper (Egaeus Press) is a collection of almost fifty pieces of flash fiction, Number VI in the publisher's Keynote Note Edition series. Twelve stories appear for the first time. *A King Called Arthor and Other Morceaux* by Donald Sidney-Fryer (Hippocampus Press) is a miscellany including a novel, and recent essays, reviews, and poetry by an author best known for his scholarship on Clark Ashton Smith. *The Road to Woop Woop* by Eugen Bacon (Meerkat Press) is a promising debut collection of twenty-four speculative fiction and fantasy tales, with some tinges of darkness. *Songs for Dark Seasons* by Lisa L. Hannett (Ticonderoga Publications) is a mostly dark fantasy collection of twelve stories and one novella (six new), all taking place in backcountry towns. Several of the stories border on horror. *London Gothic* by Nicholas Royle (Cōnfingō Publishing) features fifteen stories about London, seven of them new. Most are weird and uncanny rather than dark or horrific, but Royle's work is always a good read. This is the first in a projected series of city-based collections by Royle that Cōnfingō will be publishing. *Grotesque: Monster Stories* by Lee Murray (A 'Things in the Well' Publications) brings together an entertaining mix of eleven stories of the uncanny, dark fantasy, and horror, four of them new. *Reality, and Other Stories by* John Lanchester (Faber & Faber) is the author's first collection, and contains eight contemporary ghost stories, with the horror stemming from the technology we're so tied to. *The Impossible Weight of Life* by Michael Bailey (Written Backwards) collects thirteen weird, sometimes dark stories and thirteen poems, more than half of them published for the first time in 2020. *Underworld Dreams* by Daniel Braum (Lethe Press) is this talented author's third collection, presenting ten (two of them new) weird, sometimes dark tales. Included are an introduction and notes about each story. *These Foolish and Harmful Delights* by Cate Gardner (Fox Spirit Books) includes the title novella, plus seven weird and sometimes dark stories (four of them new). *Okamoto Kidō Master of the Uncanny* translated by Nancy H. Ross (Kurodahan Press) presents twelve stories written by a Japanese reporter and dramatist whose interests also included folklore, leading him to write more than fifty stories of the uncanny during the 1920s and '30s. Only one of the stories in this volume has been previously translated into English. Introduction by Edward Lipsett. *Untold Mayhem* by Mark Tullius (Vincere Press) has twenty-four crime, suspense, and horror stories, most of them new. *If Only Tonight We Could Sleep* by Matthew R. David (A 'Things in the Well' Publications) has thirteen stories of dark fantasy and horror, three new. *Unsafe Words* by Loren Rhoads (Automatism Press) is the author's first full-length collection, and its fifteen stories are a combination of sf, dark fantasy, and horror. It includes one new story, an introduction by Lisa Morton, and individual story notes. *Songs for Dark Seasons* by Lisa L. Hannett (Ticonderoga Publications) is a fine collection of thirteen dark fantasy and horror stories, six of them new. The final entry is a lovely, melancholy dark novella. *We All Hear Stories In the Dark* Volumes I–III by Robert Shearman (PS Publishing) is a marvelous, almost 1800-page collection of new and reprinted fantasy and dark, weird, enigmatic, sometimes horrific tales, with intertwined interstitial material that is almost like a "choose your own adventure." Fairy tales, myth, folk tales, realist stories—this is a remarkable achievement and one of the best collections of the year. *Our Elaborate Plans* by Ralph Robert Moore (self-published) has twenty stories, seven of them new. You never know what you're going to get with a story by Moore—I find his best work deeply disturbing psychological horror, but he also writes mainstream stories. *The Midnight Circus* by Jane Yolen (Tachyon Publications) features sixteen stories and related poems (the latter all new) of fantasy and dark fantasy. *The Heart is a Mirror for Sinners and Other Stories* by Angela Slatter (PS Publishing) is this prolific author's tenth collection. Her output roams between fantasy, dark fantasy, and horror with ease. This volume includes fourteen stories, two of them excellent originals. With an introduction by Kim Newman. *Nine Bar Blues: Stories From An Ancient Future* by Sheree Renée Thomas (Third Man Books) is the author and anthologist's first fiction collection, and it's a varied one, with sixteen stories, some dark enough to be considered horror, half of them new. *The Mysteries of the Faceless King* and *The Last Heretic* by Darrell Schweitzer (PS Publishing) is a two-volume retrospective of the author's best stories. The first volume, with an introduction by Michael Swanwick, has twenty stories, one of them new. The second volume, with an introduction by Paul DiFilippo, has twenty-three stories, one new. *The Traveller and Other Stories* by Neville Stuart (Soho Press) has thirteen crime and horror stories, one a new novella. With a foreword by John Connelly. *The Age of Decayed Futurity* by Mark Samuels (Hippocampus Press) collects seventeen of the author's best stories, published between 2003 and 2017. With an introduction by Michael Dirda. *A Fierce and Fertile Tomorrow* by Darren Speegle (PS Publishing) is the author's ninth short story collection and contains twelve stories (three published for the first time) of science fiction, dark fantasy, and horror. *Crepuscularks and Phantomimes: Gothic, Ghostly & Lovecraftian Tales in the Ironic Mode* by Rhys Hughes (Gloomy Seahorse Press) features eleven stories by one of the weirder purveyors of weird fiction. All but four of them are new. *Through the Storm* by Rosalie Parker (PS Publishing) is the author's fourth collection. This one contains twenty-five weird and sometimes dark stories, all but three of them new. *Umbrìa* by Santiago Eximeno, translation by Daniele Bonfanti (Independent Legions Publishing), is the first English translation from Spanish of this series of interconnected stories about the inhabitants of a surreal city.

CHAPBOOKS/NOVELLAS

Nicholas Royle's Nightjar Press continues to publish high-quality stories as chapbooks, many of which are quite dark. Alas, the series appears to be edging away from actual horror, which is a shame. *Hide* by Roberta Dewa is a dreamy, stream-of-consciousness tale of two lost souls bird watching.

Regret by Robert Stone is about a recent widower obsessed by guilt, and with Patricia Highsmith's novel *The Talented Mr. Ripley*. *The Wash* by Daniel Gothard is a brief, tense tale about the promise a man makes to his dying brother to hide his "collection." *Shannon* by Angela Goodman is a ghostly tale (without really being a ghost story) about spiritualism and communing with the dead. *House Calls* by Vlatka Horvat is clever and (to me) very funny as a homeowner becomes besieged by unwanted and increasingly bizarre people who want to make "house calls." *Signal* by Michael Walters is a moving story about a broke, depressed woman trying to survive Christmas holidays alone. *Like a Fever* by Tim Etchells is a beautiful, hallucinatory series of similes beginning "it was like" . . . creating images of dark and light. *On Blackfell* by Tom Heaton is about an engaged couple, the man's father, and a hike to an airplane crash site. *The Red Suitcase* by Hilaire is about a mysterious woman who comes to stay for a week in a guest house with a woman and her adult son. As the week goes by, the reader waits tensely for something of note to happen. Nothing does. The best of all of them is *Trick of the Light* by Andrew Humphrey, a chilling little tale inspired by M. R. James, about a couple with a broken relationship who rent a cottage by the North Sea, and encounter something weird. It's reprinted herein.

TTA Press published two novella chapbooks in 2020: *Engines Beneath Us* by Malcolm Devlin, a coming-of-age story imbued with darkness and the uncanny, and *Honeybones* by Georgina Bruce, a dreamy gothic fairy tale about fractured relationships.

Sacred Summer by Cassandra Rose Clarke (Conversation Pieces/Aqueduct Press) is a short novel—told entirely in verse—about a former dancer living in the house where a trio of young musicians encountered something dangerous twenty years earlier.

Tor.com Books published several horror and dark fantasy novellas in their novella program, including Jeffrey Ford's *Out of Body*, about a traumatized librarian whose resulting out-of-body experiences are initially joyous, but ultimately become dangerous. In the exceedingly weird and dark *Flyaway* by Kathleen Jennings, multiple mysteries come to light in a small Western Queensland town when a reserved young woman receives a note from one of her missing brothers. *Night of the Mannequins* by Stephen Graham Jones is about a teenage prank gone horribly wrong. (I acquired and edited all three.)

Ring Shout by P. Djèlí Clark is an excellent dark, historical novella embedding supernatural demonology with the real-life horror of the Ku Klux Klan. *The Tindalos Asset* by Caitlín R. Kiernan is about a broken down government agent recruited for one more job: to prevent the latest apocalypse.

Kiernan had a second novella chapbook, *La Belle Fleur Sauvage* (Dark Regions Press), which was released in 2020, although the copyright date says 2019. This one is about a parasite that infects women's wombs, destroying most of humanity. The book is intended as the first volume in a set of four plagues.

Sleepers by Gerard Houarner (Psychedelic Horror Press) is either an sf/horror story about a one man's nightmare world of office work, or about an office worker having a psychotic break. Either way, it's intriguing.

Cradle and Grave by Anya Ow (Neon Hemlock Press) is a far future dystopian horror novel about a dangerous trek into a ruined urban zone, with body horror and a constantly mutating reality.

Distinguishing Features by Kealan Patrick Burke, illustrated by Corinne Halbert (It Came From Beyond Pulp), is about a divorced man who begins to find body parts around his neighborhood.

The Girl in the Video by Michael David Wilson (Perpetual Motion Machine Publishing) begins with a teacher accidentally opening a sexually suggestive video on his phone, and becomes a novella of obsession and paranoia.

Armageddon House by Michael Griffin (Undertow Publications) is a dark, weird tale that begins with four people living in a bunker, all their needs attended to, but with no memory of where they are or how they got there.

Do You Mind If We Dance With Your Legs? by Michael Cisco (Nightscape Press Charitable Chapbooks) is a weird novella about a detective searching for a missing woman.

Poetry Journals, Webzines, Anthologies, and Collections

Spectral Realms edited by S. T. Joshi and published by Hippocampus Press is a showcase for weird and dark poetry. Two issues came out in 2020. In addition to original poems, there's a section with classic reprints and a review column. There were notable poems by Leigh Blackmore, Benjamin Blake, Ross Balcom, Richard Tierney, and Oliver Smith.

A Collection of Dreamscapes by Christina Sng (Raw Dog Screaming Press) collects several darkly fantastic series of poems, including retold fairy tales, monster tales, tales of a heroic warrior, and others. A mix of new and reprints.

Cries to Kill the Corpse Flower by Ronald J. Murray (Bizarro Pulp Press) is a debut collection of forty strong, dark poems.

Whitechapel Rhapsody by Alessandro Manzetti (Independent Regions Publishing) is a fine collection of poetry dedicated to Jack the Ripper. All these sharp, evocative poems appear for the first time in 2020. One poem is reprinted herein.

Into the Forest and All the Way Through by Cynthia Pelayo (Burial Day Books) is a riveting collection of true crime poetry focusing on the dozens of missing and murdered women across the United States.

Past the Glad and Sunlit Season: Poems For Halloween by K. A. Opperman (Jackanapes Press) includes over fifty poems, about half published for the first time. With a preface by Lisa Morton and illustrations by Dan Sauer.

HWA Poetry Showcase Volume VII edited by Stephanie M. Wytovich (Horror Writers Association) is an annual of weird and dark verse. This year's featured poets are Sara Tantlinger, Sarah Read, and K. P. Kulsk, along with almost fifty other pieces by members of the HWA. While all the poems are very fine, some of my favorites were by Annie Neugebauer, Steve Rasnic Tem, Pamela K. Kinney, Terrie Leigh Relf, and Geri Leen.

Dwarf Stars 2020 edited by Robin Mayhall (Science Fiction and Fantasy Poetry Association) collects the best very short speculative poems published in 2019. The poems are all ten lines or fewer, and the prose poems one hundred words or fewer.

Star*Line is the official newsletter of the Science Fiction and Fantasy Poetry Association. During 2020 it was edited by F. J. Bergmann. The journals regularly publish members' science fiction and fantasy poetry—and the occasional horror poem. The fall issue, edited by Melanie Stormm, was an excellent, all-Black issue filled with more horror than usual. Throughout the year there was notable dark poetry by K. Astre, Woody Dismukes, Oliver Smith, Sheree Renée Thomas, L. P. Melling, Linda D. Addison, S. T. Gibson, Sarah Grey, Soonest Nathaniel, J. L. Jones, and Marilee Pritchard.

Dreams & Nightmares edited by David C. Kopaska-Merkel has been around since 1986, regularly publishing weird and often dark poetry. Three issues were out in 2020 and notable dark work was published in them by Colleen Anderson and Michelle Muenzler.

The 2020 Rhysling Anthology: The Best Science Fiction, Fantasy & Horror Poetry of 2019 selected by the Science Fiction and Fantasy Poetry Association and edited by David C. Kopaska-Merkel (Science Fiction and Fantasy Poetry Association) is used by members to vote for the best short and long poems of the year, and can be considered—according to the editor—an annual report on the state of speculative poetry. The book is separated into two sections: Short Poems First Published in 2019, and Long Poems First Published in 2019. It's a good resource for checking out the poetic side of speculative and horror fiction.

The Withering by Ashley Dioses (Jackanapes Press) collects more than sixty poems, almost half of them new. With an introduction by John Shirley and illustrations by Mutartis Boswell.

Tenebrae in Aeternum: A Collection of Stygian Verse by Benjamin Blake (Hippocampus Press) is a powerful collection of over one hundred poems on dark themes, explored with skill. All but two are new. With an introduction by S. T. Joshi.

Cradleland of Parasites by Sarah Tantlinger (Strangehouse Books) is a fine, new collection focused on the black plague, by a former winner of the Stoker Award for poetry.

A Complex Accident of Life by Jessica McHugh (Apokrupha) is a collection of what is referred to as "blackout poetry," using Mary Shelley's *Frankenstein* as its source material. The idea is to "black out" large parts of text and create art from what remains.

Altars and Oubliettes by Angela Yuriko Smith (self-published) features forty-three dark poems, most published for the first time.

NONFICTION

End of the Road by Brian Keene (Cemetery Dance Publications) is a memoir, travelogue, and rumination on the field of horror and those involved in it. *The Brood* by Stephen R. Bissette (PS Publishing) is a 670-page entry in the Midnight Movie monograph series (series editor, Neil Snowden).

Hippocampus Press continued to publish important H. P. Lovecraft scholarship in 2020: *H. P. Lovecraft: Letters to Family and Family Friends Volumes 1 and 2* edited by S. T. Joshi and David E. Schultz collects letters by Lovecraft to his grandfather, his mother, and two aunts. Many of the letters to his aunts chronicle his two years living in New York. *H. P. Lovecraft: Letters to Alfred Galpin and Others* edited by S. T. Joshi and David E. Schultz is another ambitious volume of work collecting and annotating some of the voluminous correspondence between Lovecraft and his contemporaries. *H. P. Lovecraft: Letters to Rheinhart Kleiner and Others* edited by S. T. Joshi and David E. Schultz compiles and annotates unabridged letters from Lovecraft to Rheinhart—one of his oldest colleagues—plus letters to other amateur journalists, writers, and editors. *Eccentric, Impractical Devils: The Letters of August Derleth and Clark Ashton Smith* edited by David E. Schultz and S. T. Joshi (Hippocampus Press) is a valuable look at the lives of two working writers, and at Derleth's work as a writer and publisher of Arkham House. *It Came From . . .The Stories and Novels Behind Classic Horror, Fantasy and Science Fiction Films* by Jim Nemeth and Bob Madison (Midnight Matinee Press) is an historical overview in which the authors give their opinions on numerous adaptations of text made into film. *Sequelland: A Story of Dreams and Screams* by Jay Slayton-Joslin (Clash Books) is an examination of why so many horror movie sequels are made—bad and good—as the author holds conversations with the directors and others responsible for them. *Willful Monstrosity: Gender and Race in 21st Century Horror* by Natalie Wilson (McFarland) is organized around four types of monsters: zombies, witches, vampires, and monstrous women, and posits that today's films often subvert cultural norms and systems of power. *The Furies of Marjorie Bowen* by John C. Tibbetts (McFarland) is the first book-length examination of the life and work of the British author. *Don't Go Upstairs: A Room By Room Tour of the House in Horror Movies* by Cleaver Patterson (McFarland) explores home as a setting for horror by analyzing more than sixty films. *Fright Favorites: 31 Movies to Haunt Your Halloween and Beyond* (Turner Classic Movies) by David J. Skal (Running Press) is a profusely illustrated overview of classic horror, from *Nosferatu* to *Get Out*, with anecdotes, essays, and some cultural history. *Horror Literature From Gothic to Post-Modern Critical Essays* edited by Michele Brittany and Nicholas Diak (McFarland) contains fourteen essays adapted from 2017 and 2018 presentations at the Ann Radcliffe Academic Conference, which runs in tandem with HWA's annual StokerCon. The essays cover everything from historic works to the modern. With a foreword by Lisa Morton and afterword by Becky Spratford. *Clark Ashton Smith: A Comprehensive Bibliography* by S. T. Joshi, David E. Schultz, and Scott Connors (Hippocampus Press) is the first comprehensive bibliography of the author since Donald Sidney-Fryer's 1978 publication. *Robert E. Howard: A Closer Look* by Charles Hoffman and Marc Cerasini (Hippocampus Press) is an update and expansion of their 1987 monograph on Howard, published for the Starmont Readers Guides series. *Writing in the Dark* by Tim Waggoner (Guide Dog Books) is a textbook adapted from Waggoner's longtime blog of the same name. In addition to his own writing advice, he uses snippets of interviews from writers and editors at the end of each chapter, and includes writing exercises. *Arthur Machen: Autobiographical Writings* edited by S. T. Joshi (Hippocampus Press) includes the three volumes of Machen's autobiography, the volume of hostile reviews his works received during his lifetime, and a group of essays. With an in-depth Introduction by the editor. *20 Years of Hippocampus Press 2000-2020* by Derrick Hussey, S. T. Joshi, and David E. Schultz (Hippocampus Press) chronicles every publication the press has put out through 2020, with complete lists of the contents of each book. *The Streaming of Hill House* edited by Kevin J. Wetmore, Jr. (McFarland) is a collection of essays about the 2018 series adapted from the novel by Netflix. The contributors range from academics to fiction writers and poets. *Behind the Horror: True Stories That Inspired Horror Movies* by Dr. Lee Mellor (DK/Penguin Random House) is a combination of the overly familiar to the more interesting obscure. *Dark Archives: A Librarian's Investigation into the Science and History of Books Bound in Human Skin* by Megan Rosenbloom (FSG) investigates the history, motives, and ethics of anthropodermic bibliopegy, that is, the binding of books in human skin. The author, a librarian and journalist, has a riveting voice, which perfect fits this is a morbidly fascinating subject.

Horror Fiction in the 20th Century: Exploring Literature's Most Chilling Genre by Jesse Nevins (Praeger) is a valuable new look at what horror fiction encompassed from its beginnings through the twentieth century, including an enlightening examination of international horror, female writers, and writers of color. There has been so much change in the last twenty years that I'd love to see Nevins tackle all the new voices who have come to prominence since then. *Refractions* by Ben Baldwin (SST Publications) is the multi-award-winning Baldwin's first art book, and features previously unpublished art. With an introduction by Paul Meloy. *The Art of Pulp Horror* edited by Stephen Jones (Applause Books) is a prolifically illustrated visual history of the covers and posters of a very specific era of horror movies and books. With essays by experts including Lisa Morton, Mike Ashley, and Stefan Dziemianowicz, and a foreword by Robert Silverberg. *Wax Museum Movies: A Comprehensive Filmography* by George Higham (McFarland) is a reference guide aimed at what is likely a very limited audience.

EXHALATION #10

A. C. WISE

t's not a snuff film, at least not the traditional kind. The single miniDV cassette was recovered from the glove box of a crashed beige Ford Taurus. The car had passed through a metal guard rail and flipped at least once on its way down the incline on the other side. No body was found. The license plate had been removed, the VIN erased, no identifying information left behind.

The handwritten label on the cassette reads *Exhalation #10*. The film it contains is 57 minutes long; 57 minutes of a woman's last breaths, and her death finally at the 57:19 mark.

Henry watches the whole thing.

The padded envelope the tape arrived in bears Paul's handwriting, as does the tape's label—a replica of the original, safely tucked away in an evidence locker. It's no more than a half hour drive between them; Paul could have delivered the tape in person, but Henry understands why he would not. Even knowing this tape is not the original, even touching it only to slip it into a machine for playback, Henry feels his fingers coated with an invisible residue of filth.

Expensive equipment surrounds him—sound mixing boards, multiple screens and devices for playback, machines for converting from one format to another. Paul warned him about the tape over the phone, and still Henry wasn't prepared.

During the entire 57 minutes of play time, the woman's body slumps against a concrete wall, barely conscious. She's starved, one arm chained above her head to a thick pipe. The light is dim, the shadows thick. The angle of her head, lolled against her shoulder, hides her face. The camera watches for 57 minutes, capturing faint, involuntary movements—her body too weak for anything else—until her breathing stops.

Henry looks it up: on average, it takes a person ten days to die without food or water. The number ten on the label implies there are nine other tapes, an hour recorded every day. Or are there other tapes capturing every possible moment to ensure her death ended up on film?

"Just listen," Paul had told him. "Maybe you'll hear something we missed."

Henry's ears are golden. That's what his Sound Design professor at NYU said back in Henry's college days. As a kid, Henry's older brother Lionel had called it a superpower. By whatever name, what it means is that as Henry watches the tape, he can't help hearing every hitch, every rasp. Every time the woman's breath wants to stop, and her autonomic system forces one more gasp of air into her lungs.

He never would have agreed to watch the tape if he hadn't been a little bit drunk and a little bit in love, which he's been more or less since the day he met Paul. Paul, whose eye for framing, for details, for the perfect shot, is the equivalent of Henry's golden ear. Paul, whose cop father was shot in the line of duty three months short of graduation, causing him to abandon his own movie-making dreams and follow in his father's footsteps.

Henry has always known better than to chase after straight boys, what he knows intellectually and logically has never been a defense against Paul. So when Paul called at his wit's end and asked him to just listen to the tape, please, Henry agreed.

After 57 minutes and 19 seconds, the woman dies. After another two minutes and 41 seconds, the tape ends. Henry shuts down the screen and stops just short of pulling the plug from the wall.

"Jesus Christ, Paul, what did I just watch?"

A half-empty bottle sits at Henry's elbow in his bedroom, his phone pressed to his ear. He locked the door of the editing suite behind him, but the movie continues, crawling beneath his skin.

"I know. I'm sorry. I wouldn't ask if . . . I didn't know what else to do."

Henry catches the faint sound of Paul running his fingers through his hair, static hushing down the line. Or, at least, he imagines he hears the sound. Even after all this time he's not always sure if what he thinks he hears is just in his head, or whether he really does have a "superpower."

After watching the video of the dying woman, he's even less sure. He watched the whole thing, and didn't hear anything to help Paul. But he can't shake the feeling there *is* something there—a sound trapped on the edge of hearing, one he hasn't heard yet. A sound that's just waiting for Henry to watch the video again, which is the last thing in the world he wants to do.

"I'm sorry," Paul says again. "It's just . . . It's like I hit a brick wall. I have no goddamn idea where this woman died, who she is, or who killed her. I couldn't see anything on the tape, and you can hear things no one else can hear. You can tell which goddamn road a car is on just by the sound of the tires."

In Paul's voice—just barely ragged—is his fear, his frustration. His anger. Not at Henry, but the world for allowing a woman to die that way. The ghost of the woman's breath lingers in the whorls of Henry's ears. Do the shadows, carving the woman up into distinct segments, stain Paul's eyelids like bruises every time he blinks?

"I'll try," Henry says, because what else is there to say? Because it's Paul. He will listen to the tape a hundred times if he has to. He'll listen for the sounds that aren't there—something in the cadence of the woman's breathing, the whirr of an air duct he didn't notice the first time, something that will give her location away.

"Thank you." Paul's words are weary, frayed, and Henry knows it won't be a stray bullet for him, like the one that took his father. It'll be a broken heart.

The drug overdoses, the traffic accidents, the little boy running into the street after his ball, the old man freezing to death in an alleyway with nowhere else to go. They will erode Paul, like water wearing down stone, until there's nothing left.

Closer than Paul's sorrow is the clink of glass on glass as Henry pours another drink. The bottle's rim skips against the glass. Ice shifts with a sigh. He pictures Paul sitting on the edge of his bed, and it occurs to him too late that he didn't bother to look at the clock before he called. He listens for Maddy in the background, pretending to be asleep, rolling away and grinding her teeth in frustration at yet another of duty's late night call.

Henry likes Maddy. He loves her, even. If Paul had to marry a woman, he's glad Maddy was the one. From the first time Paul introduced them, Henry could see the places Paul and Maddy fit, the way their bodies gravitated to one another—hips bumping as they moved through the kitchen preparing dinner, fingers touching as they passed plates. They made sense in all the ways Paul and Henry did not, even though their own friendship had been instant, cemented when Paul came across Henry drunkenly trying to break into an ex-boyfriend's apartment to get his camera back, and offered to boost him through the window.

At the end of that first dinner with Maddy, Henry had sat on the deck with her finishing the last of the wine while Paul washed dishes.

"Does he know?" Maddy had asked.

Her gaze went to the kitchen window, a square of yellow light framing Paul at the sink. There was no jealousy in her voice, only sympathetic understanding.

"I don't know."

"I won't tell if you don't." Maddy reached over and squeezed Henry's hand, and from that moment, their relationship had been set, loving the same man, lamenting his choice of career.

Henry wants to tell Paul to wrap himself around Maddy, take comfort in the shape of her, and forget about the woman, but he knows Paul too well.

"I'll call you if I hear anything," Henry says.

"Henry?" Paul says as Henry moves to hang up.

"Yeah?"

"Are you still working on the—"

"The movie? Yeah. Still."

His movie. Their movie. The one they started together at NYU, back when they had dreams, back before Paul's father died. The one Henry is now making, failing to make, alone.

"Good. That's good," Paul says. "You'll have to show it to me someday."

"Yeah. Sure." Henry rubs his forehead. "Get some sleep, okay?"

Henry hangs up. In the space behind his eyes, a woman breathes and breathes and breathes until she doesn't breathe anymore.

⊸⊸

Sweat soaks thirteen-year-old Henry's sheets, sticking the t-shirt and boxer shorts he sleeps in against his skin. His mother left the windows open, but there's no breeze, only the oppressive heat they drove through to get to the rental cabin. His brother snores in the bunk above him, one hand dangling over the side.

The noise comes out of nowhere, starting as a hum, building to a scream, slamming into Henry full force. Henry claps his hands to his ears. Animal instinct sends him rabbiting from the bed. His legs tangle in the sheets, and he crashes to the floor. The sound is still there, tied to the heat, the weight and thickness of the air birthed in horrible sound.

"Henry?" Lionel's voice is sleep-muffled above him.

Henry barely hears it above the other sound, rising in pitch, inserting itself between his bones and his skin. There's another sound tucked inside it, too, worse still. A broken sound full of distress and pain.

Footsteps. His mother and father's voices join his brother's. Hands pry his hands from his ears.

"Can't you hear it?" Henry voice comes in a panicked whine, his breath in hitching gulps.

"Henry." His mother shakes him, and his eyes snap into focus.

"It's just cicadas. See?" His father points to the window.

A single insect body clings to the screen. Lionel trots over, flicking the insect away before pulling the window closed.

"What's wrong with him?" Lionel's asks.

Even with the window shut, the noise remains, filling every corner of the room.

"Can't you hear?" Henry's hands creep toward his ears again.

His mother gets him a glass of water. His father and brother watch him with wary eyes. They don't hear it. They hear the cicadas' song, but not the broken, stuttering sound that digs and scrapes at Henry's bones. No one hears it except for him.

Later, Henry learns that the sound is the cicadas' distress call, the noise they make when they're threatened or in pain. And over the course of the two weeks at the lake, Henry learns his hearing is different from the rest of his family's, possibly from almost everyone else he knows. There are tones, nuances, threads of sound that are lost to others. It's as though he's developed an extra sense and he hates it.

Lionel, however, turns it into a game, dragging Henry around to different parts of the lake, asking him what he hears, getting Henry to challenge him to see if he can hear it too. Henry's big brother grins, amazed at every sound Henry describes—birds murmuring in distant trees, small animals in the burrows, dropped fishing lines, an aluminum rowboat tapping against a dock all the way across the lake.

Henry almost allows himself to relax, to have fun, until on one of their excursions he hears the crying girl.

Henry and Lionel are deep enough in the woods surrounding the lake that the dense, mid-summer foliage screens them from the road, the water, and the other cottages. Henry scans the tree trunks, looking for shed cicada shells. The sound comes, like it did the first night, out of nowhere—a ticking, struggling sound like hitching breath. Except this time it isn't hidden in cicada song, but stark and alone, somewhere between mechanical and organic, full of pain.

Henry freezes, cold despite the sweat-slick summer air. Lionel is almost out of sight between the trees before he notices Henry is no longer with him.

"What's wrong?" Lionel trots back, touching Henry's arm.

Henry flinches. He's sharply aware of his own breath. His chest is too tight. Underneath the insect sound there is something else—distinctly human, horribly afraid. He tries to speak, and the only sound that emerges is an extended exhalation, a "hhhhhhhh" that goes on and on.

Lionel's repeated questions fall away. Henry stumbles away from his brother, half-blinded by stinging eyes, catching tree trunks for support. He follows the sound, its insistence a knife-sharp tug at his core. He needs to find the source of the sound. He needs . . .

Henry crashes to his knees, nearly falling into a hole opened up in the ground. The edges are ragged and soft, the forest floor swallowing itself in greedy mouthfuls. There's a caught breath of alarm from below him, wet with tears, weak with exhaustion, fading.

"There's someone down there." Henry pants, the words coming out between clenched teeth, his whole body shuddering. He's doubled over now, arms wrapped around his middle where the sound burrows inside him.

"What—" Lionel starts, but then he looks, seeing what Henry sees.

The girl is barely visible. The tree canopy blocks direct sunlight, and the hole is deep enough that the child is a mere smudge at the bottom.

"Get . . ." Henry's voice breaks. Tears stream on his cheeks. "Mom. Dad. Get help."

Lionel sprints away, and despite the pain, Henry stretches out flat on his stomach. Leaves crackle, branches poke at him. Things crawl through the earth underneath him, worms and beetles and blind moles further undermining its integrity, impossible things he shouldn't be able to hear. He stretches his arm as far as he can, pressing his cheek against the ground. He doesn't expect the girl to be able to reach him, but he hopes his presence might comfort her.

"It's okay." His shoulder feels like it will pop out of its socket. "I'm not going to leave you."

From the dark of the earth, the girl sniffles. Henry stretches further still, imagining small fingers reaching back for him.

"It's okay," he says again, terrified the girl will die before rescue comes. Terrified it will be his fault, his failure, if she does. "Just hold on, okay? Hold on."

⟶

The second time, Henry listens to the tape with his eyes closed. It scarcely matters. He still sees the woman, slumped and taking her last shallow breaths, but inside the theater of his mind she is so much worse. She's carved up by shadow, her skin blotched as though already rotting from within. At any moment she will raise her head and glare at Henry, his powerlessness, his voyeurism.

He stretches after any glimmer of identifying sound, wondering if his unwanted superpower has finally chosen this moment to abandon him. Then, all at once, the sound is there, sharp as a physical blow.

A faint burr, rising from nothing to a scream. The cicada song he can't help hearing as a herald of doom. It knocks the breath from his lungs, bringing in its place the heat of summer days, air heavy and close and pressed against the window screens. He shoves his chair back from the desk so hard he almost topples, and stares, wide-eyed. The image on the screen doesn't change. After a moment, he forces himself to hit rewind. Play.

Ragged breath, stuttering and catching. There's no hint of insect song. Even though Henry knows exactly when the rise and fall of the woman's chest will cease, he holds his own breath. Every time her breath falters, he finds himself wishing the painful sound would just stop. It's a horrible thought, but he can't help it, his own lungs screaming as he waits, waits, waits, to hear whether she will breathe again.

Then, a sound so faint yet so distinct Henry both can't believe he missed it, and isn't certain it's really there. He reverses the tape again, afraid the sound will vanish. Sweat prickles, sour and hot in his armpits. He barely hears the woman breathing this time, his strange powers of hearing focused on the almost imperceptible sound of a train.

A primal response of exaltation—Henry wants to shout and punch the air in triumph. And at the same time, the woman on the screen is still dying, has been dead for days, weeks, months even, and there's nothing he can do. Henry forces himself to listen one last time, just to be sure. The train is more distinct this time, the lonely howl of approaching a crossing. Goosebumps break out across Henry's skin. His body wants to tremble, and he clenches his teeth as though he's freezing cold.

He must have imagined the cicadas, even though the noise felt so real, a visceral sensation crawling beneath his skin. The train, though, the train is real. He can isolate the sound, play it for Paul. It's an actual clue.

He thinks of the summer at the lake when he was thirteen years old, Lionel snoring in the bunk above him. That first terrible night where it seemed as though all the cicadas in the trees around the lake had found their way into the room. Then, later, how their song had led him to the almost-buried girl.

Henry reaches for the phone.

"I'm going to send a sound file your way," he says when Paul answers. "It's something. I don't know if it's enough."

"What is it?" Water runs in the background, accompanied by the clatter of Paul doing dishes. Henry imagines the phone balanced precariously between Paul's ear and shoulder, the lines of concern bracketing his mouth and crowded between his eyes.

"A train. It sounds like it's coming up to a crossing."

"That's brilliant." For a moment there's genuine elation in Paul's voice, the same sense of victory Henry felt moments ago. And just as quickly, the weight settles back in. "It might give us a radius to search, based on where the car was found, and assuming the killer was somewhat local to that area."

There's a grimness to Paul's voice, a hint of distraction as though he's already half forgotten Henry is on the other end of the phone, his thoughts churning.

"Thank you" Paul says after a moment, coming back to himself.

The water stops, but Henry pictures Paul still standing at the sink, hands dripping, looking lost.

"I should—" Paul starts, and Henry says, "Wait."

He takes a breath. He knows what he's about to ask is unreasonable, but he needs to see. Without the safety and filter of a camera and a video screen in the way.

"When you go looking, I want to go with you."

"Henry, I—"

"I know," Henry interrupts. His left hand clenches and unclenches until he consciously forces himself to relax. "I know, but you probably weren't supposed to send me the tape either."

Henry waits. He doesn't say please. Paul takes a breath, wants to say no. But Henry is already in this, Paul invited him in, and he's determined to see it through.

"Fine. I'll call you, okay?"

They hang up, and Henry returns to his computer to isolate the clip and send it to Paul. Once that's done, Henry opens up another file, the one containing the jumble of clips he shot with Paul at NYU. Back when they had big dreams. Back before Paul's father died. Back before 57 minutes of a woman breathing out her last in an unknown room.

Henry chooses a clip at random, and lets it play. A young man sits in the backseat of a car, leaning his head against the window. He's traveling across the country, from a small town to a big city. The same journey Henry himself had taken, though he'd only crossed a state. There are other clips following a boy who grew up in the city, in his father's too-big shadow, but both boys' heads are full of dreams. Two halves of the same story, trying to find a way to fit together into a whole. Except now, the film will always be unfinished, missing its other half.

Even though he knows he will never finish the movie without Paul, Henry still thinks about the sounds that should accompany the clip. It's an exercise he engages in from time to time, torturing himself, unwilling to let the movie go. Here, he would put the hum of tires, but heard through the bones of the young man's skull, an echo chamber created where his forehead meets the glass.

The perfect soundscape would also evoke fields cropped to stubble, the smell of dust and baking tar and asphalt. It would convey nerves as the boy leaves behind everything he's ever known for bright lights and subway systems. Most importantly, it would also put the audience in the boy's shoes as he dreams of kissing another boy without worrying about being seen by someone he knows, without his parents' disappointment, and the judgment of neighbors' faces around him in church every Sunday.

Henry watches the reflections slide by on screen—telephone poles and clouds seen at a strange angle. His own drive was full of wind-and-road hum broken by his parents' attempts at conversation, trying to patch things already torn between them. Henry had gotten good at filtering by then, shutting out things he didn't want to hear. Maybe he should have given his parents a chance, but love offered on the condition of pretending to be someone else didn't interest him then, and it doesn't interest him now.

Between one frame and the next, the image on the screen jumps, and Henry jumps with it. Trees, jagged things like cracks in the sky, replace the cloud and telephone pole reflections. The car window itself is gone, and the camera looks up at the whip-thin branches from a low angle.

Then the image snaps back into place just as Henry slaps the pause button. He knows what he and Paul shot. He has watched the clips countless times, and everything about the trees cracking their way across the sky is wrong, wrong, wrong.

When the phone rings, Henry almost jumps out of his skin. He knocks the phone off the desk reaching for it, leaving him sounding weirdly out of breath when he finally brings it to his ear.

"I'll pick you up tomorrow around ten," Paul says. "I have an idea."

"Okay." Henry lets out a shaky breath.

His pulse judders, refusing to calm. He needs a drink and a shower. Then maybe a whole pot of coffee, because the last thing he wants to do is sleep. When he blinks, he sees thin, black branches criss-crossing the sky, and he hears the rising whine of cicada song.

◄◦►

There is a legend that says cicadas were humans once. They sang so beautifully that the Muses enchanted them to sing long past the point when they would normally grow tired, so they could provide entertainment throughout the night while the Gods feasted.

But the enchantment worked too well. The singers stopped eating. They stopped sleeping. They forgot how to do anything except sing.

They starved to death, and even then the enchantment held. They kept singing, unaware they'd died. Their bodies rotted, and their song went on, until one of the Muses took pity on them and fashioned them new bodies with chitinous shells and wings. Bodies with the illusion of immortality that could live for years underground, buried as if dead, but wake again.

Cicadas are intimately acquainted with pain, because they know what it is to die a slow death as a spectacle for someone else's pleasure. But they do not die when they are buried. They merely dream, and listen to other buried things, things that perhaps should not have been buried at all. They remember what they hear. When they wake, they are ready to tell the secrets they know. When they wake, they sing.

◄◦►

Paul drives, Henry in the passenger seat beside him, a bag of powdered donuts between them, and two steaming cups of coffee in the cup holders.

"Isn't that playing a bit to stereotype?" Henry points. Paul grins, brushing powdered sugar from his jeans.

"So sue me. They're delicious." He helps himself to another. Henry's stomach is too tight for food, but he keeps sipping his coffee, even though his nerves are already singing.

Paul mapped out a widening radius from where the car with the miniDV in the glove box was found, circling the nearby railroad crossings. It isn't much, but it's something. They're out here hoping that whoever killed the woman crashed his car on the way back to his home, which might be the place he killed the woman. Maybe they'll find her body there, or maybe he was on the way back from burying her somewhere else. Maybe they'll find him. Henry is both prepared and unprepared for this scenario.

Right now, he's not letting himself think that far ahead. He's focusing on the plan, tenuous as it is, driving around to likely locations where he will *listen.* Henry feels like a television psychic, which is to say a total fraud. He wants to enjoy the relative silence of the car, the tick of the turn signal, the engine revving up and down. He wants to enjoy spending time with Paul, catching up, just old friends. He doesn't want to be thinking of snuff films and ghosts, and on top of that there's a nervous ache in his chest that keeps him conscious of every time he glances at Paul, wondering if his gaze lingers too long.

Trees border the road. It's early fall, and most are denuded of their leaves. Henry peers between the trunks, looking for deer. The sound, when it comes, is every bit as unexpected and violent as the last time. A reverberating hum, rising to a scream—cicada song, but with another noise tucked inside it this time, one he remembers from when he was a child.

That hitching, broken sound. Like gears in a machine struggling to catch. Like a baby's cry. A wounded animal. Henry jerks, his body instinctively trying to flee. His head strikes the window, pain blooming in his forehead above his right eye.

"Are you—"

Concern tinges Paul's voice, but Henry barely hears it. The sound has hooks beneath his skin, wanting to drag him in amongst the trees.

"Turn here." Henry bites the words out through the pain, the song filling him up until there's no space left for breath.

Paul looks at him askance, but flicks the turn signal, putting them on a road that quickly gives way to gravel and dust. The trees grow closer here, their branches whip-thin, the same ones he saw in the corrupted clip of their film.

"Pull over."

Henry's breath comes easier now, the pain fading to a dull ache like a bruise. The cicada song forms an undercurrent, less urgent, but not completely gone. Paul kills the engine. His expression is full of concern. Henry wants to thank him for his trust, but whatever waits for them in the woods is no cause for either for them to be thankful.

He climbs out of the car, buries his hands in his pockets, and walks. Leaves crunch as Paul trots behind him. Nervous energy suffuses the air between. Henry hears the questions Paul wants to ask, held trapped behind his teeth. It's nothing Henry can explain so he keeps walking, head down.

When Henry stops, it's so sudden, Paul almost trips. Tree branches cross the sky in the exact configuration Henry saw in the film, only the angle is wrong. Henry should be seeing them from lower down. From the height of a child.

The burr of cicadas grow louder, the steady drone rising to an ecstatic yell. Henry forces himself to keep his eyes on the trees, turning to walk backward. He pictures a girl being led through the trees, a man's hand clamped on her upper arm. Her death waits for her among the trees, and so does a camera on a tripod.

Henry is thirteen years old again, listening to the crying girl, lost and frightened and in pain. The hours after her discovery blur in his mind, though certain moments stand out sharp as splinters beneath his skin. The scent of leaf rot and dirt, his cheek pressed to the forest floor. His parents lifting him bodily out of the way as the rescue crew arrived, and Henry scrabbling at the earth, refusing to let go, terrified of leaving the girl alone.

He remembers seeing the girl's face for the first time but not what she looked like. In his mind, her features are as blurred and indistinct as they were at the bottom of the hole—eyes and mouth dark wounds opened in her pale skin.

There were endless questions from his parents, from the rescue crew—how had he found the girl, did he see her fall, was it an accident, did someone hurt her? They called Henry a hero, and he wanted none of it. He remembers burying himself under the blankets on the bottom bunk in the cabin, wishing he could stay there for years like a cicada, only emerging with everyone long gone.

Now, as then, the insect song times itself to the blood pounding like a headache in Henry's skull. He's sharply aware of Paul watching him, eyes wide as Henry stops and turns around.

The shack is half-hidden in the trees, scarcely bigger than a garden shed. There's a catch in Paul's breath, and Henry glances over to see Paul's hand go to his service revolver.

The door isn't locked, but it sticks, warped with weather and clogged with leaves. Henry holds his breath, expecting a stench, expecting a horror movie jump scare, but there's nothing inside but more dead leaves and a pile of filthy rags. A small wooden mallet rests up against one wall.

Paul uses a flashlight to sweep the room, even though they can see every corner from the door. A seam in the floor catches the light, and once Paul points it out, Henry can't unsee it. Paul kneels, prying up boards with a kind of frantic energy, using the edge of a penknife.

"It's another tape." Paul straightens. There's dirt under his nails.

"He killed more than one person." Henry swallows against a sour taste at the back of his throat. He knew, the moment he saw the corrupted bit of film, the moment he heard the cicadas scream, but he'd wanted desperately to be wrong.

Paul holds the tape in a handkerchief, turning it so Henry can see the handwritten label—*Exsanguination*.

"I brought my camcorder. It's in the car." Henry feels the beginning of tremors, starting in the soles of his feet and working their way up his spine. Adrenaline. Animal fear. Some intuition made him pack film equipment before leaving the house, and Henry loathes that part of himself now.

Back in the car, Paul runs the heater, even though there's barely a chill in the air. Sweat builds inside Henry's sweatshirt as he fumbles with the tape, wearing the cotton gloves Paul gave him to preserve fingerprints. He flips the camcorder's small screen so they can both see, but hesitates a moment before hitting play, as if that could change the outcome. Henry knows all movies are ghost stories, frozen slices of time, endlessly replayed. Whatever will happen has already happened. The only thing he and Paul can do is witness it.

Static shoots across the screen, then the image steadies. The girl can't be more than ten years old. Her hair is very long and hangs over her shoulder in a braid. She stands in the center of the shack, dressed in shorts and a t-shirt. Dim light comes through a single grimy window. She shivers.

A man in a bulky jacket and ski mask steps into frame. He picks up the mallet leaned against the wall in the shed, now in a plastic evidence bag in the back of Paul's car, and he methodically breaks every one of the girl's fingers.

The image cuts, then the man and girl are outside. The camera sits on a tripod, watching as the man leads the girl to the spot framed by two stubby trees. The girl is barefoot. She sobs, a sound of pure exhaustion that reminds Henry of the little girl in the hole. This girl's ankles are tied. Her hands free, but useless, her fingers all wrong angles, pulped and shattered.

The man unbraids the girl's hair. He employs the same care he used breaking her fingers. Once it's unbound, it hangs well past the middle of her back. The man lifts and winds strands of it into the spindly branches of the trees growing behind her, creating a wild halo of knots and snarls and twigs.

The girl cannot flee when the man pulls out a knife. She thrashes, a panicked, trapped animal, but the knots of her hair hold her fast. He cuts. Long slashes cover her exposed thighs, her knees, her calves, her arms.

How long does it take a person to bleed to death? Henry and Paul are about to find out.

After what seems like an eternity, long after the girl has stopped struggling, the man steps out of frame. The camera watches as the trees bow, the girl slumps. Branches crack, freeing strands of her hair, but far too late.

Henry gets the door open just as bile and black coffee hits the back of his throat. He heaves and spits until his stomach is empty. Paul places a hand on his back, the only point of warmth in a world gone freezing cold. Henry leans back into the car, and Paul puts his arms around Henry, holding him until the shaking stops.

"I'm sorry," Paul says. "I shouldn't have dragged you into this."

The expression on Paul's face when he says it is a blow to Henry's freshly emptied gut. The pain in Paul's eyes is real, yes, but what accompanies it isn't quite regret. Instead, guilt underlies the pain, and Paul's gaze shifts away.

In that moment, Henry knows that Paul wouldn't change a thing if he could. He would still ask Henry to watch the tape, no matter how many times the scenario replayed. This death, among every other he's witnessed, is too big to hold alone. He needs to share the burden with someone, and that someone couldn't be Maddy. Because that kind of death spreads like rot, corrupting everything it touches, like it corrupted Henry and Paul's film, their past, their shared dream. Henry understands. If Paul shared that pain with Maddy, it would become the only thing he would see any time he looked at her, and the only thing he could do to save himself would be to let her go. And Maddy isn't someone Paul is willing to let go.

"I'm sorry," Paul says again.

"Me too." Henry reaches for the passenger side door, pulling it closed. He can't look at Paul. His face aches, like a headache in every part of his skull at once. Paul shifts the car into drive.

"Are you . . ." Paul's words fall into the silence after they've been driving for a few moments, but he stops, as if realizing the inappropriateness of what he was about to say.

Henry hears the words anyway. *"Are you seeing anyone now?"* Bitterness rises to the back of his throat even though his stomach is empty now. Paul could have asked the question any time during the drive, if he really wanted to know, if the question was genuine curiosity, and not born of guilt. Paul asked Henry to share his burden, and now it hurts him to think that Henry might have to carry it alone in turn. Henry hears the words even when Paul doesn't say them, his golden ear catching sounds no one else ever would.

"I hope you find someone," Paul says finally as he pulls back onto the road. "You shouldn't be alone. No one should."

Henry knows what Paul is saying; he should find someone to share his burden too. Henry can't imagine someone loving him enough to take on that kind of pain; he can't imagine ever wanting someone to. He knows what that kind of love feels like from the other side.

The heater makes a struggling, wheezing sound, and Paul switches it off, rolling his window down. Air roars through the cabin, and cold sweat dries on Henry's skin. If it weren't for Henry's golden ear, the wind would swallow Paul's next words whole.

"I'm sorry it couldn't be me."

⟡

It's a good two days before Henry brings himself to check the other clips he shot with Paul. The rot has spread to every single one of them. There's an open barn door looking out onto a barren field, rising up to block the buildings of Manhattan, a water stain on a ceiling spreading to cover the boy's face as he gets his first glimpse of the city, a crack of light under a closet door instead of the flickering gap between subway trains. Each new images is a hole punched in an already fragile structure, unwinding it even more.

Henry understands what the scenes are now, after watching *Exsanguination*. They are films made by ghosts, the last image each of the killer's victims saw before they died. What he doesn't understand is why he is seeing them. Is it because he had the misfortune to hear what shouldn't have been there for him to hear? The cicadas, linking him to the woman whose last sight was of trees through a grimy window. Her death linking him to the deaths of the other ghosts.

Henry shakes himself, thinking of his and Paul's drive home from their aborted attempt to find answers. Awkward silence reigned until Henry stood outside the car, looking in through the driver's window at Paul. Then their fragmentary sentences had jumbled on top of each other.

"You don't have to—" from Paul.

And, "Next time you go—" from Henry.

Standing there, trying not to shiver, Henry had extracted a promise.

"Call me before you go looking. I mean it. I'm coming with you." He almost said, *whether you like it or not,* but Henry knows it isn't a matter of like; it's a matter of need. He saw the gratitude in Paul's eyes and his self-loathing underneath it, hating the fact that he should need to ask Henry to do this thing, that he should be too cowardly to refuse and demand Henry stay home. One way or another, they will both see this through to the end.

Henry doesn't tell Paul about the images corrupting their film. But he watches them again, obsessively, alone, until each is imprinted on his eyelids. His dreams are full of doorways and trees and silvers of light. At the end of the week, Paul finally calls, his voice weary and strained.

"Tomorrow afternoon," Paul says.

Henry barely lets him get the words out before saying, "I'll be ready."

—◇—

They drive away from the city. Henry's stomach is heavy with dread and the sense of déjà vu. He clenches his jaw, already braced for the sound of cicadas, and speaks without looking Paul's way.

"We're looking for a house with a barn."

From the corner of his eye, Henry sees Paul half turn to him, a question and confusion giving a troubled look to his eyes. But he doesn't ask out loud, and Henry doesn't explain. They drive in relative silence until they reach the first railroad crossing on Paul's map, intending to circle outward from there.

It takes Henry some time to realize that the sound he's been bracing for has been there all along, a susurrus underlying the tire hum and road noise, a constant ache at the base of his skull. How long has he been listening to the cicadas? How long have they been driving?

Fragments of conversation reach him. He realizes Paul has been asking questions, and he's been answering them, but he has no sense of the words coming from his mouth, or even any idea what they're talking about. Suddenly, the noise in his head spikes and with it, the pain. Henry grinds his teeth so hard he swears his molars will crack.

"Here." The word has the same ticking, struggling quality as the cicada's distress call.

Henry is thirteen years old again, wanting to clap his hands over his ears, wanting to crawl away from the sound.

"What—"

"Turn here." Henry barks the words, harsh, and Paul obeys, the car fishtailing as Paul slews them onto a long, narrow drive. The drive rises, and when they crest the hill, Henry catches sight of a farmhouse. Paul stops the car. From this vantage point, Henry can just make out the roof of a barn where the land dips down again.

Henry is first out of the car, placing one hand against the hood to steady himself. He closes his eyes, and listens. He's queasy, breathing shallowly, but there, as if simply waiting for him to arrive, the mournful, unspooling call of a train sounds in the distance.

"You hear it too, right?" Henry opens his eyes, finally turning to Paul.

Paul inclines his head, the barest of motions. He looks shaken in a way Henry has never seen before.

"This is the place." Henry opens his eyes, moving toward the front door.

A sagging porch wraps around the house on two sides. To the right, straggly trees stretch toward the sky. Without having to look, Henry knows there is a basement window looking up at those trees.

Paul draws his service revolver. The sound of him knocking is the loudest thing Henry has ever heard. When there's no answer, Paul tries the knob. It isn't locked. Paul leads and Henry follows, stepping into the gloom of an unlit hallway. The stench hits Henry immediately, and he pulls his shirt up over his nose.

Stairs lead up to the left. Rooms open from the entryway on either side, filled with sheet-covered furniture, and windows sealed-over with plywood boards. Paul climbs the stairs, and again, Henry follows. Up here, the scent is worse. There are brownish smears on the wall, as if someone reached out a bloody hand to steady themselves and left the blood to dry.

At the top of the stairs and to the left is a door bearing a full bloody handprint. It hangs partially open, and Paul nudges it open the rest of the way. Henry's view is over Paul's shoulder, not even fully stepped into the room, and even that is too much.

The corpse on the bed is partially decomposed, lying on rumpled sheets nearly black with filth. There are no flies, the body is too far gone for that, but Henry hears them anyway, the ghostly echo of their buzz. But just because the flies are gone doesn't mean there aren't other scavengers. A beetle crawls over the man's foot.

Henry bolts down the stairs before he realizes it, back in the kitchen where unwashed dishes pile on the counter tops, with more in the sink. Garbage fills the bin by the door. The air here smells sour, but after the room upstairs, it's almost a relief.

Henry thinks of the wrecked car, and imagines the killer somehow pulling himself from the wreck, somehow managing to make it back home, only to die here, bleeding out the way the girl in the woods did. He wants to feel satisfaction for the strange twist of justice, but there's only sickness, and beneath that, a hollow still needing to be filled.

Henry turns toward the basement door. It seems to glare back at him until he makes himself cross the room and open it. Wooden steps, the kind built with boards that leave gaps of darkness between, lead down.

He finds a light switch, but he doesn't bother. Light filters in from the high basement window. It matches the light on the tape where the woman breathed and died and so it is enough.

Beneath the window, a pipe rises from the unfinished floor. There's a tripod aimed at the pipe, a camera sitting on the tripod, the door where the tape was ejected standing. At the base of the pipe, there are marks on the floor. When Henry bends close to see, they resolve into words. *Find me.*

Henry's breath emerges in a whine. For once, his ears fail him. He doesn't hear Paul descending the stairs until Paul is beside him, touching his shoulder. Henry can't bring himself to look up. He can't even bring himself to stand. He stays crouched where he is, swaying slightly. When he does finally look up, it isn't at Paul, it's at the window. On the other side of the dirty glass, stark, black branches criss-cross the grey sky. Henry looks at them for a very long time. And he breathes.

◄◦►

There are twelve more tapes. They arrive in a padded envelope, each one labeled like the originals, copies written in Paul's hand—*Exhalation 1-9, Contusion, Asphyxiation*, and *Delirium*. Henry didn't ask, but Paul knew he would need to see them. Even so, it's several weeks before Henry can bring himself to watch.

In *Asphyxiation*, a man hangs from the rafters of the barn, slowly strangling to death under his own weight. In *Contusion*, a little boy is beaten within in an inch of his life and locked in a dark closet, only the faintest silver of light showing underneath the door. In *Delirium*, an old man is strapped to a bed, injected with a syringe, and left to scream out his life with only the water spot on the ceiling for company.

Paul informs Henry by email that four bodies were unearthed on the property—the old man, the young boy, the hanged man, and the girl. But not the woman. Paul informs Henry that the search is ongoing, her body may have been dumped in the woods somewhere, buried or unburied. It may even have been on the way back that the killer crashed and crawled free of the wreck, leaving the tape behind.

What made her special? Or is she special at all? Perhaps the killer was afraid of burying yet another body so close to his home. Maybe he was planning to dig up the others and move them too, but he never got the chance. Or maybe, just maybe, he woke in the middle of the night to an insistent cicada's scream and tried to get the woman's corpse as far away as he could. As if that would ever make them stop.

Henry watches the clips one last time, the ones he and Paul shot, the ones corrupted with ghosts. The frames are back to normal, only the footage he and Paul shot of city streets and subway rides—no stark trees, no water-stained ceiling. Henry sees those things nonetheless. He will see them every time he looks at the film. The only thing he can do to save himself is let them go.

After he watches the clips for the last time, he deletes every last one.

◄◦►

When Henry finally makes his movie, his great masterpiece, it's no longer about a boy leaving the country for the city and finding his true home and meeting a boy from the city who grew up in his father's shadow. The city no longer belongs to the boy Henry used to be, and the boy who grew up in his father's shadow never belonged to him at all.

Before he begins work on the movie, Henry moves to a city on the other coast, one smelling of the sea. The trees rising up against the sky there are straight and singular; their branches do not fracture and crack across the sky. That fact goes a little way toward easing his sleep, though he still dreams.

While working on the movie that is no longer about a boy, Henry meets a very sweet assistant director of photography who smiles in a way Henry can't help return. Soon, Henry finds himself smiling constantly.

Even though the movie Henry makes isn't the one he thought he would make when he first dreamed of neon and subways and fame, it earns him an Oscar nomination. He is in love with the assistant director of photography, and he is loved in turn. He is happy in the city smelling of the sea, as happy as he can be. The love he has with the assistant director of photography—whose eye is good, but not quite golden—isn't the kind of love that would willingly take the burden of death and pain from Henry's shoulders. For that, Henry is grateful. He would crack under the weight of that kind of love, and besides, half his burden already belongs to the man he willingly took it from years ago.

At first, Maddy sends a card every Christmas, and Henry and Paul exchange emails on their respective birthdays. But Henry knew, even on the day he packed up the last of his belongings to drive to the other coast, when he said *see you later* to Paul, he was really saying *goodbye*. Paul chose, and Henry consented to his choice. Maybe Paul's relationship with Maddy could have survived the weight of his pain, but that wasn't a risk he would take.

Henry is the one to drop their email chain, "forgetting" to reply to Paul's wishes of happy birthday. When Paul's birthday rolls around, Henry "forgets" again. It's a mercy—not for him, but for their friendship. Henry can't bear to watch something else die slowly, rotting from within, struggling for one last breath to stay alive. Perhaps it isn't fair, but Henry imagines he hears Paul's sigh of relief across the miles, imagines the lines of tension in his shoulders finally slackening as he lets the last bit of the burden of the woman's death go.

For his part, Henry holds on tighter than before. The movie that earns him his Oscar nomination is about a woman, one who is a stranger, yet one he knows intimately. He saw her at her weakest. He watched her die. The words scratched in the floor where the woman breathed her last, *find me*, are also written on Henry's heart.

He cannot find the woman physically, so he transforms the words into a plea to find *her*, who she was in life or who she might have been. Henry imagines the best life he can for her, and he puts it on film. It is the only gift he can give her; it isn't enough.

When Henry wins his Oscar, his husband, the assistant director of photography, is beside him, bursting with pride. They both climb the stage, along with the rest of the crew. The score from their film plays as they arrange themselves around the microphone. Henry tries not to clench his jaw. A thread winds through the music, so faint no one else would ever hear—the faint burr of rising insect song.

Paradoxically, it is making the movie he never expected to make that finally allows Henry to understand the movie he tried to make years ago. Even though he destroyed the clips, that first movie still exists in his mind. He dreams it, asleep and waking. In the theater of his mind, it is constantly interrupted by windows seen at the wrong angle, water stains, and slivers of light, and scored entirely by insect screams.

The movie that doesn't exist isn't a coming of age story. It isn't a story about friendship. It's a love story, just not the traditional kind.

Because what else could watching so many hours of death be? How else to explain letting those frames of death corrupt his film, reach its roots back to the place where their friendship began and swallow it whole? What other name is there for Henry's lost hours of sleep, and the knowledge that he wouldn't say no, even if Paul asked for his help again. Even now. When Henry would still, always, say yes every time.

Every time Henry looks back on the film in his mind, all he sees is pain, the burden he willingly took from Paul so he wouldn't have to carry it alone. Even so, Henry will never let it go. The movie doesn't exist, he destroyed every last frame, but it will always own a piece of Henry's heart. And so will the man he made it for.

A HOTEL IN GERMANY

CATRIONA WARD

The movie star calls Cara at three thirty a.m.

Cara is dreaming of a night forest. She hears the tattoo of spongy elk hooves on the forest floor, glimpses dark hide through the lacework of foliage. The shrill of the telephone merges with the sounds of her dream, entwines with her breath and beating heart. She emerges slowly, reluctant. Perhaps it is not a dream but a memory, resurfacing. That has been happening, of late. She lifts the phone with mitten hands. 'Hello.' Her tongue is clumsy with sleep. There is no answer. But Cara recognises the resentful silence that rises between those who love one another. Family.

"Axel," she says, then, with difficulty, "Rose?" Her dead brother is calling, or maybe even her dead daughter, whose name still hurts to think or say, like a wound in her mind.

The receiver crackles with rage. "It won't work, Cara," the movie star says. "It won't be quiet. I've tried everything." She means the TV remote control. Her anger is so vast, it can only find tiny outlets, pinhole cracks in a great dam.

"I'm coming," Cara says. Reality settles around her.

She gets out of bed slowly, careful of her limbs, her elbows, her toes. Her body remembers slower than her mind and she hurts herself, sometimes.

She puts on clothes at random, plucked from the floor. The hotel corridor is dimmed for the night, with only glowing bars of soft white at floor level.

Cara lets herself into the movie star's suite. The TV plays the news at deafening volume, fighting the radio, tuned to a country station. Cucumber slices spill from a glass dish across the parquet floor. The air is filled with the scent of sandalwood. The movie star engages all her senses, day and night. Cara understands that. If you leave a space you can never predict what will arrive to fill it.

The movie star sits upright at the centre of the bed, sheets whipped up around her like meringue. Gleaming specks of gold and jet and emerald and diamond are scattered across the white. Velvet pouches and silk lined boxes are piled beside her.

"I've told you not to take your jewellery to bed," Cara says. "Something will get lost."

The movie star holds out the remote control to Cara, appealing. Her anger has melted into sadness. These mercurial shifts of feeling make her mesmerising on the screen. She is a clear pool in which dark fish swim. Cara mutes the news and puts on the shiny chrome kettle, which the movie star never leaves home without. She slices lemon and plucks mint leaves from the plant on the windowsill. As the water heats Cara returns each piece of jewellery gently to its box. Then she puts the boxes back in the safe, listing them as she does it.

"Gold collar set with pearls," she says. "Drop earrings, white gold and yellow diamond. Platinum cuff with sapphires." The movie star nods along and ticks each item off on her fingers. "Gold ring with diamond solitaire," Cara says. "Ruby pendant." The ritual imparts a pleasant sense of order.

When all eight pieces are in the safe, the movie star gets out of bed with a sigh. Cara turns her back while she enters the safe combination and locks it. The kettle begins to emit light wisps of steam. It makes no sound as it boils. Money can buy silence, even from a kettle. Cara pours out two cups and adds the lemon and mint. Their clean scent fills the air.

The movie star holds her cup tightly in both hands like a child. She gestures towards the silent screen which shows a sun-baked village and a thin man picking sticks out of the dust. "Look at this," she says. "The state of everything. It makes me so angry, keeps me up at night." She looks into the large mirror beside the bed, pulls an eyelid up, peers at her clear, white eyeball.

"You should get some sleep," Cara says. Her own eyelids give with the sandy weight of exhaustion.

"I can't," the movie star says. "This room! It faces north and the windows don't open. I can't think in here. *Smothering.* What is your room like?"

"A single," says Cara. "Not a suite like this."

"What direction does it face?"

"West, I think." Cara knows that it faces west. Some muffled instincts remain to her. She still feels the pull of sunrise and sunset like a twist in her belly.

"Let's go to your room," the movie star says.

They pad along the corridor like cats in their bare feet. The movie star leans heavily on Cara's shoulder.

◄◦►

Cara moves her discarded pyjamas off the single bed. The movie star gets into it. She pulls the sheets up to her chin. She looks very beautiful. "That's better," she says. "Can't you feel how much better the energy is in this room?" Cara sits in a chair and waits.

The movie star starts to talk in a low voice about her mother, and how she misses her. She talks about how it feels to love someone and fear them at the same time, because they can hurt you so badly. Cara listens. The movie star talks about the producer, who is messing with the script, giving her male co-star the best lines. Cara nods and makes more hot lemon. The little white hotel kettle whistles and roars. "You're lucky to be so small," the movie star says. "My legs are too long for most beds." She wiggles her toes, which peep out pink from beneath the duvet. "This is nice. I like it when it's just the two of us."

At length, the movie star's words begin to slur and her head droops. She rests her cheek on the pillow and sleeps.

Cara rises silently. She goes to the bathroom and takes the little green bottle from the cabinet. She paints her sore gums with the brush that comes with the bottle. At first it tickles, then the cold feeling rushes in, making her mouth numb and icy. She takes the pills. Blue, then white, then white and yellow. Her reflection regards her; her small thin face like a serious antelope. Dark hair cropped boy-short like all the other assistants in LA this summer. She looks too young to be taken seriously.

The movie star snores gently. Cara sets the alarm, and then curls up in the armchair by the window. *I am lucky*, she reminds herself, as she does each night before sleep and in the morning on waking. *One of the lucky ones.*

She drifts as the sun comes up, spilling shattered fragments of light on the broad running river below.

⟨⟩

The shooting day goes well. In the evening, the movie star hums as Cara makes pine needle and calendula tea. The movie star holds each butterscotch candy in her mouth for three seconds before removing it. Then she adds it to a glistening pile on the little silver plate at her side. A piece of steamed salmon sits untouched under its silver lid on the white-clothed table. "I need tomorrow's call sheet," she says.

"I'll go and copy it," Cara says. Each day the call sheet has to be taped to the movie star's mirror, to the back of her bathroom door, placed in a clear folder in her handbag, and another left on the desk. The movie star can't hold times and days in her head. Cara can. Maybe it's because she doesn't own anything. Her life is uncluttered.

"Don't take hours about it like last time." The movie star sounds imperious, but Cara sees her fear. When Cara leaves the room there will be a gap in which thoughts may creep in. Cara touches the back of the movie star's slim brown hand and goes. *Don't let it be Greta on reception*, she thinks. She is bad at human conflict. *Be the nice girl with the round pink cheeks.* As the elevator drifts down towards the lobby Cara closes her eyes and whispers, "Not Greta, not Greta, not Greta . . ." She tries to make a spell of it.

Greta's silver name badge gleams in the low light. Her false eyelashes look like peacock feathers. Her skin is smooth and beautiful. She looks tired. Before Cara can speak she holds up a pointed red nail. Her fingers fly over the nubs of the console.

Greta does not like Cara. Cara is the conduit for all the movie star's needs; three changes of suite, a screened off area in the dining room, so that no one can see her eat, silence in the corridor outside her room from 9 p.m. onwards. The movie star does not like to phone housekeeping. She needs to be seen. She prefers to go down to the lobby, glide past the people waiting at reception and ask for things in her clear voice. Despite the name tag, the movie star calls Greta "you—girl!" "You, girl—I need a bouquet of freesias in each room." Or she talks to Greta through Cara. "Tell the girl I need fresh towels."

Greta gives a final violent tap on the space bar and looks at Cara, black eyebrows raised.

"Could you please print four copies and send them up to her room?" Cara puts the memory port on the desk. It pulses gentle silver and white, as if it had a secret.

"We don't print," Greta says. "Who uses paper anymore?"

"The other receptionist did it for me yesterday," Cara says.

Greta raises her eyebrows. "And we don't print from memory ports. Hotel policy. Infection, you know."

Cara is beginning to feel a helpless panic. This has taken too long already. The movie star is waiting. "It was ok yesterday."

"Then you are very, very lucky that there was no infection." Greta's voice is filled with quiet triumph. "That member of staff will be disciplined."

Cara goes up to her room and puts the file on a data stick. She imagines the movie star's anxiety mounting. Her need for Cara seems to creep under the door like mustard gas.

Back at the desk, Greta says, "We charge a dollar a page. In cash. I can't leave reception to take it to the room, so you'll have to wait here."

Cara gives Greta eight dollars, which is all the money she has. The movie star doesn't carry it. Cara feels like explaining, "You are not hurting her by doing this, not at all." But offended dignity needs bloodshed, and Cara is available.

◄◦►

"I thought you were dead," says the movie star. The mountain of sucked butterscotch has grown. The steamed salmon fillet has been picked at and turned over to hide the gnawed places. The movie star eats like a dying animal—in secret, lashing out if discovered. "I was just about to report you absconded. Where have you been?"

"Printing the call sheet," says Cara. The movie star is always threatening to report Cara absconded. That doesn't mean she won't do it. She might, and then be very sorry afterwards. Cara smiles to cover the cold fear lancing through her chest. Then she quickly closes her lips. Her gums ache. "It was eight dollars for the printing."

"That's absurd," the movie star says. "I won't pay it. I'll dispute my bill with the manager. I need quiet now, to centre myself. Absolute quiet. You'll be in your room?"

"Of course," Cara says.

As Cara closes the door behind her the movie star is picking up the phone. She is calling the director, to tell him to change the shooting order.

◄◦►

Cara cannot leave her room, but she has a window. She can give the implant something pretty to watch. The night river runs by sleek and strong. A group of women walks along the bank, laughing. They are in their twenties perhaps, in the middle of their evening, flowing from one place to another.

One has a clever face like a raccoon. She puts an arm around her friend's waist. As she does, she lifts the back of her friend's gauzy skirt and tucks it into her belt. The raccoon faced girl laughs, the girls walking behind laugh too. The friend walks on oblivious, long brown legs ending in black panties. Cara wonders when each of the girls will die. In sixty years? Tonight? The certainty of their death, moving through them with every breath they take. Cara can't remember what it felt like.

The implant is a tiny silver node on her brow, hidden just above her hairline. Sometimes Cara thinks this is why the movie star likes her so close. Whenever she is with Cara, the movie star is being watched too.

◄◦►

The phone rings at 4 a.m., breaking her brittle sleep. "Axel?" Cara says.

"It's happening again." The movie star is crying. "*Now*, Cara."

"Don't move," Cara says. "I'm coming."

She pulls on clothes, fear coming in cold rushes.

◄◦►

The night lighting in the lobby is velvet, dusk-like. Early stars are scattered across the distant ceiling. Greta's face is serious, eerily lit by the glowing keyboard. Her fingers move like spiders. Tap, tap, tap. Greta looks up as

Cara approaches. Then she turns and vanishes through a black door behind her, leaving the desk glowing and pulsing like an undersea creature.

Cara presses the glowing blue button labelled ASSISTANCE. The alarm or bell or whatever it is rings in some distant place, out of sight. Cara presses the button again. The lobby is still. The black door does not open.

"Hello," Cara calls. "She needs a kit," she calls. "Now."

Nothing happens for a minute or so. The door opens slowly. Greta emerges smooth as a wave. "Of course," she says. "Please excuse the brief wait. We're short staffed." She puts the kit on the desk for Cara. It looks like a small black briefcase.

"This is a level ten," Cara says, looking at the label on the leather handle. "I don't want it that strong."

"This is all we have. I can send out. It will take a few hours." Cara sees in Greta's porcelain eyes that she knows what using the kit means for Cara. Cara can almost feel it already, the sick seismic movement of pain.

Cara says, "I'll take it."

"Corpse," Greta says softly, holding Cara's gaze.

"What?" asks Cara, even though she heard.

"I said, of course."

As Cara goes Greta says something else under her breath in German. It means, roughly, *knife-face*. Cara knows all those words. She has heard them many times.

Cara understands, now. Greta hates the movie star, but she hates Cara for different reasons.

◄◦►

The movie star is curled up in a corner of the bed, making herself as small as possible in the smooth expanse of white sheet. The TV and radio are silent. She grunts in time with her pulsing pain. When the cancer comes back it moves fast, blazes with unnatural speed through cartilage and bone. Tonight it is in her spine.

Cara does not waste time on words or comfort. She breaks the seal on the kit, takes the green and white pill from its plastic cartridge and swallows it.

She trembles as her body begins to purge itself. Oily, rose-scented sweat oozes from her pores. She grabs a tissue from the silver box beside the bed and coughs up grey, glistening lumps. Cara feels her insides twisting, molten. She runs for the bathroom.

"Don't go," the movie star pleads. "Don't leave m—" Cara slams the door behind her. She reaches the toilet just in time. Red and pink liquid roars out of her throat, hot, both acid and sweet. It seems to go on forever. Then everything goes quiet. Cara lifts her head. Her eyes stop watering. Her stomach settles.

It begins to happen; comes like a beam of sunlight through a deep ocean. The night takes on a velvet touch. Cara hears the fish speaking in the night river, the silent language of fin and tail. The implant is forced out of its lodging in her brow, lands with a tinkle on the marble floor. Cara's body has rejected it. The world becomes a dark flower opening, with Cara at its centre. Everything is alive—she gasps at how alive.

She is almost as she once was, now. Memory and pain wash through her. Also love. There was that, too. She feels the shape of her mouth change as the nubs grow into elegant scythes. Her tongue licks the ivory smoothness of them. She misses these, perhaps most of all.

She opens the bathroom door. She sees each mote of dust spiralling on the cold hotel air. The movie star is still curled up in the corner of the bed. She does not move as Cara approaches. She has passed out. Cara hears the dry sound of the cancer growing in her spine.

It is difficult not to drift, not to lose herself in the music of everything. But she must be fast, before her skin becomes too tough. When Cara takes her arm the movie star comes to, screaming—not with pain but with fear. Her body knows what Cara is. She hits Cara's face weakly with her fist. Cara catches the movie star's wrist with ease and inserts the IV line into her vein. She slides the cannula into the vein in her own neck. She has to stab repeatedly, and hard. In a moment, it would have been too late. Cara releases the valve and the thin plastic tube turns black. Her blood flows into the movie star.

After a few seconds the plastic tube begins to melt. They are designed to be perishable, so that no more than the legal amount of blood can be transferred. The tube disintegrates in saggy drips. It falls in smoking remains on the white sheets. Cara smells the singed sweetness, mingling with the deep earthy scent of her blood. Cara pulls the cannula from her neck. The wound closes faster than even her senses can catch.

The movie star gives a shuddering sigh. Her eyes are filled with black light. "You took so long, Cara," she whispers. "I was afraid you had left me."

Cara takes her in her arms, just as she did when the movie star was a little girl; as she did the movie star's mother, once upon a time. "I am always here," she says. "Rest, now."

The movie star's head nods wearily. "I love you," she says. "You know that, don't you, Cara?"

"I know," Cara says.

"And you love me too."

"Always," Cara says, holding her tightly. But they need each other so much that it's hard to tell.

Cara makes tea and puts it by the bed. The steam spirals, makes silk ribbons on the air. Cara gazes, then shakes herself. She could watch it for hours. Once, she would have done. All she had was time.

"They'll pick you up in an hour for the night shoot," she tells the movie star. "You should try and nap until then." She strokes the movie star's hair. The movie star grunts softly. She is lost in the dreams carried by Cara's blood.

Cara knows she is delaying the moment. She takes the last items from the kit. The pills, the bottle. Too powerful. It is going to hurt. She looks around the room one last time. She has not been this strong for many years. She wants to commemorate it somehow, before she makes herself weak and grey again. But what would be the point?

◄◦►

Back in her room Cara lays them out on the nightstand. Blue pill, then white, then white and yellow. Green bottle. This will be bad; nearly as bad as the first time, many years ago. But the thought of pain is nothing compared to Cara's sorrow at losing the world again, its myriad detail, the stark clarity of it, the thousands of warm lives she can feel for miles around, like burning stars in the night.

She fingers the long graceful points in her mouth. She lets their razor edges slice her fingertips, leaving long black bloody lines which vanish instantly. She bids them farewell.

She wonders what would happen if she didn't take the pill. She can make it to the river, she is sure. Once she's underwater the stuff they put in the air can't affect her. *I could live in the ocean*, Cara thinks. *Never surface. Or there must be remote islands, forgotten by people, where the air is clean. I could live there.* She pictures pale sand littered with the white bones of shipwrecked men. The peace of it pulls at her. *I'll do it*, Cara thinks, wild. *What else is there for me?* She had forgotten how deeply it is possible to feel. *Maybe Axel found one of those islands. Maybe Rose*—no. She cuts off the thought. She knows it leads nowhere.

They were in the forest when the mist came. Axel fought. That is why he died. Cara lay still and watched. She was allowed to live because she was useful. The movie star's grandmother, Cara's great, great, great granddaughter, was permitted to keep Cara for medical purposes. Cancer runs in the family. Cara knows that as well as anyone. *Rose.*

If the movie star has children Cara will help to raise them, as she raised the movie star, and the movie star's mother before her. She will hold the children at night when they are scared and feed them balanced diets and help them with their homework. When the movie star dies, Cara will belong to them. If the movie star does not have children maybe a distant relative will take her. The immunity will not be as perfect as with Cara's descendants. It is most powerful in the direct line. But someone might still want her. Humans are all related to some degree. The blood always helps, even if only a little.

How many like her are left? Cara doesn't know. She sees them sometimes, back home in California. People walk them on leashes in the parks like dogs. Sometimes they are missing a limb. They move slowly as though through water. Maybe the ones who are left wish they were dead too. If no one wants her when the movie star dies, the state will cull Cara like the others.

The movie star thinks of Cara as family. *I am one of the lucky ones.*

Cara takes the blue and white pill, then the white and yellow one. They go down her throat with plastic ease. She paints the ivory lengths in her mouth with the little brush.

The pain takes her. She is in its molten core. Her limbs are threaded with fire, bones jagged. Pain swills around, finds the cracks in her. Dimly she hears the phone ringing. She cannot answer. She has no hands, no arms, no voice. She is just pain. Time expands and contracts.

Through the tumult she thinks, *I'm a coward who can't bear to be alone.*

⋖◦⋗

She breaks the surface slowly. Each limb feels like lead. Cara is surprised to find that the night has passed and a cold dawn hangs over the river. She licks her smooth top gum, her blunt teeth. The grey mantel lies over the world. Everything is dulled once more. She takes a new implant from the box. It is not advisable to stay offline too long. They like to keep track. The sharp legs pierce her flesh and then flip out, fixing the little button in place on her skull. She dabs at the thin trickle of blood that runs down her brow. There is no power in it, now.

The phone rings. "I've been calling and calling," the movie star hisses. "They're gone, Cara."

-◄o►-

The TV roars, a movie about a kidnapped girl. The movie star cries and eats pistachios from a silver bowl. Pistachio shells litter nearby surfaces. A quiet man in a beautiful suit perches on the arm of a chair. He nods and listens to the movie star, draws no attention to himself. Cara understands that he is important.

"I could have been here, in bed, when they came," the movie star says. "I could have been killed in my sleep."

The hole in the safe gapes like an eye. The combination lock has been neatly cut out. "Tidy," the man says, almost approvingly. "Professional." The thief came during the three hours the movie star was on set. It suggests that they knew her schedule, somehow, knew she wouldn't be in her room in the middle of the night.

-◄o►-

The movie star moves to a different suite and the hotel stations a security guard outside her door. She tells Cara to stay with her until she falls asleep.

"Could you, you know?" the movie star lifts her lip in a snarl and taps one of her perfect canines, to show what she means.

Cara shakes her head.

"Come on," the movie star says. "You could protect me better than these idiots." Her eyes light up at the thought of Cara shedding blood for her. She doesn't seem to understand or care what would happen to Cara, after that.

Cara feeds the movie star a spoonful of sleeping draught from a gold bottle. "The car will pick you up at seven a.m.," she says. The movie star says "mmmm," not listening. She has found one of her movies on TV. Her head starts to nod. On screen the movie star churns butter and wipes sweat from her brow.

The movie star is young, but she has travelled in time and lived many lives. She has farmed wheat in Kansas; raced horses dressed as a boy; fought righteous courtroom battles trembling with conviction; walked home alone at night with footsteps following ever closer behind her; fallen in love many, many times with men and women on bridges, in diners, at parties in New York loft apartments, on buses, on a submarine, in war torn deserts and once up a tree.

But it is this movie in particular that Cara remembers. There is a moment coming soon where the woman played by the movie star discovers that the harvest is spoiled.

Cara watches. The moment, the discovery of the ruined crops, is coming now. The movie star strides across the stubbled blighted fields, skirts billowing, brave and slender as a wand, face crumpled in grief. The camera slowly, lovingly zooms in on her face. In that moment her expression is Axel's. The eyebrows like dark wings, the hurt and furious gaze, are his. And the expression is hers, Rose's, as she died, battling the disease. Infinite betrayal, high cheekbones. Rose, who has been in the ground so many long years. Her haughty, furious face passed down through the generations. Cara touches the screen, strokes the cheek with a shaking hand.

The movie star rolls over in her sleep, groaning, and Cara starts as if waking. Her hand has left a long smudge on the screen. She rubs it away with her sleeve and goes back to her room.

⁻⚬⁻

The phone wakes her again at five a.m., and she holds the receiver sleepily to her ear. "Try to go back to sleep," she says. "You have two hours until the car." Through the receiver she hears light, frightened breathing.

Cara pads along the corridor and lets herself into the movie star's suite. The movie star snores heavily, arms flung out as if in flight. Another of her movies is playing. It must be a marathon. On screen the movie star looks across a crowded bar in astonishment, at a woman who looks exactly like her. It is the one where she plays a pair of long-lost twins. She hated making that one, Cara remembers. So much work. The stand-in who read the other twin's lines was the wrong height, so the eye line was always off. The movie star is caught forever gazing slightly to the left of where her long lost sister stands, as if she can't bear to look into her face and feel so much.

Cara watches the movie star sleeping deeply for a moment. Then she closes the door silently behind her. Another one. The calls happen several times a night, now. Cara pictures Greta standing like a statue in the dim lobby, receiver pressed to her ear, as the pastel lights move over her frozen smile.

Whatever Greta means by them, the calls have become a strange comfort to Cara. She sits and listens to the silence for minutes on end, stroking the old-fashioned spiral cord. She pretends the dead are calling. Her brother or her daughter. "Rose," she whispers into the vague crackle of the line, "I miss you." And the silence seems to hold an answer.

◄◦►

The movie star picks at quartered pieces of grape. She went to a club with some of the other actors last night. She raises her dark glasses to look at Cara. She has startling white compresses under her eyes, snail venom patches to take down the puffiness. "Can we do the touch thing?"

"You're hungover," Cara says. "It will make you sick."

"If you don't do it I'll throw up in your lap." The movie star grins. Not her pretty, public smile, but the rude healthy grin of the girl she once was, who built dams in streams and caught lizards in her quick hands, who stayed out all day and almost wept when it was time to come inside at night. "Please, Mama." She called Cara that when she was little, before she understood the way things were between them.

"Ok," Cara says, "it's your funeral."

Cara thinks for a moment, then goes to the heavy earthenware jar that stops the door to the suite's vast living room. The jar is full of peacock feathers, green and sheeny blue. Cara draws out a single quill.

She concentrates, makes her mind an arrow, points it at the movie star. Slowly, Cara traces the feather over her palm, thrilling at the light touch, barely-there. Across the table, she hears the movie star catch her breath. Cara raises the peacock feather to her face, traces it over her closed eyelids, her earlobes. "Sure you can handle this?" Cara asks.

"Bring it on," the movie star says.

Cara pushes the soft silky end of the feather gently into her own ear. Her ear canal is unbearably full of whispering touch. Ten feet away the movie star shrieks and claws at her ear. "Ok, stop," she begs, almost weeping with laughter.

Cara smiles and grazes the inside of her ear with the feather, again and again, as the movie star screams and rubs furiously at the side of her head. Cara is laughing too, so she doesn't notice for a moment that the movie star has stopped. She looks at Cara with her blank blue gaze.

"You'll be there, won't you?" the movie star says. "You'll probably organise everything perfectly. My funeral."

❧

They discovered the game when she was a girl and had not yet become the movie star.

It was a hot spring day and the jacaranda threw frilled shadow on the edges of the softball field. The smell of warm earth rose up from under the bleachers. The movie star's mother sat silent like a ghost. Cara stood beside her. The leash hung silver about her neck, fastened to the bleachers. They both watched as the small figure ran base to base. She was going like the wind. Cara felt her heart swell with pride at her grace, her speed. But the ball was chasing her, and as she slid into third in a cloud of dirt, the kid on base hurled himself towards it. There was a sound like a carrot broken in two. The girl's face was a mess of blood and dirt. She didn't cry as she got up, knees dusted brown and palms bleeding. She was trying so hard not to. The movie star's mother started as if waking from a dream. She was already deep into the pills by then. She rarely saw anything that was not inside herself. Her face was blank as she walked towards her daughter, too upright, like a puppet with the string drawn tight. The mother put a vague hand on her daughter's shoulder. The girl did cry then, tears mingling with the blood on her chin.

Her mother stood for a moment longer and then walked off the field, not back to the bleachers but into the trees, in the direction of the car. She could only handle so much at a time.

Cara wanted to run out into the field, wanted to take her in her arms and soothe her. She knew she couldn't. The leash held her in her place by the bleachers. But she wished for it so hard she could almost feel the shape of the small, familiar silky skull under her hand. *Don't cry*, she thought. *Don't let them see that.* Then Cara saw the yellow-blond head move, as if leaning into a caress. She looked at Cara and smiled a little through the blood and tears. Cara caught her breath. She could feel the warmth of the sun in the hair under her palm.

Cara was scared, when they got home, that the girl would tell her mother. But she didn't—not that day, or any day since. She and Cara keep the secret.

She doesn't know if others have it; this connection, this vicarious touch. She has never had it with anyone else, not even with Rose.

—◇—

Cara is crossing the lobby with an armful of freesias when the man arrests Greta. He wears another beautiful suit of herringbone. He does it quietly with a word in Greta's ear. He does not touch her. Greta screams as if he had. Then she whispers, "I didn't do it." Her eyelash paint runs down her face in green and blue streaks.

Cara drifts nearer. She says to Greta, quietly, "I enjoyed my midnight phone calls."

Greta looks at her, mouth a skewed *o*. "What?" she says. "What phone calls?"

"She's been harassing me," Cara says to the man in the herringbone suit. "Nuisance calls to my room at all hours of the night."

"We'll make sure we go into that in due course," he says smoothly. Cara can tell that they won't. It's not important, what happens to Cara. She is property.

"I didn't call you," Greta pleads, tearful, as if that would mend all. Cara looks at her in surprise. She can see that Greta is telling the truth.

The man holds out his hand. Greta puts her silver nametag into his open palm. He follows her respectfully out of the glass doors, into the street. A black van is waiting.

As expected, they find the movie star's jewels in Greta's bag with a copy of the call sheet. That's how she knew the movie star's schedule. There are only seven pieces of jewellery, however; the platinum and sapphire cuff is missing. Greta must have sold it already. "That was my favourite," the movie star says. "These other things are just trash. I'll donate them to charity when we get home." Cara knows that whichever piece was missing, it would have been the movie star's favourite.

Cara packs the recovered jewels into their bags, into their boxes, the travel safe.

"I could have been killed," the movie star says once more, standing before the mirror. She smoothes the dark wing of her eyebrow with a licked finger. Her cheeks are plump, still luminous with the residual effects of the transfer.

◄○►

Shooting is finished. Cara packs the movie star's shoes, encasing each one in an individual silk bag. She will be glad to get back to Los Angeles. There are special parks in the city where they don't lace the air so heavily. Cara can go outside, see the sun. People in California want her to feel she has rights. The old world has no such concerns. Maybe it's more honest that way.

The travel unit is waiting in Cara's room, a long silver cylinder. Its mouth gapes wide. Cara gets in and the lid slides silently closed, sealing her in darkness. There is a brief hiss, and then the synthetic scent of roses. The hormones are designed to smell like flowers. The light mist settles. Her skin absorbs it quickly. Sleep nudges at her. She is alone at last. The implant can't see in the dark.

As she drifts, Cara recalls the tinny bite of the safe as it gave to her teeth. Dreamily she slides up her sleeve, stroking the platinum and sapphire cuff where it is fastened high on her forearm. She found a way to commemorate the moment, after all. For some reason she didn't want to leave this with the rest of the jewellery, in Greta's bag.

The cuff is valuable but that's not why Cara took it. She can't sell it—she can't even look at it in the light, unless she wants the implant to record it. She does not know exactly why she kept it. If she is caught it will be the end of her. Cara fingers the fine mesh of the platinum. She can't give it up. The movie star's voice echoes in her mind: *I love you, Cara.*

Cara thinks, *You can't love someone you own.* But she thinks of the little girl on the softball pitch, her face wet with tears. There are different kinds of bondage.

Sleep begins to take her in its dark folds. She slips into memory. Firelight on a cave wall. Elk blood runs hot between her teeth. Rose, her brother's dead smile. The time before the weak came, with their poison mist and their pills, before they hobbled her limbs and took her teeth. The fear that lived in all their eyes, then—those eyes looked up at her, not down on her as they do now. When the powerful still ruled the earth, from the dark.

Cara hopes the dead will call again; that she will hear their beloved, cold breath through the receiver, through years and time and space; feel them reaching for her with their silence, telling her that she is not forgotten. She hopes and hopes.

A DEED WITHOUT A NAME

JACK LOTHIAN

Rain falls. Heath is damp and wretched.

My sisters and I shiver as we trudge along the dirt paths. Been walking since morning, but we cannot go home, not yet, not until dark and mother is resting. Nothing else to do but follow the tracks through fields and meadows until our bones ache and our thoughts are finally quiet.

Sow gave birth to a litter just after dawn. All stillborn. Farmer found her with a bloodied snout, and their lifeless bodies torn open, half feasted upon. Farmer sliced sow's throat, dragging the carcass off to be carved and sold at market this afternoon. Yesterday sow was swollen, with child. Now just meat and gristle. I was passing, saw him haul out the body. Farmer caught me looking, muttered something under his breath, that I pretended not to hear.

We trudge on through the dank and drizzle. The men will be returning from war now, Michael among them. I have freckles. A hint of auburn in my hair. Green eyes that Michael said were like a cat.

"They're not green," says middle sister. "They're grey."

I didn't know I was speaking words out loud. Sister smiles at me as if to say maybe I wasn't. We were born within a year of each other. Oldest sister. Middle sister. Then me, with my hint of auburn and eyes of green that might really be grey.

Somewhere, beneath the October sky, men are bleeding and trembling. The rush and excitement of battle replaced by the cold, sharp fear of an end that has come too soon. Stripped of armor and pretense, they cry and beg for their mothers, like children lost amongst the grassland. I pray Michael is safe with every sodden step I take.

Older sister whispers for us to stop. Sliver of alarm in her voice. I look up, understand. Coming down the road that slices through the fields are two soldiers, bearing the king's colors. They walk with a weight and weariness, faces shaded with dirt and fatigue. The one in front has a beard, flecked white like the first drifts of snow in January. Eyes of burnt coal. The man behind is younger, but there's an age upon him, too. These are not good men.

Older sister bows her head to let them pass, and middle sister and I copy her, genuflecting as if we're not worthy to gaze upon such warriors. Perhaps we can vanish from their view. It's a trick I use too much, say my sisters. I am often elsewhere.

I stare down at my bare feet, which look powdered with the cold. A small toe missing on the right from when mother left me out in that winter when I was still just a bairn. Michael says it makes me special. Different from the rest. I focus on the smooth slip of skin as I see the boots of the men come into view, the acidic scent of their sweat hanging in the air. Footsteps come to a halt right in front of us. I can feel their eyes appraising us like the heath is another market, and we are but cattle for sale.

The squeal of the sow as the knife cut across her flabby neck. The desecrated litter scattered behind her. Picture the mother feasting up on her young. Wonder what drove her to dig in her snout, to open her mouth, bring those teeth down against barely formed skin and bone. I feel as if I am there, overwhelmed by the smell of the newborn, already rotting as they slid out. Sense the horror and panic in the sow. Stomach lurches, and I think I am going to be sick upon the ground, upon the boots of men.

Middle sister touches my arm, a quiet but firm grip, trying to settle me, and I worry that I have been speaking thoughts aloud again.

The bearded man is speaking, but it takes a second for his words to match up with his mouth as I slip back to the present.

"How now, you black and midnight hags?" he says. He is staring at us with a strange, subdued fury, even though his voice is soft and warm.

The younger man laughs, but it is forced, tinged with fear of his elder. He would laugh no matter what the words had been. These men scare me. They have taken blood today, and satiation is not yet upon them.

"What are these women?" asks the younger as he approaches me. He lays his finger under my chin, to raise my head. "So withered and wild in their attire." He runs his finger down my front, slowly, not minding the dampness of the cloth, the way I shiver not from pleasure.

"They look not like inhabitants of this earth." He presses his hand against my sex, and I try to move back. But older sister gives me a look, and I imagine her voice in my head, telling me to become no-one, to vanish off somewhere inside myself, just like I do on those nights when mother cannot find sleep nor calm.

It only ever takes a breath and a blink of an eye, and there I am. The dark forest. Skeletal black trees as far as the eyes can see. And although some might think the place is carved from nightmares, it feels warm and close to me. It is a place where man is but a memory. A place where no-one else may step.

"I know these sisters," says the younger man.

I do not recognize him. Is he from the village? No. From further away. How does he know of us? His hand is sharp below me, unwanted, not like Michael. He pulls back, bringing his hand to nose, smirking to himself, but it is an unsure smile that fades when the bearded one does not return it.

I can smell the death upon them, just as on the sow this morn. I picture the pale piglets, suddenly springing to life, their stomachs torn open, innards trailing behind them like pennants. They scramble and tumble forward, desperate for their mother's milk even in death. I can hear their frantic shrieking, and the bile rises up in me, bubbling and overflowing. I cannot stop it escaping my mouth where it splatters on the ground, and now the younger one kicks at me, cursing, disgusted. The bearded one reaches for his scabbard, but then older sister speaks, taking his arm.

She is beautiful, even in the rain.

"We were waiting for you," she says, and I almost believe her, the way she holds his eye, her voice low and calm. "We have words."

He lifts his hand to older sister's jaw. Holds it like a skull plucked from the dead fields.

"Speak," he says, and it is as much a threat as it is a command.

"Beware the Thane of Fife."

"More," he says, and those fingers tighten up her skin.

"You will have great glory. You will be named Thane of Cawdor."

He smiles at that. Good words. Good girl.

"And you all have words for me?" he says, looking to middle sister.

I realize this is a game. We all have to speak. We all have to be convincing. If we succeed, then these men will leave us alone. It is a game we play at home when storm falls upon mother, and we have no way out. Trapped with her as she howls at the faces in the walls. We try to calm her, tell her what she needs to hear, hope to bring her back to our world. We are better at this game now, but we don't always win. Thin white scars across arms and legs from all the times we are not so convincing.

Middle sister pushes wet hair from her head. She cannot look at the man. She is shaking. Her voice is barely more than a breeze. "You will be king."

"I will be king," he says, and he laughs, and the younger man joins, but I can tell that these words have sparked some deep fire within him.

And then he looks to me. I try to find words, but they will not fit my mouth. I cannot help it, there is a spark of panic and I slip away, across time and space, to the dark, quiet forest. The safe place. Yet it is not the same now; it is as if these men have infected it. Through the trees, I glimpse a fire. Pale bodies dragged towards it. Like the sow after dawn. Ready for the burning and I cannot help shout out, and then the words come in a tumble, a rush, from some unknown place.

Sisters are looking at me, as are the men. Standing on the heath, aware of my voice, speaking prophecies I could not even imagine. I tell him of his future, of his might, of how no man born of woman could ever harm him.

A brutal crack across my cheek brings me back into this world for sure. The younger one throws a clenched fist, and the sodden earth rushes up to meet me. There is the sour taste of dirt in my mouth.

It is apparent I have said something wrong. I have failed the game.

"These wayward sisters mean to mock you, General," says the young man, staring down at me. But the bearded man hushes his companion. He crouches down as if to talk to a child.

"Is this true . . .?" he asks me.

There is the iron taste of blood on my lips. I am smiling, but I cannot remember why, and I see the men are somehow afraid of me for a reason they will never quite understand. I widen my bloodied smile and tell him yes, it is true. Every word of it.

I do not know why, but I put my finger to my lips and then place it upon his, a trace of blood passing from me to him. The blackness in his eyes grows small, and his breathing becomes shallow. There is only us in this moment, only his devouring of my words, of a future laid out before him.

Then he is risen and gone, down the road, never looking back. The younger man hurries to keep pace.

Older sister helps me up.

"Where did that come from?" she asks, but I wouldn't answer her, even if I could.

Three sisters, on the damp heath, shivering in the cold, waiting for night to fall, so they can return home once their mother is safely asleep. We think we have done well, said the right things, played the game and won.

Within two months, a hundred men will lie dead, and the blame shall be upon us.

◦

Father was taken. That is what mother tells us, night after night. Sometimes she is speaking directly to us, her darling daughters. Other times she is talking to a bottle or a smudged glass. Then there are the nights she hisses at the faces in the walls. Arguing with them. Screaming at them. Striking out until hands are bloody. And then she begins on us.

She tells us the story many times of how we lost our father. A shadow crept into the house and slipped into his mouth while he slept. The shadow would not leave him. Mother never says where this shadow came from or why it chose him; she only reiterates her despair at how nobody in the village noticed the transformation. The idiot townsfolk saw something that walked and breathed and ate and spoke like man, and they never looked any closer. Mother says he was hollow. Something else lived in him. No longer father, no longer husband, no longer even man.

Yet he still puts his seed in her, and from that, I was born forth. For that sin alone, I must take the beatings and whippings, I must not react when she spits at my face and claws at my eyes. Dirty girl. Stupid girl. Wrong to be born.

Then one morning, father awoke, walked out of our failing house, and down the road. He disappeared into nothing. Mother says he vanished into the air in front of her, burning up, ash and dust caught, twisting in the beams of an early sunrise.

One day she will be dead, and I will be free. I will no longer need to hide in the darkened forests of my head. I will no longer have to play the games of saying the words that she needs to hear. Yes, father was taken. Yes, father was changed. Yes, that shadow could return, so we must lock the doors and keep out the light. Without light there can be no shadow. Yes, mother. Yes.

On that day, my face will light up, just like Michael says, and never grow dull again. It starts with my smile, and then the brightness spreads to my eyes and my skin, and I am like an angel. This is what he tells me, in quiet moments we steal together.

Some days he waits around the corner from the marketplace, near the edge of the village. He lets me walk past him and pretends to pay no heed. I feel sparks of fire flicker through me as I walk the paths to the woods. Green thick forest, not like the place in my head, but still pleasing to escape to. Still safe.

I walk, and he follows, stalking me like prey. Sometimes I run to make things more difficult for him, but most times, I wait for him to get closer and closer. The beast yearning for the hunter. Those lost afternoons, when he pulls me close, puts himself inside me, whispers my name over and over. Buries himself in my scent, my neck, my skin, my body. Sometimes it hurts, and sometimes I feel like a something rather than a someone, but even on those odd, strange days I grow excited at this power I hold, to start such a burning within him.

He is to be wed to Beatrice, the daughter of a merchant. A woman who gives me looks of pity and vague disgust should she ever have the misfortune to pass me on the road. Aye, I am beneath her, but her man is on top of me, and that gives me a pleasure I cannot describe. Imagine Beatrice naked and watching us. Imagine that cruel curl of her lip trembling as she sees the wild fire he has for me. Sees us bleed together as one, skin on skin, body on body.

He could never be hers like he is mine.

"Things are getting worse," he says as we lie on the forest floor. Curled together, his arms around me, his warm chest behind. He talks of how there is a new King, how the sons of the deceased ruler have taken flight, how there is a rebellion of sorts brewing.

Michael is a good man. He does not believe in this new regent. When men raise arms, he will join them in rebellion.

And then he mentions the name of the king, and I see a man in armor, listening to the mutterings of a shivering girl.

I feel a cold wind pass through me from some unknown place.

I think of the damp heath, and the words we had to say to make the men go away.

I want to talk of something else. I don't want to hear of the new king, with his white-flecked beard and dead, black eyes.

So I tell Michael a secret. The day by the water, six months before. I had spent the morning walking, letting myself become lost in back roads and pathways, old trails and lanes where folk rarely walk anymore. All the way across the hills down to the winding river.

I saw older sister sitting by the bank, with a boy and girl, younger than her, younger than me. They were laughing. I crept closer to see what caused such contentment. Older sister rarely laughs at home. And she has no friends. None of us do. We only have each other.

I heard her call the boy "brother" and then my foot pressed against loose stone and she turned, saw me, and I fled. Though I had done no wrong, her look was such that it filled me with some odd shame. She came back later and said nothing of it. When I pressed her on who these people were, if our father was dead how dare she call one brother, and she said that I must have seen something else, the way I do sometimes when my eyes go strange, and my body is elsewhere, that this was just imaginations. But no, this was not one of those times.

Michael says nothing. He just breathes deeply, his mouth against the nape of my neck. I feel him stiffen and slowly buck against me.

A man is watching us. For a moment, I think he is not real. Perhaps made of twig and branch, come to life, to try to join this pageantry of humanity. I smile at the sight, imagining the leaves swirling around, forming a foot and then a leg, and the roots winding around like twine, holding in place the bark and the greenery. Then my eyes move to the face, and I see two eyes staring back across the forest floor. I realize that this is a man, this is real, and he seems momentarily shocked. Then he is striding forward, shouting, angry, and Michael is cowering before his father, naked, his manhood still strong but fading fast. I run, still unclothed, through the woods, fear turning to a strange joy. I know Michael is in trouble, but it is good for us. It means things will be forced to change. He cannot wed Beatrice now. And we will be together, the whole world can be our woods.

‹o›

Then the world changes again. Moon rises and falls, over and over. There are battles fought, and fields of blood. Folk say the false king lies dead. They say the man who killed him was ripped from his mother's womb as an infant. I think of the sow, with her bright red snout, her little ones beneath her as she furrowed away desperately.

Maybe she wanted them back inside. Maybe she wanted them safe.

I have not seen Michael since the day in the forest. I heard he went to fight, and I heard he came home safe, and I hope my prayers guided him in some way, even if I could not remember the right words.

I go to his house, but his father comes out and blocks my way. His eyes look me from head to toe and back for a long time. I think of how long he must have stood in the forest, watching us.

"Do not come here again," he says. His voice is thick, and the warning is clear.

‹o›

Last night I woke from dreamless slumber to feel someone lying down next to me. For a moment, I thought of Michael, but in the dark, I knew that was not true. It was mother.

She whispered that I had a shadow in me. Then she put her arms around me, and I was scared, for I have never known her touch gentle. I felt like a rabbit in the mouth of a dog. Though I feared the worst, she stroked my hair like a mother should, and her voice stayed soft. She told me how she was sorry she could not protect me, could not guide me to the light. Then she sang a song far older than any of us, and sleep lulled me back into the dark.

And before the dawn, there is the cracking of the door, like a great thunder. Wood splinters. Sisters scream. Men come for us, iron and steel in hands.

They have heard what we told the false king on that day. They say we bewitched his mind. That our foul and dank deeds polluted a once-great man. Michael had cried before them and talked of how I used some enchantment on him, how my filthy body corrupted his pure soul. Beatrice stood behind him, tears rolling down her face at the horrors her man has endured, far worse than any war.

Mother yells and urges us to run and tries to stop them. I see the fear in her, for these men are shadows. She fights for us with a ferocity I could never have imagined, but she is only a woman and has no place in this. They toss her aside like a doll as they drag us outside.

I want to tell her that it is fine as they lead us out through the village, towards the flames that burn and crackle in the dark. I want to let her know that I understand, that there are dark, deserted places in many of these hollow men where shadows can thrive.

Closer and closer to the fire. My sisters are numb with the terror of the flames. I find my voice, and I find the words, and they come out, sharp and clear in the winter air.

"It was only me," I say, and then everyone is quiet as if this is a play, and they have been waiting for my line.

I tell them of the foulness within me. I tell them of consorting with goat-like men and men-like goats. I laugh as I recount the sins I forced Michael to commit upon my defiled skin, and I talk black tales of Beatrice lying with us too. I boast to the ears of this innocent village about how I drove a good man to murder. How I bewitched him, this kind and good man with the white-flecked beard.

I tell them my sisters are pathetic and have no knowledge of my ways.

I keep talking and talking. Sometimes I am not even using language, only sounds, growls, and barks. I lose myself in the guttural noise. I let them drag me in a rage towards the pyre, as they beat and shove me on, trying to silence this abhorrent tongue of mine, trying to protect themselves from my cracked words and violent phrases. My sisters are sobbing, pleading with me to be silent. Michael can only stare at the ground, but his face is filled with wrath like the others, demanding my burning, my end.

They can do what they want. I am not there anymore.

I have slipped away. I am elsewhere.

I am in the dark forest, watching the fire, a moonless clouded sky above me. I see the men force me towards the blaze. I could stay and watch some more, but what is the point?

As the flames rise, I turn my back on them all, looking to these blackened woods, these skeletal trees. I understand there is a freedom here, of a different kind. I run into the darkness, a smile upon my face now, leaving the village behind, the smoke rising in the distance, further and further and until there is no trace of it left.

LORDS OF THE MATINEE

STEPHEN GRAHAM JONES

I t's not that my seventy-two-year old father-in-law is actually going deaf, it's that he's a, in my former mother-in-law's words, "lazy-ass listener." I say 'former' for her because she passed three years ago, kind of right on schedule as far as I'm concerned, but my wife Sheila's still kind of torn up . . . not so much about her mom being gone, her insides chewed up, bubbling up red down her chin, all that, as that the two of them never made up proper before she went. Which, again: nothing all that surprising, this is the way things go about ninety-nine percent of the time between moms and daughters, as far as I can tell.

Either way, the result of all *this* is that, with his wife gone, Sheila's dad's been kind of letting their apartment go to hell. Crusty dishes tottering on every flat surface, newspapers and engineering journals stacking up into fire hazard after fire hazard, the whole place an ashtray, pretty much. So, to pick up her dead mom's slack—though it's also her two brothers' slack if you ask me—Sheila commits to cleaning her dad's place up one Sunday. I offer to help, of course, it's what you do when you're married, when you're shouldering burdens together, when it's a team effort, and then it turns out that the best way I can help out is by ushering her father out of the apartment for the afternoon.

"So what do I do with him?" I say to Sheila. We're standing before the open hatchback of her car, her mentally going through the two tubs of cleaning supplies arrayed before us. I haul one up, swing it onto my hip, and she takes the other, shuts the hatchback and beeps the lock in one efficient motion.

"He just can't be there," she says, already getting her grim attitude on for the coming mess.

I look out into the haze of the city, trying to imagine her father and me muttering to each other over a Chinese food buffet for four or five hours, or the two of us doddering through a museum or art gallery, neither of which we'd know what to really do with.

"Does he like movies?" I ask, some fake cheer to my delivery.

I should say here, he and my mother-in-law were at the wedding, of course, but that was sixteen years ago. I shook their hands and called them Mom and Dad and took all the necessary pictures that day, but, since then, I've successfully avoided any meaningful interactions with them. Just the usual holiday stuff, here's a pot roast, thanks for the shoeshine kit I love it, no we don't have any secret kids yet ha ha, yeah I like my new job too, your daughter's the best, sure I can install that new washing machine, thanks, thanks.

Which is to say: who was this musty geezer I was now to spend an afternoon with?

All the same, my time for this had probably come. You can only dodge bullets for so long. And, I told myself, it's not like he's completely checked in anymore, right? I might even just be a nurse to him, a helper, some shadowy presence holding him by the elbow, steering him away from traffic, saying completely unintelligible bullshit to him.

"He used to like action movies, yeah," Sheila answers, a tinge of unexpected hopefulness to her voice, to match my fake cheer. It's not for the afternoon I'm about to lead her father through, I don't think, but for the father he used to be, who probably played his action movies too loud too late, his way of having the last word for the day.

It's settled then.

I haul my assigned tub of cleaning supplies up, Sheila keys us in, announcing our presence until her father creaks forward in his chair, his whole face squinting about us, and, after taking inventory, Sheila says back to me, "A *long* movie?"

"A loud one," I tell her, since maybe her father *is* going deaf—I'm pretty sure he didn't turn his head to the sound we are, but to the flurry of motion we were in his peripheral vision.

"Nothing scary," she tells me, doing her important eyes.

"Luck," I say, one hand to her shoulder, and kiss her on the side of her face, her eyes hard for the coming work.

Next I'm guiding her father down the dark hall of his building, to the elevator, and right before we get there he chicken-wings his arm out, the one I'm holding, effectively telling me he doesn't need me to keep him from falling.

Still, when he's stepping over that thin deep chasm between the carpet of the hall and the hard floor of the elevator car, I hover close, ready to be there should he need me.

"Where's she having us go then?" he says, aiming the unsteady rubber foot of his cane at the pad of buttons, which can't be anything like hygienic for anyone else who might have to touch those buttons. Instead of helping, though—instead of *interfering*—I hang back, wait for him to find the L by himself, which is, I guess, both the third and fourth letters of *Hell*.

Not that I'm thinking like that.

Yet.

"We're going to the *movies*," I tell him loud enough that he can hopefully catch at least part of it, and like that we're descending down into the afternoon, which is where him being a lazy-ass listener comes into play.

◄◦►

The theatre is a four-screen job, kind of on the backside of thirty. It's seen better days; the same sixteen-year-old who sold us the ticket also filled my popcorn bucket, and the carpet is all threadbare in the middle of the halls from thousands of shoes scraping, and the urinals are the kind that are those big yawning porcelain mouths that stretch all the way to the floor, so you're practically standing in them.

We're forty minutes early for the movie, but it's the first showing too, so we sit there and wait, me crunching popcorn and watching the slideshow commercials and quizzes cycling on-screen, him nodding off since I'm guessing he can only see the static ads and questions up there, not hear them so well.

By the second trailer—we're sitting in the handicapped seats—he's leaning forward to the screen, like that's where all the sound is coming from. He turns his head to the side to better funnel these voices in, and the way his cane is spiked down in front of him, both hands on the handle to pull forward with, it's like he's hauling back on a big lever.

I don't mean to make fun. Someday that's me, I know. I already find myself sleeping through parts of television shows I would have been awake for ten years ago. It's the natural progression, and so what. Bring it. I'm ready.

Not that I'll ever have a son-in-law to dodder me down to the movies, but oh well. If I'm any indication, we're overrated.

Anyway, if there were an usher making the rounds through the theater to keep everything kosher, I'd flag him or her down for assistance about this hearing problem, but as it is, I have to pat my father-in-law on the shoulder like telling him to stay put, then go to the concession stand to solve it myself, see if they have something to get him to hear the movie as well as see it.

When I come back it's to an empty house, an old-man-less house, and my heart thumps once in my chest, kind of lurches to a soft stop, my head already reeling excuses out to Sheila, a future version of myself already scouring the men's restrooms and the other theaters for her father, then widening the search out to all the concrete and sidewalks of the city, and finally, inevitably, the hospitals and morgues.

But then I'm just standing in the wrong theater, because this action movie's playing on half the screens here. I exhale from deep in my chest and rush fast to the right theater, where the next trailer is already booming.

My father-in-law's sitting there squinting up at the screen in a way that tells me this is a bad idea, that taking him to a movie at this stage of his life, and a modern action movie at that, the third installment of a series geared for thirteen-year-old boys, is an exercise in stupidity. There's nothing for him here, and there won't be.

Still, it's where we are.

I settle into my seat and offer him the assisted listening device they had behind the counter. He takes it, holds it up against the light of the screen to properly inspect it, then recognizes it as a version of the wireless television headphones Sheila got for him a couple of years ago, so he could blare his news at whatever volume he wanted, without including his neighbors.

He grunts thanks, ducks into the rig and looks up at the screen, waiting for the magic to happen. When it doesn't, I reach over under his chin, click the green light on, and it must start receiving then, since his eyes change like he's hearing something.

What his wife meant by "lazy listener" was, I have to think, pretty much the same thing Sheila says about me: that I check out a few words in, start thinking my own thoughts, only staying involved enough in whatever she's saying to nod at the appropriate moments, pretend to play along. She's right, I guess. Maybe it's a man/woman thing, maybe it's a husband/wife thing, or maybe she just, as happens, married a minor version of the asshole she grew up with.

Either way, with the movie piping directly into his ears now, my father-in-law is pacified. I can tell because the cane he's still holding under both hands angles back and back, the curved handle at his chest now, which is kind of like a visual definition for "contentment," which, to me, translates across as "success," or, in the mental checklist I've got going, "two hours."

After this it'll be me swinging us by the corner store for any groceries he might need, which I trust will take another forty minutes *and* involve a carton of the cigarettes he's not supposed to have. Taking travel-time into account between here and there and his place, if we're moving slow and careful like I plan to, that's a whole afternoon, ta-daa. We'll come back to a rejuvenated apartment, a tired but satisfied woman, and then I'll be free.

Right on schedule, then, twenty, twenty-five minutes into the movie, I'm watching the movie alone, my father-in-law's head lolled forward in sleep, the green light glowing against his throat like a visible heartbeat.

By now I'm as into the movie as it's possible to get, considering the fare. It's all car chases followed by car wrecks, with sporadic gunfire and bikinis stitching it all together in the least likely ways. Not complaining, it's not like it was false advertising or anything, you get what you're paying for, but still, it could be in another language and I'd be watching the same movie.

Just because it's one of my assigned duties to conserve any and all battery life whenever I encounter it—Sheila says I'm the battery police, the hall monitor for charging—I contort myself to reach over, into my father-in-law's sleeping space, to turn that green light off. At which point, my fingers having to see by feel, I discover a notch that turns out to be a headphone jack.

It makes sense, I guess. If you and your movie date are sitting together, then one unit can receive for the both of you, if the kid at concessions can supply you with an auxiliary set of headphones to string between the two of you.

Instead of turning the unit off, I untangle my own headphones from my jacket pocket, reach across with both hands to hold the assisted listening device steady while I plug in.

Why not, right?

I lean back, want to chock my knees up on the seat in front of me except this is handicapped, there's just open space before us. I tilt my head over to thumb one earbud in, then the other.

Thirty seconds later, my face goes slack with wonder.

I'd assumed, the way anybody would, that what piped into a device like this would be the same thing coming through the surround sound.

Wrong.

It's—it's so much better, so much fuller. And of course it is. This isn't for hearing-*impaired* people, dummy, this is for the blind, who want to experience the movie the only way they can: through running description, while still hearing everything coming through the speakers mounted all around.

This description, though, it's . . . I've never heard anything quite like it. It's not that it's a woman's voice, an older woman it sounds like, one I guess I would call "Mom-class," as in, the kind I'd expect to be reading to the boy I still am inside, it's what she's saying, and how she's saying it. I lean up, to be closer to the screen, but then, finally, I close my eyes like I'm supposed to.

What the woman in my head is telling me is "A white convertible Jaguar skids in from the left, from a road that's suddenly just there, and it's already sliding, it's going to hit our red Charger, but the driver, whoever she is, she's hauling the wheel back over hard, she's shifting down, and from right above we can see the passenger side door handle of the Jag just touching the driver's side door handle of the Charger, slow motion, and in that moment the two evenly matched drivers look across into each other's eyes and smile, each knowing how many miles of open road are waiting before them."

At which point the speakers in the *theater* deliver the Charger driver's line, "Welcome to the party, babe," and then the narrator is back, saying "the Charger's rear tires smoke, his hand guides the shifter deep into the next gear, and we stay in place behind the two cars as they race away."

And, the thing is, with my eyes closed, I can see this *so*, so clearly, so much better than if I was just watching it with my eyes. Which, I know, it's not quite cool of me to say "look how the other half lives" when I'm doing it by choice, not by accident or birth or whatever—I'm just a tourist in the land of the blind, of course it's fun if I can leave whenever I want—but still, this woman painting the scene for me, all the sounds of the movie still coming in, it's a way of watching I'd never considered, a way of seeing I'd never guessed was possible.

I close my eyes tighter and suck air in deep, to relish this.

The bar fight at the strip club is something else, but I don't even peek, just surreptitiously guide my popcorn bucket onto my lap, in case other moviegoers have filtered in.

At the high rise scene I already saw in the trailer, my chest actually hollows out to be this high, and when the gold Lamborghini is crashing through the golden window in even slower motion, the narrator practically showing me each piece of flying glass, I cue in to a sound that . . . what *is* that? Kind of an undertone, that I guess must have been there the whole time, since I started this.

It's like . . . it's not steady, but it's constant. A grinding? Metal on metal?

I open my eyes to the comparatively bright theatre, to see if, I don't know, to see if some woman is standing before me, filing her fingernails on an emery board, her *metal* fingernails, and using a file, not sandpaper and cardboard, but there's no one. I chance a look around, and we're alone in here in the middle of the day.

Beside me, my father-in-law is still sleeping.

I pull my left earbud out, listen to the theater, but there's only that glass from the high rise, whuffing down onto the white umbrellas set up around the pool, so many stories below the action.

It's an old device, I tell myself. An old device at a crappy, soon-to-be-retired theater, and we're probably the first person to use it in years. There's dust in the transmitter, there's bleed over from a competing signal, or—or the headphones for this particular jack are *proprietary*, that must be it. Whatever I'm hearing, it's because the grooves in my plug don't line up perfect with the internal ridges in the device. I'm not even supposed to be listening like this. Of course something's going to sound a little off. What was I thinking?

Mystery solved, I thumb my earbuds back in, lean back, close my eyes to try to make this movie not so terrible.

After the pool scene, which the visual-assist somehow makes believable—it's all about if you want to enjoy or not—in a moment of comparative silence when the hero is just cruising along in what turns out to be an electric car, which means a *quiet* car, I hear it again, that undertone of metal on metal.

This time when I turn my head toward it, toward my father-in-law, I keep my eyes closed, and my whole body goes cold.

I'm in his apartment with him.

And—and I haven't been actually hearing that sound, it's that, this woman's voice, it's split in half somehow, has a top level, the stuff she's supposed to be saying, the stuff she's reading from her script, but somehow she's whispering under that, asking me "Can't I *hear* that, can't I hear that metal-on-metal grinding?"

My first impulse, my almost-reaction, it's to open my eyes and push away from whatever this is, what this can't possibly be, but, but—I *do* push away, both my hands firmly on the armrest, the cable between us tightening, but I don't open my eyes.

This . . . I'm with him, somehow, my sleeping father-in-law. Like, his memory, his mind, his self, it's leaking out through his ears, it's infecting the device, it's crawling across the headphone cable into my mind's eye.

I shake my head no, no, but at the same time, in a sort of wonder, I *look*.

⊸⊙⊳

He's standing in the kitchen, the television blaring from the living room. It's the Turner Classic stuff Sheila's mother was always so in love with, that she always insisted on instead of my father-in-law's blarey news programs. Meaning this is from then, from before, from when she was alive. Before she died.

Why I keep watching now, it's because I want to see how old she is in this. And, because, I don't know, maybe we're all voyeurs? Or we all have that tendency, will all sneak a look if given the chance, if there's no real risk involved? If there's no way to get caught doing the Peeping Tom thing?

All I'm doing is listening to a movie through a pair of earbuds, man. Completely innocent, here.

I close my eyes even more, to see better.

Judging by my father-in-law's gnarled, liver-spotted hands, this can't be more than five years ago. What he's doing in the kitchen is . . . it's dinner? Sort of. Maybe. Which, I never knew he was capable of that, of dinner, of being the one to prepare the food, of bringing it instead of having it brought.

But, what this means, what I know it has to mean, it's that Sheila's mom is already sick, that she's already been coughing up blood for a few months.

That grinding sound, though, that metal-tearing sound, I can finally attach it to something that completely makes sense, now that I'm seeing it: a can opener, one of the old-fashioned wall-mount electric ones, that slowly turn the can around, biting perforations into its top. I guess I've maybe even seen it there in their kitchen tucked under the counter right by the doorway to the living room, the wallpaper all stained under it, I just never actually *noticed* it. And I assume its motor or chassis or whatever must be mostly in the wall, since all that's showing is a square white plate and then the silver arm that holds the can while the little saw blade teeth chew into it.

Sheila's father is opening a can of generic creamed corn, holding it with his right hand to keep it from dropping when it's done, I guess—to keep more splashes from happening. But it's not built to be guided like that. The pressure he's applying to the side of the can is changing the tilt of the can, is slowing it down, is making the sharp teeth dig in at a slightly different angle, and maybe into the same place in the lid, even.

In the living room, the music swells for some romantic moment or another.

Next door, the action movie roars on, as if on the neighbor's incredibly up-to-date sound system.

I start to turn that way, to the bright lights and screeching tires, but I come back to this slowly rotating can of corn, and the visual-assist narrator says, as if speaking just and only to me, for me, "And we can see what his hand on that rotating can of corn is resulting in, can't we?"

I look closer, can't, no.

Not until my father-in-law lowers the can from the magnet that stays latched onto the lid.

"Glittering there in the yellow kernels," the narrator says, rapt on this detail, highlighting it for me, "are little . . . are those metal *shavings?*"

They are.

The ancient can opener would have worked fine, done its job like it's supposed to, probably works just like advertised every time my father-in-law uses it for his own meals, but by angling the can over just enough, and slowing it down, he's turned it into a weapon.

He sees these metal shavings, too, I mean. And he nods about them, humming in his mouth contentedly.

They're so obvious, now that I've seen them. Before he stirs them in.

Then he's walking into the living room but "We stay behind, don't we?" the narrator says right into my mind. "We stay behind, and we look over to the pantry. The door's open, isn't it? Go on, lean in, see what's there."

It's the trash can, overflowing with the torn-open cans of food my father-in-law's been feeding my wife's mother for weeks now, it looks like. For months. That he's been killing her with.

I suck a harsh chestful of air in and open my eyes, find myself staring right into my father-in-law's face, his saggy eyes wide open.

He smiles at me then chuckles, turns back to the screen, clapping me once on the thigh and leaving his hand there, like initiating me into a new place. Like ushering me in and keeping me there.

On-screen, a car explodes on landing from an impossible jump and the sound of the explosion is muted and distant for me, is happening in some land far, far away from where I am now.

◀◦▶

Walking down the sidewalk when the movie's over, ready to catch my father-in-law should he stumble, what I'm really doing is rewinding through my mother-in-law's last couple of years. The doctors diagnosing ulcers and "nonspecific intestinal hemorrhaging" or whatever it was. It didn't matter then. What mattered was that she eat only bland foods. What mattered was all the prescriptions meant to quell the digestive storm raging inside her.

What she was doing was watching TCM and eating tiny slivers of metal. If her health plan paid for more or better imaging, maybe the jig would have been up, and it all could have been an accident, bad luck, one failing kitchen appliance trying to kill her, her husband unwittingly involved.

As it was, she just kept getting chewed up from the inside.

And nobody suspected anything, least of all Sheila. Her mom was the right age for her body to be failing in unexpected ways, wasn't she? It was a tragedy, it was sad, but it wasn't any kind of real surprise. It's what we all have waiting for us, surely.

Only, it didn't have to be. Not for my mother-in-law.

Did she know right at the end, too? Did she finally see a glittering shard in her corn or peas, and look up to her husband, watching her spoon this in?

At that point, coughing up blood, blood in the toilet, her stomach and intestines in revolt, all failing, did she just guide that next bite in anyway, and turn back to her classic movie?

I don't know.

She was from that long-suffering generation, though. The one that would rather hide a thing like this than involve her own daughter. The one that would rather her daughter keep a father she could believe in.

"And now he's walking along the sidewalk close to the building," the narrator now whispering in my head says, "reaching forward with his brown cane as if pulling the sidewalk to him rather than pulling himself forward on the sidewalk."

And no one knows, I add, my heart beating in my throat, nearly choking me.

Do I tell Sheila, though?

I mean, first, before that, how do I even say I know this, right? I 'saw' it in the audio description for that car movie I took your father to? A woman reading a script in a sound booth months ago whispered it to me?

More like I dreamed it. More like I zoned out in the movie as a form of self-defense, and in that zoned-out state I worked up this grand story for how your father, he *killed your mother*, Sheel, really, serious, I solved the case. Also, there *is* a case.

As proof, of course, I could take a can from the pantry, it doesn't matter what, and mess with its angle in the can opener until it leaves sharp little slivers of metal behind.

At which point Sheila would look up from the bowl I've just poured, study me long and hard.

"Are you accusing him?" she would say to me. "Do you really think my father's capable of this?"

It's as unlikely a scenario as a car crashing out the high window of a building, landing in the pool in a way that doesn't kill everybody involved.

It doesn't mean I don't believe it with every fiber of my being, though.

I saw it. With my ears, sure, but in a more pure way, too: in my head, leaked across through a headphone cable.

Whenever my father-in-law is sitting in the room with us, nodding like catching his head from falling over and over again, now I know that what he's doing is congratulating himself on having gotten away with it, with killing his wife of forty-five years. And for no reason I can come up with other than that one day he saw that he *could*.

Can that happen, at the end of your life? Can you become a killer in your dotage, in your golden years? Can you want control of the remote enough that murder's your best option?

Nobody will suspect you. There's no motivation anybody can claim, there's no first attempt, there's no bad history, there's no evidence anybody can find. Just, one day you saw a bright, curled piece of silver in some sliced pears you'd just opened, and you looked up from them to the horrible old movie filling the living room, and you nodded maybe. Maybe.

It can happen, I think. It *did* happen.

I've never considered doing anything even remotely like that to Sheila, but I'd be lying if I said I hadn't imagined her dying in a car crash or a mall shooting. Not just imagining it, but fantasizing over it. Not like I wanted it to happen, but like . . . I don't know. Like the pity that would result after that, for me, and how I wasn't involved at all in this, could just start over now, start clean, it was attractive somehow. In a dull, never-going-to-happen, please-never-happen way.

I love Sheila, I mean. I want us to grow old together, to watch our television shows together until the end. I want it to be her and me, a team. We'll be the ones who make it, together. That's what I've always intended, what I've always dreamed.

But if this ever surfaces, what her father did to her mother, I don't know.

It'll send her into a spiral, I know. One she might never pull out of all the way. One that might take me down with her.

And I can't have that.

◦

"He punches the button for the third floor with his cane on the third try," the visual-assist in my head narrates when we're back to the building.

We stopped at the store and went up and down every aisle, so now I have two paper bags of groceries, *not* including a secret carton of smokes, thank you.

"Did you two have a good afternoon?" Sheila asks, opening the door while I'm still trying to get the key into the lock.

"Lords of the matinee," I tell her, stepping aside to present her father, safe and sound.

Sheila's hair is in a scarf, her sleeves rolled up, her shirt tied at her stomach like Rosie the Riveter. The stringent scent of cleaner washes out past us.

While she gets her father settled I quietly haul all the trash bags down to the trash. When I get back, Sheila's unfolding a blanket over her father's lap and working the big-button television remote into his right hand. There's not an ashtray in the room, not a newspaper left. For him it has to feel like his life's been dialed back to five, ten years ago. Sheila's beaming, glowing, bright and smiling. It's been a successful Sunday for her. She's a good daughter.

The television comes on under her father's trembling index finger and the commercial that blares into the room is for the movie we just sat through. The one we just listened to.

"What did the two of you see?" Sheila asks, her face somehow blank, as if there's no wrong answer.

"Period piece," I say with a shrug, lying for no reason I can claim, "that one with that one girl with the hair?"

Sheila considers tracking this down with me but then shrugs it away, looks around the place as if proud.

"Looks great," I tell her. "You found the way it used to be."

"I give it two weeks," she says back, and that's probably about right. "See the kitchen?"

I pretend I didn't, go back in. The counters are gleaming, the handles of everything catching the light.

"Couldn't be better," I tell her, and she proceeds to unpack the groceries we just got, line them in the pantry, and, while she's doing that, I find myself studying the wall-mounted can opener.

It's an ugly, unwieldy appliance, one I can't imagine was ever considered normal. It's like—it's like those old hatches or flaps or whatever that you still find in old houses, that you can plug a vacuum cleaner hose into, that are connected to some sucker-pump in another part of the house, that are supposed to make keeping the carpets clean so much easier.

Can openers should just be something you stash in the drawer, twist with your hand.

"Did you like it?" Sheila says, half in the pantry.

The movie.

"Love story," I say, "turned into murder, you know," and now my hand's to this wall-mounted can opener.

All it takes is a slight push to bend the top arm down not even five degrees, two or three of which it still has enough spring to recover on its own. It'll still function, will still open cans. Just, well. I'm not going to be here every meal like he was for his wife. I can't guide every can. Except like this, by messing with the machine, making it where it doesn't even know how to open can without turning it into a weapon.

Thirty minutes later, being the good son-in-law, I use it on some canned beets, my father-in-law's professed favorite, what we just bought twenty-four of in a flat box.

He's watching his news, his headphones on so we don't have to hear it.

"He looks so good," Sheila says, speaking freely since there's no chance of him tuning us in.

"I liked spending time with him," I say back, guiding the bowl of beets in, stirring the clumps with the spoon, hiding the bright slivers in deep. "I wish—I mean. I should have been doing it all along."

"You know," Sheila says, absolving me, "life."

It's our usual call and response.

I settle the dark purple beets down into my father-in-law's left hand.

I reach past him, pull the chain on the lamp beside him off, in case the silver in his meaty purple might try to glint, give away what's going on here.

The look he gives me about the light going away is hard, uncompromising, and that it lasts one bit longer than it should that tells me he probably also turned the lamp off on his wife, didn't he? Of course he did. Otherwise she might have seen what he was doing. Otherwise she might have known how he was killing her.

I hold his eyes, trying not to tell him anything, trying to just make him guess, because I imagine that has to be worse, more what he deserves, but then

Sheila's there at my side, her hand on my shoulder, her voice up on tippy-toes because she's being a good daughter, because I'm such a perfect son-in-law.

"Do you need anything else?" she's asking her father.

Her father looks from her to me, and then to his beets, and then he stabs his spoon in, brings it up to his mouth, and by the time we're leaving, I'm the last one in the room with him, the one carrying his empty bowl back to the kitchen.

His mouth is purple, the juice leaking down his chin.

I come back with a napkin, dab that color away, and the assist in my head settles back in, says, "And after the son-in-law leaves the room, the deadbolt clicking over, the grinding undertone comes back, doesn't it? That metal on metal sound, and when the old man on the chair chocks his headphones back and looks into the kitchen, what he sees, just partially, is *me*, standing at the can opener, bringing him his next meal, and his next, because his wife loves him enough to feed him, and keep feeding him, even when he tells her he's full, even when he tells her it hurts. 'Just one more bite, dear,' she'll tell him, holding her hand under the spoon as she guides it to his mouth. 'Just one more bite, and then you'll be all done, won't you?'"

On the way out, balancing a tub of cleaning supplies on my hip, I reach back in, switch the overhead light off with finality.

"It was a good time this afternoon, wasn't it?" Sheila says to me on the elevator.

"I should go to the movies more often," I tell her, and use my knee to push the button to deliver us down, away from this, into whatever wonders our old age might have waiting for us.

CLEAVER, MEAT, AND BLOCK

MARIA HASKINS

The first thing Hannah learned when she came to live with her grandparents after the Plague, was how to wield the meat cleaver. Grandma taught her, guiding her hands in the backroom of the old butcher shop on Main Street. Showing her how to wrap her fingers around the handle, how to put her thumb on the spine of the handle for extra power and precision, how to let her wrist pivot when she cuts.

"You don't need to be strong," Grandma said. "The weight of the blade, the sharpness of the edge, is enough."

This past Christmas, Grandma and Grandpa gave Hannah a cleaver of her own. When she unwrapped it, Grandpa was already apologizing for not getting her new clothes or makeup or jewelry, even though such things are hard to come by these days. Hannah didn't know how to tell him she'd never received a better gift in all her fourteen years.

The cleaver is real and useful in a way few other objects in Hannah's life have ever been, and she loves everything about it. She loves the dark, smooth wooden handle; the solid *thunk* of the wide, rectangular blade when it shears through meat and bone and hits the wooden chopping block; the way the steel edge glistens beneath the lights.

Sometimes, when Hannah works in the butcher shop, she thinks about her parents and baby Daniel. They've been gone for three years, and she knows it's better not to dwell on the past, yet she cannot help it. Sometimes she thinks about Meg, their old dog, too. About Meg's silvered muzzle and silky, pointy ears. About the way Meg would sigh when she lay down on Hannah's bed every night. About Meg's pink and bloody guts torn out all over the driveway when the raveners fed on her.

Sometimes, though rarely, Hannah thinks about a stifling attic space above a hall closet, wooden beams digging into her back and legs, a trapdoor barred with a garden rake, and the sounds that came from the house below.

More often, though she tries not to, she thinks about Pete from school, and the way he looks at her.

◄◦►

Every day after school, Pete follows Hannah home. He trails behind her along the paths and streets, regardless of which way she chooses to go. When she enters her grandparents' house, two blocks away from the butcher shop, he lingers across the street, staring at the living room window as if he knows she's watching him from behind the heavy yellow drapes.

Every day, Hannah stands behind those drapes, waiting for Pete to skive off down the lane to his parents' house. She waits with Rosko, her grandparents' spaniel, beside her; her hands stroking the dog's silky, caramel-coloured fur until Pete is out of sight.

◄◦►

Rosko sleeps in Hannah's bed. That's the way it's been since she first got here. Every night he curls up beside her, so close she feels each quiver of fragile life beneath his ribs. She lays there beneath the pink and white quilt Grandma picked out for this room back when it was still the guestroom rather than Hannah's room, and whenever Rosko whimpers in his sleep, she puts her arm around him.

Hannah doesn't want to love Rosko, and yet she cannot help it.

◄◦►

Before the Plague and the raveners, Pete and Hannah lived in the same neighbourhood in the same city. It's not like they were friends, but they went to the same school, though he was a grade ahead of her. Now, they both live in this run-down sawmill town full of old pickup trucks, faded strip malls, and resettled Plague-survivors, but they never speak to each other. Hannah rarely speaks to anyone at all, but she knows the silence between her and Pete is different. It's more than an absence of words. It's like the steel blade of the cleaver, bright and hard and sharp enough to cut.

◄◦►

Pete's family moved to town two months after Hannah arrived with the other Plague orphans. First time she saw him, he rode his red bike with a group of friends past the butcher shop, on their way to buy home-made candy from the re-purposed Tim Hortons down the street. She shouldn't have been surprised. Lots of survivors end up in this town because it's one of the few in the region that survived the Plague with most of its infrastructure intact. On days when the electricity works, residents can almost pretend the world is functional again.

Her grandparents have lived in this town all their lives, running the same butcher shop on Main Street since before Hannah's mom was born. Even though the government-run supply store opened down the block last year, selling dry and canned goods, hygiene products, medicines, and second-hand clothes, people still come to the butcher shop to buy meat. They stand at the shiny glass counter, chatting with Grandpa about the weather and the rationing and the freight trains that have just started moving through a couple of times per week. Hannah stays in the backroom with the cleaver, trying not to listen, trying not to think of which customers were raveners during the Plague, and which were not.

◄◦►

When Hannah wields the cleaver exactly right, when her grip is firm and her wrist pivots the way it is supposed to, then, all her memories are sheared away until nothing exists except the meat and the cleaver and the *thunk* of steel against the block.

In those rare moments, Hannah can almost forget. She can almost forget the Plague. She can almost forget that her dog and her parents and Daniel were killed and eaten by Pete and his parents. Almost. But not quite.

⟶◇⟵

Hannah hides beneath the fir trees at recess while Pete and his friends play tag in the schoolyard. They *call* it tag but it's really a game of chase, and no matter how it starts, it always ends with the kids who were raveners chasing those who weren't.

Crouched beneath the drooping branches, knees and hands touching wet dirt and roots, Hannah watches as Pete knocks Alexa to the ground under the swings. Alexa doesn't try to fight once she's down. She doesn't scream even though her face is a mask of terror. Pete grabs her arms, pushes one knee into her midriff, opens his mouth and leans close to her face, jaws snapping. Hannah's heart thuds hard and fast in her chest, watching as Pete leans in to rip Alexa's throat open, as his fingers curl into claws.

Then he laughs and shouts, "Gotcha!" before he lets Alexa go and runs after someone else.

Alexa stays down. Hannah can't see her face, but she knows Alexa's crying.

Pete and the others chase Oscar next. Oscar is tall and fast, and it takes a big group of them to bring him down, all of them falling on top of him, clawing at his back, screeching and hollering, tearing at his clothes.

Hannah picks up a rock and holds it in her right hand, knuckles gone white.

That day in the city when the raveners came loping up the driveway, that day when baby Daniel wouldn't stop screaming, that day when dad hoisted her up into the attic as the backdoor was pushed off its hinges, and the front door bent and shivered, that day, she held a pair of scissors in her hand. Huddled in the gloom beneath the rafters, she wasn't sure what she'd do if the trapdoor opened from below. Would she fight? Or would she let them kill her? Holding the scissors, she listened as baby Daniel went silent, as the raveners tore and swallowed.

Under the fir-trees, Hannah holds on to the rock until the bell rings.

⟶◇⟵

It's been two years since Hannah was found in the woods by a rescue and retrieval team, eighteen months since she came to stay with her grandparents.

She's learned a lot in eighteen months.

How to sharpen knives, how to mop the butcher shop's black and white tile floor, how to skim the fat and foam off Grandma's stock pot, how to put scraps and lard into the meat grinder, pushing the pieces down the hopper, turning the crank until everything is pushed out through the grinding plate, pale-pink curls of sausage meat dropping into the stainless-steel bowl below.

But nothing holds her interest like the cleaver.

Working at the counter in the backroom, she grips the cleaver in her right hand while she holds the meat in place with her left. Grandma taught her how to wield the cleaver, but Grandpa taught her how to cut. How to turn a loin of pork into chops and roasts and stew meat. How to turn a slab of beef into steaks and brisket, blade roast, sirloin. How to separate a chicken into all its parts.

Before the Plague, Hannah would have never thought she'd end up working in her grandparents' butcher shop. Mom and dad only brought her here for visits at Christmas, sometimes for a week in summer. Back then, Hannah dreamt of traveling the world and becoming a dog groomer or maybe a cartoonist.

These days, the butcher shop seems as good a place as any to make a life. There is nowhere to go, nothing to become. The world beyond the highway, beyond the train tracks, beyond the ocean, is broken, rent asunder by the Plague and the raveners and the riots and disasters that followed in their wake. Even now, no one knows how many died, how many lived, how many turned ravener, how many turned to meat.

Hannah knows it's best to look ahead. There's a vaccine now and a cure. People will never turn into raveners again. It was a virus that crept into people's brains, made the infected crave living flesh and blood, made them gather in hordes, made them break down doors and windows to get to the living people hiding inside, made them rip through ribs and skin and skulls with their teeth and fingers.

Look ahead. Make the best of things. That's what people say.

What they mean is, forget.

◄◦►

It's Saturday, and Hannah has been working in the butcher shop since breakfast.

She helps out every weekend and most weekday evenings after homework. Her grandparents worry about how much she works and her lack of friends, but it doesn't bother her.

Hannah works, cleaver in hand. The meat on the block is cold and slippery. It's been bled already, the carcass gutted and skinned, made ready for eating.

She is not thinking about school. Not about Pete. Not about waking in the night with Rosko beside her, listening for furtive noises outside. She is not thinking about mom and dad and Daniel. Not thinking about raveners, clawing at the scraps of plywood covering the windows. Not thinking about the stifling dusk that engulfed her, once the trapdoor closed. The smell of blood and offal wafting up from below, hours after the raveners had left the house. The wet gleam of blood on asphalt once she got outside. Moonlight on the pavement where the last bits of Meg had been ground into the pitted surface. Ragged taste of salt and bile in her mouth as she ran from the city, folding herself into the darkness of the woods beyond the highway.

Her vision blurs, making it hard to see, but the cleaver knows enough for both of them. It keeps cutting, through bone and gristle and slippery meat while Hannah remembers.

She remembers everything. That is the curse of those who did not turn into raveners, to remember.

The raveners don't remember being raveners. Once the cure burned the virus out of them, they had no memory of what they'd done, they could not recall their hunger, guts and brains ripped out, limbs cracked, flesh chewed and swallowed.

The vaccine absolved them. There is no blame or guilt, no justice either. But Hannah can't forget. Can't look ahead, can't make the best of things. That's her secret, the one she dare not speak out loud to anyone.

Pete, and the others who were raveners mostly look like ordinary people now. Except, when she catches sight of them at the edges of her vision, their faces slip like melting rubber masks, revealing other faces, leering and snarling, teeth and gullets.

She isn't sure how to tell masks from faces. Maybe there is no difference. Maybe no one, no matter who they are or what they did, have real faces. Maybe there are only masks, and nothing but the hollow darkness beneath.

Hannah looks down at the hand holding the meat, and for a moment it doesn't seem as if it belongs to her. The pale skin, the veins beneath, the bones covered in flesh and sinew. It's just another piece of meat for the cleaver to sort out on the block.

"Hannah, come have some lunch."

Grandma's voice stops the descending cleaver, the steely blade quivering above the wrist where the bones and joints hold it in place. Hannah puts the cleaver away and takes off her apron, hanging it on the hook beside the stove. She washes her hands and sits down with Grandma.

"You work too much," Grandma says as they dig into the flaky crust of the homemade chicken pie. Hannah watches the pale, creamy filling spilling out—chunks of chicken, green peas and golden carrots from the garden, flecks of fragrant thyme that Grandma dries in bunches in her kitchen.

"I like working," Hannah says.

Grandma doesn't say anything else and neither does Hannah, but the unspoken words—the words they both might say if they could find voices strong and gentle enough to hold them without shattering—are there in the warmth between them when Grandma touches her arm.

You do what you need to, that's what Grandma said that first night when Hannah couldn't fall asleep in the guestroom. *I'm not going to tell you how to deal with it, because I don't know either.*

—◇—

The house where Hannah's grandparents live is small and square, with a black tar-papered roof and white stucco walls. In the front garden, fading daisies and cat mint peek out between sage and thyme, peas and beans. Like the backyard-garden, it's ready for the last harvest. In summer, zucchini and onion, carrots and potatoes, tomatoes and beets, crowd together where the flower beds and the lawn used to be before the Plague, but it's autumn now, and everything will soon turn brown.

Inside, the house is all flowery wallpaper, chintz, and polished wood. It smells of firewood and lavender sachets. The back of the house looks out over the greenbelt and the gravel road beside the creek, and from her window on the second floor, Hannah sees the river, the highway, and the train tracks.

Sometimes, when she stands in the window, breath catching on the glass, Hannah sees Pete down by the river, walking or riding his bike on the trails through the old scrapyards and abandoned buildings. Sometimes, he's with his friends, usually he's alone. She'd recognize him anywhere. That lopsided slope of his shoulders. The swing of his arms. The way he cocks his head when he looks around.

Along the river, there's a warren of run-down industrial properties, an old sawmill and a cement factory, a heap of rusted car remains and a scrapyard. From her vantage point, Hannah sees the tangled rolls of barbed wire and debris heaped up in that scrapyard. It was part of the barricade around the town during the Plague, when guards patrolled the perimeter 24/7, armed and ready.

The Plague never reached this town. Not one single ravener ever roamed its streets, though other communities along the highway were wiped out. No one knows why some places were spared. Maybe it was God's will, like the priest tells them in church. Maybe it's because there's no airport or harbour nearby, like their teacher says. Maybe it was just dumb luck, like Grandma thinks.

No one had time to build barricades around the city where Hannah lived. By the time people realized there was a Plague, it was already on the inside, inside the suburbs and the downtown core, inside the houses and trains and subway stations, inside hospitals and schools and preschools. One Tuesday, everything was fine with school and lasagna and mom going to a yoga class at the rec-center. Next Tuesday dad was boarding up the windows, and most of the neighbourhood had turned ravener. The Tuesday after that, Hannah was all alone, in the woods.

Grandpa and Grandma only ever saw the Plague on TV, until the TV-broadcasts stopped, the internet went down, and that big winter storm hit in the midst of everything, knocking out the electricity. After that, "everything went bonkers," like Grandpa says, for about a year.

They know what happened, everyone does, but knowing is not remembering. They don't lie awake at night, listening to the wind but hearing the raveners breathing outside the door, scratching at the walls and windows. They don't hear Daniel shrieking even though mom is trying, trying, trying to make him shut the hell up, they don't hear the heavy thud when dad falls to the floor. They don't know what it sounds like when raveners eat someone.

Hannah remembers, but cannot speak of it. Her memories are like a thousand thousand thousand screaming, bleeding mouths, and if she were to reveal them in the daylight, if she were to lay them bare in this house, she fears the horror of it might devour not just her, but Grandma and Grandpa and the street and the river and the entire world.

⋖⋗

Hannah is chopping pork in the backroom, setting aside the scraps for a batch of Grandma's sage and onion sausage, when she hears the entry-bell jingling.

"How's business?" someone asks Grandpa in the shop.

Hannah knows that voice. It's Pete's mom. She doesn't need to look to know what the woman looks like, neat hair, neat clothes, red lipstick and a smile. Her face so clean and polished you'd never know she ever tore raw meat off the bones.

"Can't complain," Grandpa answers. "People always need to eat."

Pete's mom laughs. In the backroom, the cleaver stops.

Grandma is standing next to Hannah at the counter, turning the crank on the meat grinder, and for a moment the grinder too goes silent. Hannah glances at Grandma, and before they both look away, Hannah catches a gleam of the cleaver's steel in Grandma's eyes. It's so brief that afterward she is not sure whether it was real, or whether she imagined it.

Then, the bell jingles again and Pete's mom leaves, carrying the meat she bought in a brown paper bag. In the backroom, Hannah closes her eyes, but the cleaver keeps working, moving with more speed and accuracy than she could ever manage on her own.

⋖⋗

One October day, after school, Pete follows Hannah all the way to her door. He comes right up to the house behind her. The key slips between her fingers when she tries to get inside, away from Pete, and then Rosko is out on the porch before she can stop him. He's too happy, too wiggly, to contain. Same as Meg was, once.

"I like your new dog." Hannah turns and looks at Pete, really looks. His face is pale and smooth around the wet cave of his mouth, and she catches the glint of his teeth and tongue. He stares back at her, blue eyes shiny and blank. "I remember you," he says, and puts his hand on Rosko's head. It's just a brief touch, fingers curling into Rosko's caramel coloured fur. "We went to the same school, remember?"

Rosko backs away from Pete, a growl lurking in his throat. Hannah feels the weight of her empty hands. If she had a rock, or a pair of scissors, she'd know what to do with her hands. But they are empty.

Looking at Pete, Hannah sees her fist go through his face, breaking it, smashing it to pieces, until she reveals the true face beneath. But instead she grips Rosko's collar and drags him inside, pulling the door shut behind her, locking it with the deadbolt and chain. The dog wiggles around her and she holds onto him, sitting there in the hallway, back braced against the door, waiting for the raveners to come.

She waits for a long time.

-◇-

Once, and only once, Grandpa asked Hannah how she survived. She told him the truth. She hid. She hid when she could and ran when she had to. That's all. She wasn't smart or brave or strong, just lucky.

Grandpa didn't ask for details, but Hannah remembers the details. She remembers dad telling mom the army would surely come and get them out. She remembers how the raveners mostly roamed the cities and towns at first, so the woods and fields were safer. But eventually, the hordes headed out to hunt elsewhere. She remembers the places where it's harder for the raveners to find you. Narrow concrete pipes half-filled with fetid water and dead things. Root cellars barred from inside. Garages with metal doors. Shipping containers at the dock. She remembers what to eat to keep yourself alive even when you think you want to die.

Hannah remembers being found, too. She remembers the army truck and the smell of biodiesel and disinfectant and hot chocolate, the people in hazmat suits swabbing her arm, drawing blood, testing her for infection, telling her she was "clean" before they administered the vaccine. She remembers the months of boredom and half-decent meals at the quarantine camp, watching raveners be brought in each day on trucks, howling and scratching at each other, before they were penned, swabbed, cured, and put into a separate section of the camp.

Hannah dreams of the past every night. Sometimes, she's in the camp. Sometimes, she's in the woods. Sometimes, she's huddled beneath the roof, listening to dad moaning below.

Every time she wakes up in her grandparents' house and sees the pink and white quilt, the world seems more unreal than what she left behind. Maybe she only dreamed that she was saved. Maybe she is still curled up in a concrete pipe by the river, gnawing on raw fish and worse.

Yet, every day she gets out of bed, puts on her clothes, and acts as if she believes this is real. Every day, she wraps the shreds of what is left of the old Hannah around the emptiness that is Hannah now, and no one seems to notice that there's nothing left of her beneath the rags.

◄◦►

The day when Pete finds her hiding beneath the trees at recess, Hannah doesn't have a rock. Her second mistake is to run. She should have just stood still and let him knock her down, get it over with, but when he comes for her, she bolts. Pete knocks her off her feet, pins her down, his breath warm and wet on her face and neck.

Hannah doesn't scream. Screaming will only bring more of them, she's seen it happen enough times. She knows she is going to die, knows she is already dead, that she died in that gloomy attic, that whatever came out of there, whatever hid in the woods for all those months, was not really Hannah, but someone, *something*, else.

But Pete does not rip her throat out. Instead he leans close and whispers in her ear, words as slippery as meat.

"I remember," he whispers. "I remember what they tasted like."

Then he's up and running again, chasing someone else. Hannah doesn't move. She looks up at the blue sky that is so thin and worn it might be ripped asunder by a gust of wind, or a scream, and reveal the black cold void beyond.

◄◦►

After work in the butcher shop that evening, Hannah cleans the meat cleaver and the knives and the chopping block. She scrubs the counters and mops the floor. It's the first time she brings the meat cleaver home with her. She wraps it in a towel and tucks it into her backpack.

That night, with the steel beneath her pillow, it's easier to sleep.

I remember.

She knows it's the truth, because it's sharp and it hurts and it cuts through every lie she has been told—about the Plague, about the cure, about the raveners. It reveals the world as it is, as it always was: a place where everyone is meat.

◄◦►

Rosko sometimes whines at night, wanting Hannah to let him out in the backyard, but she keeps him inside as much as she can after dark. Pets disappear all the time in this town. Cats. Dogs. Caged rabbits and chickens.

"It's coyotes," people say, "they're everywhere these days."

But Hannah hasn't seen any coyotes from her window or on the way home from school. Not a single one moving in the greenbelt, or by the river. She has just seen Pete, and his friends, riding or walking through the tall grass and scrub, sometimes venturing into the woods beyond.

One night in late October when Rosko wakes her, he's growling rather than whining. Hannah pulls the cleaver from beneath the pillow and when they get downstairs, Rosko stands stiff and trembling, staring at the backdoor, hackles raised.

There are voices outside, low and muffled. Close.

Outside the kitchen window, the night is moonlit and frosty. Hannah shivers in her blue flannel pyjamas. She sees a thousand shadows in the yard, crouched and looming, hunched and menacing, fanged and clawed. She stands very still, listening, with the cleaver in her hand.

The cleaver is still warm from being in her bed, and when she raises it slightly, it feels light and quick in her hand, almost happy. Hannah understands. It's eager. Eager to cut, to chop, to slice. The weight and heft of it settles her heart and breathing, allows anger to come through, burning away the fear.

She opens the door a crack, keeping Rosko behind her.

"Go away," she shouts, and her voice sounds deeper and stronger when she holds the cleaver. "Go away, you fuckers!"

It's the cleaver that makes her swear. She never has before. But now she wants to.

There is rustling, there is wind, the creak of the fence. Maybe something scrambles over it. Maybe there are footsteps, disappearing down the narrow path along the greenbelt.

Coyotes, that's what people will say, but the cleaver knows the truth and so does Hannah.

Afterward, Hannah lies awake, holding Rosko. He's smaller than Meg was when she slipped out while dad tried to reinforce their front door. He weighs only a little more than Daniel did the last time she held him.

Mom wouldn't let Hannah take Daniel with her in the attic when she hid. "There's no time, and he might cry," mom shouted at dad as the raveners pounded on the doors. It was true, maybe he would have cried, but he was a good baby, and Hannah tried so hard to make him understand how important it was to be quiet. Maybe she could have saved him.

Hannah lies awake with the cleaver underneath her pillow until jaundiced morning light filters through the pink and yellow curtains.

I remember.

Of course Pete remembers. They all do, and everyone knows it, even if they pretend otherwise. It's easier to pretend. Because so many of the survivors were raveners. Because no one knows what else to do. Because it's over now, and everyone should get on with their lives.

Hannah wraps the cleaver in a towel and puts it in her backpack.

She's tired. Tired of being scared. Tired of wrapping the shreds of old Hannah around the emptiness. Tired of not screaming.

She knows what she must do, and so does the cleaver.

The rest of the week, Hannah walks a different way home from school every day. It takes longer, because she avoids the roads and streets, staying closer to the river and the woods, but for two days Pete does not find her. On the third day, he's back, following her through a copse of trees by the train tracks, past the old sawmill, through the mess of wrecked cars near the greenbelt. The clouds hang low, fat with rain, and Hannah runs the last bit home, cleaver bouncing in her pack, heart thumping in her chest until she is safe inside with Rosko.

She walks new routes every day after that, knowing Pete will follow.

It's October, then November, and the sun goes down earlier every evening. There is only a slip of light left after school, and dusk lurks all around while Pete follows her. Hannah stretches out the walks home until there is barely enough light to see by. Some days, she doesn't make it to work in the butcher shop at all. Other days, she hides from Pete in the wreckage of old buildings or the hulks of rusted cars, watching as he searches for her, waiting to see what he will do. Those days, she gets home so late that Grandma and Grandpa have already gone to bed.

She knows they're worried, but they don't ask where she's been.

Hannah wonders if they're scared that she would lie, or if they're scared she'd tell the truth.

◄◦►

It's late November. The air smells like frost and snow and Hannah's breath hangs in the air in ragged tufts on the way home from school. She chooses the longest route, and Pete follows about a hundred meters behind. Whenever Hannah turns and looks at him, she shivers—a bit from the cold, not so much from fear.

Near the river, she starts to run. Not fast enough to really get away. Just fast enough to make Pete follow, but once they've left the houses and the streets behind, the chase is real. It's like the day she fled the city with a pack of raveners at her back. That time, the raveners found an old woman hiding in a car and dragged her out, giving Hannah enough time to escape.

Pete chases and Hannah runs, heading for the scrapyard. It's a jumble of old machinery, rusting metal, sagging storage sheds, busted cars, and no one is watching except the broken eyes of the buildings.

Even though Hannah has it all planned out—where to hide, where to wait for him if he falls behind—Pete catches her unaware, jumping out from a pile of old tires and knocking her to the ground. In the gathering dusk, Hannah fights silently, but Pete is strong, and there's no other meat here to divert his attention. His hands grip tight, pinning her down, her right arm trapped underneath her at a painful angle. Panting, Pete leans close.

"Not so tough now, are you." His breath smells sour and sickly and Hannah tries to knee him in the groin, but he holds her down. "Don't you think I see the way you look at me? Like you're better than me. Like you didn't hide in the mud and eat bugs and worms and roadkill to survive. Like that makes you better than me."

Hannah tries to buck him off, but he's too heavy. She wriggles her right arm halfway free and feels around for the backpack stuck underneath her legs, its zipper half open.

"You *should* be scared of me." Pete's voice is harsher now. "All of you should be. You shouldn't have made it out of that house. I looked for you after we ate your dog and your brother. I looked and looked, and I knew I smelled you but then . . ." His voice wavers, his face crumples. "I remember it. Every day. Every night. All the time. What do you think that's like? Mom says I can't talk about it, not even to her, but . . . I . . ."

Hannah stares at his pale, flushed face. There are tears in his eyes, snot dribbling from his nose. As if *he* has anything to mourn. As if *he* has lost anything. Then Pete sees her looking and he growls, slipping a grin back on his face before grabbing her by the throat. His mouth flaps open, wet and pink and full of teeth, and the memories ignite in Hannah's head, burning through her, a conflagration consuming doubt and fear, consuming the girl she was before, consuming everything but meat and steel.

The backpack is pinned below her thighs. She reaches into it for the cleaver, and the cleaver does not hesitate. It's sharp and efficient. It's useful and reliable even when Hannah is not, and Pete doesn't see it, doesn't know the blade is coming, doesn't realize it's there, until the steel bites into his face.

You don't need to be strong. The weight of the blade, the sharpness of the edge, is enough.

Closing her eyes, Hannah folds herself into emptiness that has grown inside her since she hid in that attic. The cleaver doesn't need her help. It knows what to do. It knows what to do with every piece of slippery wet meat held down on the block, and here in the scrapyard, the cleaver does its work while the world inside and around Hannah screams, a thousand thousand thousand mouths yawning wide, shrieking in terror and despair, wrath and ruin, grief and devastation. So many mouths: her own, mom's, dad's, Daniel's, Meg's, all of them, the whole world, crying out in agony and triumph while the cleaver goes about its business.

◄○►

Afterward, it's quiet, and for a single, razor-thin sliver of time—a sliver so thin and fine Hannah can see both past and future through it—no one is screaming. Not in Hannah's head, not elsewhere either. The world's gone mute, watching Pete in the gravel. Hannah watches as the last of the bruised daylight fades. She watches closely, hoping to see the moment when he turns into meat, but it doesn't happen. It already happened. He was always meat. Just like mom and Meg. Just like dad and Daniel. Just like she is.

There's a culvert of corrugated steel nearby where the creek spills into the river, its tarnished vault high enough to stand inside and she drags the body there. If Hannah were alone, she might have left it in the open, to be found. But the cleaver knows best. It knows how to sort out the meat beneath the blade, and it knows what they can do, together.

◄○►

Grandma finds her in the backroom of the butcher shop early next morning. Worry and relief chase across her face as she looks at Hannah's bloody shirt and torn jeans, her dirty shoes, her heavy, wet backpack.

Hannah holds Grandma's gaze and Grandma does not look away.

"Pete told me he remembered," Hannah whispers while the cleaver keeps working. "Maybe they all do."

Even then, Grandma does not look away. She *sees*. She sees the meat on the block, and the meat on the floor, she sees it for what it is, sees the world as it is, and Hannah, in turn, sees the exact moment when Grandma understands, when she understands everything—cleaver, meat, and block.

Maybe her old hands tremble. Maybe not.

"Right," Grandma says, fumbling with her apron. "Pies and sausages it is. But they're not for everyone," she adds sharply, and there's a glint of steel behind her glasses when she gets the meatgrinder ready. "Only for those that might remember and appreciate the taste."

Hannah nods and wraps her hand around the handle as the cleaver goes back to work.

THE EIGHT-THOUSANDERS

JASON SANFORD

He spoke once, the words whispered by frozen lips on a face so frostbitten he looked like a porcelain doll. I found him below the summit as our expedition bottlenecked before the Hillary Step on our final ascent of Mount Everest.

And above the bottleneck, more climbers. Dozens of people snaking to the top in their insulated red and orange and bright-color parkas and boots and backpacks.

As if the mountain bled a trickle of rainbow-neon blood.

I leaned against a rock overhang, numb and cold and exhausted and focused only on climbing higher. I thought the man sitting under the overhang dead until I saw condensation rise from his lips. Spindrift snow danced around him.

"Don't let me die," the man whispered.

No one else had noticed the man. Or they'd ignored him like all the dead bodies we passed on Everest.

I waved for Ronnie Chait, my boss and our expedition's leader. Ronnie stumbled over in his red high-tech coat and pants. He was attempting his fifth summit of Everest and his first without a supplemental oxygen system. Back at base camp other expedition leaders had grumbled about Ronnie leading people to the summit while not using oxygen. But no one had dared confront Ronnie. He was one of the richest men in the world and known for both his love of mountain climbing and his hard-ass attitude toward business and life.

Ronnie knelt before the freezing man.

"He's too far gone," Ronnie said. "Must have been up here overnight."

More climbers stepped past us. The longer we waited, the longer it'd take to summit. In one of Ronnie's viral Ted Talks he'd recounted what he'd learned during decades of venture capital and mountain climbing. How rescue was impossible on Everest. How if you died on Everest your body stayed on Everest.

His point was to live your life as if every day was Everest. That you couldn't rely on others to save you.

"Nothing to be done, Keller," Ronnie said as he laid his hand on my shoulder. "We can't help him. But staying here will keep us from reaching the summit."

Ronnie's eyes hid behind his sunglasses, but it felt as if he glared into me. As if this moment decided my future with him. I owed my career to Ronnie. He was helping me reach Everest.

He turned and climbed up the ropes, daring me to back out.

I hesitated. The freezing man looked at me with a desperate gaze. I remembered my little brother's final hours. How I'd wished I'd been there with him.

I couldn't leave this man to die alone.

Could I?

Nyima Sherpa, Ronnie's main guide, hiked over. Nyima rubbed the frozen man's legs and arms, trying to return circulation, but his extremities were already too far gone. We tried to help him stand, but the man couldn't move.

"He's already half dead," Nyima said.

I should have felt something, but didn't. I was exhausted and numb, not merely my body but my emotions. I knew logically that this was because my oxygen mask and cylinder couldn't provide enough air to be clear-headed in the mountain's death zone. But even knowing that, I didn't care. All that mattered was to keep climbing.

"I'll stay with him," a voice said above the hiss of my regulator.

A short woman stood beside Nyima Sherpa. She wore a parka so faded the red was nearly pink. Her insulated pants and boots were black and also faded while massive mountain goggles covered the top of her face in one big rainbow-reflecting lens. An older-style rubber oxygen mask covered her mouth, nose and chin, ensuring no skin was exposed to the sun or the cold. But the line leading from the mask dangled loose, unattached to any oxygen canister.

"Truth," the woman said. "I'll stay. Continue your climb."

Nyima stared at the woman through his icy goggles. His oxygen mask shivered as if he couldn't gasp enough air. He muttered something in the Sherpa language before grabbing my arm and hustling me to the line of waiting climbers.

When I glanced back the woman knelt beside the dying man in the shade under the rock overhang. Now out of the dazzling sunlight, she removed her rubber oxygen mask and gloves, revealing deathly pale skin. When she opened her mouth, I saw large fangs. She leaned against the man and whispered into his icy ears while gently running a finger along his neck.

"Keep climbing, Keller," Nyima yelled. "Just climb, damn it."

◄◦►

For the last decade I've reached toward Everest. Summiting larger and larger mountains. Exercising daily. Working forever-long hours for Ronnie's venture capital company. Begging for a taste of the stock offerings in the new tech start-ups he continually funded and spun off.

Because it wasn't good enough to want to climb. You had to have the means to climb. And that's what working for Ronnie gave me.

Not that I hated Ronnie. Working for him was like aiming for Everest—it didn't matter what we created, only that we reached the top. And in our spare time we bonded over mountain climbing. Tech bros convincing ourselves it was our genius and hard work which carried us here.

But I sometimes wondered. Now that I was actually on Everest the mountain felt like that gourmet burger restaurant Ronnie had bought a few years back. Bad decor and overpriced food yet always filled with tech bros and hedge fund managers whose haircuts cost more than a hundred bucks. Ronnie loved the place and took his top people there most weekends for beers and laughs. No matter that we were sick of the damn place. That we couldn't eat another of those fancy burgers even if our mommies kissed our cheeks and begged us to swallow.

But eat them we did. And convinced ourselves we loved them. Because Ronnie did.

As I climbed the last few meters to the top of Everest, I wondered why summiting felt like another weekend at that damn burger place.

My body was so weak it felt as if I swam through wet concrete. I gasped at the oxygen streaming into my mask. I stepped to the top behind Ronnie. We were the last to summit. Nyima was already descending with the others in our group.

Ronnie took a photo of me at the summit. When I offered to take one of him he shook his head and said we needed to descend.

I stared at the distant Tibetan plateau. At the other nearby eight-thousanders. Lhotse. Makalu. Chomo Lonzo. All mountains nearly as tall as Everest. All their peaks in the same death zone which was killing me, my body unable to grasp enough oxygen even with this mask.

"Someday we'll climb them all," Ronnie yelled. "We need to go."

Distant clouds swirled one of the mountain ranges. For a moment Ronnie looked worried. He stepped forward and slipped, only his climbing axe keeping him from sliding toward the edge of the mountain. I wondered if the effect of not using oxygen was getting to him.

But I said nothing and followed him. Because at this point what else could I do?

-◦-

By the time we climbed down the Hillary Step the clouds were closer. From this distance they looked pretty. But darkness was also falling, with the sun so low that the side of the mountain we climbed down was now in a giant shadow. We had to reach the temporary camp at South Col before the pending storm reached us. Below us in the distance I saw Nyima and the other expedition climbers—it looked like they'd make our overnight camp before the storm hit.

We turned on our headlamps and staggered forward.

I focused on following Ronnie, forcing my exhausted body to take step after step, and almost ran into him when he suddenly stopped. We stood near the rock overhang where the climber had been freezing to death. Maybe Ronnie wanted to see if we could still help.

But there was no one under the overhang.

Ronnie stumbled backward, knocking me down. I slammed my climbing axe into the snow to steady myself as Ronnie backed up even more.

The woman in the faded red coat stood before us on the mountain's edge, right beside a sheer drop of a thousand meters or more. Her face and hands were no longer covered now that the sun was hidden by shadows. She cradled the frozen man in her arms like a child and bit into his neck. Red sprayed across the spindrift snow. The man didn't move, either dead or so far gone he felt no pain.

The woman turned toward Ronnie and me and smiled, the blood on her lips and chin instantly freezing.

"I waited for you two," she said. "You're already dead, you know."

Ronnie held his climbing axe before him like a weapon, but I didn't move. We barely had the strength to reach camp let alone fight. Besides, it would be so simple for her to knock us right off the mountain if she desired.

The woman shook her head. "Don't worry—I won't kill you. But you started your descent too late. The jet stream's shifting. The storm and wind will hit before you reach camp."

Ronnie stepped forward as if to swing his axe at the woman. I grabbed his shoulder, stopping him. She was right. Down below us I saw the other climbers already blurring as the increasing wind stirred up the snow.

The woman turned back to the mountain's edge. She held the frozen man out as if offering him to the sky before tossing his body into the air as if he weighed nothing. The man soared for a moment before dropping out of sight.

The woman stepped back to the rock overhang, allowing us enough room to pass. "You idiots call that the Rainbow Valley," she said, pointing to the dropoff. "From all the dead climbers in their bright parkas and gear. For what it's worth, I didn't kill any of them."

Ronnie staggered past the woman, keeping as far from her as he could without falling.

I crept by closer to the woman, afraid I'd fall if I hiked that close to the edge. As I passed she said, "I'm Ferri."

"Keller," I said back, whispering inside my oxygen mask. I didn't think she'd hear me. But she nodded as if she'd had and followed me as I climbed down.

◂◦▸

Ronnie and I made it to the South Summit before darkness and the full storm hit. But my oxygen tank had run out minutes before. I gasped at the dry air, my body hyperventilating but still not getting enough oxygen. Panic shook me. I felt like I was drowning. I prayed I wouldn't pass out.

Nyima and the other Sherpas had cached oxygen bottles here yesterday, but I didn't know if I'd last long enough to reach them. As Ronnie lead me toward the cache between two rocks, the weather cleared for a moment. I saw the headlamps and illuminated tents at South Col and the lights of the other climbers who were nearly to the camp. Then the wind shifted and I again saw only a half-dozen meters in the swirling snow.

"There's only empty bottles," Ronnie screamed, leaning over the cache. A number of red bottles lay scattered across the snow and rock, left from when the other members of our expedition changed out their oxygen earlier. But one of the bottles still had the seal over the threads to keep out ice and snow—it hadn't been used.

"That one," I said, pointing at the full bottle. "They left that for me."

Ronnie picked up the bottle. But instead of handing it to me he threw it with a strength he shouldn't have had. The bottle bounced off a rock below us and tumbled over the edge of the mountain.

"It's empty," Ronnie yelled. "Empty. But there's air all around us. Breathe it, Keller. Breathe!"

I fell to my knees, lightheaded, as Ronnie began descending again. Was he going to leave me here? I collapsed onto the empty bottles, my gloves smacking each one, begging for one to have oxygen in it. Unlike Ronnie, I hadn't trained my body to climb Everest without extra oxygen. I gasped for air, desperate to breathe. I couldn't die here. I couldn't.

"Your friend's an asshole," the woman in faded red yelled as she sat on one of the rocks beside me. "Yeah, he's addled from oxygen deprivation, but he's still an asshole."

Ferri. That was her name. I tried to stand but my vision swirled and I crashed to the frozen ground.

Ferri leaned over and stared into my face. Her lips were glazed in frozen blood. She pulled her worn backpack off and opened it. Inside were the gloves and sunglasses and mask she'd worn earlier along with a fresh oxygen bottle. She replaced my bottle with the new one. My mind and vision cleared as oxygen again flowed into my mask.

"Thank you," I whispered.

"I only did it to keep your blood fresh."

Ferri stared at me with a blank expression, the right side of her mouth open slightly so I could see a single long fang.

"Sorry, bad joke. I always carry an extra bottle in case someone needs it."

I stood up on shaking legs. "If I die out here . . ."

"If you die out here I'll drink your blood."

"Then maybe I shouldn't die."

"Always a good idea."

I staggered after Ronnie as Ferri followed.

‹o›

Wind and cold and snow bled the mountain and ripped through my thermal coat and gloves and boots. I had to make camp or die. But in the blizzard I couldn't see anything. I'd already lost sight of Ronnie in the howling snow and could easily walk off the side of the mountain. Fall a thousand meters, my body never to be found.

Ferri walked behind me. When I stopped she stopped. When I struggled against the white-out wind and snow, she followed. Never giving me a hint on which way to go to reach camp.

For a moment the snow above me parted and I saw the stars, bright as a million spotlights in the thin air. I glanced down and saw, a few meters away, Ronnie crouching next to a small boulder.

I stumbled over and collapsed beside him. His face was porcelain, his nose and cheeks polished into white river stones with frostbite like the dying man we'd seen earlier high up on Everest. He must have lost his insulated facemask at some point.

"Where's camp?" I yelled over the wind.

Ronnie shook his head.

The boulder partly protected us from the jet stream but we couldn't stay here. We'd be dead in an hour if we didn't get out of the storm. The camp was likely only a hundred meters away. But if we stumbled around we'd more likely fall off the nearby cliffs.

Ferri sat down beside us. Ronnie glared at her. "Where's the camp?" he yelled.

"She won't help us," I said.

Ronnie yanked my facemask off, the precious oxygen bleeding into the blizzard. "She found you an oxygen tank," he yelled, point his ice axe at her. "Where the hell's our camp?"

I shook my head, not knowing. Ronnie turned his anger on Ferri, shifting his ice axe so the pick end pointed at her chest. His eyes, which had seemed hopeless moments before, sharpened into the fire that anyone who opposed him in the tech world knew only too well.

Ferri stared blankly at Ronnie before she smiled. But not a real smile. More a smile given by someone who'd copied smiles she'd seen on the faces of others. As if Ferri had long ago given up on feeling any actual emotions.

Ferri blandly pointed into the whiteout around us. Ronnie staggered to his feet and stumbled in that direction. But was he heading toward camp, or had she directed him toward a cliff?

"You'll die if you stay here," Ferri said in a flat voice barely heard over the howling wind.

"I thought we were already dead."

"You are. But if you follow him you may end up dying later."

I stood and staggered after Ronnie.

◄◦►

We stumbled through the white. With each step I expected Ronnie to vanish before my eyes, falling to his death down some forever cliff.

I shook my head, trying to focus.

Ronnie stopped and I stood next to him. We heard a faint clanking.

"Move it or die," Ronnie yelled as he grabbed my arm. As if he was again in charge of his own destiny.

We shuffled through the snows and wind until we saw a bright orange tent. Then a red tent. The wind blasted the tents so they barely stood, but I didn't care if they were about to collapse as long as I could climb inside one.

A western climber stood beside the red tent banging an ice axe against an empty oxygen tank. Nyima argued with the climber, trying to convince the man to go out into the blizzard with him to find us.

They both stopped when they saw us.

"You two are damn lucky," Nyima said as he shoved us into our tent. "Did you hear our banging?"

I fell on my sleeping bag, not even able to take off my boots or crampons. "Only heard it . . . right before we saw camp," I said, my words shivering like my body.

"Then how'd you find us?" Nyima asked. He handed me a thermos of lukewarm tea, which I swallowed desperately.

Ronnie stared out the open tent flap as if looking for Ferri. We could only see a meter or two with the blowing snow. Who knew where she'd gone.

"We took a chance," Ronnie said. "Took a chance."

Ronnie wiped his frozen face and paused, reevaluating his words.

"No," he said. "We made it work."

◄◦►

The situation at camp wasn't much better than what we'd experienced coming down the mountain. Despite the best weather forecasts used by Ronnie and the other expedition leaders, the jet stream had unexpectedly shifted and now blasted the camp at full speed. Nyima said that so far the tents were holding up, but no one knew if they'd last through the night.

"It'll clear by morning," Ronnie announced.

"How do you know?" Nyima asked.

"It will." Ronnie pulled his sleeping bag around himself and didn't move.

Nyima returned to his tent. The tent fabric beside my head rattled and howled, the support rods bending dangerously close to breaking. I rolled over and looked at Ronnie, whose face showed severe frostbite. Nyima had wanted to bandage Ronnie's face, but Ronnie had waved him away. I still wore my oxygen mask and, for a moment, considered offering him some of my air. Oxygen helped the body fight frostbite. If Ronnie used some, he'd have a better chance of avoiding permanent damage.

I would even swear to Ronnie that I'd tell no one. Anyone who asked would be told he'd climbed Everest without supplemental oxygen.

But I knew Ronnie. If I helped him he'd grow angry. Not today—today he'd be grateful. But back home, at work . . . when we returned to life . . . he'd find a way to hurt me. To show that he didn't need to rely on me for anything.

That he was the master and I was nothing.

I rolled back over, breathed a deep gasp of fresh oxygen, and fell into a fitful sleep.

⭒

The storm continued the next day.

When I'd first seen Everest several weeks ago from base camp, I'd watched beautiful wisps of cloud and snow spiral off the summit. Only later did I discover those wisps were hurricane-force winds. Ronnie always paid for the best forecasting and had assured me we'd never be in the death zone when the weather was this bad. That this was something that only happened decades before when people had climbed the mountain without adequate technological support.

I wanted to laugh but was too exhausted.

Even with a tent and sleeping bag it's nearly impossible to sleep in the death zone. The oxygen mask gripped my face like a stranger's hand trying to suffocate me. But when I removed it I couldn't get enough air.

Still, I drifted in and out of something like consciousness. I remembered Nyima coming to the tent and telling Ronnie the other expedition leaders wanted to meet with him. The two of them crawled into snow blowing by like a jet engine, unable to stand without being knocked over. After crawling barely a meter they vanished in the blizzard.

They'd left the tent flap open and I tried to raise enough energy to sit up and zip it shut. Before I could, Ferri climbed into the tent and closed the flap for me. The tent was being blown almost flat and she lay on Ronnie's sleeping bag so she could look into my face.

"This tent isn't much protection," Ferri said. "The wind's blowing at more than 100 kilometers an hour. Your tent could parachute in the wind and drag you over a cliff before you'd know what's happening."

I stared at Ferri as I gasped at oxygen inside my mask. I remembered all the times my little brother was sick when we were children. He told me once his body felt so numb and exhausted that he pretended it was a puppet he controlled. Twitch a string and his arm moved. Touch another string and he'd smile to allay our mother's concern.

I felt the same right now. My mind tugged a string and my head nodded to Ferri's words.

Ferri leaned over me and sniffed my blinking eyes. "You're dying," she said. "I can smell it. Your body's so weak your digestive system shut down. Every second your cells wink out by the thousands, all of them angry as they scream for more oxygen."

Ferri stuck her tongue out as if to lick my eyeballs before pulling back. "If you stay here much longer you'll die. If you go out in this blizzard you'll die. What are you going to do?"

"Ronnie said the forecasts are for the jet stream to shift again. The winds will stop and we'll descend out of the death zone."

"That what he told you?" Ferri asked. "Before I came here I listened outside the tent where Ronnie and the other expedition leaders are meeting. Turns out the forecast was always iffy but Ronnie convinced everyone to push to the top. And now the forecast isn't supposed to change for several days."

I twitched the strings holding my body together, making my body shiver slightly. Every climber knew what happened if you stayed for days and days in the death zone.

While Ferri stared at me the entrance unzipped and Ronnie climbed into the tent, pausing halfway in. He glared at Ferri, backed partly out, stopped again in the doorway.

"Want me to move over?" Ferri asked. "There's room for all of us."

Ronnie glanced outside at the snow gusting past.

Ferri picked herself off Ronnie's sleeping bag and kicked it toward him. "I don't need it," she said.

Ronnie took the bag and disappeared into the blowing snow to find another tent.

"He doesn't like you," I said.

"He shouldn't," Ferri said. "But it doesn't matter because he'll be dead before he gets off this mountain."

"He won't like that."

"Most men don't."

◄◊►

My oxygen tank emptied before nightfall. Nyima brought me another one, but refused to enter the tent to hand it to me so I crawled outside.

"She's dangerous," Nyima yelled over the howling wind. "Bring your bag and we'll double-up in my tent."

I shook my head and climbed back inside. Nyima shrugged and crawled to his own tent.

I clicked the oxygen tank into my regulator and breathed sweet, deep air again. I collapsed back on my sleeping bag.

Ferri grinned her fake smile. "Should I like being called dangerous?" she asked.

"Does Nyima know you?"

"I've seen him up here many times. Seen most of the Sherpas and westerners over the years. Sometimes they recognize me. Most of the time they think I'm just another climber."

"You from here?"

"No. From what you now call Italy, but centuries ago. I've been climbing this mountain for the last forty years."

"Why?"

Ferri reached up and pushed against the tent fabric that the wind shoved down at our faces. "I mislike killing people. But I must feed. So many people die climbing this mountain that I can feed without killing. I come here every year or two."

Ferri pushed harder against the sagging fabric. "No, I misspoke. When I say I mislike killing, that's a lie. I don't like or dislike anything. What I am precludes emotion. I exist. I have desires. But my emotions are dull and cold. Just like the people who climb into this dead zone. They're exhausted. Shells of who they'd be elsewhere. It's my only chance to be around others who behave like myself."

"If you don't like or dislike killing, why do you avoid it?"

"It's a choice. One I decided a long time ago to follow."

I thought of following Ronnie up this damn mountain. How I felt I had no other choice once I started our climb. Was Ferri mocking me? Was she serious?

But then I thought of that man freezing to death under the rock overhang. How he'd reminded me of my brother. Even though I still felt exhausted and numb, a shiver of sadness raced through me.

"That was an emotion you just felt," Ferri said. "I could almost taste it."

I rolled over so I didn't have to look at her.

"What made you feel that?" she asked, crawling on top of my body so I couldn't look away from her face. "Tell me. I'm always curious when emotions are strong enough that people still feel them up here."

I looked at Ferri's fangs, which hovered right above my eyes. But I felt no fear. And the sadness I'd felt a moment before had already fled, leaving me numb again. Was this how she lived all the time?

"My little brother," I said. "The man under that overhang reminded me of him. My brother battled leukemia for most of his life, always in and out of hospitals as a kid. He loved reading about mountain climbing—I think he dreamed of one day being strong enough to climb. But one night he died by himself in the hospital, before my family and I could arrive to be with him."

Ferri clicked her fangs against my cheek's cold skin. "Too predictable," she said. "I suppose now you'll say you're climbing Everest to honor your brother? That he's why you work with Ronnie and risk your life doing this silly stuff?"

I pushed Ferri off me. I had been about to say that. I had always believed that.

"Fuck you," I said.

"It's okay," Ferri replied. "I don't care what lies you spin to rationalize following Ronnie up here. But at least you felt something for a moment. That's all that truly matters, right?"

Unable to answer, unable to know how to answer, I rolled back over and slipped into something that was close to, but never quite the same as, sleep.

◄◦►

In the morning the winds hadn't let up. Our expedition was running low on oxygen and supplies, as were climbers from other expeditions. Nyima came by my tent and said we were all going to try climbing down before we got any weaker.

"The winds will die down if we climb low enough to get out of the jet stream," Nyima said. "Get ready. We leave in thirty minutes."

I cleared the ice from my oxygen mask and pulled on my boots and crampons. Ferri lay on the tent floor and watched me with a mix of both interest and a deep lack of caring.

"Any thought on what I should do if I want to live?" I asked.

"I have no suggestions. You live and die on your own."

"But you helped us earlier. You told Ronnie how to find the camp in that white out."

"Did that actually help?"

I shivered. She'd said she didn't have emotions and didn't care what happened to us, aside from her choice to avoiding killing if she could. If I lay back down on my sleeping bag, would Ferri stay with me as I slowly died in the coming days? Would the last thing I saw be her lips on my neck?

I stumbled out of the tent into the blizzard.

Nyima was readying our expedition's climbers while Ronnie looked on in irritation. When Nyima saw me he looked past me at Ferri emerging from the tent.

"You're short roping Keller," Nyima yelled at Ronnie.

I paused. Was I in such bad shape that I needed to be roped to Ronnie to help me get down the mountain?

"I'm not doing that!" Ronnie said. "It's on him to get down."

"I don't care if you use oxygen or not," Nyima said, "but you brought Keller up here and you're getting him down."

Nyima roped me to Ronnie with several meters of cord. To my surprise Ronnie glared at Nyima but didn't protest again. If Ronnie wasn't so exhausted from not using oxygen he'd likely have refused to do this. And I knew he'd fire Nyima for this embarrassment once we got to safety and he returned to being his old self.

But for now that didn't matter. We started down the mountain.

Each climber quickly disappeared in the white out conditions. Nyima led the main part of our expedition down the mountain but Ronnie and I were far slower. It didn't take long to realize that Ronnie and I weren't roped together to help me, but for me to help him. After going so long without supplemental oxygen, Ronnie couldn't climb off the mountain on his own.

"Nyima knew if he tried to get you to short-rope Ronnie, the fool'd say no," Ferri yelled as she climbed beside me. "This way his ego is safe because he thinks he's helping you."

Because the storm blocked the sun Ferri didn't wear her glasses or facemask. She stood straight up in the howling wind as she climbed down while I hunched over, using my ice axe to keep from sliding down the slope. Two meters below me Ronnie also hunched over, the rope between us tight as if that was all that kept him from losing his grip and tumbling off the mountain.

Ronnie glanced back and saw Ferri standing beside me. He tried to hurry faster down the mountain but slipped. The rope jerked forward and was about to yank me after Ronnie when Ferri grabbed the rope, stopping both of us.

Ronnie struggled to his feet and moved on. Ferri released the rope.

"He's endangering both of you," Ferri said. "That's why Nyima put you two by yourselves—he didn't want you or Ronnie taking other climbers with you when you die."

"Fuck Nyima for leaving us."

"He didn't leave you. He merely realized you two were already dead."

"How did he know that?"

Ferri blocked the wind with her body and leaned in so she could talk without yelling. "Because I'm with you."

-◦-

I was as dead as Ferri claimed to be. No emotions. No life. Nothing but one boot in front of the other. One gloved hand on the rope between me and Ronnie. The other slamming my ice axe into the mountain over and over to keep from sliding.

The whiteout completed my isolation. I saw Ferri beside me, striding against the wind as if daring it to blow her off Everest. Aside from Ferri, I was perfectly alone. Even Ronnie, only two meters before me, slipped in and out of the whiteout.

Why had I done this, I wondered. Ferri had been correct—I used my brother as little more than an excuse for risking my life. As rationalization for following Ronnie as we marked off mountains like sexual conquests. I'd always told myself I was better than Ronnie. That I had an actual reason for doing this.

But in the end, mountains didn't care why we climbed or whether we won or lost.

I paused, causing Ronnie to yank against the rope. He looked back at me. He waved for us to continue.

We had to keep struggling. We had to . . .

Ferri looked at me and smiled her emotionless smile.

We climbed on.

◄◦►

Ronnie and I crouched in a windbreak created by a rock overhang as snow howled past. We drank our remaining water but it didn't help our exhaustion.

"It can't be much further," Ronnie yelled. "The jet stream will end if we climb low enough."

I wanted to believe that, but couldn't. All I could focus on was how hard it'd be to leave this windbreak and continue on.

Ferri stood above us on the overhang, leaning into the wind like an airplane wing. I didn't know why she did it because she didn't look like she was having fun. According to her, she couldn't even have fun. But still, there she was, leaning into the wind.

Ronnie ignored her. "This will amaze people," he said. "How we escaped death. How we refused to give up."

I nodded, already imagining Ronnie's next Ted Talk sweeping the world with his version of survival. Not that I cared. And Ronnie was in far rougher shape than me. He'd collapsed into the windbreak when he reached it. I knew if I got him to stand up I might be able to help him climb a little further down the mountain. Maybe even to safety.

But helping him was also exhausting me.

And *if* we reached safety, he wouldn't be grateful. He'd hate that I'd helped him. Hate that he hadn't survived because of only himself. He'd find ways to hurt me.

I tried to remember my brother. To remember my pain when he died. To remember why I'd wanted to help the freezing man under the rock overhang. To force myself to feel anything.

But I couldn't.

"We need to go," Ronnie yelled.

I stood up. Ferri looked down at me.

With my ice axe's saw tool, I cut the rope between me and Ronnie and stepped away.

Ronnie grabbed the overhang, trying to stand, but was too weak. He glared at me from behind his snow goggles. His frostbitten lips opened, closed, opened again without saying anything.

"Don't worry," Ferri yelled, hopping down and sitting beside Ronnie. "I'll stay with him."

Ronnie pushed himself back into the small cave created by the overhang, as if trying to escape Ferri. She patted his leg.

I hiked on.

An hour later I cleared the jet stream and the worst of the storm.

—◇—

I woke in the medical tent at base camp with bandages on my frostbitten face and hands. I vaguely remembered stumbling down the mountain after clearing the storm. At some point a rescue team found me, but I didn't remember when or how.

In the tent the base camp doctor and two nurses worked on a dozen members of various expeditions. The doctor leaned over the face of a women who'd summitted Everest an hour before I did. The doctor said the woman's frostbite was the worst he'd ever seen.

"You're lucky to be alive," Nyima said as he pulled a camp chair up to my cot and sat down. His face was also bandaged, although not as badly as mine. "They're landing a helicopter to medivac that climber out first—she's in worse shape. You'll be on the next flight."

I whispered, unable to speak louder. Nyima leaned over and I repeated myself.

"She took Ronnie," I said.

"Before or after you abandoned him?" he asked quietly so no one else could hear.

I looked away from Nyima and watched the doctor and nurses trying to save the other climber. So many people hurt. And another expedition of seven people had vanished during the storm and were presumed dead.

But even though Ronnie died, Nyima was already being praised for saving the rest of the climbers in our group.

"One of us Sherpas gets killed, no one cares," Nyima muttered. "But you western fools die and the whole world pays attention. And Ronnie's death will be big because of who he was."

I understood. Everyone would be watching. If I admitted what I did, the world's anger would crash down on me.

"You tried to save him," Nyima whispered. "But some people refuse to be saved by others. Remember that."

I nodded. Nyima patted my chest and walked out of the tent.

The tent fell quiet as the doctor and nurses carried the severely injured climber to the first medivac. That's when Ferri entered. She wore a brand-new red coat and snow pants, both too big for her body. Ronnie's clothes.

Ferri walked among the other injured climbers, tasting the air over each person's cot before stopping at mine. She leaned over so her tongue almost licked my right ear. She pointed at her new red coat.

"Ronnie stripped naked before the end," she whispered. "So delirious from cold he thought he was burning up."

I nodded, even though I didn't want to know details like this.

Ferri sniffed my right eyeball. "You're going to lose your nose. And half your fingers and toes. But you climbed Everest. Was it worth it?"

I started to cry, the emotions that had been repressed by exhaustion and lack of oxygen flooding out of me. Ferri watched dispassionately. She was the same as she'd been on the mountain. No emotions. No cares on the choices she made.

She stood up as the *chuck chuck* sound of another helicopter echoed across base camp. "I'll see you when you return," she said. "People like you always come back."

I laughed weakly. "You mean people like *us* always come back."

Ferri tapped her tongue to one of her fangs and nodded.

She walked out of the tent as the doctor and nurses rushed in and carried me toward the waiting helicopter. I wanted to yell at Ferri. To say I was lying—that I'd never see this damn mountain again. That I'd never return.

But would I?

The doctor and nurses strapped me into the helicopter's spare seat and closed the door. I watched out the window as the machine struggled to gain altitude in the thin air.

As the helicopter flew higher I saw Ferri walking back toward the mountain. She'd again covered her face with her sunglasses and unused oxygen mask so the sun couldn't hurt her. She passed the tents of hundreds of other climbers.

No one saw her as anything more than another person waiting for a chance to reach the top.

She was right—I'd be back. I wouldn't let this stop me. And when I returned she'd be here, waiting.

I cursed. I was as stupid as Ronnie. I hated myself for that. But I also realized it didn't matter.

Because in the end, once I finally killed myself on this mountain, she'd be there. I wouldn't die alone like my brother. Even if she never felt a single emotion over anything I did in my sorry-ass life, I wouldn't die alone.

SCOLD'S BRIDLE: A CRUELTY

RICHARD GAVIN

Do we have an understanding then, Mr. Biskup?"

Ivan Biskup disliked the way the smile was growing across the face of Peters; his neighbour, the unbidden guest to his garage workshop.

"No," Ivan returned. "No, we don't. Not yet at least." He plucked a rag from the pocket of his trousers to wipe away the perspiration that jeweled his weathered face. The iron workshop was a stifling cell. The open garage door afforded no breeze but only the rays of the Dog Day sun to pour in like molten slag. "I don't even understand why you, why *anybody*, would want a book like this, let alone have something made from it."

The chunky volume reposed upon one of Biskup's worn workbenches. The book's gold-leaf edging sparkled under the fluorescent lights. *Cruel & Unusual: An Illustrated History of Torture Devices* was the book's title. The cover seemed to shout these words, with its thick, ominous typeface. Beneath the title was an arrangement of four photographs, each showcasing a different invention born of humanity's boundless creativity and cruelty. Ivan recognized one of the items as an iron maiden. The other, he assumed, was a gallows, or some hideous rack-and-rope contraption designed to dislocate living limbs like corks popping from bottled champagne. The other two were line drawings of devices too esoteric for Ivan. He scratched the back of his neck.

"I teach history," answered Peters, though Ivan had forgotten his question, "I want a device for a visual aid. It will help me teach a lesson. The neighbours tell me you work wonders with wrought iron."

There was a fluttering noise as Peters flicked open the book to an ear-marked leaf. He tapped his finger on the page, coaxing Ivan to look.

The image might have been of a helmet. Ivan squinted his eyes and studied closer, concluding at last that the contraption was a mask of some description. Its frame was of curved iron bands and jutting screws and a few ornamental curlicues. Poking up from the top of the mask was a pair of donkey's ears, fashioned in crudely hammered metal.

"You're either joking or crazy," Ivan said. His indignation had been made plain. "Folks around here aren't going to let their kids see something like this in school. I don't care if it is from some fancy history book. What's this thing supposed to be anyway?"

"It's called a scold's bridle. It's also sometimes referred to as a brank. In medieval times, authorities would employ it to remind certain people of their station in life."

At that instant, a young mother pushed a pram along the sidewalk in front of Ivan's exposed workshop. The woman gently rocked the carriage with one hand while with the other she waved a blue teddy bear before the open hood. Neither action consoled the infant, whose cries were piercing and persistent.

"Good morning, Allison!" Peters cried. He waved and grinned at her. Allison waved back tiredly. Peters then turned back to Ivan and mumbled, "That kid sounds like a boiled cat. Imagine hearing that at three in the morning?" He shuddered with disgust.

Ivan reached over and closed the book.

"I'll pay you," announced Peters. "I know you need the money."

When he saw the expression on Ivan's face, saw the way the older man puffed up his sizeable frame, Peters raised his hands in a gesture of peacekeeping.

"Please," he began, "don't take offence. It's just . . .well, I watch. I see things. I'm good at taking little pieces of detail and seeing how they fit into a larger mosaic. This workshop, for instance. When my wife and I first moved onto this street, we'd see throngs of people on your driveway every Saturday and Sunday."

Ivan nodded mournfully. "My sales. My Edwina used to help me every weekend . . ."

"I remember. I think almost every house on the block had at least one piece of your ironwork; fireplace tools, patio furniture, garden gates."

"Every house except yours," Ivan replied. He, too, was good at noting details.

"That's why I'm here; to correct that. Besides, it's been a long time since you've had one of your sales. I'd imagine your bills are piling up. And before you ask, I deduced this after your wife passed last year. My condolences, by the way. You haven't hosted a sale since. I remember that day in January when your car wouldn't start. You had it towed and I haven't seen it since. The repairs must have been outside your budget. You've been practically housebound."

Ivan emitted an unintentional sigh of lament. "*If* I make that mask," he began, "what were you thinking of paying?"

Peters named a sum that stole Ivan's breath.

"I don't believe you," Ivan said thinly.

Peters produced an envelope plump with bills.

At Peters' insistence, Ivan counted them, fumblingly.

"How does a schoolteacher come up with that kind of money?"

"Family," Peters said plainly. "Now, let me go over a few of the key details." He once again opened the torture book to the chosen page.

"The scold's bridle shown here is modelled on a donkey's head. I gather this was a pretty common design; make the guilty party resemble a jackass, that sort of idea. But I came up with this rough sketch on this paper." He produced a sheet from his shirt pocket. "The bridle I want is made to look more like a rabbit. See the ears?"

Ivan moved his head vaguely.

"As for the mouth clamp, the book suggests an iron band lined with adjustable screws, points facing inward. These can be tightened to various lengths, depending on how deeply the punisher wants to push the screws into the wearer's gums . . ." Peters continued to explain gleefully, before finally asking, "Do we have a deal then, Mr. Biskup?"

Ivan's gaze was tethered to the bulging envelope on his workbench. "Yes . . . yes, I suppose we do."

-◆-

He did not begin to work on the project until the sun had begun to sink, dragging with it some of the swelter. After a pauper's supper of canned soup and an apple, Ivan wended his way to the garage.

The iron muzzle was the most labour-intensive of the bridle's components. Mr. Peters had requested that the bit be lined with a gravel-like coating of barbs. A pair of chains linked the mouthpiece to the muzzle, and the whole contraption was framed by a network of flat iron bars bent to fit the exact measurements Mr. Peters had left on his sketch.

The following evening Ivan went about ornamenting the scold's bridle with the jackrabbit ears of thin metal. He even added six pieces of jutting copper wire to the muzzle; whiskers for the bunny's polished metal nose. The gum clamp was lined with double rows of screws and the mask's interior was enhanced with thick spiky bolts. He scored the interior of the eyeholes and peeled back the pointed metal jags so that the wearer's eyelids would, theoretically speaking of course, be nicked with each blink.

The third night was just a matter of tightening and buffering.

On the appointed morning, Peters came to collect. The metal monstrosity was secreted inside a white cardboard box that bore the insignia of a wine Ivan had never drunk. Peters peeked into the top, then gave what might have been a very faint nod. He neatly folded over the carton's flaps, picked up his spoil and strolled down Ivan's driveway without so much as a word.

-◆-

From that day onward, guilt—inexplicable, burning, ever-present—became Ivan's erstwhile companion. It weighted his frame like a millstone. When he did manage to steal a few hours of sleep it chewed on his psyche, causing dreams of tortures too gorgeous to be ever be recalled by a civilized mind. Indeed, Ivan felt as if he was trapped in one of the devices from Peters' book. He thought of the schoolchildren seeing what he'd wrought. He found that thought unbearable.

However, he paid his bills and still had cash left over, enough to keep himself in drink for several weeks.

Finally, his guilt crested over into burning curiosity.

Ivan lay on the bed, listening to the windup alarm clock ticking at him from the nightstand like a clucking tongue. It punished him until daylight finally broke.

He sat up too quickly and for a moment the room lilted, yet it did not rob him of his clarity. He needed to know, needed to be reassured that he had done nothing wrong. Of course, his mask had been fashioned in good faith, as a teaching tool, but nevertheless, this rationale could not keep the ugly guilt at bay.

He rose and dressed. This morning he would have closure.

Not until he was out in the street did it occur to Ivan that he hadn't bothered to check the time. It was early but clearly not too early; women and men on the street were jogging or were beginning their morning commute in their smart-looking business attire.

He thought he'd made it all the way to Peters' house without being seen when the front door was startlingly flung open. Peters stared hard at him. His white Oxford shirt was buttoned to the collar, but the tie was hanging from his right hand like a limp scourge.

"Ivan!" he said with audible shock.

"I . . ." he began, clearing his throat as he struggled to find the words, "I just came to . . ."

Peters raised his hand and chortled softly. "I know why you're here." He pushed the door open wide. "You want to see your creation in its new home, yes?"

"Something like that, yes."

Inside, the house was warm and stale. Heavy drapes kept out the light, kept the rooms obscured.

"Nice place you've got here," lied Ivan.

"Come with me," Peters said. "You'll appreciate this. The scold's bridle is not only beautiful, it works. Come. Wifey's in the kitchen making breakfast." The wave of his hand was childlike, playful.

Dread retarded Ivan's rounding of the corner. When he finally willed himself to advance, his fear became manifest in the shape of the woman at the stove. Ivan could no longer move. His breath leaked out in a low moan. It felt like his organs had been replaced with ice.

She was seated at the kitchen table whose single place-setting was for her husband, who casually sat, took up his fork.

The scold's bridle crowned the woman like some gruesome headdress. The metal ears jutted up as though she was a startled hare listening intently for some encroaching predator. Aside from the cage on her head, the woman's attire was quite normal, almost banal. She wore a robe of lavender satin. She was looking at Ivan, looking into him. Ivan could see her brilliant blue eyes, shimmering with tears of agony, shining out from the shadows of the Lepus mask.

"Dear, we have a guest," said Peters. "Set another place at the table." His tone was noticeably firmer now, more like a military commander than a spouse. "Have a seat, Ivan."

Ivan nodded. Thoughtlessly he pulled one of the high-backed chairs out from under the kitchen table and sat down. He was happy for the support, for his legs seemed to have lost all their strength.

Peters' wife retrieved a plate, coffee mug and juice glass from the cupboard.

"Here, let me . . ." Ivan said as he attempted to stand.

"No," Peters said coldly. Ivan looked at him and Peters shook his head. "No," he repeated.

She was facing them now. The metal bands that Ivan himself had manipulated so cunningly were revealed in all their hideousness. The morning sun shone through the window with ironic brightness, causing the torture tool to gleam.

Ivan could only suppose that the woman was pretty, so smothered were her features. Through the slats Ivan could see her eyes, wide and wet with tears. They were the only human feature he could discern inside that orgy of cold metal.

"She likes rabbits," Peters explained. "A jackass mask would have been too harsh."

She stepped closer in order to set his place. As she leaned in Ivan was able to hear faint gagging sounds and the awful chink of teeth-on-metal. Her breathing was sharp but uneven, drawn and exhaled solely through her nostrils. A dark wet thread suddenly sprouted from the muzzle. It left a small red stain on the linen tablecloth.

"My god," Ivan gasped before pushing himself erect. He turned and began toward the front door.

"I told you it was for teaching," Peters called, but Ivan was already out the door. The rest of Peters' spiel fell on deaf ears, for Ivan was too absorbed in shock and self-loathing to hear. The only words that managed to rise above the murmur were "You're culpable, you know!"

Ivan rushed out into the day and squinting from the accusatory sunlight. He staggered back to his home. Once inside he went straight to the garage where the cordless phone was perched near his workbench. He had it in his fist and was about to dial when Peters' words bored into him. He had been desperate, yes, but even this and playing up the grieving widower routine would only get him so far with the authorities.

Panic set in. The garage became stifling. Ivan flung the track door open. He breathed in greedily, his mind racing.

Ivan was so lost in his panic he did not hear the approaching footsteps.

"Are you Mr. Biskup?" a strange voice called. Ivan jumped at the sound of it. "Sorry, I didn't mean to startle you."

The woman in his driveway was not wholly unfamiliar to him. He'd seen her before: the young mother from the basement apartment down the road.

"Mr. Peters said I should talk to you," she said.

"Talk to me?" Ivan sputtered.

Allison. Was that the name Peters had called her?

"He said you'd understand," she continued. She moved to him, revealing her fatigue-ravaged face, her teary, reddened eyes. "It's my baby," she said. "He won't stop crying. Day and night. I've tried everything; singing to him, midnight feedings, taking him for long drives. Nothing works."

Ivan's hand autonomously found his mouth and gripped it.

The woman held out a tattered envelope. "It's all I can afford. I don't need anything as elaborate as what Mr. Peters ordered. Here, I drew a sketch."

She unfolded a colourful paper from inside the envelope. It was an ad from a magazine or catalogue. The infant in the photograph had been distorted, its wide and innocent grin gagged by a hectic thumbnail drawing of a chin strap and blinders and a spiked ball-gag forced between the tiny lips.

"I love my son, you understand? I love him. I'm not doing this to punish him. I just need some peace and quiet. I'll only need this for a while . . . just a little while . . . just until he learns."

COME CLOSER

GEMMA FILES

A path opens in the trees before you, and you have to tread it. You *have* to. It's not a decision. It comes from somewhere else, outside of you. It's not the sort of call that can be ignored.

That's what we tell ourselves sometimes, when we're about to make a mistake. Or when we're already halfway through making one.

―◦―

The first time you take its picture, the house is on another street entirely, around the corner, up towards the underpass. By June, it's on your street.

By October, it's next door.

―◦―

You're keeping a dream diary the day you notice the house, just as Dr. Batmasian told you to, back when you still thought your insomnia was curable. That morning you dream you're in what you feel absolutely sure is your home, but in hindsight is a completely different apartment—a compilation of other people's, maybe, larger, and with spaces you've never used because they don't exist. It's the sort of dream where you think you're awake and start going through the motions of an ordinary day . . . in this case, taking dishes out of the dishwasher. Except every time you're "done," you go to shut it and suddenly find it's full again, with a different set of dishes every time. And all the while you're thinking: *This is wrong, this isn't right. This has happened before, over and over.*

At which point another version of you entirely walks in, dressed in what you only now recognize as your father's clothes. *I think I'm dreaming,* you tell her, and she simply nods, replying: *Yeah, you probably are. So you should do something that'd really hurt in real life, and if it doesn't, you'll know you're asleep.*

Which sounds logical, so you step back a bit, sigh, tuck your hair behind your ears, and slam your head face-down onto the granite countertop. And since you do indeed barely feel it, you just go ahead and keep on doing it again and again until you wake up at last—kick your way to the surface between various peeled-back layers of sleep, up through untold fathoms, out into the real world once more. Until you come to back in your own bed, your own condo, exhausted and sticky and alone.

Annoyingly mundane, but as recurring dreams go it certainly beats the one where you're desperately trying to kill somebody with a sharp object, stabbing them till your hands are sore while they just stand there laughing at you. Not to mention giving you reason enough to at least get you upright, dressed and clean and through the door, so you can make it to work on time for once and thus leave comparatively "early"—i.e., at the time you normally would if you ever bothered to get there when your contract specifies you should in the first place.

Spend all day copying and filing on demand, handing out mail, making coffee; it's a glorified intern's job, if this place could actually afford to pay interns, or anybody actually ever took unpaid internships anymore. You got it by virtue of having a degree in Library Sciences, hoping one day it'll get you the job you really want. But if the day's a grind, there's always the evening: twilight in the Distillery District, magic hour, everything touched with cool blue and gold, making even the most degraded objects pop as if they're Pixar-painted. And then, right there on your way over to the weekly meet-up with Joe and Anjit, there's the house.

"Take a look," you say maybe ten minutes later, plopping your phone down on the restaurant table between them. "Either of you ever remember seeing this place before?"

"Nope," Joe says without even looking, but Anjit narrows her eyes. "Is this one of those postwar bungalows?" she asks.

You shrug. "Might be, I guess—I don't know much about architecture. Looks old enough to be, though."

Anjit agrees, peering closer. "Where *is* this?"

"Just 'round the corner from my place, like halfway up the block. Almost to the China Lily Soy Sauce factory."

"Oh God, yes; that place is so gross. Like . . . right near that little bridge, the underpass?"

"That's the one. Weird how I never really saw it before, though; must've walked past it a million times, right? Maybe it just never registered how there was an actual *house* under all that other crap."

The other crap in question is however many years' worth of overgrowth, *Life After People* style—ivy everywhere, weeds to the waist, a drooping chestnut tree that probably hasn't been cut back since Dutch Elm disease blew through Toronto. The house is a classic one-storey with a later addition slapped on top, a box on top of a box, the second floor only slightly smaller; there's one of those eye-shaped windows at the front, half-blinded by leaves. Whole place is in obvious disrepair, if not quite a ruin; windows dark with dust and cracked to boot, paint peeling leprous.

Artificial, not natural, and yet—the house looks as if it grew up out of the ground, like roots. It looks . . . immutable.

Maybe it's all the green.

You tap the phone's screen, asking: "Okay, improv time, bitches—who you think *lives* here, just off the top of your head?"

Joe snorts, still not looking. "Nobody, Lin, Jesus. Not for a *long* damn time."

A passing waitress: "Serial killers, for sure."

Anjit studies it a moment, then glances back up, grinning. *"Witches,"* she suggests, then whoops as you high-five her, signalling the waitress as she swings back around. "One more for my friend!" you yell, finally getting Joe's attention, at least momentarily.

"I'll have whatever they're having, and make it a double," he tells her, before going back to editing his Grindr picks queue.

◄◦►

That night you dream you find a tiny box, no longer than your finger, no wider. But when you open it up it turns out to be a window, and when you put your eye to it you see an entire landscape, some grey-on-grey moor under a stormy overhanging sky, moonless, pelting rain. Strange grasses occupied by dark motion, hidden eyes, the wet bones of long-dead things. And an over-whelming fear comes washing up over you, this sudden dread that you might somehow slip through, end up stranded in that bleak field under that same lowering thunderhead, trapped in another world entirely—unable to glimpse the way back into your peaceful room, your familiar bed, except through that tiny, lidded rectangle. Always and forever from then on at the mercy of any stranger who might decide to slam the lid shut over your only way back out.

A week passes, or maybe a couple; you can't help seeing the house out of the corner of your eye as you go by, even when you're not looking for it. Which is how, slowly, you start to notice it isn't in the same place anymore.

"That house is moving," you tell Anjit eventually, after your usual weekly hookup. The two of you are lying in bed, sharing a joint; Joe's in the shower, sponging away sex-traces and singing loudly along with Marvin Gaye, but that place between you where he most often lies is still warm, still slightly depressed. "The vine house. You remember."

She inhales, holds the smoke in her lungs a moment, then blows out a little plume of it, miniature dragon style. "The one on your phone," she says, black eyes cast up and shining, watching the last of her toke dissipate into darkness. "Yes, well, that's . . . what do you *mean* by that, Lin, exactly?"

"That it's not where it used to be when I took the picture. It's—somewhere else now."

"Another part of the city?"

"No, still on that block, just . . . closer to the corner, I guess. A lot closer. As if it's about to turn onto my street, or something."

Anjit turns on her side, frowning. "That really doesn't seem possible, though, does it?"

You shrug, not really able to disagree. "Took some more pictures, if you want to see," you offer, reaching for your phone. And by the time Joe comes back out, humming, you and Anjit are sitting cross-legged together poring over the evidence, swiping back and forth to run it forward or back, the world's slowest little movie.

"The hell're you doing?" he demands, then snorts when you try to tell him. Scoffing: "Oh Jesus, *that* thing again? You need to get yourself some Netflix."

Anjit shakes her head, hair flipping. "What I don't get," she says, to you, "is what happens to the house right next to it, when it does move. I mean—look at this, here, and here: house, house, *the* house. And then, in this next one . . ."

". . . it's where the second house was," you finish, nodding. "But there's nothing behind it, nothing new; that other house where it used to be hasn't been pushed on like beads on a string, or switched around. It's just *gone*, supplanted."

"Yet here, in this next one—the previous house is back, but on the other side, switched from left to right. And now it's the house that *used* to be in front of our mystery bungalow—the *previous* right-hand house—that's gone."

Joe stands there naked, arms crossed in annoyance yet swinging free; you catch sidelong sight of him and snicker, which probably isn't the effect he was looking to have on you. "Well, that's impossible, obviously. But either way, who cares?"

"Lin," Anjit tells him, eyebrow hiking. "Equally obviously. And why the hell not?"

Joe strikes a pose and makes himself jolt, abruptly tumescent, as if he's pointing at her hands-free. "'Cause it's rude to turn down a Greek bearing gifts?" he suggests theatrically, and watches her dissolve into giggles.

"He does have a point," you concede, which just makes her laugh all the harder.

⋯

A week later you round the corner onto your street, only to find the house waiting for you.

⋯

"So when does it move?" Anjit asks a few days later, when you show her the latest snaps.

"I don't know," you reply, resisting the urge to shiver, automatically, while at the same time swiping through with your eyes kept peeled for ones pretty enough to maybe fix up and post. "When I'm asleep, maybe."

"And you don't see it doing it, obviously."

"Never. It creeps, the same as ivy."

"Apt." A beat. "So what happens to the other houses, you think, while they're gone? I mean . . . do they look any different when they come back?"

You frown, considering this. "Kind of, yeah," you say, at last. "When the houses reappear, they seem more decrepit—drained, reduced, empty. Like everyone just left in the middle of the night, and somehow you just didn't notice until now. And meanwhile, the vine house itself seems bigger every time, as if it's absorbed part of the house it replaced: a cornice, or a floor, or a room. It seems more *inhabited*."

"Inhabited how?"

"Oh, I don't know, it just . . . like sometimes I'm walking by, coming home late at night, and there's music inside. Weird music. Weird music, plus weird lights." You pause again. "I mean, no surprise there. 'Cause everything about that damn *place* is weird, inside and out."

Now it's Anjit's turn to frown. "Thought you said you hadn't ever been inside."

"Oh, I haven't. It just—strikes me that way."

Anjit nods. But: "This is ridiculous," Joe breaks in finally, impatiently dismissive, as if you've neither of you ever had that exact thought. "You're both stuck on this damn thing, Lin, and it's eating up your brains. We need to—"

"Need to *what*, Joe? What do 'we' need to do about it, exactly?"

It comes out snappish, perhaps more so than you originally intend it to, since it definitely seems to slap him across the face a bit, as—from across the room—Anjit raises her eyebrows appraisingly; takes him aback, if only for a second. Still, rotating bedroom-centric polyamorous circuit show he co-stars in aside, Joe's never exactly been the kind of guy to take that sort of thing lying down.

"Okay, then," he says, at last. "Not we, so much; me. *I'll* do something."

"Again, like what?"

"Watch and see."

-◦-

Which is how the three of you end up back on the street at roughly 3:00 a.m., approaching the house in question sidelong, like a sleeping dog of uncertain provenance. As if you somewhat expect it to wake up and come for you, teeth bared and barking.

The vines seem fresher, full of bright new growth; the path to the house slopes gently downwards through a "garden" of weeds, dusty, unscuffed, blank. There's a black-barked tree almost at the bottom, its groin bulging with tumorous roots, next to a gate without a fence that stands there alone and ridiculous, a concrete metaphor—just a post and a latch on one side plus a post and hinges on the other, pewter-coloured, decorously locked against intruders. Joe snorts, then steps around it, while you and Anjit hover uncomfortably on the other side.

"You coming up, or what?" he demands.

"No, thanks," Anjit shoots back coolly. "Honour's *all* yours."

You think about agreeing, but don't. There's something about this place, the sudden nearness of it, that dries your mouth out. You swallow instead, hearing your throat click.

Weird music, weird lights, figures moving behind shades: your own words come back to you, tone ironic, like a stranger's. None of the above tonight, though—just the windows' black, cracked gaze, eyeing you sidelong. Just that disapproving mouth of a door, pursed shut.

Joe stomps up the path, leaving visible prints. "Hey," he calls. "Yo, serial killers, witches. *Nobody.* Anyone home?"

You hiss, abruptly mortified, voice a strangled stage whisper. *"Jesus,* Joe—keep it down, for Christ's sake! It's the middle of the fucking night."

"Uh-huh, middle of the night, downtown Toronto. Where everybody's perfectly free to call the Neighbourhood Watch anytime, not that I notice it happening."

"Well, you wouldn't, would you?" Anjit points out helpfully. "Not until the cops got here."

"Oh, I'm setting my watch."

He's up the path's top now, almost to the vine house's greyly sagging bottom step, its water-stained middle rucked like lichen. Just two more steps and he'll be up onto the tiny porch, barely more than a verandah-topped portico. No knocker, but there's a doorbell's button-topped plastic rectangle half-hidden underneath that empty patch where the mailbox used to hang, its outlines faint-sketched in dirt, now all but indistinguishable from the rest of the house's gangrenous paint-job or its encrusting foliage, the leaves' shifting shadows.

"Don't you dare ring that," you warn him, and Joe gives a five-year-old's grin, hand already in mid-reach with the pointer finger extended, as if he's looking to get caught. But before he can make contact, something rings out from deep inside—not a chime so much as a tone, a drone, a breath. An exhalation.

Joe hears it and perks up; Anjit hears it and blanches. You hear it and think of . . . what? Something distant, something cold, plucking at the very edges of familiarity. A hoarse wind blown from far off rattling across the window-frames, making them moan. A glass harmonica touched after midnight, its waters murky, singing with disease.

(There are instruments made of human bone, you've heard, in places like Tibet; they play them in temples to frighten away evil spirits. But this doesn't sound like that, not exactly. This sounds more like—

(—something you play to *welcome* them. To call them closer.)

And now there are shadows, too, set against light, making the drawn shades flicker, same way a dreaming man's pupils do behind shut lids. "See?" Joe announces, to no one in particular. "Normal-ass people, exactly where you'd expect to find them—inside, listening to music, watching . . . TV, or something. Like *normal.*"

"Doesn't sound much like music to me," Anjit murmurs from behind you. To which you'd probably agree, if that exact moment didn't happen to be right when the front door suddenly snaps open.

◄⊙►

Afterward, Joe claims he couldn't see anything, that the door simply flung itself wide too fast and briefly for any additional details to register, then slammed in his face. But both you and Anjit know that can't possibly be true, because—*you* saw it. Both of you. Because Anjit described it unprompted, using exactly the same words you would have, long before it ever occurred to you to ask her to. Because she did it haltingly, between gasps: described the door's inner edge, worn and seemingly tooth-worried, grey as a dead man's wound; described the tiny slice of lintel thus exposed, the bare, unpainted post with its worm-track hieroglyphics, its flayed and peeling lip of general decay.

And that thin, thin hand reaching forth to stroke itself down the side of Joe's face, quick and gentle—barely resolved, an almost subliminal image, aside from the simultaneous suggestion of far too much bone cut with far too few fingers.

All this followed by Joe stumbling back, sitting down with a thud on the curbside as if he couldn't physically go any further, sitting there shivering. Joe's skeptical eyes rolling helpless, a spooked horse's, thrown back again and again towards the house only to skitter away like a flinch, helplessly tethered; his hands both fisted, drumming on his thighs, face sweat-slick and pale. As if he'd have given a million bucks to get up and walk away if he'd had it, let alone been capable.

"What happened?" you demand, as he stares back and away, back and away. "Nothing," he claims—*lies*—angrily, before literally biting his lip, hard enough to bruise. But: "Oh Joe, that's *so* much crap," Anjit interjects, equally pissed, before you can. "Who was *in* there? You must've seen—"

"No one. Nothing. I don't . . ." Joe trails off. "I just don't want to talk about it, okay? *Ever.* Wasted enough of my time on this shit as it is, goddamnit. I mean, *fuck.*" And without giving either of you time for further words he rolls to his feet, power-walks away, still muttering curses under his breath.

You can't get him on the phone the next day, which isn't surprising, not at first. But—you can't reach him the next day either. Nor the next, nor the next after that, not any. Not you and not Anjit either. Not at his home, at work, on any of his phones . . . not at all.

Then again, it *is* August. Vacation season. Maybe he just went to Cabo. Maybe.

◄◦►

Come away with me, Lin, Anjit keeps suggesting, as the house creeps closer; *up north, just until it passes by. My cousin has a house outside of Bracebridge, right on the river.* And eventually you give way, mainly to make her happy, or so you tell yourself—because what the hell do you have to be afraid of anyhow, after all? You live in a damn condo.

The river is beautiful, though. Quiet. The pine trees whisper. There's just something about being near water, watching it ripple, rise and fall, current bearing everything steadily away, forever . . .

When you step out of the Uber with Anjit at your side, you study the street up and down as she settles with the driver, afraid of what you'll find. But the house is nowhere to be seen—not up, not down, not left, not right. You make her walk around the block with you, exploring the side-streets further and further, as if you're mapping the area. You don't think you've ever paid this much attention to where you live before, barring that time somebody got shot down the block.

It's gone, entirely, no trace left behind. Such a relief. As if a headache you've had for years is finally over.

The vine house is *gone*.

◄◦►

Anjit and you order in, have a nice dinner together, after which you see her off with a kiss and go to bed early—alone but not lonely, having already taken a long, lavender-scented bath, washed and oiled your hair, then wrapped it securely enough it won't stain your pillows, just as your mama taught you to. You're so deliciously tired by the time the whole routine is done, you almost have to remind yourself to turn out the light. You fall asleep, humming.

You either don't dream or don't think you do, falling from dark to dark. But you do wake up eventually: still alone, on the floor, someplace so dark you can barely tell if your eyes are open. A place you've never been, and never wanted to be—elsewhere, elsewhen. Other, with a capital "o."

You already know where, though. You can tell without looking, without having to. You can tell it by the smell.

Lie there in the dark, planks stretching your back, making your hips displace and your pelvis feel as if it's cracking open, aching in every cold bone at once. Lie there with your skin crawling, your muscles bunching, a feverish chill making your stomach bunch and your cheeks burn. Lie there sick and scared, horrified far beyond your own capacity to fully feel it, with nothing but the same four words running through your brain—emphasis shifting each to each before looping back around forever, again, and again, and again, and again.

This *isn't my house.*

This isn't *my house.*

This isn't my *house.*

This isn't—

And then, right then, that's when the very worst thing of all happens: you realize you can hear your friends calling to you, desperate, the both of them here in this awful house as well. Anjit's screams appear to come filtering vaguely down somewhere to your right, probably from up on the second floor; Joe's seem to echo closer yet simultaneously further away, thrumming through the wall nearby, the very floor you're sprawled on. You can feel them inside you, knotting around your heart, tugging hard.

I did this, you think, knowing there's no way in hell you possibly could have—no way, Jesus, that's fucking *insane*; that's *crazy*. And yet . . .

I did this to you, me, you can't stop yourself from thinking. *Just by noticing. By making* you *notice*.

Oh God, I did this to all of us.

You're up, then, knees popping, almost falling—lunge forward, grabbing for the wall, the door. Find it, or what you think might be it. A knob in your hand; you twist it, yank. It opens. You propel yourself through it, into the space beyond. Choke out: "Joe?" and hear your throat creak with it, a strangled whisper running to a whimper, as if you've been throat-punched; God, everything just *hurts* in here, for no reason. It's so *cold*.

"Lin?"

Someone stumbles into you, hands clawing at your arms, burying her face in your neck—you know that perfume, those sobs. It's Anjit. "Where the hell is Joe?" you ask her, feel her shake her head, skull grinding painfully against your collarbone. "I don't *know*," she weeps back. "I don't, I just—I thought he was here, next door. I thought he was with you."

(That's what it sounded like, anyhow.)

Which is when Joe starts screaming again, of course, from above or below, you'll never be able to tell; as if he can hear you too, as if he recognizes your voices. As if he's being torn apart with somebody's bare fucking hands, piece by goddamn piece.

"HELP ME, YOU GUYS HAVE TO HELP ME, *CHRIST!* I'VE BEEN HERE SO LONG, SO *LONG*, OH JESUS, *PLEASE*—"

You join hands, knit fingers till your knuckles crack, Anjit dragging you headlong in her wake from room to room as she howls Joe's name back at him, barely pausing for breath: *Oh my God Joe, just hold on, we're here, we're here!* But you already know you'll never find him, either of you. Just all these other people, more and more through every new door, catching and clawing at you as if you're their only possible means of escape, their last shred of hope. Some of them young and some old but all in pain, the same terrible pain *you* feel, borne incalculably longer—long enough for them to be uniformly insane, caught inside a shriek, their lungs raw from constant screaming. These mad, moon-blind bastards, pleading for something you can never give; how long can they have they *been* here, for God's sake? If God even applies . . .

Almost none of them seem to speak English, but it's the last who finally calls out in Hindi, startling Anjit into answering—he gives a shout and rushes you, rips you apart, drags her backwards by her hair screaming *Lin, Lin, LIN*! And you go after her, of course you do, but—

—the next room's smaller, and the next, and the next. Smaller and more silent. You're getting further, not closer. You can't hear her anymore, nor Joe. You can't hear anything but your own heart, banging at your ribs like a crazed bird caged in bone. Feel its claws, its beak: that's your fear, made flesh. It's going to eat you alive, from inside out.

You turn, or try to. Fight your way from a room into a corridor, a nook, a cranny. Open the last knob onto what seems like barely a closet, then pivot to find the door has nothing inside it at all—that there *is* no door, no frame or hinges, barely a seam. The plaster simply sealed over behind you, *around* you, like a fold of scar, a cocoon.

There in the dark and cold, held rigid, unable to move an inch; your skin gone sub-zero, so bad it almost doesn't hurt anymore, as if the nerves are dying all at once. That's when it takes hold of you at last, the house's true occupant: hugs you close, breathes into your mouth with gentle, loving ease, as if it's trying to infect you. As if it wants nothing more in the whole wide world than to keep you alive, just as long as it possibly can.

So glad you came, it tells you then, smiling, its teeth against your lips, tongue printing yours. *So very, very glad.*

◄◦►

A path, and this is where it ends. A mistake, unfixable, made without even knowing you did.

A fenceless gate, forever left open.

IT DOESN'T FEEL RIGHT

MICHAEL MARSHALL SMITH

I t was all going so well.

Monday had been a debacle, and so we approached Tuesday morning with dedication, focus, and a willingness to play nice. I leapt out of bed at the first sound of activity, jammed my feet into slippers and wriggled into a sweatshirt, moving swiftly so as to give Helena a chance to keep dozing. I hurried next door and ushered Tim out of his bedroom as quickly and quietly as possible. Once downstairs I engaged our son in cheerful banter—or so it seemed to me—while making him a boiled egg and soldiers. He sat at the table (after only about ten minutes' encouragement) and ate it without making it into *too much* of an issue. I heard the distant sounds of my wife going into the bathroom to shower, and checked my watch. 07:24—a little ahead of a schedule designed to see wife and child departing for school at 08:15, at the latest.

Good, good.

Tim declared himself sufficiently full of egg, asked for and was given permission to get down and go into the family room, where he further requested to be allowed to watch an episode of *Ben 10*. This was denied as part of a long-standing attempt to avoid TV early in the day, especially a show which—while not entirely pointless—involves too much shouting, posturing and inter-species violence for my liking. Tim made it clear that he found this denial unacceptable. We reached a compromise that saw the TV going on, but for an episode of *Postman Pat SDS*, a spin-off of *Postman Pat*, which finds our plucky mailperson upgraded to parcel-delivery troubleshooter—solid, wholesome entertainment from the BBC which has no shooting or death in it whatsoever.

I tried to hammer out a further deal in which Tim got dressed in his school uniform before I pressed PLAY, but couldn't get any traction on even the broad outlines of such a proposal. Instead I settled for a good faith verbal agreement that as soon as the show finished—approximately 07:49—we would jointly tackle the donning of clothes in a spirit of cooperation and cheerfulness.

He watched the show. Helena tromped downstairs and made herself some tea and a piece of toast. I hovered in the background, still pajama-clad, waiting for the TV programme to finish, like a poorly-dressed junior member of the servant classes held in limbo until the ruling classes were ready to get onto the next thing.

The show finished. "Okay," I said, brightly, in the tone parents use when there's a mountain to scale but they're determined to believe they have a chance of achieving it without heavy casualties. "Let's get dressed! Let's see if we can break our record!"

And that's where it all unraveled.

⊰⊶

Tim's school attire is simple. It involves pants, a vest, a pair of grey trousers, a greyish shirt, a tie (fastened with a piece of elastic; you don't have to actually tie the damned thing, thank god), a sweater. And socks, of course, and shoes—but I'll come back to those. It's not a complicated outfit. It can be donned (as I know from the handful of times when the process has unfolded without incident), in three minutes flat.

It can also take the whole of your life.

Eventually, after following him around the living room, cheerleading with increasingly leaden politeness, I had him dressed (despite Tim feeling that the collar of the shirt felt "scratchy," and taking it off again, twice). I had his teeth brushed (I wound up doing it for him, which I *know* I shouldn't, but sometimes you just have to get the sodding thing done). And while my tone had become clipped, things were more or less proceeding according to plan or at least along lines of quotidian shittiness. All that remained was the socks and shoes. Or, as it's known privately between Helena and I . . .

Footwear Vietnam.

I don't know what the problem is. I've investigated every possibility I can think of, including suggesting we have Tim checked out by a doctor to ensure that he genuinely doesn't have some kind of skin disorder or a bizarre neuralgia affecting the skin on his feet.

The bottom line is that socks . . . *are a problem.*

For three months Tim has complained that they have "lumps" in them. These "lumps" were originally only discernable once shoes had been put on over the top. He'd claim the socks felt uncomfortable, "lumpy"—and would kick off, full bore: shouting, crying, yanking off his shoes and throwing them away. Over time the flash-point slipped earlier and earlier, until the lumps began to present before the shoes went on, and eventually as soon as the socks were in place. He can now look at a pair of socks before they're even on his feet and tell that they will have lumps when they've been put on.

We can't see or feel any lumps, naturally.

We are inclined, if I'm absolutely honest, to believe they don't exist. We have nonetheless bought three extra pairs of shoes, and *god knows* how many socks, from every outlet we can find. Some, for a time, seem to have made a difference. There were a couple of sets from Gap which were golden, for a while, lumpless and magical.

But then, just as you're starting to relax and think the problem is fading, one morning those socks just don't work anymore.

"It doesn't *feel* right," he'll say, kicking his legs out with sudden, spastic force. "It *doesn't feel right.*"

Full-blown hysteria is only seconds away by that point, accompanied by crying of such violence that I find it impossible to dismiss the whole thing as bad behaviour or difficulty in transitioning or merely proof of what lousy parents we are. We've tried coaxing. We've tried shouting. We've tried being icily polite. We've tried ignoring bad behaviour and rewarding good. We've tried massaging his feet and warming the socks on the radiator and telling him that every sock on the planet has stitching in it and that's *just the way it is and you have to get used to it.* We've threatened to tell his teachers why he's late every morning. We've actually told them. We've done everything we can think of, basically, and still the mornings work like this: one out of five—not too bad; two out of five, pretty bad; the other two, Total Sock Armageddon, and Footwear Vietnam.

This morning was one of the latter kind.

Screaming, shouting. Socks being pulled back off and thrown down the stairs, four times. In the end the two of us had to hold him down and stuff the socks back on (I don't know if you've tried getting socks on a strong and semi-hysterical five-year-old, but it's really, *really* hard, and can be painful, and it is a depressing and deeply crap way to start the day—especially when you love the little *fucker* very much and hate to see him upset, no matter how firmly you have come to suspect that the whole affair is a way of asserting power and has nothing to do with socks at all).

Eventually I wound up carrying a shouting child out to the car without his shoes on (with me still in my pajamas, of course, hair sticking up as crazy as you like, a real treat for the neighbours, and not for the first time) and shoving him bad-temperedly into his car seat. He banged his head very slightly on the way in, which made me feel terrible. I put on his seatbelt and made sure it was secure, Helena strapped herself in, and they drove away. I stomped furiously back into the house, the time still only 8:32, and went to have a shower.

Parenthood—it's not for everyone.

◦►

Tim is a lovely child most of the time. Sweet, funny, bright, and sometimes even helpful. There are these flashpoints, however, and living with them hanging over you the whole time is like playing an especially ill-advised style of Russian Roulette where instead of a single bullet, there's only one *empty* chamber, and thus a very, very high chance of the whole thing kicking off.

That sounds ludicrous, possibly, but it feels that way sometimes, because there's just *such* a difference in quality of experience between a child deciding to be sweet and tractable and him or her electing to go to the Dark Side. A five year old on the warpath—with their total lack of care for (or absence of understanding of) punishment or incentive—can make you understand all too well why our prisons are full. The scariest thing is when incentives don't work, the promise of sweets when they get home or a seven hour *Ben 10* marathon if they'll just consent to you putting on their fucking shoes. Our lives are based on incentives, often hypothetical, long in coming, frankly hard to put your faith in. If incentives are not going to make you behave then you're going to have terrible problems forging a pleasant life.

The biggest challenge for me is nothing else seems to help. No amount of talking or shoe-buying or sock stretching/warming makes any difference—which you can't help feeling means the whole thing must be at best psychosomatic, and possibly completely made up, a line drawn in the sand over which inter-generational strife has been pre-established and can be returned to at the drop of a hat. I have many faults but I am a fundamentally reasonable man, and a rational one. I can roll with the punches and suck it up, so long as the problems make sense. It is the forces of unreason, and irrational acts, that bring me to my knees.

And these *fucking* socks.

-◦-

Thankfully, the whole episode ended on an upswing. After I'd had my shower and stomped back downstairs, I made a cup of tea and took it onto the front step for my ritual first cigarette, the time then being about 8:45. I stopped smoking in the house long before Tim was born, and now try hard not to do it anywhere near him, for any number of reasons (including having recently been sternly informed by Tim, as he observed a stranger with a cigarette in the park, that smoking was bad for the environment). As I stood on the step watching the street, I saw a few parents walking by with their own children, en route to local schools. Some of these little groups were chatting nicely, others passed in affable silence; some wore uniform, others smartish casual clothes.

Then I heard the sound of childish dudgeon from the left, the source initially hidden by the next house.

A small boy, perhaps three and a half, was the first to enter frame—cruising along on a scooter, casting an occasional glance back, as if rubber-necking a traffic accident in which no-one had been hurt.

Then his mother appeared, pulling another child reasonably gently along the pavement. This little girl—who looked to my not-very-expert eye to be around five years old, the same age as Tim—was wailing at medium volume and intensity, and hopping along.

"I can't do anything about it now," the children's mother said, a well-dressed but harried-looking blonde in her mid-thirties. "We're *late*. I'll look when we get to school."

The child wailed afresh, hopping with exaggerated discomfort, as though the world were a harsh and insupportable place and her mother a graceless harridan who wanted nothing but for her to suffer.

The group slowly proceeded to the right, disappearing from view a couple of minutes later. *Thank Christ*, I thought. *At least it's not just us.*

The sad truth of it is that many of the better moments you have as a parent boil down to that: the promise or hope that at least it's not just you who is making a total pig's ear of the whole business.

Significantly buoyed by this reassurance, I went back indoors and started my day's work.

At the end of which Tim came home, bursting into my study to tell me about something he'd seen out of the window on the journey home, and I picked him up and we went downstairs and watched a *Ben 10* together. I remembered that a threat/promise he'd never watch the show ever again had been a core part of my attempt to get him dressed that very morning, but while sitting on the sofa, the two of us comfortable and content, I didn't care, and there was nowhere else I wanted to be.

At one point he looked up at me and said, as he sometimes does, "I love you, Daddy."

And that's the point where you know that there's nothing better in the world, and nothing you would not do to protect them, and how very lucky you are.

◂◦▸

The next morning—Wednesday—followed about the same course. Part of the problem is that once you've had a bad morning you brace yourself for the run to continue, and I'm convinced that this anxiety is audible on some psychic wavelength to which children are finely tuned. They can smell your fear, basically.

On Wednesday it didn't even *start* well.

The boiled egg went largely uneaten. My attempts to get Tim into his clothes—the six articles of which are graven in my mind, like dispiritingly tough levels of a video game that's too hard to be any fun—were immediate failures. My son informed me that school was boring, that he didn't care what his teachers thought if I told them about how he was behaving, and nur nur ne nur-nur.

Then he glanced up at me, with the smug look that says, "I know that cultural mores stand against you giving me the sharp cuff around the head I so richly deserve, so let's not even pretend you've got anything in your armory, dickhead" (or at least, that's what the look says to me) and went running out of the room.

So then it became:

Chase him around the house.

Put each item of clothing on him two or three times.

Eventually have to carry him downstairs under my arm, screaming.

Child deposited in the car without shoes *or* socks this time, strapped into seat, wailing.

Wife drives off with stormy expression.

Stomp back indoors.

Helena and I broadly see eye to eye on all this stuff, including the feeling/hope that it's just a phase, an attempt to establish power in a family where Tim is an only child faced with an army of two adults bent on oppressing him at all times. You can still get on each other's nerves—especially when you're tired. One parent tries to do something out of sync with the other, or accidently undermines something said out of his or her hearing, and suddenly you're being snippy with each other, the child slipping out of your grasp, cunning enough to know that this division in the enemy ranks has given him a chance to escape, to regroup, and to take his *fucking* socks off for the *fifth fucking time.*

I had a furious shower afterwards, then calmed myself down while making the subsequent cup of tea and rolling myself a cigarette. I actually don't like rollies very much. The swap was intended to help me cut down. In fact, of course, it merely means I'm now incredibly good at rolling cigarettes. The extra tar and the desiccating qualities also mean that I seem to have aged more over the last nine months than in the previous three years, but this could be down to parenthood: to being woken too early every day of every week; to all of the sentences you never get to finish through being interrupted by either child, or wife admonishing child; to the swallowed frustrations and the anger that goes unexpressed; to the abused-parent daily routine of being perpetually on edge, and on your best behaviour, in the hope of prolonging an unexpectedly good burst of good humour from the child who (despite your declared intentions, and best efforts) basically rules the household.

"Lumps?" I sometimes want to snarl at Tim, "*Lumps?* You want me to tell you about lumps? Try being a grown-up for a while. Try walking in my socks for a day, sonny, and see how you feel about lumps then."

Yes, I should give up smoking. For the sake of my child. I'll get around to it, probably round about the time the child gets round to giving me a break.

I took the cigarette and the tea out onto the step. I was there about the same time as I had been the day before and so the view was much the same. I did notice some kind of confrontation taking place between a red-haired mother I've seen before, and her boy, on the other side of the road: he stopped walking, shouted something, pointing apparently at the pavement. She kept enviably calm and used everything possible in body language to reassure him that she was on his side in whatever debate or problem he was having with reality.

He thumped her on the arm, and there was a lot of screaming, but she held firm, and eventually he went limping after her down the street and out of sight.

A minute later, I heard shouting from the left—and the group of three that I'd seen yesterday appeared, in eerie déjà vu. The younger child, coasting along on his scooter. The mother, looking even more tired than the day before, again dragging the elder child. She was less gentle this morning, and the girl was making a lot more noise, hobbling along in a ludicrous parody of pain.

"I checked them *three times* before we left the house," the mother snarled. "I'm *not* having you make me late for work *again*. Let's just *go.*"

The child whacked her on the back, hard, and tried to pull away. She tightened her grip, pulled to a standstill just outside the gate to our path.

"It doesn't feel right," the child wailed, evidently not for the first time. "It doesn't *feel* right."

The woman opened her mouth. I could feel from fifteen feet away just how much she wanted to shout at her, to tell her daughter to stop making it up, to *stop being such a little shit*. Then she caught sight of me, standing on my step, and her mouth closed like a trap.

I shrugged, with a half-smile, trying to load both actions with as much 'Sister, I've been there and I share your pain' as possible.

She smiled back, but it was a short, sad expression. It's *quite* good when another parent signals that they know the score, but it's not great. You feel that you should be able to do all this stuff effortlessly. You don't want sympathy, however well meant—you want admiration for how well it's going.

Eventually she dragged her daughter out of sight.

I went indoors. Worked.

The day passed.

◄◦►

Thursday was about the same as Wednesday. At one point, having caught him as he tried to dodge past me on the main landing, I sat Tim roughly down on the stair and asked him straight out, "Why are you doing this? Do you enjoy the attention, the drama? Do you think you're winning something?" He shouted back that his socks were lumpy, and it didn't feel right—nebulous but battle-tested weapons for which he knew I had no defense. He wrenched away and ran into my study, where he threw himself on the ground and writhed, yanking his socks off, again.

Fifteen minutes later a wild-haired man in a dressing gown—yes, that would be me—carried his kid out to the car once more, stuffed him into his child seat, and made sure his seat-belt was secure. Helena had seen me do everything in my power to keep an even temper, and when she caught my eye through the windshield as she started to drive off there was no tetchiness there. Merely tiredness, sadness and a slight look of fear.

I knew what she was thinking, because the same thought was going through my own head:

Is it always going to be like this? Is this what our lives are now, perpetual skirmishes, this endless trench warfare leavened with unpredictable moments of ineffable love, the battle lines doubtless changing as he gets older, but with no cease-fire ever in sight?

I gave her a smile, and tried to make it a big one. She did the same, and off they went.

We weren't the only ones having those thoughts that morning, I suspect. Red-haired mother was having more trouble than the day before, too. Her child lay down on the pavement for a while, kicking at her, shouting. It took her ten minutes to get him back upright and tug him along the road.

The weird thing was that something almost identical happened with another kid, moments later—another boy ranting about his feet, at a brunette woman I'd never seen (or never noticed) before. She managed to get him past, eventually. I'd finished my cigarette and was turning to head back indoors when I heard the sound of a voice I now recognised.

"Please," it said, the tone more pleading, less authoritative than the last two mornings, "*Please*, Nadja. Please just come along."

There was an incoherent shout, then a burst of tears. I walked down a couple of steps, looked left—and saw the blonde of the last couple of mornings.

She was gazing down at something, impotently, shoulders bowed. She heard my feet on the path and closed her eyes—feeling the shame of having another adult witnessing her powerlessness and rage. The final straw.

I took a gamble and walked further down the path.

At the gateway I could see that the woman's son stood to one side, with his scooter. The daughter was lying full length on the ground, screaming histrionically while she tugged off one of her shoes. The other had already been thrown into the road.

"Yikes," I said. "You look like you're having exactly the same kind of morning we did."

The woman looked at me gratefully. "Really?"

"Oh yes. I had to carry our kid out to the car. No shoes, no socks. Screaming. Before that, I had to brush his teeth while my wife literally *held him down*."

"I'm sorry."

"Most of the time he's lovely. But the mornings . . . the clothes, the shoes and socks. It is . . . *not fun*."

"I worry it's us," the woman said. "Sometimes my husband and I sit staring at each other at the end of the day and wonder what we're doing wrong."

"It's how they keep us on our toes. That, and once in a while being so wonderful that you realise without them your life would now be nothing."

She smiled, a little, and the two of us watched as her daughter took her socks off, and threw them away too.

"My feet are cold!" she wailed, immediately.

"Well, yes," her mother said, patiently. "That would be because you've taken your shoes and socks off."

"They're *cold,*" she screamed. "It's *your fault.*"

"Well, if you put your socks and shoes back on," her mother said, calmly, pleasantly, sweetly, "maybe they'll warm up. Shall we try that?"

"No!" she shouted. "It doesn't *feel* right."

"So. You're upset that your feet are cold because you took your socks and shoes off, but you won't consider putting them back on again, is that it?"

The kid just wailed.

"Good luck," I said, and retreated back to our pathway. This wasn't due to lack of courage. It's what you do. You can't get involved helping discipline someone else's child. It's not the done thing, and you can't let children see adults appearing to gang up against them (nice though it would be, every now and then, to feel you were part of the superior forces, for a change).

You have to let other parents do their thing: give them the space and privacy to snarl rude words under their breath, to tug their child a little harder than they're supposed to. It's all very well banning physical chastisement, but that's like entering a war zone and disarming yourself on the way in. If one of your fellow grunts occasionally lets off a harsher word than they're supposed to, while under heavy enemy fire, you turn your head and let it go.

She eventually got the girl to her feet, still snuffling, still ranting. She coaxed her off down the street, the mother's back straight, and head held high.

And just before they got to the corner and left my sight, her daughter did something odd.

She turned her head, looked back at me.

And smiled.

◄o►

And then it was Friday.

I had high hopes. Tim had come back from school in a lovely mood the afternoon before. Instead of watching TV we played with Lego and did some drawing together. I made him the pasta dish that he appears to like and he ate a lot of it without having to be constantly reminded to follow one mouthful with another. He went up to his bath fairly promptly, denied himself the traditional splashing spasm which sends water up over the MDF surround and will eventually ruin it completely, and got out after only ten minutes' token resistance. He didn't even shout for us much after I'd read him his stories and turned out the light. In general it was what passes for a textbook evening, and when Helena and I crashed out on the sofa in front of valium television afterwards, it was with a feeling of a job moderately well done.

But then, Friday.

He wrong-footed me by being extremely good for the first forty minutes. He ate his egg. He didn't ask for a *Ben 10*. He acquiesced—like some pampered Restoration nobleman—to being put into his school uniform, while humming an odd tune to himself.

By 8:10 it was looking like plain sailing, which always, in a pathetic way, makes me want to cry.

And then it span off into the woods.

I approached, smiling, holding his toothbrush—already laden with the toothpaste he prefers. I handed it to him thinking that things were going so swimmingly this morning that he might even wield the implement himself.

He threw it back at me.

"Uh, Tim, no," I said. "We don't throw things at people, do we."

He ran past, heading upstairs. I took a deep breath and decided to leave him to it, hoping the moment would pass (as it does sometimes, to be replaced with eerie calm and helpfulness). Meanwhile I retrieved the toothbrush, wiped the toothpaste off the carpet, and calmed myself down. When I started—oh so very calmly—up the stairs in the direction he'd run, I saw first his sweater, then the tie, then the shirt . . .

He'd taken it all off.

He was back down to his pants.

It took twenty minutes to corner him and get it all back on. While we were brushing his teeth he pulled Helena's hair hard enough to make her eyes water, and refused to let go. It got so out of hand that in the end I rapped him on the back of his hand, barely a slap, but enough to show things were in danger of going critical.

He stared up at me, eyes suddenly full of tears and dismay. "You didn't warn me," he wailed.

"I don't have to," I said, through teeth that were gritted half in anger, and half with appalled guilt at having struck him. "You *know* you don't pull people's hair, especially mummy's. It *hurts*. How would you like it if I pulled *your* hair?"

He wailed.

The socks came off again.

It was bad. It was a *really bad one*.

It kept getting later and later and he kept getting louder and louder and closer to hysterical and the worst of it was, as always, that every now and then, through all the crap and the shouting, I kept getting glimpses of my son when he was not like this, when he was sweet and lovable and *my child*, instead of this uncontrollable creature—and all I wanted was the best for him, and for him to be nice enough, for long enough, for me to show him how very much I loved him.

In the end, a full half hour behind schedule—late enough that he was likely to get written up in a book at school, and his parents called to account—I carried him out to the car.

He wasn't shouting any more, however. Not wailing, nor crying. He was silent. I put him not too roughly into his car seat and stepped back.

"You haven't done my seat belt," he said.

"Do it yourself," I snapped.

It was a mistake.

He's perfectly capable of doing his belt up by himself—just as he's capable of dressing himself, and brushing his teeth, and eating his boiled egg without having to be motivated on every sodding mouthful—but yes, it was a mistake.

I heard Helena saying something irritably, but I'd had enough. I slammed the door (making sure, of course, that his fingers were nowhere near; you get used to taking that kind of care even when the red mist is descending), and stomped away up the path.

◄○►

By the time I'd got to the front door I'd realised it had been a stupid thing to do. In his current mood Tim simply wouldn't do the seatbelt up. Helena would have to get out of the car and come around to do it, which was the last thing she needed. I was turning round to go back and set things right when I stopped in my tracks.

We were so far behind schedule that it was around the time I'd normally be having my cup of tea and a cigarette, and I saw both the red-haired and the brown-haired mothers on the other side of the road.

Both their little boys were shouting, one lying on his back on the sidewalk, kicking his feet, pulling off his shoes.

Then I heard a voice.

The blonde woman's voice.

She sounded desperate, near tears.

I walked quickly back down the path, my mind on going to put Tim's seatbelt on, but then saw the blonde woman's daughter was lying on her back on the pavement too. Her feet were bare. She was silent, staring up at her mother with an expression that was hard to interpret.

"Please," her mother said, kneeling next to her to try to help, to be loving, to do whatever it took to break this deadlock. "Please, darling. I've *got* to get to work. Please just put your socks back on. Please."

Still she looked up at her.

And then a shape came running from behind me.

Tim had leapt onto the woman's back before I even realised it was my son I was watching. His weight was enough to knock her forward so that her face smacked into the cold pavement, very hard.

Her daughter was immediately in movement, grabbing her mother's face in both hands and pulling it toward her, or her face towards her mother's, I couldn't be sure.

Tim looped his arm around the woman's neck and started beating at the back of her head with his other fist. The woman's little boy stood neatly beside his scooter and watched—as his sister lunged forward and took a bite out of their mother's cheek.

I shouted something incoherent.

Then I saw that on the other side of the street the brunette woman was sprawled face-down in the gutter, three children on top of her, beating, biting.

The red-haired mother was trying to run, but a crowd of five children had appeared from around the corner and were after her. None of them wore any shoes or socks.

All were running very fast.

I started toward the blonde woman, who was screaming, a ragged strip of cheek hanging down off her face, her daughter and my son pulling at her hair and gnawing at her throat.

But then I saw the windscreen of our car, and the blood splatter across the inside, and the shape of Helena's head slumped over the steering wheel.

I shouted. Something. I don't know what.

The three kids on the other side of the road raised their heads from the body of the brown-haired woman, and looked at me.

I backed away up the path. Then turned and ran.

I got the door shut behind me, put on the chain, drew the bolt.

Their bodies hit the door half a second later.

◄◦►

You know the rest.

Or if you don't, you soon will.

It is dark now. The sound of sirens has died away for the moment. If the experience of the last fourteen hours is anything to go by, it will get louder again soon. I'm still in my dressing gown. I'm smoking, inside the house. I don't know what I'm waiting for, or what I'm going to do. I do know what I'm hearing, however, beyond the windows, and I know whose small, dark shape is moving restlessly out there, crawling around the house, trying to find a way in.

I love that shape. I have nurtured it, tried to do the right thing by it, for five long years. I'd know that shape even if it didn't keep saying the same thing.

"I love you, Daddy," it says. It doesn't say it often, but once in a while it repeats this thing, in a voice that is not cracked with hysteria now, just low and hard and cold. "But it doesn't feel right."

MINE SEVEN

ELANA GOMEL

Black sky, white snow, yellow light.

Lena felt that her vision was being starved of some essential nutrient. She longed for fire-engine red, viridian green, shocking purple. But the electric glow in the Funken Lodge leached brightness out of everything, slashing the entire spectrum down to the uncompromising contrast of arctic winter: darkness and light. It repelled and attracted her in equal measure. She spent most of her time staring out of the curving floor-to-ceiling windows of the lounge, seeing the pale blob of her face surrounded by reflections of the chandeliers like jellyfish swimming in a sea of tar.

Bill, on the other hand, happily mined the darkness for Instagram posts. He would go out with his cameras and come back hours later, stomping his chain-wreathed boots to shake off the snow, removing his multilayered parka, fur hat, and face protector in the side-room the hotel provided for its guests' winter equipment. Then he would bound up the stairs into the lounge to show her his latest pictures. The black sky at midday; the sparkle of fairy lights in downtown Longyearbyen; clumps of ice crystals growing where no plants ever grew. He was gleeful about having caught the Northern Lights on camera. Lena found the greenish smears against the pitch background less than impressive. Tomorrow, though, the Aurora forecast predicted a better display.

Tomorrow was a relative term. In mid-January in Svalbard the sun never rose above the horizon. Darkness was the same whether one was asleep or awake; in the middle of breakfast or having a nightcap. It was like being in a fever dream. The sluggishness of time thickened Lena's blood. She was perpetually cold, her body repelling the generous warmth of the hotel's blazing radiator heaters.

Bill made fun of her. After all, he said, she should feel at home here. Spitsbergen, though a Norwegian territory, had a Russian mining settlement, Barentsburg, and an abandoned Soviet-era ghost town, Pyramiden. Chukchi people were not Russians, she would remind him, but such distinctions were lost on Americans. Most of the time they were lost on Lena herself.

This arctic vacation had been Bill's idea, with Lena tagging along, partly out of curiosity about her heritage but mostly based on the simple "why not?" They had the money: Bill's startup dividends. Her social-media post about their plans had elicited a flurry of envious likes. But now she felt like a prisoner in the bright lodge surrounded by the encroaching dark, held at bay only by the incandescence of the electric lights that never went out in Longyearbyen.

Until they did.

◄◦►

They were as unlike as two women could possibly be: the waitress blonde and thin, with washed-out blue eyes; Lena dark and round-cheeked. But when the waitress, whose name was Irina, took her orders, Lena heard an echo of her mother's liquid vowels and hard consonants in her speech. Irina was overjoyed when addressed in Russian.

They chatted about the hardships and pleasures of living in the northernmost town in the world. One got used to the cold, Irina said. And it was getting warmer too.

"Adventfjorden used to be frozen in winter," Irina continued. "Now it's ice-free all year round. Whales come. Fish too, lots of cod. People go fishing in January."

"Why would they?" Lena asked. "Isn't it too cold?"

Irina shrugged.

"People need jobs," she said. "Mines are gone."

Longyearbyen used to be a mining town. Spitsbergen's greasy coal, dug out of the permafrost, had, once upon a time, been the best in the world. Americans, Norwegians, and Russians had competed for the black gold. Lena and Bill had gone to see one of the decommissioned mines, now trying to pass itself off as a tourist attraction. Lena could not imagine anything less attractive than the narrow tunnels flooded with thick darkness and festooned with ice spears, broken machinery frozen into the unyielding ground like sinners in Dante's hell. But men had crawled through these wormholes, hacked blackness out of coal-seams, and coughed their lungs out in the meagre air.

Five of the six mines were closed now. The remaining one provided the electricity that kept Longyearbyen lit and netted the miners a million kroner a year.

"Do you miss Russia?" Lena asked.

A faraway look on Irina's face reminded Lena of her mother's expression on the rare occasions when she spoke of her childhood in the Siberian town of Anadyr. Her mother swore she had nothing to be nostalgic about. But Lena had seen her on more than one occasion furtively go through yellowed pictures of unsmiling men and women in front of deerskin yurts.

Before she could answer, Bill showed up, his face ruddy from his morning photo-excursion. They switched back to English. Lena regretted it, even though her Russian was rusty. As for Chukchi, a native Siberian language spoken by a few thousands in the world, she only knew a hypnotic litany that her Nana had made her learn by heart, telling her it was a powerful spell made up by her shaman grandfather. Lena understood not a word of it but cherished it as a memory of Nana, whose wrinkled-apple face and kind hands presided over her childhood.

Lena picked up Bill's phone, scrolling through the pictures. She paused, staring at a close-up of garishly lit snow piled up against the Falun-red wall of an apartment building. Sharp shadows drew a cartoon sketch of a snarling face on the powdery surface.

Irina refilled their coffee cups.

"My Northern Lights app says we'll have a great display today," Bill declared. "I have arranged for a dogsled ride!"

They had visited a dogs' compound, where big huskies bedded placidly in snowdrifts and puppies who had never been indoors played in the frozen glare of spotlights. Lena looked longingly at the overstuffed armchairs of the library nook.

"All right," she said.

"I went to Svald-bar for coffee," Bill continued (Svald-bar being the cute name of his favorite downtown hangout). "I saw that guy drinking aquavit. I thought I would have some but then I realized it was only 8a.m. Darkness really messes up your biological clock."

He laughed raucously.

"It is Old Sven," Irina said. "He used to be a miner. At Mine Seven."

"What's Mine Seven?" Bill asked. "I thought there were six mines on Spitsbergen."

"It's locked."

"You mean closed," Bill corrected. Irina smiled, tight-lipped, and flitted to the next table. The Funken Lodge had few guests, mostly from Norway and the UK. Svalbard winter tourism was still a niche industry.

Lena reluctantly followed Bill down the stairway that looked magical in the soft glow of the hanging clusters of pearly lights. She would be happy to stay in the lodge, poring over the old volumes of the history of Spitsbergen and nibbling on a cloudberry jam toast. A dogsled ride would take them outside the perimeter of lights, into the unrelieved darkness of the rest of the island. It felt final.

She took her time, putting on her outer trousers, her padded parka, and fixing the chains to her fur-lined boots, dreading the slap of the frozen air. But when they finally stepped outside, she realized she must have become inured to the brutal cold. She felt numb rather than frozen. Hypothermia setting in? Lena told Bill she wanted a cup of hot chocolate before heading out on the dogsled.

They walked downtown, following the thin setting moon, which was surrounded by a hazy halo. The streets shone like a handful of jewels set in dull black velvet. Longyearbyen had a shopping center, a library, and a museum, all limned in garish electric garlands. The town was positively profligate in its use of lighting. Tall pylons that lined its streets were topped with blinding spotlights, each shedding enough illumination for an average American block. Apartment houses had large windows, defiantly kept un-curtained, that dripped pools of multicolored radiance onto the snow.

There were fairy lights and bright shop signs everywhere. Electricity was not a problem. The coal was still there.

Nobody was supposed to venture outside the lit zone alone and unarmed. Polar bears lurked there in increasing numbers, spurred on to migration by the melting ice-fields and warming seas. A polar bear had killed a child in the schoolyard a year ago. Since then, more and more people carried guns everywhere. Lena looked at the giant whitish ghosts surrounding the town, leaning into its bright core, and shivered. What good would bullets do against these somnolent monsters?

These were mountains, of course, not enormous beasts. Just mountains where the coal slept.

A man staggered toward them. At first Lena thought he was slipping on the iced pavement, even though most inhabitants of Longyearbyen were surprisingly sure-footed. But then she realized the man was drunk. He swayed and mumbled to himself as he passed by.

"That's the guy I saw in the bar!" Bill said.

The man folded into the snow. They tried to lift him up but he was surprisingly heavy, his parka too tight on his swollen body, bursting at the seams.

Bill frowned.

"He looked smaller in the bar," he muttered. "But it's him."

Two figures materialized out of the gloom, pulled the fallen man up and hustled him away, their wrapped-up heads giving them the appearance of strange insects.

Lena and Bill walked on toward the local bakery. Childishly, she hoped that if she procrastinated enough, the dark day would seamlessly melt into the night and the dogsled ride would be cancelled.

Her hope was realized, though not in the way she had intended.

⊰⊙⊱

The owner of the Fruene café, a stocky Norwegian named Bjorn, poured two steaming cups of what was advertised as the only gourmet chocolate made beyond the Arctic Circle. Lena swirled the thick liquid in her cup, staring at the stuffed polar bear mounted with its paws waving in the air as if about to slap down a customer. The sign at the entrance said in English: "This bear is already dead. Please leave your gun at the counter."

"Who is Old Sven?" she asked Bjorn.

"Old Sven? A miner. A former miner. He has been in Longyearbyen forever. One of our oldest residents."

"Doesn't he have a family on the mainland? To go somewhere warmer?"

"It's getting warmer here."

"Really?" Bill interjected skeptically.

"*Ja*. Permafrost is melting."

"Did he work in Mine Seven?" Lena asked.

She caught a grimace of distaste on Bjorn's face as he pondered how to fib her off. But he never had the chance. The lights went out.

◂◦▸

Lena pushed a rolled-up map into the purple maw of the fire and coughed when acrid smoke stung her sinuses. It was fortunate that the Funken Lodge had an actual fireplace in its lounge, even though previously it had been used for decoration only. Now the survivors huddled in front of it, watching the sputtering flame. They had burned all the books and greetings cards in the small hotel shop and started on the fat volumes in the library. The Scandinavian décor had promised a plentiful supply of wood, but it turned out that the glossy blond tables and armchairs were plastic. Somebody tried to burn bedclothes and almost choked the fire.

She was not sure how she had made it back to the hotel. At some point, she had found herself crawling on the frigid pavement without a parka or gloves. Her fingers refused to bend and she thought, distantly, that she might lose them to frostbite. But this did not feel real or urgent enough. She was humming Nana's chant as if it could make the lurkers in the dark acknowledge her as one of their own and let her pass. It was an insane thought and she embraced it because sanity no longer had any place here.

The snow had turned anthracite-black, the town dissolving in the night as thick as treacle. The Funken Lodge was an indistinct smear. Lena's eyelashes hung in broken clumps, the frozen tear-tracks on her cheeks burned like acid. The gaping hole of the entrance was veiled by a swarm of tiny snowflakes, stinging like angry bees. She stumbled over a body on the floor in the changing room. The man was not dead as she had first assumed but in shock, gasping and mumbling. She dragged him into the lounge where

Nigel, a British skier who never skied, managed to get a fire going. The man, another tourist, was thawing out while Lena stood on top of the staircase, waiting for more people to come in. "More people" were a euphemism for Bill, even though she knew he was not coming back. Eventually she gave up and helped the handful of other survivors to barricade the entrance door that was stuck halfway because its electrical mechanism had shorted out.

⋖⊶

In the café, when the lights had blinked out, Lena was momentarily sure she had gone blind. Even if the wiring had failed there should have been enough illumination coming in from the brightly lit street. But instead she was plunged into the murk ringing with the tinkle of broken glass and Bill's cursing.

"What the hell?"

So, it was not her eyes. Bill's voice was mingling with a whole array of incomprehensible noises that filled the dark: a shuffle; liquid gulping; choking sputter.

"Bjorn?"

The floor under her feet shook as if somebody else had walked into the shop, somebody with a giant's tread. Bill grasped her hand and pulled her to where he assumed the door was.

"We are getting out of here!"

A wave of hot stink assaulted her nose. Mothballs? Wet dog?

Blood?

She was bumping into sharp invisible angles. There was a growling and a wallowing in the dark, sounds like a leaky faucet, like a legion of cats, like sobbing, like dying; her brain desperately sorting through a medley of images to put a name to what she was hearing. But the only image that kept coming back was the sign that said: "This bear is already dead."

Bill's hand slid from hers.

She blundered through the writhing shadow and then she brushed something, something shaggy and unclean. A cold spasm doubled her up, and the shaggy mass receded. She slipped on steaming wetness crusted with ice. And then she was outside, hatless and without her parka, crawling through the snow and refusing to look back.

But even if she had, she would have seen nothing.

—◦—

The survivors of the Funken Lodge were few. Besides Nigel who had come to Spitsbergen after a messy divorce with a pair of skis and spent most of his time at the bar, there was a Danish woman who sobbed unceasingly, a Norwegian engineer named Oscar, and several Germans whose limited English seemed to have abandoned them altogether. But no administrative staff was around. Where were the receptionist, the waiters, the shop lady, the cleaners, all the human nuts and bolts that kept the machine of civilization running? They had gone out together with the lights and had not come back.

Nigel tried his cellphone for the hundredth time. It was useless, all signal having disappeared the moment the darkness came. He turned on the flashlight app and let loose a swarm of bluish afterimages in Lena's field of vision. The glare suddenly felt dangerous.

"Turn it off!" the Danish woman whose name Lena could not remember said venomously. "We need to conserve batteries."

"Much good it'll do!" Nigel muttered but complied. Perhaps he too felt that bright light could attract unwelcome attention.

A crash of glass resounded in the restaurant, making everybody jump, but then Oscar emerged, carrying a bottle of wine and a loaf of rye bread. They were in no danger of starvation with the fully stocked kitchen, but they had to eat cold food—"cold" as in "frozen."

The man plunked down by the dwindling fire and slurped wine out of the bottle. The rest cast irritated glances in his direction but nobody said anything. It was strange, Lena reflected, how in all post-apocalyptic movies and books the survivors either banded together or turned against each other in a Battle Royale. Neither was happening here; they were just a handful of shell-shocked individuals rather than an emerging tribe or a gladiators' arena.

From outside came a crunching noise.

It was the sound fresh snow makes when it is crushed underfoot. It had become familiar to Lena and for a moment she was glad because it meant somebody was walking outside, somebody was coming in, perhaps Bill, miraculously returning . . . and then it hit her. It must have hit the rest of them at the same time because the Danish woman whimpered, and Oscar paused with the bottle lifted to his mouth, the black wine trickling down his chin.

They should not have been able to hear the footsteps through the triple-glazed windows of the Lodge. Not unless the walker was large and heavy—*very* large and heavy.

Lena knew she should be screaming or hiding under a chair—but all she felt was a glacial numbness. It was as if Bill's absence (*death*) had spelled an end to the American Lena, cracked her identity open like a shell and whatever was emerging was as unfamiliar to herself as it would have been to him.

She found herself with her face pressed to the window. Darkness had restored transparency to the glass walls of the lounge, which used to reflect back the shine of the multiple light fixtures. But now she could see outside, into the thick murk diluted by white swirls of snow. And something moved in the murk, a core of deeper darkness trailing wisps of rotten black. The shapeless shape blundered through the drifts and was gone.

Oscar swore. The Danish woman clapped her hand to her mouth.

"A polar bear . . .?" Nigel suggested uncertainly.

"Come on, man!" Oscar spat. "Even after Brexit you should know that polar bears are white!"

Something shifted in the sky, filmy green streaks of Northern Lights crossing the starless vault. The snow grew brighter, reflecting the scattered glow.

"Look!" Lena pointed to the drifts under the window.

The snow was deeply dented by oval footprints, large enough to have been left by one of those famous Svalbard bears whose images decorated every mug and T-shirt in the shop. But these footprints bore the unmistakable crisscross pattern of snow chains.

⟶⟨◦⟩⟵

The Northern Lights winked out and then came back.

Lena regretted that Bill could not see them. Her thoughts moved slowly, wrapped up in the insulation of the hotel's excellent Chablis. At least she had not drunk straight from the bottle like Oscar, she told herself with maudlin self-pride. She had found a glass. Alcohol *really* was fire-water, just like Nana had said. A momentary return of warmth was worth a hangover.

The rest had made a similar discovery because they were all dozing in drunken stupor in front of the dying fire, buried under their piled-up parkas and blankets as the windows bloomed with rime on the inside. But the Northern Lights were bright enough to call her to the glass wall again and gape at the greenish arc that pulsed in irregular gasps of ghostly fire.

Nana had told her that the Chukchi called Aurora Borealis "the eyes of the dead." She had told her about other things as well: the persecution under Stalin; the scattering of tribal encampments and the confiscation of their reindeer; death from alcoholism, poverty, and despair. Lena had not listened. The American Lena had not wanted to know. And when Nana told her about the shamanic power of her grandfather Sergei who had died in the post-Soviet turmoil, she chalked it up to an immigrants' pathetic pride, clinging to the useless heritage she could not wait to be rid of.

But history has a way of catching up with you, she thought. *History is etched in every cell of your body.*

Nana had told her Sergei could call blizzards upon his enemies, could freeze blood in their veins, could make their bones shatter like icicles. She had thought it was as useless a superpower as they come. What was the need for ice magic in the ice-bound land? Why call the curse of cold upon your foes if nature did it for you?

But what if the curse was lifting and another, bigger, curse was following in its footsteps?

The giant had not come back. A short snowstorm had erased the footprints and the rest of the survivors had agreed that it was a polar bear, after all. Lena did not argue with this conclusion. The book she had rescued from the fuel pile and hidden under a pillow, the book in Russian, remained her secret. They would not believe her, in any case. And even if they did, what good would that do?

The book, with the fading logo of the USSR state publishing company "Young Guard," was called *Arctic Labour Heroes: Coalmining on Spitsbergen.*

◄◦►

The knock on the door came at 5:15 p.m.

Lena knew it because this was the last time she looked at her cellphone. The battery was down to 1%. She scrolled through the album Bill had shared with her, looking at the faces in the snow, the toothed maws of dark houses, the indistinct figure crawling among the dogs' shelters. Why had he refused to see what was in his photographs?

The tiny screen blinked out, echoing the darkness outside. The fire in the fireplace was still alive, but only just, anemically licking the wooden planks Nigel had found in the storage closet. Besides Lena, he was the only one awake; the rest were hibernating, as if sliding down the evolutionary scale, adapting to winter-sleep.

The lounge was above the entryway. When the lights had been on, one could see all the way down. Now darkness lapped at the landing like stagnant water.

Lena and Nigel exchanged glances. The Brit pulled out his own cellphone which still had enough battery to produce a flickering yellow beam.

"Don't go," Lena said.

The barricaded entrance door drummed under a rain of blows. Nigel started down the stairs, carrying his pathetic puddle of light with him. And then a voice.

"Lena!"

Nigel paused, his upturned face a playground of skittering shadows.

"Your husband?" he asked and afterwards Lena recalled a hesitation in his voice as if he knew the answer and did not want to say it. And so did she but she hesitated too, unwilling to put it into words because if she did it would all be over, and her world—the normal ordinary world of suburban California, work, marriage, exotic vacations—would be gone, flooded, submerged.

Her hesitation lasted only a couple of heartbeats, but it cost Nigel his life. He was down in the entryway when the door burst open in an explosion of glass fragments and an arm reached for him. It was an arm, not a paw, wrapped up in tatters of padded parka fabric. It was as thick as Lena's waist and its rough skin was peppered with black hair and dotted with crudely done tattoos: blue hearts, and vodka bottles, and crossed shovels, and red stars. The black-rimmed fingernails, each the size of a postal envelope, tore into Nigel's throat as he choked on his own blood, and pulled him through the hole in the door, his screams dying into a liquid gurgle.

Lena did not remember running down but here she was, the icy blast from the outside lacerating her face, as she picked up Nigel's cellphone and focused its light on the figure that still waited outside, standing there silently as if it wanted to be seen by her—as perhaps it did.

The creature—the *kelet*, the forgotten name of the Siberian evil spirit popping up in her head uninvited—was so tall that its head disappeared into the gloom and she could not see its face. But she could see the faces that grew out of its broad chest like clusters of grapes: faces of men, hard and frostbitten, ravaged by weather and smoke; men who had laboured in the black bowels of the island for the hidden light. Men who had been crushed when a coal seam collapsed or suffocated when methane flooded the tunnels. Men of Mine Seven.

And Bill's face was among them, even though he had never worked in a mine, had never put his gym-toned body through the meat grinder of physical labor as these men had. Slack and empty, his face recognized her and grinned idiotically.

Had the *kelet* reached in and dragged her out like live bait from a fisherman's tin she would not have resisted. The enormity of what she was seeing silenced the instinct of self-preservation. But it turned around and walked away, revealing the broad back into which bodies of sled-dogs were frozen like fish into the ice on the surface of a winter lake. The clothes that its human core had worn barely clung to its gnarled contours. Its feet were horny and splayed, the snow-chains ingrown like nails. It trailed a ragged mass of something like torn skins or quasi-human silhouettes, or three-dimensional shadows . . . but the cellphone blinked out, and Lena was left standing in the numbing stream of black air.

She might have literally frozen in place had not the snow brightened to improbable pink and looking up, she saw the Northern Lights again, purplish lavender this time, undulating in the sky like a cosmic opera curtain. It was rare, such a display, and even now the wonder of it made her move.

She went to the changing room where outer gear was kept. Her own parka was not there anymore but there were plenty of others, belonging to the guests and personnel who would not be coming back. She bundled up and put on fur-lined boots with snow chains. They were too big but it hardly mattered.

The Northern Lights flickered out, then on again, enough illumination to keep her on the track that led away from the sightless corpse of the Funken Lodge up into the mountains. She found that her eyes had adjusted enough that she could see their white humps against the clear jet sky. She was staring at them, trying to remember if there was a moon tonight, when she collided with another bundled-up figure coming down from the heights.

They avoided falling into the snow by clutching at each other. The newcomer's face was hidden under the layers of scarves, but she saw the blue eyes.

Irina dragged her to a barn mantled in white. There was an equally mantled snowmobile parked nearby. Somebody in the hotel had tried a snowmobile after the lights went out but it had not worked. Nothing worked: cars and minibuses in the Lodge's garage were so much useless junk.

They stood in the nook of the doorway. Irina pulled down her face protector.

"Did you see it?" she whispered.

Lena nodded.

"It's because of the melt," Irina went on feverishly. "I heard old people talking . . . but I thought it was *chepukha*. Nonsense."

"I found a book," Lena said. "Russian. An old one, Soviet times. Mine Seven was theirs, wasn't it?"

"It collapsed. Tunnels were flooded. People killed."

"They called them Heroes of Labor in the book, but the medals were awarded posthumously."

"Old Sven was the only Norwegian there. He worked in the office. He said, one of the miners was . . . Chukchi. From Siberia. A powerful shaman, so he said. He put a spell on the mine. A curse. But it was frozen into the ice. Just like their bodies. They were never recovered. The families got empty coffins and medals."

"And now the ice is melting . . ." Lena said.

"Yes. The ice is melting."

"Old Sven . . . they grew on him. Like frost on a tree."

Their eyes met.

"I was in the gallery when it happened," Irina said. "Having coffee with Sveta."

Sveta was another Russian girl who worked in the art gallery shop.

"Anybody alive?" Lena asked.

Irina shook her head.

"What are you going to do?"

"I will go down to the harbor. Maybe . . ."

Adventfjorden was free of ice; perhaps a ship would come in. Or a plane—Longyearbyen had an airport, and somebody on the mainland was bound to raise the alarm.

If they did not have bigger things to worry about. Ice was melting everywhere, oceans rising, carrying tides of old diseases and old curses, the mud of the past flooding the present.

"Come with me," Irina said.

Lena stared toward the mountains where the red banner of Northern Lights was unfurling once again.

"Where is Mine Seven?"

"Up there. But you . . . there is nothing you can do."

"I am from Siberia," Lena said. "My family lived in the Arctic. My grandfather was a Chukchi."

"But . . . do you know how . . .?"

She did not. The legend that Grandfather Sergei had been a shaman may have been just that: a family legend. Nana's chant may have been a lullaby, for all she knew. But if magic was melting, could not another kind of magic freeze it back, put it in the permafrost where it belonged?

This was a slender hope. But it was all she had now: the Chukchi Lena emerging from under the melting slush of her American identity. She had to try.

They embraced, kissing each other on frozen cheeks. And Lena climbed the shivering mountain toward the black maw of Mine Seven, where rusting pieces of broken metal lay in puddles of inky water.

SICKO

STEPHEN VOLK

The moment Marion stepped into the shower the world changed forever. She felt the water hit her forehead and run over her closed eyelids. It had been icy on her fingers when she'd first turned it on. Now it was lukewarm. Good. Cooler was best, to wash away the Phoenix heat. The heat of a long drive. Perspiration the young man may have noticed, but she hoped he hadn't. *Not very lady like.* But did it matter, really, what the young man thought? She'd never see him again. Apart from checking out the next morning.

She revolved, away from the spray. It hit her shoulders and calmed her, slightly. Didn't get rid of the stress entirely. That would be asking too much. Maybe she wouldn't get rid of that stress in her shoulders for the rest of her life. What a thought! Maybe it would never go away. How about that?

She asked herself what had made her do it in the first place. Was she crazy? Or did those lunchtime sessions with Stan in that featureless downtown hotel room, slats of sun intruding through the blinds, knotted limbs, trading saliva, make her feel crazy a little bit? Of *course* they did. God knows, that's what they were *for*. She needed an escape, or the office would have made her scream. Watching that clock go round. Waiting for you-know-who to come out and hand her back her typing, telling her there was a spelling mistake, not just one, but *I think you'll find* . . . like she's back in school, and his fingernails, too long for a man, they needed attending to, as she nodded, contrite, and smiled sweetly, rolling a fresh sheet into the typewriter.

Her previous shower had been earlier that day, after Stan had been inside her. Not his real name, but the one he wrote in the register. Stanley *Kowalski*. They joked about it! *Streetcar Named Desire.* "Punk downstairs wouldn't know Tennessee Williams from a hole in the ground." She'd lain there and lit a cigarette, as he did, from his own packet, but she wasn't worried about taking the smell of the cigarette back to her desk. She was worried about taking the smell of him.

Under the shower, back then, a world ago, she'd thought, wet, rotating, dreamy, of those commercials with the perfect housewives who held up for scrutiny their dirty linen and immaculate lives. Who said to her every day: *Don't get jealous, get even. You too can be like me. Seemingly unattainable but actually far more sexually accomplished than you might presume.*

Doris Day. Grace Kelly. If she couldn't *be* them, she could at least look like them. That was a form of advertising, too, really. *A message from our sponsor* . . . Available, but not easy. And if she couldn't afford new stockings, she could use that pencil line up the back of the leg trick her mother taught her.

He'd cupped her breasts from behind, then helped her on with her white *Tide clean* bra, kissing her neck hairs before hooking it up, taking a suck on the cigarette and giving her a halo of smoke. He declared he was hard again. Donning earrings, she'd pointed out with an arched eyebrow she'd just taken a shower.

"Showers are overrated," he'd replied. "I like dirty."

"I know you do." Grinning, she'd pushed him away, splayed fingers against hairy chest.

He'd sat on the bed, one sock on and one in his hands, and his face drooped, as it always did when their liaisons came to an end. He became a little boy again, sad to say goodbye. That saddened her, too, but cheered her at the same time, because she at least meant something to him, and she didn't always feel that with men. Stan was different. Even if they had to sign in under bogus names. That was something of a thrill in a childish way, but it also made it not real, not serious, impermanent, and somehow trivial, like a prank. Something silly, to him. . . . Was it?

She didn't know *what* she thought. It was probably just *too much thinking* getting in the way, like he said it was. Fretting that things could go wrong because they'd always gone wrong in the past, but they wouldn't this time. He said he loved her and wanted to marry her, hadn't he? What more did she want?

All they needed, before they walked down that aisle, was some money to settle his debts—and it wasn't like they were *debts*, as such, so much as mistakes, so much as people who had let him down, who promised him things would happen, and hadn't. Stan was too trusting like that. He saw the best in people, and suffered for it. It wasn't fair. But then the world wasn't fair.

This is what she'd been thinking as she walked back to the office earlier that Friday afternoon. As she sat at her desk straightening her skirt, as her boss tapped his watch and she apologized for being two minutes late, it wouldn't happen again, tidying her hair, coughing into her hand, turning the roller of the typewriter. Not even aware of the meeting he'd had behind closed doors with a client, thinking only of Stan's body tangled in a bed sheet, one knee raised, his lips coming closer to hers, until her boss placed the brown paper package on her desk.

Until he said it was a *$40,000 cash payment* for a property, just brought in by a valued customer and friend.

She hadn't even noticed the person leaving. She'd been in a post-coital daze. Her boss had said the name of the customer. He'd said the address of the property. But after he'd mentioned the quantity of cash, which hit her like a weapon—the way money did to those who didn't have it—the rest became a blur, a kind of dull thudding hum in her head, monotonous and overwhelming, like the giant hive buzz of a drag race.

She *did* hear him telling her to *Put the cash in the safe, Marion, please . . . It's the weekend . . . You can take the money to the bank first thing Monday morning.* She did hear *that*—loud and clear.

"Yes, sir. Yes, sir. Yes, sir."

$40,000! House for his baby daughter—a wedding present!

"Yes, sir."

Her boss returned to his office, shaking his head. She could hear him on the telephone as she opened the metal door hidden behind the painting that adorned one wall.

She had her purse with her, the straps over one forearm.

Nobody was watching. The other desk was empty. Wittering Peggy was off buying a wedding dress. (Peggy, so plain, but so full of confidence now she had an engagement ring on her finger.)

Using the combination entrusted to her, Marion opened the safe.

Felt a hollowness growing inside and didn't know if it was her stomach churning or her uterus aching, but part of her was crying out. Crying out for Stan. Crying out for him to tell her what to do. But she knew what to do, didn't she? Didn't she know what to do, all on her own, without a man telling her? *Do it!*

She slipped the brown paper package *not onto the shelf of the safe* but down into her purse. Tugged the zip closed over it. Clunked the safe door closed. Spun the rings of the combination lock with three jerks of her wrist.

Back stiff as a rod, she walked into her boss's office. He looked up, startled, standing, saying she didn't look well. No color in her cheeks. Gosh. She really didn't look well at all.

"No—No, I don't feel well, actually, sir. I don't. I've got the most awful headache."

Well, gracious . . . In that case, she'd better go home, hadn't she? Go home, Marion, dear. Right away!

But—

She protested, diligent, dutiful. A good employee. (A good actress. Grace Kelly . . .)

"No buts! Go home this instant, young lady!"

Coat. Purse.

$40,000!

"Thank you, sir. Goodbye, sir. Have a nice weekend, sir."

"You too, Marion. And Marion? . . . Do rest up, won't you?"

"Oh, I think I'll be spending the weekend in bed, sir."

The memory of her own small, tight laugh made the sweat come out of her pores again, and she stood with her hands flat against the shower walls.

She remembered stepping out of the office onto the sidewalk, into the oven-hot sunlight, looking back at the word REALTY painted on its front window. Recalled, when she was a little girl of about five or six, and inno-cent—asking why that shop sold REALITY? And her momma telling her, no, silly pig, it wasn't REALITY, it was *REALTY*, and that meant REAL ESTATE—which somehow, to her mind, back then, still meant something was real and something wasn't.

And walking away with the package in her purse, she'd felt she was leaving REALITY behind. But perhaps that was what *$40,000* bought you. The fantasy you always dreamed of. The perfection of the commercials. The perfect marriage that, in America, only money could buy. And if she didn't deserve it—who did?

Her back was straight. Her poise immaculate. Daring not to run and give the game away, she almost slowed to a stop, and so paused and touched up her lipstick, which didn't need it.

She walked straight home—five blocks, so convenient!—where she packed a suitcase since she'd already decided to take herself and the *$40,000* to Fielden, California, where Stan lived. *Airport check-in closes 3 p.m.* she'd remembered him saying. *Come with me. Hang work.* Fieden, California— where he now sat, or stood at a bar, not even remotely guessing their troubles were over. that black curl hanging over his brow, striking a match, she could smell the phosphorus, she loved that smell, and became deliriously happy for a moment, imagining his face as he rips open the package and sees the wads. His jaw dropping before he grips her face in his hands and smashes her lips with his.

Her Ford Customline slid out into the road.

She drove.

Not that it was easy at first. Just as when she walked back from lunch she thought everybody could see that she'd had sex, now she thought everybody could see she was a thief. Of course they couldn't. Of course there wasn't a great big sign on her vehicle saying STOLEN MONEY ON BOARD.

Of course. Of course. She knew. She knew.

She stopped at a red light. Flexed her fingers on the steering wheel. *$40,000!*

Nobody could tell by looking at someone whether they'd done something bad. Not that woman pushing the stroller, not the fat, bald man crossing the crosswalk, not the skinny old man with a mustache who looked a lot like . . . oh *God*, looked *exactly* like—and stopping, doing a double-take, staring right at her. Her boss—*right at her*!

The lights changed and she floored the gas.

Her back sank into the seat as the car took off. She imagined her boss turning his head, perplexed, doubting his eyes, watching her powder blue Ford sedan go. *No, it couldn't have been. Could it?*

Her face was in shadow, she told herself. He'd never have made out her face. Maybe the blonde hair. That was all, she thought, as the city peeled away.

One thing she did know . . . no turning back now. *No turning back, kiddo,* she could hear Stan telling her. Proud of her, taking her hand.

She hit the highway for as long as she could, eyes always flitting to the mirror, too often probably, more there than out front probably, and the steering suffering from her jitters, because she got honked at more than once, and more than one car swerved to overtake her. But she kept her cool. *Relax,* Stan kept saying in her mind. *Just relax, baby. You're doing just fine.* And she *was* doing just fine. If she could just hold it together and keep her eyes on the asphalt.

The one thing she didn't want to happen is to get a fender bender or to get pulled in. If Mustache *had* recognized her, he'd have wondered why she wasn't laid up in bed like she said. He'd have grown suspicious, checked the safe, found the *$40,000!* gone, and phoned the police instantly, so she could be all over the police radio by now.

He didn't recognize you, baby.

I know, but—what if?

What if nothing.

A howl like a bear in a trap went through her. Her eyes flashed wide as a long hood Peterbilt loomed in the back window. Her head almost went through the roof. The wheel spun in her hands. She grabbed it hard. Her tyres whined. The massive bulk of the truck sailed by. Spooked her so much she pulled over to the side of the road.

Her body was telling her to sleep, so she'd best listen to it and catch forty winks or else end up in a ditch. Some broad in the morgue being ogled and prodded by the glee of men perusing the enemy. For what? Money? *Stupid bitch.*

And at her funeral . . . who?

Next thing she remembered, being woken up by the knuckle-rap of a state trooper. Long face filling the side window. Sunglasses filling the face. Herself filling the sunglasses. A blonde hitching herself upright elbow by elbow, tousled hair like a tramp—in both senses. To the black orbits of a skull.

His lips, desert dry. Desert wry. Non committal.

Questions.

Answers.

Did they satisfy him? Did she satisfy this man? If not, what would it take? Why didn't he wet his lips with his tongue? What was a tongue for anyway? He looked at her from behind the blackness. The look that was always the look. Never scared in the way a woman was scared every day.

But she wouldn't show him she was scared. She wouldn't show him she was powerful either. Men didn't like that, and cops didn't like that especially. They liked, Yes sir. Sorry, sir. I won't let it happen again, sir. I won't do anything this stupid again, sir, said the *widdle girl* to the *big bwave man*.

His face didn't move. His body didn't move. She wondered how he moved in bed. Whether he kept his uniform and sunglasses on.

He touched the peak of his hat, let her go. *Allowed* her to go. She wondered if he wanted to take her to bed the whole time he was talking to her. She wondered whether the whole time he was comparing her to his wife.

She drove, and noticed he was following her at a prowl. At worst, suspicious. At best, protective. *Daddy gonna look after you, sweet pig.* She lay off the accelerator as a mark of obedience. They liked you to obey them. It was the main thing they were interested in, when it came down to it.

Her neck was red hot and damp.

He was still on her tail when she pulled in to the gas station in Blocksville to fill her tank. Paid with her own last few dollars. Considered a while trading in her auto for one with California tags. Then she saw the state patrolman standing, watching her from the edge of the forecourt, leaning against his black and white, arms crossed as she left. Watching him in the rear view as he pulled into the space she left beside the pump, filled his own tank and didn't follow. Grew tiny.

She drove, then the heavens opened. Gushed over her windshield like the water ran down her hips and behind now thinking about it.

Her headache should have told her the air pressure was building and a storm was due. She was a witch like that. Expected it to be a shower—*shower, ha!*—ten, fifteen minute downpour, but it failed to desist after thirty. Forty-five and counting.

The road was layered with a mirror-like sheen pocked by machine-gun holes that refused to relent. *Biblical*, Marion thought. And, as in the Holy Book, lo, did appear a Good Samaritan—or was it the Angel Gabriel glowing up ahead?

Bright illumination broke through the gloom.

Two words. One of them . . . MOTEL.

A letter flickering between life and death, right and wrong. Electricity debating her fate.

The parking lot was empty, its spaces ill-delineated in the dark. Rain sparkling in the glare of the beacon that she saw turn away from her as she arced the Ford to a halt near the cabin at the far end of the chalets, its window the only one lit, and switched off her engine, surprised how loud the rain was on her hood. Louder still on her purse and fingers, her purse being over her head as she ran to the building, throwing herself through the screen door, and shaking the water from her like a dog.

The desk was unmanned. She rang the bell. *Unmanned.* Funny word. Meaning emasculated. In a different context. Obviously in a different context. But no one was there. Not a soul. She could see through to the back—an old typewriter, really old, an Underwood, which made her think of her IBM electric in work, which had made her feel efficient, modern. But she didn't have work anymore, did she? That was behind her. She supposed this was called "the office" was it? She saw a bunk bed of an in/out tray, a spike with checks impaled on it, and a Howdy Doody Ovaltine mug holding pens.

She turned and looked at the rain through the window. Beyond it, a path snaked up to a grotesque, crippled-looking building atop of a slope. Only half-believing her eyes, she squinted then laughed. *The House on Haunted Hill.* Vincent Price would be right at home. She couldn't think anyone else in their right mind would be. She didn't think houses like that existed anymore outside of movies. Mustache, her boss, would have pulled it down in an instant and built a condo.

$40,000!

The screen door banged. The young man used a newspaper as a roof. It was now sodden. He dumped it in the bin next to the umbrella he now held, apologizing for not coming out to greet her. She shook her head, shrugged, laughed. It no longer served a purpose in his hand so he put it down, buckling under a little self-applied shame. He hadn't met her eyes with his own. That told her pretty much everything.

He said he hadn't seen it much worse than this. Er, the weather.

She said, I know.

She confirmed—Yes, just one night, please. She had to make an early start in the morning. Had someone she had to meet in . . . *No, don't tell him. If the police come* . . . She quickly replaced the rest of the sentence with a smile. He smiled back, hesitant and gauche. Poor kid. Flummoxed in the presence of a female. Had he ever seen one before? Didn't he go to the high school dance?

He looked up—not at her, *past* her—said she was the only resident tonight. She had the pick of the bunch. "What's it to be?" Like a game show host. She gave him her lucky number. He said that was absolutely fine, though he didn't believe in luck. "Luck is just a word people use to blame something for things going wrong."

She swallowed and said, "Bright boy . . . Man, I mean."

He didn't take offence. Rummaged in his paperwork a while before dangling the key, escorting her under the covered way, unlocking the door to her temporary abode. She expected to hear the army of cockroaches run for cover, but it was well cared for. Clean, but sparse. The bed was soft. The shower worked. As he demonstrated, swishing the plastic curtain back and forth proudly. It was all she wanted right now. A box to rest in.

He tossed the key from hand to hand, then placed it on the night stand. She asked if there was anywhere to get something to eat? He said, "Not really." He said he'd just made a sandwich and she was welcome to have it. She said that wasn't necessary. He said it wasn't a problem, he could make another one when he went back up to the house.

She imagined the kitchen in the house and Vincent Price, or rats, at the very least. Which was stupid.

"That's kind," she said.

"You can watch TV too, he said, if you want to watch TV." Beckoning her to follow him back to the office.

"No, that's fine. Just a sandwich is fine."

While she eyed the stuffed birds—and they eyed her—he puffed up the cushions of an arm chair. Sat opposite, hands clasped between knees and hunched forward, eager for praise. Egg mayo. What kind of praise was he expecting? *Yum yum.* Did she want a soda? Coffee?

"*Uh-uh.* Coffee will keep me awake."

He produced two bottles of 7-Up from a refrigerator. Handed her one. Offered to get her a glass. She told him not to worry, she'd drink from the bottle. "Wouldn't be the first time." His eyebrow jumped and he nodded away.

To fill the space, she asked his favorite show.

"*I Love Lucy.* Isn't she great?"

"Sure, she's the best."

"You know she's married to that guy who's her husband on screen? Desi Arnaz? In real life? Can you imagine the money they have? That house . . . I mean that house on TV is incredible, but her house in real life? Do you think she has a swimming pool?"

"Well," she said. "You've got a swimming pool out front, too, if you look." He didn't understand. Then he did. He said, "You're funny!"

"Sure," she said. "I'm Lucille fucking Ball."

He didn't seem to like the *fucking* and flinched slightly, then pretended it hadn't bothered him, and squared his shoulders, grinning away his unease. The chasm that opened between them filled her with desolation. She rubbed her eyes.

"Look, I'm sorry, I'm bushed. I appreciate your hospitality but I need to hit the sack."

"That's okay." He stood too. "Was the sandwich okay?"

"The sandwich was perfect. Thank you. You're very sweet."

Shit.

With the opening of the screen door the air was cold.

"I'm, er, sorry I wasn't here when you arrived," the young man said, hands shoved in his jean pockets. "Mother . . . she takes a lot of looking after, and I have to split my time between here and the house. If she hollers . . ."

"I get it."

"She's not well. Not at all well. Hasn't been for years. Never gets out. Which means I don't get out much either. I don't mind. That's my job. Caring for her. That's what I'm here for."

"I'm sorry about that."

"Don't be. Not much to expect, is it? In return for a mother's love?"

"I guess not," Marion breathed.

"I try not to worry. About the medical bills mounting up. About the loan from the bank. About the warning letters. About them coming knocking someday. About what I'll do when that happens. When something happens to her. About this place. Where someone stops for one night, then moves on. That must be nice."

That must be nice, she thought later, back in her room, as she turned on the shower. *Must be nice to have a future. Must be nice getting away from being trapped.* Yeah, she knew what *that* felt like. But had she escaped? Had she really? Her boyfriend was out there somewhere, sleeping in his ignorance, but till she hooked up with him, where was she? Pretty alone, that's where.

The spout sounded like a cat with a hairball before the water came, dredged up from who knows where below the Californ-*ai-ay* desert, trilling against the glass.

She let it run as she slipped out of her dress, smoothing it flat on the cheap, ignominious bed. That was her now, cheap and ignominious as she uncoupled her white *Tide white* bra. Thinking of Stan again as she listened to the water outside and in and needing his touch, and hating that she did, sliding her panties down past her knees to her feet.

Naked, she took the money from her purse and stared at it in its fat brown envelope, as if it might impart some revelation to her, or frog-like be prince-like with a wish. She was way beyond that now. Way beyond fairy tales and princes. She wasn't waiting to be rescued. She could control everything. She could have everything she wanted. The rest of her life was just a build up to this moment. This opportunity. And she was going to take it.

She wished to hell she believed that . . . any of it.

As she stepped under the spray everything was just pounding and hurting and deafening and making no sense. If it all made sense and she was doing the right thing, why did she feel like crap?

Because she'd been *selfish*—that's why. It had been total greed that had motivated her. The greed to have a better life. To snatch it up whatever the cost. Was that the person she was now? Hard, callous, uncaring?

Did she need that money more than the poor young guy who ran this motel, with his sick mother and the bank loans mounting up? Did she need it more than Mustache, even—a man nearing retirement, maybe tearing his hair out right now, having a sleepless night, taking his ulcer medication, whose reputation was on the line, whose *responsibility* was to look *after that money*, and what had he done? *Trusted her.* That was his only mistake. *Trusting her.*

And what about the guy whose money it was? *Cash payment* on a house. A *$40,000 house* for his daughter to live in, raise a family in, make love in, have Thanksgiving in—*gone*. Stolen. All of it. Their savings—*$40,000!*—up in smoke. Their futures ruined. *All* their futures, *destroyed*.

She turned to the shower head, shoulders shaking, skin rippling in goose flesh, her tears mixing with the rivulets as she wept.

She couldn't. Couldn't do it. Didn't *have* to do it.

She could change her mind.

Handle on the lever of the shower. It was up to her.

And she thought: *This was where it all changes.* All she had to do was turn around. Go back. Put things as they were. Nothing was stopping her. *Nothing.*

She yanked the controls to STOP and the flow of water cut out abruptly. Silence fell over her.

Good silence. Happy silence. Decorated only by her breathing. Yes. *Now. Yes.*

The shrill rattle of metal rings along a metal rod.

◄◦►

She stepped out of the shower.

Drew the plastic curtain closed after her. Quickly wrapped herself in the cardboard-stiff towel—*hey, everything* stiff *here, young man?*—tucking it in over her breasts, like she always did, since a child really, how many thousands of times covering herself up, patting herself down, left arm, right arm, armpits and ass, the time honored ritual, using the second towel to adorn her head with the flourish of a turban, and, still damp in places, picked up the money, thrust it deep in her purse, dried her hair with rough, impatient hands—still wet, no shape, spiky, a mess, a blonde *mess*, but who was going to see her, who was going to judge?—and, body only half-dry, feeling the patches of water still on her calves and between her toes as she dressed, the frock sticky, not sliding on, plucked and tugged by her fingers to cooperate, she left the room after a circuit of scrutiny, suitcase packed, key fob dangling.

In the motel office a light was on. Inert birds stared from the back room, but the desk was empty. Nobody home. Except he *had* gone home—O, virgin mine—up the wooden hill to . . . Mother.

Plucking a pen and pad, Marion decided to leave a note for him to find next morning. To say thank you, at least. No . . . Explain? No—not explain.

She looked out again at the ghost train pile where an old woman was dying, half a cent from a Halloween joke, crappy clapboard tower of a time long bulldozed, made from every cheated yesterday with how many nails of regret, how many mortared joints that couldn't be undone?

She took two hundred from the first wad her fingers found in the depths of her purse. Reconsidered. Made it a round five. The message she left with the banknotes read: "Good luck." She paused before adding an X.

The parking lot was mirror-like with puddles, but the rain had ceased, as if she'd turned off that flow, too. The night accepted her car back without question. She pictured the young man running down the snaky steps after her, fearing she'd run off without paying. But that didn't happen and she was glad. His surprise would come in the morning and it'd be a pleasant one. She smiled. It was the kind of thing people did if they were a good person. And she was a good person. She was sure of that now, as she drove.

To keep herself awake she tuned the car radio to 90.7 FM. Harry Belafonte singing "Scarlet Ribbons (For Her Hair)." She turned it up, though that voice was so soft you couldn't turn it up. It soothed her like ointment on a graze, and the surrounding darkness now seemed a comfort not a threat.

She hadn't left her name, and realized now that she'd never asked his—the young man's—and he had never given it. To pass the time she asked herself, was he a Roy or a Ray? A Deke or a Dennis? A Freddie? Fred? Alfred? It didn't matter. She'd never see him again. She might never even *think* of him again, and that made her a little sad. She told herself to snap out of it. Not to go into those *crappy thoughts* again like she always did. Keep firm! Keep a grip of the wheel!

Not long now and it would be over. The record would be off the turntable. The lid would be closed. But for now the music was taking her there.

Phoenix. The sign fled past. Twenty *miles.*

She almost mouthed it to make it real. But it *was* real.

REALITY.

Frog-hopping from crosswalk to crosswalk, traffic light to traffic light, she crept downtown, where it seemed they'd depopulated the city just for her. Leaving the street she knew so well, she swung round back of the real estate office. Five spaces for her company, five for the liquor store, five for the attorney. The RESERVED FOR sign ballooned in her headlights, then died.

She could've driven straight home, held onto the money for the weekend, and put it back in the safe before her boss came in the next morning—but what if he came in early? Before her? *Real* early. He did sometimes. How would she do it then, without being noticed? Or explain it, after walking in, if he'd already found the money had disappeared?

No. She couldn't risk it.

She dropped her set of keys on her desk.

Crossed the room. Hinged back the framed copy of Whistler's Mother. Behind it found the bland grey door of the safe. Her mouth an O, she spun the combination to the numbers she knew, back and forth, clockwise and anticlockwise.

What if he had recognized her at the crosswalk, though? No—that hadn't been her. It couldn't have been. *Why, I was at home sleeping off my headache, sir. You must've been mistaken. It must've been someone who* looked *like* me.

The safe opened without protest. The sigh was hers. She reached for her purse. Took out the brown paper package.

$40,000 . . . *less the five hundred.*

She felt light-headed with shock. *God.* He's sure to notice *that* on the cashing-in slip—*$500 short!* How on earth was she going to explain that? Maybe she could doctor the slip on Monday, but he'd still see it on his bank statement sooner or later. How the—?

"Well, well, employee of the month."

Marion spun around, holding the brown paper package against her chest.

Stepping out of his office, Mustache switched on the overhead light with a limp hand and it blinded her. She tried not to writhe like a rabbit throttled by a wire. Tried to formulate the story in her head, the answers she'd gone through a million times—

But he knew. She could tell. He *knew!*

"I . . . I just . . ."

"You just *what*, Marion?" Skeleton in a charcoal grey suit. Sallow eyes, so like her father's, gliding closer, so full of disappointment, so full of the feeling he knew it would amount to this. "Just thought you might get away with it?"

"No! No, it was just—just a loan," she stammered. "I just needed to borrow it, for a short while. I can explain."

"Good." Mustache said she could explain everything to the police. He was sure they'd understand completely. Picking up the phone, he'd see what they said about this whole *sorry affair* when they got here.

"No, please!" She killed the call he was dialing. Told him in a rush, a fountain, he'd always been good to her—not a lie—given her a job when nobody else did. Shoe store girl, fired. No qualifications, no good in school. She'd always be grateful for that. His kindness. *And she knew he'd be kind now, when she needed it. Knew he'd understand.* The one person who had faith in her.

His laugh a grunt. "And this is what you do to me?"

"Not to you! *Not to you!*" Feeling his hurt, but feeling her own hurt more. "I . . . I wanted to get married."

He laughed. "Well, congratulations. But I wouldn't set the date just yet. You know you'll do time for this?"

"Please. Listen to me. Please, sir. I'm not a bad person. I just made a mistake, that's all. Is a person not allowed to make a mistake? Have you never made a mistake in your whole life?"

"Like stealing $40,000? No. I can tell you I most certainly haven't! Nor would I!" Skull face filling her vision. Too close. Making her giddy. "I have too much respect for the law, and I have too much respect for myself. And people who don't have that end up where you're going. To jail!" He grabbed the phone off her, trailing it away from her grasp.

"If that happens," she stated, for avoidance of doubt, "my life will be over."

"Well, quite frankly, you should have thought of that."

She showed him her palms, voice breaking. "You know if I go to prison I'll be finished. I'll have nothing."

"Young lady, you *always* had nothing. And you always *were* nothing." He was coming forward—skinny, a Charles Atlas "before" picture under the clothes—and Marion found herself walking backwards, almost tripping over her heels, until her back hit the wall and the breath out of her. "Don't you think I always *knew* that?" He looked down from her head to the tips of her toes, eyeballs rolling over every inch of her. "Look at you," he said, lower lip glistening under that used bathroom-brush. "Yes, I took pity on you because you're easy on the eye, you *decorate* the place. But you're nothing but a cheap tramp with dyed hair and the pretense of a respectable job. The truth is you're not respectable at all, are you? And never will be."

Marion moved to get past him but he caught her forearm, so hard it drew a gasp. He clasped it to his chest like a possession. Nicotine breath reaching her flexing nostrils.

"Relax, dear."

She tried to pull back her anatomy but couldn't.

"Hey, hey. We're both grown-ups, aren't we? There's a way out of this, and you know it. Don't you?" His free hand lifted her chin from her chest. "Sure you do. Look at me."

Not taking puzzlement for an answer. But if she needed a ribbon tied on it . . .

"You need to be nice to me, Marion. I'd say you need to be *very* nice to me indeed."

And then it was clear. She understood, because she was a *cheap tramp* and only had the *pretense of a respectable job* because that was all she deserved—*a lie*—and wasn't expected to be nice—*a thief!*—was just expected to obey. Understood the only way for it all to end, now.

"It's okay. It'll be fine, you'll see," he whispered, mockery of a Romeo, between dry pecks to her mouth.

"Put your lipstick on."

She did.

This was the price, the cost, the punishment she had created for herself.

This opening of gangrenous lips fastening onto hers. This jabbing jaw, once, twice. This odor of after shave on his collar turned stale with the Arizona sweat. Skin the texture of a turtle's rubbing against her cheek.

This belt unbuckling from the bag of bones—this *respectable* man—draped in the boss's chair under the boss's desk lamp, its glare glinting off his gold tie pin. This kicking off of her high heels. This kneeling on the office carpet.

This blackness in her mind . . . a prayed-for blackness as she shut her eyes but still had the picture in her head of his open pants, the parting of the folds of his underwear like a vagina, having to hold it, having to caress it, for hours, for days, clammy, hot, vile, until she had to . . .

—try to replace the image with memories of Stan, of his body, of their own activities, the nice ones, but the pictures wouldn't stick. Her boyfriend's

Kowalski smile cut into his seven o'clock shadow and the way he kissed her hand so tender, so true, fingertip by fingertip—*oh baby!*—but her mouth tasted not of him but of the pulsation of corpses. The hands on her scalp placed there like a foul benediction, fingers raking through her platinum curls as something filled her mouth with its flesh.

Scarlet ribbons . . . Scarlet ribbons (for her hair) . . .

After he was done, Mustache gave her the handkerchief he'd used to wipe. Told her she could keep it. Quipped he sure wasn't going to give it to his wife for the laundry. "It's monogrammed. Worth something."

Marion tidied her dress as best she could. Wanted to rinse herself out with bleach, to throw up. Dreamt of doing both as she put back on her earrings, but mainly just wanted to be out of there, gone.

Mustache came back from washing his hands and looked at his watch. "I'd better get home," he said, lifting his jacket from the back of his chair. "I told my wife I was working late, but there's late and late." He placed the parcel of money in the safe, shielding it with his back as he slammed its door and twisted the lock. "I've re-set the combination, so don't go getting any more bright ideas."

His look was one of disdain. Of power. Well, she wouldn't let him have that. Not completely. She took a cigarette from the box on his desk and lit it with his airplane lighter.

"Happy now?"

"Happy?" He actually grinned. "Oh I think happiness is relative, don't you?" He snatched the cigarette out of her mouth and stubbed it out in the ash tray.

"I did what you asked," Marion said. "We made a deal. We forget what happened. Both of us. This is over."

"Oh, you think so?" He smiled with one side of his mouth. A Dick Powell smile. Just needed the tuxedo. "I think that's up to me. I think the terms of our arrangement need to be defined more clearly." He sat on the edge of his desk, knees angular in the baggy pants. "Let's say once a week. Maybe twice. Hell, even three times if I'm in the mood for it and I don't mind looking at that sour mug of yours. What say let's just leave it you're at my beck and call, day and night? That seems fair, don't you think?"

Her stomach turned over. The cancerous smell devoured her again and bile rose in her gullet, hot as a wildfire. *And what if not*, she wanted to say, but she knew what if not. His hand was stroking the phone receiver.

"Now get out."

She did get out. Couldn't wait to get out. Wanting the night air of the parking lot. Thinking of the trail she left and he left, of viscid substances, of liquids. Liquid brimming in her eyes and no, not wanting to give him the satisfaction of that, no way, keeping her cool, her *fucking* cool, her *fucking* strength as she reversed past the Cadillac Eldorado he stood next to, smirk bidding her farewell, smirk saying: *You'll repay my generosity for some time to come, young lady.*

No, that wasn't ALL. Not by a long chalk.

Home, door closed, locked, safe, safe now, and sleep. Her pills saw to that. Tempted to take the whole damn bottle. But Stan, darling Stan—he would be sad. He would pine. She couldn't inflict that on the man she loved. *Love!* That's what she had to remember. Facing her boss the next morning. *Love!* Taking his dictation. *Love!* Touching up her lipstick so she looked presentable. *Love!* Getting the Dick Powell grin again. The glint on the tie pin. Typing a contract when what she wanted to type was—

No. It was private, what had happened. It was their *secret*, the old man's hand on her shoulder said. The liver-spotted hand that had run through her blonde hair, and now patted her shoulder like a father, the father who she never knew much and then was gone. Two years old, and a figment. *REALITY.*

She wanted to talk to Stan on the phone, so she did, like she always did, except for the night before, when she'd been driving to the motel. He asked how come, and she said, "No reason." After a while he said, "Shoot, you don't have much to say tonight." She said sorry. He said, "In that case I'll go. This call is costing money." The burr of the dead line made her tummy flip again. She hated that sound. The sound of him not being there.

But she couldn't *tell* him, could she?

What would he think of her? Not much. *Tramp. Blonde. Nothing.*

She kept silent for a week.

Even when they hooked up the next lunch time in that same hotel, that same concrete box with the same squeaky fan, in the same unclean sheets, and she kissed, but didn't want to do more, not this time, honey, please. Just wanted to lie there, just hold each other, was that all right? Did he mind just doing that?

But a week later she couldn't hold it inside any longer. The pictures, the sensations, the knotted, horrible feelings carving her empty like a hollowed log from the inside out. Couldn't keep silent with them swirling around in her brain anymore, jostling there amongst the sweetest memories of childhood, tainting those other memories like a stain that spread and spread.

Stan half-lay against the off-white pillow, striped by the sun—Phoenix, 6.09 p. m.—sucking the cigarette to its root as he listened to what she said, then gave a long blue exhale. She wondered if she'd upset him, because when she opened her mouth to speak he showed her his palm.

"Let me think about this for a goddamned minute, okay?"

He sat up, arc of his long spine over the sheet that covered his legs, which he tore off and strode, naked, to the window. Hand through his black hair. Looking out, not looking at her.

She went to the bathroom and washed her face. She'd predicted he'd be angry. Of course he would. She wiped away the salty lines that streaked her make-up. Hitching her breath, applied it afresh, a duty. Max Factor. The way a woman ought to look, wasn't that right? The way a woman needed to look for her man. No rawness in her throat. No horrors in her mind. No sick feeling of worthlessness in her soul. Just like in the movies.

He didn't turn when she walked back in.

"You know what this means? This means we've got him," he said. "Forty grand is nothing to what we can squeeze out of that old goat now."

She frowned.

Almost laughing, he held her by the upper arms—soft, not hard, not brutal—as if about to shake sense into her. "You think his wife wants to find out about what he's been doing? You think his friends in the golf club do? It's called blackmail, baby! And we've got him over a goddamn barrel. We can bleed him for—what? A thousand a week? Three thousand? It doesn't have to stop when I pay off my loan, either. This can go on forever. This is a cash cow, right here! And the beauty is, he'll never go to the police about the money because it'll all come out about you." He held her heart-shaped face in his palms and his lips met hers, but it wasn't the kiss that she'd be waiting for, or the embrace she craved. Instead, he just tittered like he'd backed a winning pony at the races. "This is beautiful. *You're* beautiful!"

Was she? *Was* she beautiful?

White shirt slung on unbuttoned, he asked did she want to go for pizza, dim sum, or a burrito? Her choice, he said, arms wide and magnanimous.

Later, watching the pointed end of a wedge of dough slide into his mouth, and the Bourbon after it, and the grease of mozzarella and pepperoni shining on his chin and lips as he spoke, and the finger that wiped it as he laughed, and as they clinked glasses, she realized he was celebrating. To him it didn't matter whether she was using her body for love of for profit. So what? They loved each other. This other thing was about money. What difference did it make, if it meant they could be happy?

And she thought, *Fuck you.*

Fuck you, and when he looked up, puzzled, she was gone. The chair opposite, empty.

She drove.

Foot on the gas. No suitcase. No map. Passing the city limit signs. Not knowing which highway she was on, whether she was heading for Hollywood or the Grand Canyon. They said that Grand Canyon was deep. Real deep. Maybe deep enough for her.

And her thoughts went round and round till a cop car wailed. The sky in her rear view streaked with the bruises of sundown. The blue lights blasting into her eyes slowed her down to a halt. Her tires kicked up a cloak of dust as she braked. In her side mirror the figure approached through a sandstorm. Emerging, squat, broad.

"Hands on the steering wheel, ma'am," said a high pitched voice.

A woman's face lowered to the side window, asking politely but firmly if she knew she'd been driving 10 m.p.h. over the speed limit for the last ten miles.

Highway patrol uniform. No sunglasses. Blue gray eyes. Pale skin. Freckles peppering her cheeks. She'd never seen a female one before. Didn't know there was such a thing. Like unicorns. She almost smiled. Almost.

Ma'am, is there something wrong? . . . Ma'am?

Marion opened her mouth, and spoke.

MOUSELODE MAZE

CHRISTOPHER HARMAN

The Maze? Been here since Henry VIII. I've been told it's grown like Topsy this Spring. Not been looking myself. It's of historic interest apparently, along with the rest. It's listed on the *Register of Parks and Gardens*."

From the project manager's distracted responses to Maurice's and Trevor's questions, the refurbishment of the sprawling ivy-clad Tudor pile, Mouselode House, was his main concern. The hotel was due to open in a couple of months.

Maurice and Trevor were sitting in a deep, ugly sofa in the long lounge backing onto the immense rear garden. Tavener was standing, his face stressed behind round-lensed glasses. He'd been on the way to somewhere else. Hammering, laughter and banter of workmen had punctuated their talk. Paint fumes were giving Maurice an ache in his sinuses.

"It doesn't mention the maze," Trevor reminded Maurice, brandishing his copy of the specification.

"Work your ideas around it. That's what we advise."

With that dampening reminder that other firms were putting in proposals to get the contract, Tavener left, saying he'd be in his office if they had any matters to ask about or wished to discuss. Maurice had the impression he'd prefer it if they didn't.

He stood and faced the mullioned window. The maze was about three hundred yards away. Trevor got up laboriously.

"That yew––it'd take some pruning." He shook his head, sucked in a breath between his teeth. "Could be a third of a mile of hedging. The cost in man-hours . . . Looks dense as an earthwork. It challenges the house. I'd grub it up if it was up to me."

"Isn't up to either of us," Maurice said. He agreed with Trevor but wasn't about to admit it. He'd always liked the idea of working on an ancient garden, and the maze should have given it even greater appeal. But it loomed, threatened, a dense bank of gloomy greenness.

Not liking the maze didn't matter, what did was Trevor's negativity about the whole project. Surprising, as for months he'd agreed with Maurice that they needed something high-profile with big money to go with it. Two years on from setting up *Viridian Vistas*, turnover was shaky; they'd been surviving on mainly residential jobs and barely breaking even for the past six months. It was timely, an associate informing Maurice about the hotel chain seeking proposals from firms. He'd emailed to express an interest and included a link to the *Viridian Vistas* website.

Way off our patch, Trevor pointed out––about eighty miles. Maurice suggested they could relocate for a period if necessary (easy for Trevor following his recent divorce, though Maurice didn't say so). A question for later was whether their own crew or local labour would do the spade work. Not our speciality, big upper-crust estates, Trevor said. Maurice didn't deny that, but where was the harm in going to Mouselode even if just to see 'the lie of the land'? Trevor acquiesced––though, as the date approached, he'd grumbled at the cost of two nights in the Oakshott Inn, the tight deadline for working out a proposal that had a chance of success. He'd been subdued on the train up from Stoke-on-Trent.

"Standing here won't butter the parsnips," Trevor said, sounding stoical as he headed to the rear vestibule. Maurice followed, reassured that Trevor was being professional and putting his reservations to one side.

In the garden they separated. Weak sunshine mitigated the neglect and air of indifference. He noted overgrown rhododendrons, chipped balustrades, ragged box hedging, bindweed in the beds, moss and algae on the paths; and the lawns were overdue a mowing. The title of the specification, *Paradise*

Garden, suggested what the owners had in mind, and the garden itself seemed to be striving for that, here and there in mists of bluebells, banks of dandelions. Willows whispered pleasantly. Maurice had overheard talk of the hotel, like others in the chain, being promoted as a spa. In a converted barn complex behind a stand of beech trees, there was already a gym and pool.

He came to a grassy slope ending at low bushes which mostly disguised the western boundary wall and obscured where the garden became meadow and scattered copses extending to hazy distances. He wrote into his pad: '*Replace the rotted bench on west margin with pergola?*' Something he'd like to do, sit here and contemplate the illusion of boundlessness.

Half an hour later, reading his notes, he thought the sky had clouded over. It hadn't, but the maze was startlingly before him, a dark green, immense mass. There were persons in it. He doubted he would have heard them but for the silence of the willows. What was she saying: "Come on" or "Come in"? A muffled quality, as if the voice was buried in the total density of yew. Another voice, just as murky, a deliberation in each separate word like a knife sawing tough meat: the word "Ear" or "hear" or "here" coming through. Demanding something? Or were the speakers lost? Trying to find each other? Needle-like leaves came into focus before him. Why should it seem he was the subject of whatever was being said, when nobody inside could see through the dense hedging, three feet in width to judge from the entrance arch about ten yards away. Now light, restless impacts accompanied the voices, a faint jangle. Was that a lead; did they have a pet dog with them? His heart laboured. He eyed the entrance, sure the voices' owners were about to reveal themselves, and he didn't think he could bear that.

Trevor's voice was a shove at his back. "Not supposed to be thinking about the maze."

The fading of the voices was like waking from a troubling dream. Nobody was going to appear in the maze entrance, he knew that with an iron and welcome certainty.

"I'm not." He looked at his watch.

"Yeah. Time for some grub."

◄◦►

"You're the garden guys, aren't you?" The youngish woman wore a fixed-look-
ing smile and, over her lanky figure, a knee-length woollen one-piece of
horizontal bands of bright colours. Her companion was in jeans and a black
suit jacket, chestnut hair bisected by a turquoise stripe. Salads and herbal
teas on their trays. Maurice and Trevor had mostly finished eating.

"Hope to be," Maurice said, gesturing for the two women to take the empty
seats at their table. *Cath's Caff* was full, mainly of workers from Mouselode.

Fierce-eyed, Trevor grinned at the women. "Hey Maurice, *The Garden
Guys* sounds better than *Viridian Vistas*." He thumbed at Maurice. "'*Viridian*'
was his idea. I wanted '*green*,' but it had already been taken."

Maurice stretched his lips towards a smile. The women's were politely
non-committal as they weighed Trevor up. "Trevor," Trevor said, jabbing
his hand across the table. A bit much, Maurice thought, joining in the hand
shaking. Three other first names followed.

"We're *Hi-Class Interiors*," Thelma, the darker one, said in an accent more
at home in Mouselode House than in *Cath's Caff*. She was as unsmiling as
her partner was the opposite.

Tessa gamely filled a beat of silence. "We've been looking at some old
photographs this morning."

"Any of the garden?" Maurice asked.

"A few. We were thinking of blowing some up for the dining room."

"We *were*," Thelma said, picking at her salad. "They're pretty ropey. Been
in a tea chest for a hundred years, we think. Only found the other day.
Workmen were clearing out a dark corner of the basement."

"They date from the early nineteen-twenties if other old documents and
papers are anything to go by," Tessa said, persisting in her enthusiasm.
"That's when the last family owners lived there, though they were pretty
distant. Dunlop, they were called. Couple of sisters, from Bristol. Inherited
1919. Died a few years later in the flu epidemic. They didn't exactly endear
themselves to the local community from what I've heard."

"Incomers rarely do," Maurice said; a statement for which he'd no particular
evidence.

As the conversation moved towards the highs and lows of running mid-
dle-sized businesses, Maurice felt restless.

"Have you been in the maze?" He wasn't sure he'd caught a tone of idle interest.

"They haven't got time to muck around in mazes, Maurice." Trevor did an ingratiating eye-roll at the women.

Thelma said, "No, we haven't."

While Maurice was trying to work out if she was agreeing they hadn't time to 'muck around in mazes' or confirming that she and Tessa simply hadn't entered this one, Tessa said:

"But we plan to," a timidly triumphant smile, "because we've . . . got a plan."

"Got a plan, eh?" Devilish amusement in Trevor's eyes.

Thelma sighed, eyed Maurice, and said dismissively, "A plan of the maze. It was with the stuff in the basement. Cheating if you ask me. So, who does what?"

Maurice was glad of the swerve away from the subject of the maze.

"Let me guess. You're the practical one." Thelma nodded at Trevor, who looked pleased she'd got him so right. Now an exaggerated frown of enquiry at Maurice.

"Me?" He acted false modesty. "Just flair, imagination . . ."

"I make sure the work gets done," Trevor said, making a grab for more attention. "Practical ideas, nothing too fancy. Work done well and to cost." Then he said, managing to sound lubricious, "Like to get my hands dirty."

Maurice wondered if the women noticed there were tiny threads of ingrained dirt around Trevor's fingernails.

Trevor was saying how he'd "done it all"––tree work, green-housing, hedging, running a garden centre. He didn't mention the latter going bankrupt.

◄◦►

Back in the Mouselode grounds Trevor moved off, pushing the wheel measuring device that was like a wheelbarrow without the barrow. Over the next forty minutes or so Maurice would hear its ticking and occasionally see Trevor, thickset in his donkey jacket, trundling the thing, half his attention on the digital counter, stopping now and then to write down figures.

As he strolled, Maurice wrote down colour schemes, keeping in mind seasonal flowering, suitable shrub varieties. Gravel or paved pathways linking uniquely characterised spaces? A scent garden? Sunken garden? Croquet lawn? All paths lead to the maze, he thought, as green needle leaves filled his vision. Somewhere Trevor's wheel ticked. His heart was as quick and light. Voices again, this time deeper inside the maze, soft and dry. Tick, tick, went his heart. The ticking ceased and Trevor was beside him.

"So. You're here again," Trevor said.

"Can you hear them?" Maurice asked.

Listening, Trevor started to nod confidently. "Obviously they do have time to mess about in mazes."

Tessa and Thelma. Maurice wanted Trevor to be right.

"Maybe following that plan."

"Like a maze this size needs a plan," Trevor said.

"Somebody must have thought so," Maurice said. "Wonder how they're getting on."

Trevor passed his wheel to Maurice. "I'll ask them——and if they fancy a meal with us at the Oakshott tonight."

"Why not just wait here? They'll be out in no time." There was tension in Maurice's voice.

"Wait to pounce you mean? Not a good look." Trevor listened, shook his head, chuckled condescendingly. "Deary me. Sounds like they're stuck. I'll go and fish them out. Shouldn't take long. We're not talking Hampton Court here."

Maurice heard no voices now, lost or otherwise. Trevor was looking up at the entrance arch, rubbing his hands together. Stopping short of spitting on his palms, which Maurice had half-expected, Trevor passed through and the hedges rustled as if noticing him.

Maurice could have got back to work but felt inclined to wait. He laid down the wheel. There was nobody else in the garden, as far as he was aware, and to judge from the silence the maze could have been just as deserted. Trevor seemed profoundly absent, the maze a network of utterly empty corridors. Five minutes gone and Maurice heard no exchange of greetings. He went and sat on the stone plinth of a crumbling bird-table some yards off. More time passed. He strolled towards the house. Air hissed through the willows. He stepped over a snake-like length of perished rubber hosepipe. He looked back to the maze, returned reluctantly to the entrance. He called out Trevor's name at an inner layer of hedging that imposed like a prison wall. With no shouted reply, an uneasy sense of obligation had him crossing the threshold.

He walked left, took a right after several yards, then another left. A right turn, another. "Trevor!" and the silence swallowed the name as if the narrow ways had ceilings as well as walls of yew. More passageways and he had an unreasonable sense of enormity.

Trevor's appearance was at once startling and a relief. He shook off a dull perplexity in his flushed features.

"That went well," he said, admitting defeat with a feeble breath of laughter.

"Maybe they found another way out," Maurice said. Whoever 'they' were.

"They're still in there," Trevor said, and Maurice was convinced he was right. "Their voices were like cuckoo calls—all over the place. Obviously got time to act daft." His voice went thin, peevish. "I'll bet interior decoration's their hobby, not their bread and butter like our thing is for us. Family money behind them. Posh and rich." A sharp glance upwards, as if suddenly intimidated by the height of the hedges. "Heard an animal too. Running thumps. Hare maybe? How would I know? Right, lead on."

Trevor following, Maurice knew the route back until a passageway seemed an exact repetition of the one before. The blanket of cloud and his vanished sense of direction hid the house. After a series of random choices, he expelled a breath of relief at an opening ahead affording a column of grass and willow unstable as an image on an old television. They stepped out from an airless dryness into a downpour, ran to red brick and mullioned glass scored through with slanting rain.

In the rear vestibule, Trevor said, "Great. How long's this going to last?" He sounded glad of something concrete to complain about. They stared. The maze was like a low, drear, green-grey cloud. To Maurice, it didn't feel like they'd discovered the way out; it seemed more like the exit had found them, that the maze had deigned to release them.

In the lounge Trevor played *Angry Birds* on his tablet while Maurice read a biography of "Capability" Brown on his. After an hour with no sign of the rain letting up, Trevor said he was off to the Oakshott. "Need a pint. That maze dried me out."

"I want to see those photographs," Maurice said.

"Yeah, fill your boots," Trevor said, stalking in the direction of the front exit from the building.

Looking for *Hi-class Interiors*, Maurice entered a room with ping-pong and pool tables. The latter was a third covered with photographs.

Half a dozen views of the garden. There might have been vibrant colours, sunshine, but there was no way of telling from the drab, faded black and white. Plant varieties and even trees weren't clearly identifiable, nor locations in the garden. But a section of maze wall was unmistakeable, like the leading edge of a dirty glacier. No people on any of the pictures until he spotted two, and they weren't in the garden.

He didn't doubt that the women must be the Dunlop sisters. He recognised the main street of the village. They were turned inward and back, clearly surprised and furious at the impertinence of the photographer snapping them from behind. Both were tallish in straight, tubular, twenties-style 'flapper' dresses, faintly grubby, unless that was the poor quality of the photograph, though hems were unmistakably frayed. The shorter woman wore a beret from which her uncombed hair clasped her features in a narrow arch. The taller one's hair was in a bob that straggled out from a cloche hat. Curious how the enormous holdall-type bag suspended between them from looping handles held his attention more than the women did. It was misshapen, its contents pushing out the sides, bizarrely suggestive of knees or elbows. The women might have been broadly heading in the direction of an antique shop a few yards ahead. Was that where they intended to add to whatever the bag contained?

Sunshine brought Trevor back to the Mouselode lounge about an hour later. Maurice joined him at the makeshift food and drinks table where Elsie, elderly and big in her blue housecoat, served them mugs of tea and coffee. They took their drinks outside where *Hi-class Interiors* were sitting in plastic seats at a round, rusted metal table on the rain-glazed, broken paving of a patio. Soft drinks in tall glasses were before them.

"Look at these two ladies of the manor," Trevor said with heavy good-humour. Tessa's smile faltered. Thelma's lit cigarette twitched between her fingers.

"Mind if we join you?" Maurice said as Trevor lowered himself into a spare seat.

He rose again, "Damn." Tessa passed him a filthy rag to wipe off rain droplets.

"Saw you hurtling out of the maze earlier," Thelma said, little puffs of smoke exhaled in time with her words. "Like something was after you."

"Rain was," Trevor said. He took a gulp of coffee.

Maurice didn't want to talk about the maze. "I only went in to rescue him," he said, genially.

"I didn't need rescuing," Trevor said, casting Maurice a sour glance. "Looking for you two, *actually*. Thought we heard you . . ."

"You heard wrong. Some of us have work to do," Thelma said.

Trevor appeared to grudgingly accept her explanation and stared out into the garden.

"I've seen the photos," Maurice said. "Not a lot of use to us, I'm afraid. Recognised a bit of the outer wall of the maze but not much else."

"They were taken by a local man, 'Gerald Picton, Professional Photographer' —it's stamped on the backs," Thelma said. "Presume he was invited into the grounds to make a record round about when the sisters were in residence. But the photo of them in the village looking decidedly miffed is a bit of a mystery."

"'Miffed' is putting it mildly," Maurice said. "Giving him quite the 'evil eye.'"

"How about joining us for a meal tonight at the Oakshott?" Trevor interrupted with determination.

Thelma cut in as Tessa was about to reply, saying they were due at an art exhibition opening in Liverpool that evening. Trevor's face clouded over.

"Wine and nibbles," Tessa said sheepishly as if that might soften the blow. She drew herself up in her chair. "I've heard the maze's days might be numbered."

An abrupt change of subject, though Maurice would have chosen another.

Tessa went on. "Someone in the village has written anonymously to the board about a body found in the maze around the time of the Dunlops."

Thelma took a long drag from her cigarette, her eyes squinting.

"As if that's going to change their minds."

"You've got that right," Trevor said, matching her disdain. "Folk have been dropping dead in and around old places like this for centuries."

Neither of the women could provide Maurice and Trevor with any other details about the 'body'. After more inconsequential chat, Maurice muttered something about needing to catch Tavener and left. He took his empty mug back to the lounge and commented in a jocular undertone to Elsie, a long-time resident in the village: "Just heard about the body in the maze."

Elsie pursed her lips like a school dinner lady. "Oh that. Well, you heard right."

"Old news, I suppose. Hundred years back."

"Poacher he was. People think he wandered in at night and got lost. Died naturally, they say. Happen got frightened and his heart gave out. He wasn't young." Spoken like it happened a month ago. "An animal got at him before he was found. A big 'un, with big teeth." She beamed sweetly past Maurice's shoulder. "Mr. T., what can I do you for?"

"You wanted a word?" Tavener said to Maurice.

"No, the question has been answered," Maurice said, his expression upbeat and positive as always in the man's presence.

◄◦►

He lay awake in his room in the Oakshott. Creaks from different points on the floor of Trevor's room next door had too much of a hesitant, almost searching quality to be sleepwalking. They merged into his own pounding footfall as he fled along stuffy leaf-lined alleyways, his heart in his mouth as something pursued him. A lightly thundering gait, a snap of jaws. Exiting a passageway he glimpsed a dark, baggy body enter it from another yards away. Running was like swimming; he clawed to escape. A balloon of terror inside him burst and he awoke. Fading in his mind's eye, a fastness of yew, the terror boxed into it.

Selecting Delius from the playlist on his phone and attaching the tiny earpieces, Maurice walked through the garden after breakfast. The sun sprawled indistinctly in soapy white cloud with the faintest tinge of green, as if cast up from his surroundings. With *The Walk to the Paradise Garden* in his ears, he wrote into his notebook: "*rhododendrons like outposts of maze (cut back), silver birch to counter-balance?*" At the edge of his vision, the maze's darkness conjured a low humming bass-line under Delius's serene, sliding harmonies.

He ate lunch alone in *Cath's Caff* as Trevor had already eaten. Returning to Mouselode, he saw him checking soil acidity. In the house, Maurice signed into the *Gardeners World* app on his tablet and worked up a 3D plan of the grounds. Later he found Trevor rolling the measuring wheel back and forth as he joked with plasterers in the reception area. His smile slipped as Maurice approached.

"Thought you'd done all the measuring," Maurice said.

"Not in the maze I haven't."

"What's the point?" Maurice said, the wrongness of it a wire in his chest.

"To get the measure of it. Flummoxed me yesterday. Won't this time."

They went to the lounge where Trevor pulled a packet of folded, thick, discoloured paper from an inside pocket. "Got this off Tessa."

'Tessa' now was it? The rejection of his invitation to join them in the Oakshott forgotten? He handed Maurice the item. Maurice grimaced as he opened it out. The stiff, yellowish paper could have been the thick heel skin off a monstrous foot. The interlocking passageways in the plan doubled, blurred, rotated in his swimming vision. He blinked hard, swallowed, looked again. "Doesn't even show the entrance. And what's that figure eight?" It floated in the two-inch wide margin surrounding the maze. "Page number?" He peered for signs of a razor-blade cut. "If the plan is from a book, it's not been torn out."

"Might make sense when I'm inside," Trevor said.

Maurice thrust the plan at Trevor who took it and left. After a moment Maurice watched him pass through the maze entrance and out of sight. Elsie, polishing the hot water urn, had been watching too. "Not again," she said with a click of her tongue.

Maurice attempted a breezy insouciance. "Almost addictive, that maze. It's like the Tudor equivalent of a computer game."

"Well, I wouldn't know about that," Elsie said. "But I know it's bad news." Biting her thumbnail, she glanced about. "My husband, when he was alive, said he wanted to put a torch to it. We sneaked here before we were married. Early evening, light going, house empty, up for sale. It was his idea, but we only got to the entrance. This breeze struck up. Hedges were all a-quiver with it, hissing. Only that wasn't it at all. Whispering it was, like a whole crowd of people. The sound built up then faded like they were moving, and

I mean quick, like there was bees swarming along the runnels, really fast. Well, we were fast. Out of there and back in the village in no time."

"Like it," Maurice said, as if she'd benefited him with a well-honed humorous anecdote.

"Yeah, bet you do," she said with a sigh, as if used to listeners' disbelief.

Sometime later, as he was dozing off in the lounge, Maurice's phone rang. It was their admin assistant Monica complaining that she'd texted Trevor three times regarding an urgent technical enquiry from a contractor client and he hadn't replied.

"He's on another planet at the moment. I'll have a word when he's free," Maurice said and rang off.

Almost immediately there was an alert on his phone screen. What now? And on WhatsApp?

But it was Trevor, with a picture and some accompanying words.

"Me at the centre. Result!"

The photograph was a selfie. Behind Trevor's beaming face, a slight incline of bare earth and a hedge border with an opening into a shadowy parallel passageway. Maurice brought the screen close up to his eyes. With two separating fingers, he expanded the image. The scream of the hot water urn became a faint shriek on a bed of humming voices.

A squat, dark shape was a blurred blot against that inner wall of spiny leafage. Wait a minute——were they slender trunks of yew or the pipe-like legs of some animal? Was Trevor about to find out?

He ran out of the room, not caring about the turning heads. He slowed, approaching the maze. The entrance seemed the threshold of a malignant forest. Entering, heading down one passageway, then a parallel one, and onwards through a series of turns, he could finally let out an enormous exhalation of relief.

A familiar easy beat, not the rapid ticks of the measuring wheel pushed in a panic; sounding a dozen yards away, but possibly many times that, taking account of the confounding layout of passageways. As he listened, the ticking ceased.

Around him the air was inert, dead. It felt like time had stopped. Maurice moved to make it start again.

Passing through an opening he paused, snatched a breath. For a second or two he wasn't alone and wished he were. But the figure wasn't moving and wasn't about to. Not someone, but an item of statuary in a dead-end like an alcove. If it was intended as relief or as a point of interest in the monotony of the maze, it was a failure. Chanced on unexpectedly, the slender, life-sized, all too human shape was bound to startle. The long, pale drapes of stone resembled the 'twenties fashion adorning the Dunlop sisters in the photograph. This figure reminded him of the taller one in the cloche hat, though weathering rendered the head-covering indistinct. He doubted there was an actual likeness of her—but he'd have to see the face to ascertain that. That raised the question, *Why would a statue be placed facing directly into the hedge*? There was no way he was going to check, but with the old stone probably pre-dating the Dunlops, the face was probably as worn away as the hat.

He realised he hadn't heard Trevor's wheel for several minutes when a noise, as of someone crashing into foliage, came from somewhere behind him. It knocked away his edgy consideration of the statue. He walked tentatively to an opening further off than the one through which he'd entered. Through that and beyond two or three more, he found Trevor.

He was stooped, hands on his knees as if he'd run to that point. He jerked back, shocked, before realising it was Maurice.

"Congratulations, you got to the centre," Maurice said, the hardness in his voice an attempt to compensate for the nervy weakness he felt.

"Not with any help from this." Trevor pulled the maze plan from his jacket pocket. Maurice noticed he didn't have the wheel with him.

"There was a woman," Trevor said wonderingly, as if it had been an extraordinary and disturbing eventuality. "Other side of a hedge."

Just a woman then. If there had been a beast near the centre, it had been a harmless one. Trevor clearly hadn't noticed anything amiss in his own selfie.

"*Hi-Class* . . ."

"No!" Trevor said irritably, violently shaking his head. "Someone else. Saw her through a thin section of hedge. Very slim, she was. Grey-whitish gear down to her knees . . ."

"Was it a statue?" Maurice asked, not sure he wanted it to have been. The one he'd seen was enough to contend with.

"Statue? What *are* you talking about?" Trevor didn't wait for an answer, and Maurice thought he'd be pushed to provide one he'd be comfortable with.

"There was a dog with her." Trevor looked at Maurice as if for confirmation that it could have been. "I mean . . . the size."

A shadowy, indeterminate alternative creature trundled through Maurice's head; a bulky, baggy piece of nonsense the stress of the maze must have created. He'd think the same of the statue if not for recalling its solidity.

"Leaping around her," Trevor went on. "Not barking."

The same animal Maurice thought he'd seen against the hedge in the selfie? He showed Trevor the picture on his phone, pointed out the questionable shape. "Was that it?"

Trevor gave it an irritable, cursory glance. "That's leafage and shadows."

Maurice so wanted him to be right. "Did you say anything?"

"What––through a hedge to a complete stranger?"

"'I seem to be lost'?" Maurice suggested.

"I wasn't." He emitted a small cough. "I was just puzzling how to get to the entrance."

"And how's that working out?" Maurice said, folding his arms.

Trevor considered the ground, gestured vaguely at the opening Maurice had emerged from. "After you, as you seem to be in your element."

Retracing his steps as well as he could remember them, Maurice entered each new passageway with a caution he hoped Trevor wouldn't pick up on. Trevor walked close behind, breathing heavily. Maurice was glad there wasn't the metallic ticking of the wheel to give them away in the dead silence. No birdsong must mean nothing nested here. Though the animal lurked in his mind, more than anything he didn't want to encounter the statue again. They were far past it, surely, though such was the confusion of passageways there was no guarantee it wouldn't reappear. And it already had in his imagination, facing him now from the end of a long perspective, its face corroded.

A sharp, hopeless turn on Maurice's part and they burst out into sunshine and birdsong. Without a word, Trevor hurried ahead of him towards the house. Maurice didn't feel aggrieved, as he had no sense of something personally achieved.

In the lounge he suggested Trevor should check his phone for texts from Monica. Trevor mumbled some reply and disappeared towards the front entrance.

Tessa and Thelma were testing wood stain on a section of panelling. Others were packing equipment away. Maurice looked at his watch. Ten minutes past five. Time had quickened in the maze, or seemed to have. He checked his phone to work out when Trevor had sent that selfie of himself at the centre. Nearly two hours ago. Well, his phone couldn't lie. Thelma saw him.

"What's the food like at the Oakshott Inn? We're fussy eaters. Should be finished in half an hour." Brusque but with a slight air of making amends for her and Tessa's previous refusal. Maurice said their meals the previous evening had been excellent, though in truth they'd been merely adequate. They agreed that the four of them should meet at the Oakshott at six-thirty.

⋅◦⋅

He had to concur with Thelma and Tessa's expert and amused assessment, in low voices, of the decor in the Oakshott's dining room. Too much brass on the walls, too many stuffed animals staring down at them from glass cases, from cross beams. After they gave their orders, Maurice broke the silence. "Trevor got to the centre of the maze."

"All by myself. This . . ." He rooted in his pocket and brought out the maze plan. "Was useless." Unhappy with the plan or the women for giving it to him, or both, he proffered it to whichever of them would take it. Thelma considered him, tight-lipped. Tessa took the plan and began to turn it around in her hands. She got her phone out and started to tap with her forefinger. She glanced up bashfully. "Don't mind me, just had a thought."

"Wonder if the book it's taken from makes sense," Trevor said.

The Oakshott manager was serving that evening. He placed down two starter dishes before Maurice and Thelma. He had a name badge: "Clive Picton: Oakshott Inn."

Maurice pointed at the badge. "There was a photographer here . . ."

"Yes, my great-granddad. Vanished early twenties, nobody knew where. He'd had dealings with the Dunlop sisters. Some say he's buried under the maze—there's not a scrap of evidence though. The family never liked that kind of talk. And nobody was ever going to dig up the whole maze to find out. What's all this about?" He looked wary of what he might hear.

Maurice deferred to Thelma who said, "Photographs, found at Mouselode the other day. His name is on the backs. There's one of the Dunlop sisters on this very street, not looking pleased with the photographer."

Picton's expression darkened. "Carrying a bag? Huge, shapeless thing?"

Thelma nodded. Picton blew out and stalked off.

"I've got a theory," Tessa said. She showed them the display on her phone, rows of symbols. "If you turn that eight on its side, it's more like the symbol used in mathematics for infinity." She held up the plan and phone screen for them to see for themselves.

Thelma looked unconvinced. Picton returned with the remaining starters, his expression closed. When he'd gone she said, "A jokey suggestion that you can wander in the maze forever? Why is it placed outside then?"

Trevor didn't contribute much to conversation during the rest of the meal. Maurice took up the slack, not always holding the women's attention as they glanced, trying to work out Trevor's mood. His face was like a heavy mask as he ate as unthinkingly as an animal. He left without a word after stolidly consuming his bread-and-butter pudding. Thelma and Tessa departed soon after.

"Everyone's jumping ship," Picton observed, as Maurice stepped up to the bar. Facing away, Picton fixed him a whisky and water.

"That bag––it was discovered between their beds when the women were found dead of the flu. When the police opened it there was this disgusting smell of rot. It was full of corpses of little animals, ferrets, mice, moles, all dried up, mummified or pickled, or so the story goes. There were bloodstains in it too, and some big candles. Ragged holes at the bottom of the bag, at each corner and midway along, like acid had burnt through." He turned, placed Maurice's drink down.

"What happened to it?"

"Nobody knows. Chucked? Burned? Probably best thing. God knows what it was for, all that weird stuff inside."

◄◦►

Maurice was finishing breakfast and chatting with Mrs. Picton when Trevor came in, greeting them cheerfully. He sat, snapped open his napkin and ordered porridge, a full English fry-up, toast, coffee.

"Lottery come up for you?" Maurice asked. There was a striking contrast to last night in Trevor's demeanour.

"Next best thing." He swigged his glass of orange juice in one go. "Going home. Glad about that."

Maurice said he'd booked a taxi to pick them up here at the inn at eleven-thirty. They could eat lunch at Preston railway station. Mrs. Picton brought in a bowl of porridge.

"I'm taking a last walk around the garden. I suggest we try and have a few words with Tavener," Maurice said.

Trevor was concentrating on parallel grooves he was making with the edge of his spoon in his porridge. "Yeah, could do."

"Before then, let's get some ideas together, an overall theme that'll get his ears pricking up. He might put a good word in with hotel group board if we play our cards right."

His heart hadn't been in what he'd said, but he doubted Trevor noticed. He just stared at the patterned surface of porridge, uncomfortably maze-like it seemed to Maurice. "Yep, he might at that."

"See you about ten?"

"Ten. Yes," Trevor said, with a rapid nod of his head. "Don't *worry*," he went on, in a testy, placating tone. Taken aback by Trevor's direct stare from eyes that shone wetly, Maurice nevertheless thought he was right about 'going home'. The sooner the better. He wasn't even sure he wanted *Viridian Vistas* to get the contract.

Packing in his room, Maurice heard Trevor enter next door. If he was getting ready to leave, he did so silently. They had to vacate their rooms by eleven, so Maurice took his wheelie luggage bag down to the reception where he was permitted to leave it behind the counter.

⫸

Maurice strolled the garden but his critical thinking had come to a stop. He went into the house where Elsie served him a coffee. Ten o'clock and no sign of Trevor. He rang Trevor's mobile number and was dolefully unsurprised at the recorded message.

Thelma came up. "Glad to see your colleague has cheered up."

Maurice nodded, recalling Trevor's brittle brightness. "Just wondering where he is now."

"Told me he had to fetch something he'd left in the maze."

Maurice leapt up, spilling his coffee, startling her. "When was this?"

"Five minutes ago." Thelma looked mystified at the bad news she'd apparently delivered. And Maurice couldn't have enlightened her.

He looked out at the high outer green wall. Ten minutes went by and, as he'd predicted, Trevor didn't appear. Maurice left the house and walked to the entrance. He stepped over the threshold.

No answer to his shouted "Trevor?!" *Too far away to hear.* No, that was stupid. He walked into the body of the maze, determined to prove that to himself.

Minutes and green corridors later, with a sense of the entrance becoming more remote behind him, a leap in his chest at the ticking of Trevor's measuring wheel. Of course, it was easier to push than carry. He wished he could place its direction. There was an opening, yards in from of him, another yards behind, but no clue as to which, if either, might take him towards Trevor. He shouted his name again, listened. The wheel didn't cease to tick and if he could hear it, his shouts should be all the more audible to Trevor.

Anxiety and anguish, he felt both distorting his face. If Trevor wasn't oblivious to Maurice's calls, was he choosing to ignore them?

"What are you playing at, Trevor?" If the maze was a game, was Trevor a willing player? "The taxi's due in . . ." He checked his watch. Where had the minutes gone? "In three-quarters of an hour. We haven't even spoken to Tavener yet."

Nothing, just nothing apart from the ticking of the wheel. There was a baleful silent malice in the spiky leafage walling him in.

"I tell you what. I'll speak to Tavener, and I'll take the taxi by myself. You make your own way." His voice had emerged high and strained and he wondered if it had alerted the creature he heard now.

A light-footed gallop, leaves whispering as if in its slipstream. A direction away from him, but would that bring the animal to that distant opening he could barely make out in the perspective? He froze until he was sure nothing was about to charge out. But now there was a dread inside him that the diminishing impacts were heading towards a rendezvous with the source of the ticking.

Listening until he could hear neither the ticking nor the busy steps, he moved on, his heart stumbling like his feet in a low murk of trepidation. The sun's position might have clarified his own, but between the high hedges the sky was reduced to a pathway of luminous, lumpy cloud.

A scream was abruptly cut short before it had barely registered in his mind. Behind the din of his pulse in his ears, a ripping, bony snaps, wet sounds.

Maurice ran through passageway after passageway, felt a savage leap of salvation on seeing in a gap no immediate layer of hedge waiting beyond it. Nearer, a slump, a rockfall inside him.

He entered the open space, the *only* empty space other than the passage-ways . . . the centre. It was about fifty feet across; the bare earth rose in a low blister that would afford a view over the hedges to the world outside, the garden, Mouselode House, and a general direction towards them.

He climbed the incline, turned a full circle. He laughed. *You've got to laugh*, he thought. He closed his eyes, opened them again. No, not laughing now. No trees, no upper reaches of Mouselode House. He could maybe have dealt with that, but not the runnels of the maze extending way beyond where any rational being would expect the outer wall to be. In every direction, narrower and narrower alternations of hedge tops and thin dark furrows between them. Further still the maze was corduroy, blending to an indistinct greenish murk and eventually a faint merging into the sky. If the maze had a perimeter, it was beyond every vague horizon.

He recalled the plan, the infinity symbol in the margin outside the maze. But he wouldn't believe this mathematical horror. It had taken only the twisty complexity of a conventional maze, the troubling presence of the running creature, Trevor's elusiveness, to send him temporarily mad. Infinity didn't exist on the human level of things.

Would Trevor's reappearance dismiss this insanity? No, these weren't his running steps—too irregular, too many limbs. They described a roughly concentric passage, a radius between fifty and sixty yards, around the centre of the maze. A spasmodic motion with intermittent complete stops. Following a scent? Whose? Whatever or whoever the creature sought, it was gradually closing in.

He wouldn't stay here to be found, or inadvertently discovered. He just needed to strike out. A modicum of comfort that the centre of the maze logically entailed a boundary, and it wasn't far off. If the maze went on forever it wouldn't have a centre. Infinity didn't have a centre.

He strode down the incline and back into the maze. He could search too, for Trevor, for the way out. With endeavour and energy coursing through his blood and thoughts, maybe reality would reassert itself.

Trotting the narrow highways, he tried to maintain a broadly single direction but had no notion if he was succeeding. Maybe the exit would surprise him—it had before.

The mess stopped him in his tracks. He was shocked beyond measure. He covered his mouth, nauseous. A big and bloody heap. He could have avoided identifying it but for the measuring wheel abandoned to one side. He would have leapt over it all but for the bulk of darkness that sidestepped out from an opening several yards further on.

Supporting the large bulk of the leathery bag, a cluster of thin limbs dancing on the spot; not exactly feet, not exactly hands thudded against the ground. He recalled the sisters in the photograph, the bag suspended between them by its long, looping handles. Here it was again, complete with buttons, rusted metal satchel-type clasps, projecting outer pockets. Now the flaps of the pockets fluttered like trollish eyelids over cruel black buttons. A seam near the base opened on a snaggle of pale lengths like candles shaved to points and stained red.

Maurice spun around, prepared to flee the way he'd come. His legs braked, arms whirring to stop himself falling into the square pit that had appeared, filling the gap between the hedges. He looked away, as aghast at the motion in it as he was at the presence of the sisters behind.

They were almost skeletal in their long pale gowns. The taller one had a straw-like bob, clasped in a cloche hat, her face a matter of bone and shades of onionskin. The shorter sister's hair, under a fungoid beret, was like dead bracken curtaining even less of a face. An odour of old dustbins, dead vegetation, and rose water came to him.

The thing with the straw-like hair gestured into the pit. "Here, down here." Her voice, strained through soft obstructions, seemed to be offering an escape.

He gazed down, tottered at the sight of tops of heads. Skulls, rags of hair. Packed close together, the bodies milled on the spot like grubs in a tobacco tin.

Maurice wanted to be stone like the statue he realised he'd mistaken the taller sister for yesterday. In sympathy, or a simulacrum of it, the other sister, in the beret, tilted her head.

From between her stiff curtains of hair her voice emerged like turned earth. "It's the only way out."

At the prancing impacts closer behind him, the smack of leathery jaws, Maurice made his choice.

HEATH CRAWLER

SAM HICKS

Ahead, a figure made unreadably black by the winter sun was walking between the palisades of gorse. Despite the obscurity, I recognized him by his distinctive gait and by the small black mongrel dog, which trotted leadless at his feet, and by his walking stick, which I knew to be a handsome piece, whorled with the polished stumps of severances and knots. I'd observed much about the man's appearance when we'd passed earlier that week: the stick, the vintage coat and high-laced boots, the modishly long beard and side-shaved hair. We'd exchanged heath walkers' hellos, and he in his turn must have observed my worn-out shoes and rainproof jacket and drawn his own conclusions.

My Jack Russell terrier, Arnie, twitched his ears, although, curiously, so far, the man's dog had failed to provoke the usual warning barks. In fact, as the man began heading towards my bench, Arnie seemed oddly content to leave me undefended.

"I hope you don't mind," the man said. "I don't want to disturb you, but this bloody ankle's killing me. I need to rest it for a minute." He sat down, smoothing his coat with leather-gloved hands. "I broke the bloody thing a year ago, and it's been playing up ever since. The cold doesn't help, of course."

I was surprised that there was still no reaction from Arnie; he wasn't a dog's dog and regarded his own kind with profound and aggressive suspicion. But it was as though the stranger's dog, now settled in front of me, didn't announce itself as kin.

"Not at all," I lied. "So long as you don't mind me smoking." I took out my pack and lit up—I'd cut down to two a day, but in emergencies might add a third, and I was confident that, in this smoke-free world, it would speed the man's departure.

But he replied, "Of course not," and I thought I heard a touch of an accent—German? Dutch?—and again when he said, "One of life's pleasures, isn't it?" He produced his own pack—crumpled, blue, French —and lit a pale-tipped cigarette with the flip of a Zippo lighter. "An improvement on breathing, don't you agree?"

"Oh. Yes. Maybe," I said.

I knew it would seem too theatrical, too obvious a snub, to get up and walk away. Protocol demanded I give it a moment, and, resigned to this, I turned my attention to the man's dog, which so far I'd only glanced at.

Did the man see my face? Perhaps not, since he was already talking and looking straight ahead as he said things like "beauty of the morning frost" and "dew in spiders' webs," and by the time he turned his head to face me I had, I think, reset myself to neutral. It wasn't only that the dog was disfigured. What prompted my revulsion wasn't its protruding yellow teeth or the shining welts that razed across its muzzle, but the expression of its wet and pink-rimmed eyes, the nauseating dissonance of its effect. What I saw there, in those black spheres, was not the curious, submissive, or wary look of a kept animal, but something I'd seen once in the street in the eyes of a collapsed, half-conscious drinker. It was spent and lonely rage. I'd seen it in the eyes of a gambler, stumbling from the betting shop, the glassy lostness of one with nothing precious left. And on the television news, I'd seen it there, the dazed outsider wrongly accused of acts of horror, staring at a world made hell. We anthropomorphize our pets and read all kinds into their expressions, but here, peering through this animal mask, was the most uncanny, the most unnerving and subtle, human parody I had ever seen.

"There's nothing to compare to it, is there?" the man was saying.

"I'm sorry?"

"What I just said—the bond between dog and owner? Don't you think? And in my work, they make good subjects. I mean, how their lives intersect with ours."

"They do? What work is that?"

"I'm an artist," he said. "Among other things. I like to say that all I do is take what's already there and reshape it."

What was it about the way he spoke that made me feel he wanted something from me? I threw my cigarette butt to the ground, grinding it to death with my shoe and gave Arnie's lead a tug.

"Well, nice to meet you," I said, rising from the bench.

"And you. I'm Emile by the way—and you? Your name?"

I didn't want to offer it but didn't know how refuse. "Simon," I said.

"Simon. Yes. Thanks for the loan of your bench. Much appreciated."

It's strange how the heath is at once an open space yet one in which you are constantly subject to containment. Each pathway runs through or opens into clearings closed about with high gorse or groves of trees, and when another person appears, they have often just rounded a corner, and bring unintentional surprise. I walked away in the direction from which Emile had arrived, and I'd just reached the mouth of the wide track when such a meeting occurred. A woman appeared from a narrow path cut between the bushes on my right, one on which the frost was still sparkling, untouched by the morning sun. It was unusual to see someone without a dog, and I spoke my hello with some hesitation, unsure if the code still applied to solitary souls. But the woman didn't reciprocate. She stopped and stared at me quite openly, as though she'd been expecting someone else and couldn't grasp that I wasn't them. There was about her appearance the same meticulous curation as Emile's: a cinched waist, fur-collared coat, a red tartan beret set on severely bobbed black hair, and the bold, emphatic make-up of 1950s Hollywood. I moved on, but in a few seconds, turned my head. Emile was still on my bench and the woman, her back towards me, hadn't shifted from the middle of the track. Some intuition told me that the two of them must be together or know each other in some close way, and I was doubly convinced when the woman raised her hand and slowly wagged a scolding finger towards Emile.

◄◦►

I usually walked Arnie at the north end of the heath, wary of the south side where certain locals are known to behave in a way the local paper, reporting an arrest, claimed to have "no inoffensive words for." The south side, like the north, has that same sense of a series of enclosures within a greater expanse, yet there the clearings are smaller, and the paths leading off through the gorse and the groves of trees are narrower and more numerous, and the ground between is irregular with the small craters left by the old chalk mines. I've read that, in the nineteenth century, a part fell through, revealing tunnels and rooms and pillared chambers, which sadly, by order of the town, were quickly sealed again. But a few days after meeting Emile, I took Arnie to this south side for his morning walk, guessing that it was currently too cold for anything too shocking. The morning and evening walks of the past two days had been ruined by a creeping tension, an anxiety as we rounded a corner or approached a branching path. It was the thought of seeing Emile and his disfigured dog that troubled me, even though I knew I could so easily avoid them. I could turn back if I saw them ahead. Or if they appeared too suddenly, and I was forced to speak, I could make some excuse to hurry off.

The way he spoke, and the way he moved, haunted me. That slow way he'd limped towards me, gaining color as he emerged from the dark of the oblique sun. His unsmooth movements suggested a crawling thing, an insect dragging a wing as it traveled painfully across a wall. I had taken a dislike to him and wasn't pleased that he knew my name and might treat this as an invitation. He might think he'd the right to talk to me now, to interrupt me, to accompany me as I went. And that dog—my God. Had it been rescued from an abusive home or worse, had Emile caused its injuries? And how did it learn to use its eyes as it did? And then there was that woman in the tartan beret, wagging her finger, as if to say, "Naughty. You naughty, naughty boy." And was he? Was he her naughty boy? The thought made me feel quite sick. And so, on the south side, nearer the four-lane road which bypasses the town, I felt a little easier, thinking that he, as I had been, might be loyal to the north.

I'd stopped beside a mature oak tree, waiting for Arnie as he performed a snuffling circuit. Behind it stood a copse of younger oaks, naked in the February sun, hopeful, straight-growing in their clean smooth skin. A bright-breasted bullfinch flew down to a small branchlet that could barely hold its weight and took off again across the clearing, high above the yellow-flowered cumulus of gorse, and as I tracked it with my eyes, I saw what I'd hoped I wouldn't.

"Arnie," I called, and then more masterfully, "Arnie, come here now." Arnie lifted his nose from a clump of roots and bounded to me. I fumbled to attach his lead, looking hurriedly around. Not far away, where a path opened into the almost circular space, beside a bush whose bare thin branches, heavy with dew, seemed made of threads of spittle, were Emile and another man. The other man was heavily built in a muscular way, clad in a black tracksuit and woolen hat, his thick arms crossed, his deeply tendoned neck bent forward as he listened to Emile, who leaned in close, gloved hand on the bigger man's elbow. Emile's dog was on high tiptoe, front paws pressed against the man's leg like the hands of a clinging child. Nearby, a brown whippet gazed away, as if the other dog weren't there.

I drew up my hood and shortened Arnie's lead, starting us off in the direction of the car park. He fixed me with the hurt expression that always melted my heart, upset to be rushed, not understanding as I diverted him from the tempting openings at the base of the gorse bushes, those low and living tunnels that draw small animals in.

At the line of blackthorns that marked the car park's edge, I dared to look behind me. It was on higher ground I saw them, in the blackened patch left by the summer fires, where only reddish bracken broke through the cinders, seeming lit from the inside. She was following him, her tartan beret the brightest thing in the whole scene, while he walked haltingly ahead downhill, keeping distance between them, black dog at his heels.

◄◦►

I don't enjoy walking on the marsh by the river, but we went there the next morning. I find it eerie up there, the watery shushing of the reeds, the abandoned buildings, the strange men you come across doing inexplicable things, like emptying rocks from the backs of trucks into the middle of boggy fields. The wind whipped across and muddy ponies loitered on the path, and I was scared to let Arnie off the lead in case he fell into the thick mud or black water of the creek. But a change of routine can clear the mind, and, indeed, as we walked under the white sky towards the gray line of the river, I had what seemed a minor revelation: I'd only ever seen Emile a couple of times on the north side of the heath because he was a creature of the south. That would explain what made me uncomfortable about him, what I instinctively disliked. It was a personal atmosphere of sleaze, only detectable up close. I bet he usually hung out on the south side, approaching men, as I'd seen him doing yesterday. And that woman—well, who knew what people got up to together? It made perfect sense now, the finger wagging. Perhaps they were meant to be off duty the day he approached me, and he'd annoyed her by bending the rules. He'd tried his luck away from the usual stamping ground, and, having failed, had gone back to the place they knew best. They'd gone back to their normal routine, their south side activities. I'd have nothing to worry about, if I kept away from there.

That afternoon, Arnie and I returned to the north side of the heath. I let him off the lead, and he ran around the leafless trees and in and out of the low tunnels beneath the gorse. I said my hellos to fellow dog walkers, none of whom knew my name, and apologized with my usual bashful pride when Arnie barked at their little charges. We restrained our pets and continued on our walks, laughing sympathetically.

On the way back, the path dipped through an overgrown copse. The light was fading, and its last gleam shone through the tight twigs and branches which grew so closely that, in their complexity and chaos, they seemed to move without the slightest breath of wind. Looking through, black lines and circles drew within and across in a web of retreating perspective, and just visible through it all, deep within its heart, I saw something red, quite large, maybe a scarf that had been lost on a windy day and become trapped there, irretrievable. I guessed it was the sight of that which set Arnie barking again. He trembled as he stared into the trees, and I wondered what he dreamed was there.

-‹o›-

The next morning on the north side of the heath, after a heavy frost, we turned a corner, me cracking a puddle's ice underfoot, and came face to face with Emile. I didn't have a chance to speak or step aside before his gloved hand was on me, his breath warm on my skin as he leaned in confidingly, and said, "Simon. What luck. I forgot to give you my card last time. You must come along and have a look around."

I felt something being slipped into my pocket, and on my leg, the soft pressure of his dog's front paws, braced against me. That corrupted face would be searching mine as I stood imprisoned by its master's hand.

"Oh, really?" I said, moving my elbow slightly, only to feel the man's grip tighten, almost affectionately, on my arm. His eyes were blue and clear, untroubled, and from one of them the ghost of a scar ran down, like the white track of a tear.

"My shop," he said. "And gallery. In the town. You're very welcome to come and have a look. I meant to say when we talked. There's no compulsion to buy, mind you. We all like to browse, don't we? Now," he released my arm, "I've got to get back to the car. I'd love to stay and chat, but there's a delivery coming today. Something special."

The gentle pressure on my leg eased. I looked down and seeing the black dog's face in profile I couldn't help imagining a rope around its neck and its small body swinging from a gibbet, perhaps on a windswept moor.

Emile moved away and the dog followed him, its pace set by the slow fall of the polished walking stick, its tail obscenely erect, curled almost like a pig's.

"Arnie," I called, not seeing him. But Arnie didn't come.

He wouldn't have gone far without me. He never did. He was a good boy. I walked around; the way we'd come, the way ahead, and then off in new directions. I became frantic. I ran over to the car park and then back to where my search had started, but when you're searching for something dear that is lost, the world becomes breathless and outpaces you, however hard you try to keep up. The white bark of the silver birches, the oaks, the leaf-scattered holes and slopes, spun ahead of me, and I seemed unable to catch them, to reach the place I needed to be.

"Have you seen a Jack Russell?" I asked anyone who passed. They shook their heads.

"Run off, has he?" they said. "What we have to put up with, eh?"

And, "Mine does that a lot, but he always finds me."

And, "How old is he? Is he a young one?" as if that would make any difference.

"Arnie," I called. "Come here, Arnie. Come to me now."

I stood at the top of the earth steps running down through the thicket where we'd lingered yesterday. Might he have gone back there, to bark at the invisible foe? An animal could get trapped in that puzzled mass, as unyielding, as hard, as iron. He would make a noise though. He would howl. I swung round at the sound of someone climbing the steps:

"Have you seen my dog? He's a Jack—"

She shook her head, and the black wings of her hair brushed her cheek.

"Don't go to him," she said. "I know he asked you." And there was that accent again, but harsher than Emile's. Was it Eastern European?

"What? I'm looking for my dog, Arnie. What are you talking about? Are you talking about Emile? Why would I want to go to him? I've got no intention."

She didn't stop walking. It almost seemed like she was talking to herself, leaving words trailing behind her: "You're wrong for us. I told him that. We've already got what we want. You're all wrong. Don't go to him. I might not be able to do anything about it."

I watched her cross the clearing and turn away into a hidden path.

⟶

I'm not ashamed to admit that I cried when I finally got home. That is, after I'd tried to leave the heath then turned the car around, going back to scour the same paths.

The day was almost done by the time I'd spent a panicked hour phoning vets and animal rescue places to see if he was there. Then I made up some lost dog posters—grainy things with scanned photographs—and I drove back to the heath with them. It behaved differently at night. It rustled and gathered and watched, and the towering bushes terrified me with the intensity of their presence, their nocturnal seething sound. When I tried to fix a poster to a tree, I heard laughter somewhere close, and at that I gave the whole thing up and took my barely lessened pile back to the car. But as soon as it was light, I returned, and pinned my appeals from north to south, seeing no one, still calling out for Arnie.

I drove to the center of town and worked up and down the high street, and then along the minor road that led to the park. And there, by a disused phone box, I noticed a narrow lane that, in all the years I'd lived around there, had never registered its existence with me. Of course, I knew its name from Emile's business card. The address of his gallery and shop. Had *he* taken Arnie? Perhaps in collusion with his girlfriend? To make a fool of me?

Arnie had been there until I talked to him, and then, as if by supernatural means, he'd vanished.

Why anyone would open a business down there confounded me. It was so easy to miss, a dead end lined with the uglier sides or rears of buildings, and further on, the shadowed yards of small workshops. At the very last building, a gold-lettered sign above a window read "Emile's." Not a shop window as such, more the size that would be quite generous for a town house, and revealing within an unlit, shadowed space, with at the back, something blacker than the rest, perhaps a door. It was impossible to make out what the room held, or even its full dimensions. Here and there was a glint of gilt or a dimmer sheen, but these were few, and beyond the weak reach of the daylight the main impression was of shrouded shapes, perhaps furniture or maybe artwork for the gallery. But what business could he expect to do down there?

The yellow lichen on the brick around the door, I thought, was the very yellow of the gorse flowers on the heath. And then it was as if I could smell the coconut fragrance of those flowers, filling that lane which was as cold, as strange, as suggestive of pitfalls, as the dark and paths and clearings of the nighttime heath.

Pushing the door and finding it open, I took a step inside. But was the place open for business at all? The gallery and shop? I edged forward but knocked into a hard something draped in sheeting which held a scent at once sulfurous and sweet. Wary of causing damage in that cryptic gloom, I took out my phone and shone its light around.

There was someone sitting there, only a few feet away. Startled, I backed away towards the door, hitting the object again, releasing another cloud of sickly scent. Why didn't they say something?

"Hello," I said, keeping my voice low. "Are you okay? I was looking for Emile, but if the shop's not open . . ."

The seated figure didn't answer. Did I know him? Yes—the black tracksuit, the broad shoulders, the arms as thick as girders. He was the man Emile had been speaking to on the heath. He was starkly solid in the light of the phone, blunt-faced and rugged. I could see the rapid rise of his chest, the pulse beating in his neck, but he didn't seem aware of me. He looked ahead sightlessly, unblinking and vacant. He was like a clever facsimile, a heavyweight puppet constructed by a master of the craft.

I spoke again: "Mate, are you all right? Can I help you?" Was he sleeping with his eyes wide open, as I'd heard some people did? Was he drugged?

A low growl sounded from the dark. I swung my phone, and the white light found the liquid luster of its scars, its black and open jaws, and its eyes. The dog moved forward one pace and fixed me with its stare, knowing I would be held there, unresisting, as it showed me its new trick, its newest gut-wrenching impersonation, its variation on a theme. And in its shining eyes I saw the bewilderment of the bloodied, punch-drunk fighter who can't tell if the pain he feels is his or his opponent's or if it hangs outside himself, in the baying of the crowd. I beheld the cold horror of the man who surveys the violent death wrought by his manicured hands in one unforeseen and unwanted moment of madness.

Her voice broke the spell, a sharp string of unfamiliar words, and then her hands were upon my shoulders, pulling me towards the open door.

"Didn't I tell you not to come? You're lucky I was here. You're not right, but he'd take you anyway. Why didn't you listen?"

"Listen?" I repeated, grabbing the door frame, trying to obstruct her. "What's wrong with that man? Who are you?"

As she moved to loosen my hands, I glimpsed the woman's face. Fleetingly, it disclosed the signs of an immense and unsettling self-control, an inner battle to maintain command of impulses, desires, visions and powers that were completely and utterly alien to me. I stepped back into the lane, suddenly disarmed.

"We're moving on today," she said. "Be glad you're free."

And the shop door slammed behind her.

I wandered, dazed, back to the high street. At first I couldn't understand why Arnie's image was everywhere, and then I realized it was to let me know that I'd never see my little friend again. My misery at this understanding, and the shock of what had happened in Emile's shop, overwhelmed me so much that I can't say what I intended, what my motives were for going back, for turning back to follow the road that led down to the park, and then walking down that narrow dead-end lane.

The building, the adjacent workshops, were boarded up as though long abandoned, as if years had passed within the hour. But this mystifying discovery was not the only cause of the havoc in my heart. I felt the pounding heat of what I can only describe as jealousy, a cruel blow to the pride that I didn't know I possessed. Why did she say I wasn't right for them? What did I lack that the other man had? What quality was demanded by their unfathomable art? What formless substance?

THE DEVIL WILL BE AT THE DOOR

DAVID SURFACE

I always wanted to believe in ghost stories. It was easy to do, growing up in the church. On my knees every Sunday, I'd close my eyes and reach out to the invisible world. The invisible world never spoke back, but I knew it was there. As Saint Paul said, *We fix our eyes not on what is seen, but on what is unseen.* It was the unseen world that I was drawn to. The stories of ghosts and monsters that I loved were not so different from the stories I heard in church every week—miracles and curses, blood sacrifice, even the dead being raised up. It was all the story of an unseen power, and the promise that one day I could become part of that story.

There was one story that my father used to tell that was unlike all the others. He'd tell it on the long bus ride home from church-school trips to the cathedral in Louisville where we brought our Lent offerings. About an hour into the trip, when the bus was in that dark stretch of two-lane highway about halfway home, my father would rise up from his seat, walk to the middle of the bus, reach up and hold onto the luggage rack with one hand to steady himself. Then he'd begin to tell a story about a group of friends and a haunted house. One by one, the friends would dare each other to enter the haunted house alone. Then the others would go in and find their friend butchered, each time in more explicitly horrible ways. It was, quite simply, the most violent, gory story I'd ever heard. He told the same story every year, and we all came to expect it with an excitement mixed with dread and nausea. At the end of the story, all the friends are butchered like sheep, except for the last one who knows that he too is doomed. "I know I have to go back there. There's something there. It's waiting for me . . ." Every time, my father would end the story with a loud shout that always made us jump and scream, even though we knew it was coming.

My father never explained how the house came to be haunted, who or what was doing the killing. Or why anyone would keep returning to that house, knowing what was waiting for them there. That was not the point of the story. The point was the cold wave of raw-nerve horror and dread that rose up and rushed through that dark bus, taking all of us with it. Listening to his warm, familiar voice turn hard and cold as an ice pick, it was hard to believe that the man telling this story was the same man who stood in the pulpit and talked about Easter morning and God's forgiveness. It seemed like someone or something else had taken his place.

About a year before my father retired, he stopped telling this story. A boy from our church had gone crazy and killed four other kids in an abandoned house they'd broken into. The details were so horrible that the police and district attorney tried to keep them out of the news, but they leaked out anyway, rumors of young bodies hacked into pieces and strewn in every room, floors awash with blood. It was horrible, and horribly familiar. The boy who'd done all that killing had been on those church trips with us, and had heard my father tell his story many times—enough to memorize it, just as I had.

It was around this time when I started to notice all the mystery leaving the world. Old abandoned houses were no longer ghostly habitations; they were rusty nails and rotten lumber, empty shells where terrible human mistakes were made. It was no longer the unseen presences they once evoked that terrified me; it was the absence of any such presence, the complete void of anything felt or unseen. I think I spent some time in mourning for the unseen world, for that sense of something beyond what the eye can see.

By the time I entered college, I'd decided that if there was any real mystery left in the world, it was inside the human mind. Not in sacred caves or woodland grottos. Not in churches. Certainly not in haunted houses.

◄◦►

Greta was at least twenty-eight when I first met her in the university cafeteria. I knew she was a graduate student from up north, and that she'd taught some intro psych classes. There were a few grey strands in her kinky halo of black hair. When she peered down at me through her round granny-spectacles, I wondered if she could tell that I was almost ten years younger than she was.

"You like Neruda?" she said, glancing at a fat volume of poetry that I'd placed, perhaps deliberately, next to my food tray.

"Yeah," I said. "I do."

"Have you read him in the original Spanish?" I don't recall how I responded to this challenge—my Spanish was terrible—but it did start a conversation about poetry. The truth was, I was surprised and excited that she was even talking with me. I'd changed my major from English to Psychology only a month ago, and still felt like a pretentious young romantic hiding behind a long beard and a thick book of poetry. But the longer we sat and talked, for every moment that she didn't get up and walk away from me, the more I felt like part of this new and more practical world.

The one area where Greta conceded that I may have known more than she did was the spiritual. She seemed very curious about the fact that I'd grown up as the son of a minister, and from time to time I'd catch her looking at me as if she was surprised that I wasn't more straight-laced or completely insane.

Greta once asked if I believed in God. "It depends on what you mean by God," I replied. It wasn't much of an answer, and Greta, typically, was not satisfied with it.

"What do *you* mean by God?"

"Well," I began, "Not an old guy with a white beard sitting on a big throne up in the sky . . ."

"Alright. Then what?"

"I don't know," I said. "It's just that . . . sometimes I feel like there's something. I can't describe it, but I just feel like it's there."

"But if you can't see it," Greta said, "and you can't describe it, how do you know it's God? How do you know it's not something else?"

"What do you mean?"

"I mean . . . what if it's not good? This thing that you can't see, but you know it's there . . . what if it's something bad?"

I didn't have an answer for that. I knew Greta didn't believe in God, but what she'd just said seemed even worse. It was one thing to believe that that universe doesn't care about us—to believe that the universe means us harm was something else entirely.

One day Greta asked if I knew Doctor Mandel. Doctor Mandel was the head of the folklore department. He was famous, among other things, for his books of traditional ghost stories he'd collected from old folks in the country. I even had a few of those books that my mother had given me for Christmas over the years.

"He has a tape he wants someone in the psych department to listen to."

"What kind of tape?"

"Interviews. He interviews people. You know, collects their stories. He says a man came to him about a week ago and wanted to talk to him. About a house he says is really haunted."

"What, are you kidding? Was he like messing with him or something?"

"No. Mandel says he was serious. He told him he couldn't help him, but the guy wouldn't listen. Mandel said he was kind of desperate. So he agreed to record him. Now he wants someone from the psychology department to listen to it. He says he's concerned about the guy."

"Have you heard it?"

"Not yet. I thought maybe you might want to come with me." Greta must have known how this sounded, because she looked down for a moment, and I thought I saw her blush. "I mean, I just kind of thought it sounded like something you might be interested in."

Of course, I thought. After all, I was probably the only person Greta knew who believed in invisible things. It was an easy connection for her to make.

Doctor Mandel's office was in Cooper Hall, a hundred-year-old limestone building on the opposite side of the campus. The moment we walked in the door, the smell of old wood and furniture polish took my mind back to my father's church. If I'd seen candles flickering at the end of the hallway and heard the mournful rumbling of a pipe organ, I would not have been surprised.

Doctor Mandel received us politely and invited us to sit down. The sun had set and his office was dark. As if our arrival had made him notice the darkness, he went around and turned on a couple of lamps that failed to push back most of the gloom.

"I appreciate the both of you coming," he said. "I know this is a little unusual. It's just that I wanted to hear . . ." he searched for the right words. " . . .a psychological perspective on this."

"So there's a tape you want us to hear," Greta said, getting right to the point as usual. I'd said nothing so far. I was flattered that Greta had invited me to come along, but I still felt more than a little like an imposter.

"Yes. It's on the machine over there . . ." Dr. Mandel nodded toward an old reel-to-reel. "It's pretty easy to operate. Just turn it off and close the door when you're through."

"You mean you're not going to stay?" Greta asked. Doctor Mandel had picked up his jacket and was moving toward the door.

"No," he said. "I've heard it." He didn't have to say *and I don't want to hear it again.* I could tell by how quickly he left and closed the door behind him.

After a moment, Greta walked over to the tape player and pushed a button. A loud hiss rose up from the speakers, then Doctor Mandel's booming voice stating the date and time of the recording. Greta adjusted the volume and returned to her chair.

The voice of a man came from the speakers. At first it was hard to tell what he was saying, his voice was so low. Greta turned up the volume. I could hear a tremble in the man's voice that he was probably trying to hide, the catch of breath in his throat.

It was supposed to be a good day, the man said. *I took my kids for a hike in the woods. We were only out there for about an hour when this big rainstorm hit. It came up out of nowhere.* The man paused, like he was reliving that moment, the surprise of it. It was supposed to be a good day, the man said again, like he was fixating on that small sense of wrongness to delay moving on to what happened next.

The rain came down fast and hard, so when they saw an old white house through the trees, they ran toward it. When they got closer, they could tell it was abandoned. There were no vehicles, and whatever driveway had been there was choked with tall grass and weeds. Kudzu vines crawled up the walls, twisting their way under loose boards and shingles, and the glass was long gone from all the windows that gaped open darkly. The plan was to wait out the rain on the dilapidated old porch. *We never meant to go inside,* the man said. They huddled together under the eaves, pressing close to the house to stay dry. The man described how he could feel the house at his back, how it didn't feel right, and how he eventually had to step away from it, even though it meant getting drenched in the rain—anything was better than feeling that old house pressing close against him. His kids got cold and restless. *Why can't we go inside*, his daughter kept complaining. *Because*, his son said, *it's not safe.* The daughter started teasing her brother. She told him he was scared and kept daring him to go inside. *I dare you. Go on, I dare you*, until the boy finally got angry, pulled open the rotten front door and stepped through it. Right away, the man knew something was wrong. *We should have heard something. Some kind of sounds of him walking around in there.* But there was no sound. Just the final dripping of the rain that had suddenly stopped. The daughter got nervous and asked the man why he wasn't going in to look for his son.

I wanted to go in there, but I couldn't. I tried, but it felt like my legs were frozen. She kept asking, "Why don't you go in and look for him?" It made me angry, so I told her, "You made him do it. You made him go in there. Go look for him yourself." Then I said, "I dare you." I don't know what made me say that. It was like something else was talking through me. She looked at me like she didn't know who I was. Then she went inside . . .

At this point, there was a long silence. I was sure that the tape had run out, until I heard the scratchy sound of the man's breathing. At first I thought he was crying, until I realized that he was struggling to breathe.

I thought it was going to be quiet. Like when my boy went in before. But it wasn't. The sounds that came out of that house . . . it was like animals being skinned alive . . .

When the man started talking again, he sounded exhausted, his voice stretched thinner and weaker, like he'd aged years in the telling of his story. *I don't know how I did it, but I made myself go in there. I was afraid of what I was going to see. The second I went through that door, the screaming stopped. I looked for my kids, but they weren't there. There was no blood, no footprints, nothing. It was like they were never even there . . .*

There was another long pause.

Now I know . . . I have to go back. There's something in there. It's waiting for me . . .

When the tape was over, I managed to turn my head toward Greta. I was surprised to see her head resting face down in her folded arms on the table.

I said her name and she looked up, her face paler than I'd ever seen it. She'd removed her spectacles, and her eyes looked naked and defenseless.

"Are you alright?" I asked.

"I don't know . . . she said, rubbing her eyes with one hand. "It's just . . . I don't think I've ever heard a man sound . . . so *afraid* before."

The office door swung open slowly. Doctor Mandel stood in the doorway, looking back and forth between the two of us. "So," he said, "It's over? You heard it all?"

I nodded. I was still finding it difficult to speak.

"So," Doctor Mandel continued. "I suppose you can see why I was so concerned."

"What about his children?" Greta asked. "Have the police been called?"

"Yes. That's just it," Doctor Mandel said, sinking wearily into his desk chair. "There aren't any."

"What do you mean?" Greta asked.

"I mean there are none. The police confirmed it," Doctor Mandel said. "He doesn't have any children."

Later over a couple of beers, Greta told me that she wanted to interview the man on the tape herself. At first I thought she was kidding, until I saw the look on her face. She still looked a little pale, but there was a determined set to her lips that was almost grim.

"Why?" was all I could ask.

"Don't you want to?"

The truth was, I did not. Like Doctor Mandel, I'd heard all I wanted to hear. It had been fun at first, a return visit to the mysteries of the world. But the man's voice had left a kind of raw, open place in my mind, and all I wanted now was to leave it alone and let it heal.

"I don't know," I said. "I mean, he's already told his story once. Why would he agree to talk with us?"

"We could say we're following up on his first interview. You know, just a few more questions."

"Shouldn't we tell Doctor Mandel?"

"No," she said, a little too quickly, I thought. She also hadn't answered my question. *Why?* Why did she want to find and talk with this man who was obviously deeply deluded, possibly dangerous?

"How would we even find him?" I asked, still hoping it was not going to happen. Greta reached into her shirt pocket and pulled out a folded scrap of paper with a phone number hastily scrawled on it.

"It was on the tape label," she said with a slight smile that almost looked mischievous.

I don't know what Greta actually said when she made the call. The man, whose name was Bill Carson, agreed to meet us at his apartment. Greta and I arrived there just as the sun was going down. It was one of those prefab one-story brick complexes that looks like a motel, a few beat-up cars and children's bicycles scattered in the cracked asphalt parking lot.

Bill Carson was a tired-looking man who looked older than he probably was. He was still wearing an oil-stained gray jumpsuit with his last name stitched over the breast pocket from whatever job he'd just left. "You're the people who called?" he said, looking at us cautiously. "The ones from the college?"

"Yes," I said, forcing a friendly smile—so far, it wasn't a lie.

"Come in, then," he said.

I expected the inside of the apartment to be a total wreck, the furniture covered with dirty clothes and food containers. But there was no furniture. The carpet, which was a faded ugly green, was bare. The only evidence that someone lived here were a few photographs hanging from the walls in cheap drugstore frames. The curtains were drawn shut and it was already fairly dark inside. Carson made no move to turn on the lights.

"So," he said, looking back and forth between the two of us. "Are you here to help me?" The question broke my heart, and for a moment I thought about leaving.

"We'd just like to ask you a few more questions if you don't mind, Mister Carson," Greta began. "On the recording, you talk about your children . . ."

"Yes," I interrupted. "Tell us about your children. Please. If that's alright."

I didn't turn to see the surprised look I knew Greta was giving me, but I saw it register in Carson's face as his eyes kept moving back and forth from her to me. Finally, he gave a ragged sigh. "They were good kids. Good kids. Better than me."

I nodded and tried to look sympathetic. The truth was, I wasn't sure how I felt—I just wanted to hear how far he was going to take this.

"You know the hardest thing?" he said. "They trusted me. I led them right to that damn place, and they followed me. All the way. Right up to the door. I guess no matter how scared they were, they figured nothing bad was really gonna happen as long as their daddy was there . . ."

At this point, Carson stopped talking. I nodded toward the photographs on the walls. "So," I said, hesitantly, "Those are your kids?"

Carson started like I'd woken him from a dream. He glanced where I was looking, then glared back at me. "Are you serious?" he said. "Are you fucking serious?"

I opened my mouth but my mind had gone blank. I stood there stupidly while Carson pulled one of the framed photos from the wall, walked up and thrust it at me. When he spoke, his voice was tight with anger. "What does this look like to you?"

I glanced down and confirmed what I thought I'd seen when we entered the room. It was one of those generic, mass-produced photos of model-families that come packaged inside cheap frames.

"You think I don't know what this is?" He shook the framed piece of paper at me. "This is all I've got now. And you come here and talk to me like I'm crazy or something? Get out. Both of you. Get the hell out of here."

I took Greta by the arm and quickly walked her out of the building. I could hear the door slam behind us, but we didn't stop walking until we reached the car. We got inside and locked the doors, then sat there for a moment before I said what I'd been thinking.

"I think he's telling the truth."

"What do you mean? Telling the truth about what?"

"About his kids. When he was talking about them. I could tell. He's telling the truth."

"Well, he thinks he is . . ."

"No. I mean . . . he's right. It's true."

Greta stared at me like I'd gone insane. We'd both heard what Doctor Mandel said, what the police had said too—there were no children. But it didn't matter. I knew the man was telling the truth. That every word he said was true. I don't know why I was so sure, or how it was even possible. But I knew it.

Here is where you might ask why we didn't just stop at this point. Just drop it and walk away. There was no real reason for us to keep going. But I think that's why we did it. There was no reason for us to keep going, and no reason not to keep going. It felt like some kind of big black hole had opened when we weren't looking, and we were already falling into it.

◄o►

The road we took out of town was familiar. It was the kind of road where the new cheap brick homes become fewer and fewer, and the old dark country takes over. I'd been on many roads like it, but there was something about this one that felt familiar in a deep-down way I could feel in my guts. It felt like I was heading toward something I'd been heading toward all my life, something I could not stop from happening.

"Pull over," I said.

Greta saw my face and pulled the car over to the side of the road. I walked into the weeds and vomited.

"Are you okay?" Greta called out to me. She'd gotten out of the car and was standing next to it, looking at me apprehensively as if she was afraid to come too near.

When I could stand upright again, the sky already looked darker. We'd agreed to do what we had to do in the daylight, and had started out with plenty of time to not let darkness overtake us. But now the light was almost drained from the sky. "Why is the sky so dark?" I asked. "It shouldn't be this dark."

The countryside grew starker; a few decrepit barns, then nothing but trees and empty fields. Then the shell of a rusted-out car appeared on the left side of the road, a gnarled tree growing up through the hood where the engine used to be. Next to the ruined car, the faint traces of a rutted trail. Greta slowed the car down until we'd come to a full stop in the middle of the road. "This is it," she said.

"How do you know?"

"It's the way the guy described it."

We sat there, still not turning in, the engine vibrating underneath us. I felt cold inside, and wondered if I was going to be sick again.

"So," Greta said, "Are we gonna do this?"

I didn't know what she meant. Why had we come here? We'd been acting like this was all some kind of research project, but now I wasn't sure. I just felt that same heavy sense of inevitability weighing me down, crushing me. I didn't know what was going to happen. But I knew we had to see it through to the end.

Greta turned the wheel and we rolled into the trees, the car bouncing and rocking on the hard ruts in the ground. Sooner than I expected, the house came into view; first a flash of weathered white through the trees, then the empty black mouth of a window gaping at us. As the road curved around to the right, the house seemed to retreat for a moment and almost vanish, then move toward us. Greta stopped the car and we both sat in silence, looking through the windshield at the thing in front of us, neither of us making a move to get out.

And just as quickly as the fear and nausea had come over me, it went away, and I felt a twinge of impatience. It was just a house. And old, empty house with nothing in it. Nothing but rusty nails and rotten wood. I opened the car door first to show Greta that I wasn't afraid, and to prove it to myself.

We walked through the high weeds toward the house, briars scratching our arms, burrs clinging to the cuffs of our jeans. Up close, the house looked in even worse shape. Weeds and small trees reached up through the floorboards of the porch that split and sagged. The lower windows had been boarded up with plywood, but the upper windows gaped open blackly, the glass and frames long gone. As I stared up at the old house, I had the feeling that I'd seen it before, although I knew that couldn't be true. Now that I was closer to it, the familiar feeling of nausea and dread started to return.

Greta and I climbed up onto the rotten porch, the boards sagging and groaning under our feet. We stopped in front of the door that for some reason had not been boarded up. "Look at this," Greta said. "Look how all the windows are boarded-up to keep out trespassers—why would they leave the front door like that?"

The answer came to me right away, and it terrified me, so I tried to turn it into a joke, and spoke in a spooky voice, *"Maybe it's a trap . . ."*

"Don't," she said, her voice suddenly sharp, "It's not funny." I looked and saw that Greta was scared too, all the hard, confident light gone from her eyes.

The door gaped open, breathing it's cold breath of mildew and raw earth. Neither of us moved to enter.

"Are you scared?" Greta asked. I knew she wasn't trying to accuse or humiliate me—I'd heard the note of anxiety in her voice—but the anger rose up inside of me anyway.

"You're the one who wanted to come here," I said. The rest of what I wanted to say stuck in my throat, but Greta knew what I meant. The reason we were here, and whatever was going to happen to us—it would all be her fault.

I saw a flash of anger in her eyes, then she turned her back on me and disappeared through the doorway. I hesitated, for a moment, then went in after her.

Inside, the dank, raw smell was even stronger, like we were in a cave miles below the surface of the earth. A sickly gray light filtered down from one of the shattered windows above. I half-expected Greta to have vanished, but I found her standing just inside the doorway with her back to me. She was staring at something on the wall. I stepped closer and saw what she was looking at: big spray-painted words on the wall, the dried paint drooling down.

GOD WANTS TO KILL US ALL.

I thought I saw Greta tremble. I put one hand on her arm and she shook it off. "Come on," she said, making her voice sound hard and commanding again, but I knew it was an act. She was becoming less and less like the Greta I knew with every step she took.

The deeper we went into the house, the colder it got. It wasn't just the temperature—there was something in the air itself that I could feel entering through my skin and reaching my heart, a cold malignant feeing that came from the walls around me.

"Do you feel that?" Greta asked. She felt it too. I felt startled, then a wave of relief; I wasn't crazy—but that also meant it was real.

"Yes . . . what *is* it?"

I could hear her trying to keep her voice steady. "The power of suggestion. All those stories we've been listening to . . ."

We turned a corner into an empty room. It was darker because of the boarded windows, and it took a few minutes for my eyes to adjust. When they did, I saw small objects attached to the mildewed walls. I stepped closer and saw what they were: dozens of tiny nooses made of twine, nailed in a row to all four walls, surrounding us. Hanging from some of them were the corpses of small animals.

Greta spoke, her voice grim and tight. "I think we need to go now."

That was when we heard the sound. Somewhere above us, something heavy was dragging itself over the rotting floorboards toward the stairs.

Then we were running, breathing hard and tripping over the trash and rotted leaves under our feet. But the room we came out into was not the one we recognized.

"Where's the door?" I said. "Jesus, where's the fucking door?"

"Wait," Greta gasped. "Wait. Listen . . ." I tried to quiet my breath and listened. The dragging noise from above had stopped. I looked at Greta. Her face was deathly white, but her voice was firm. "Okay, listen to me. Animals live in abandoned houses like this all the time. That's probably what we heard. An animal."

"Okay," I said. "Why can't we find the door?"

"We just got disoriented," Greta said. "Let's calm down and get our bearings. It's got to be here. Doors don't vanish . . ."

I watched Greta turn from one direction to another. "This way," she said. I knew it wasn't the same way we came, and she probably knew it too. I don't know how long we circled around in the dark, looking for that door.

"It's not here," I finally said.

"It's got to be."

"Greta, *it's not fucking here.*"

I could hear her breath coming faster in the dark. "Alright," she said, "those windows upstairs are open, right? We'll have to go through them and climb down."

We looked around until we found the staircase. At the stop of the stairs was a blackness thicker and more impenetrable than any I'd ever seen. I looked up into that blackness and felt that familiar cold sensation of dread deep in my guts. *Sick with fear.* I'd heard that phrase before; now I knew what it meant. *Sick with fear.*

A sudden bright flash of light burst through the holes in the ceiling and the cracks in the walls, illuminating the wretched room around us for an instant. But no thunder. Heat lightning, I thought. I was looking up the stairs at the thick blackness gathered there when the flash came again, and

I saw that the blackness did not disappear with the lightning. It remained there, heavy and solid, like a living thing.

"I'm going up," Greta said. "Are you coming?" My throat had closed and I couldn't speak. I could only shake my head. Greta stared at me. "Alright. I'll climb down and try to get the door open from the outside."

There is no door, I wanted to tell her. *Not anymore.*

She turned and walked up the stairs, the rotten wood groaning under her feet. The second she passed into the blackness at the top, everything fell silent again. I listened hard for the sound of Greta's feet walking on the floor above, but there was no sound. I was alone. All the cold dread in that place reached right through my skin and into my heart.

The lightning flashed, and I saw them. Silent, motionless figures, standing on the stairs above me. When the lightning flashed again, they were gone. But I could feel them waiting in the dark.

Then the screaming began. Not from just one throat, but many, until it seemed like the whole house itself was screaming. *Like animals being skinned alive.* I clutched my head in my hands and fell to the floor, screaming myself to drown out the terrible noise. When I realized that mine was the only voice still screaming, I stopped and listened.

In the darkness above, I heard something coming down the stairs. I wanted to run but I couldn't move. I lay there, curled up on the floor, hearing the uncertain shuffling steps coming closer, then stop. A voice spoke. It was Greta's voice, but horribly changed; a wet, ragged hissing noise.

"Look what they did to me!"

I wouldn't look. I felt a hand on my arm; it was warm and wet. *"Look what they did to me!"* the voice said again, raising in pitch to a kind of shrill hissing cry that tore into my brain. Something hot dripped onto the back of my neck.

That's when I ran. I ran with my eyes closed so I wouldn't have to see the thing that I knew was right behind me. I ran blind, colliding into walls, until I dared to open my eyes and saw an open window in front of me and leapt through it, knowing that dying when I fell to the ground would be better than what was waiting for me inside that house.

◄◦►

But I didn't die. Not yet, anyway. Somehow I survived that fall. Although sometimes I wish I hadn't.

Of course I went to the police, even though I knew it would do no good. I knew they would tell me that there was no such person as Greta Hartman—I'd heard this story before. There was no use in asking them to search the house, because I knew the house would not be there. Until the next time.

I know what I have to do now. But first, I'm going to take some time and go on a long trip. I'm going to visit all the people who know me and still remember me. I won't tell them why I've come, about the things that happened and the things I've seen. Why should I make them unhappy?

I know I wasn't supposed to go into that house with Greta. One at a time—that's the way it's supposed to happen, the way it's always been. I broke the rules, but I know that doesn't mean I've gotten away with anything. It just means that it's going to be that much worse when it's my turn.

Because I know how this story ends. I've known it all my life.

LET YOUR HINGED JAW DO THE TALKING

TOM JOHNSTONE

Dance with me," he said.

"You're bold," she said.

That was what Mary loved about him though. He was bold, but not too bold.

Old too, but not too old. The silver hairs combed back over his head stretched like the rain-slicked roads out of the small town.

I say "Mary," but I mean my mother. It helps if I call her "Mary." That makes it a story.

He was in Carluke on a business trip, he said. She didn't ask what his business was. That was one of the first things she learned about him: that it didn't do to ask too many questions. If she had done so, she felt she sure he'd have said something like *Ask me no questions and I'll tell you no lies.*

Instead she let him let her do all the talking. He asked her about herself and she told him: about how her pregnant mother walked from Lanark to Carluke after Mary's father died in the pit explosion. He was a good listener, nodded in all the right places. When she spotted him smiling, she said "What?"

"Nothing. I like your accent."

She looked away, embarrassed by the glint in his blue eyes and the way he smiled at her, kept looking at her mouth when she talked.

"I thought you wanted to dance," she said, pursing her lips. It was his turn to look away.

"I didn't do very well the first time. This is nothing like the tea dances back in Sidcup."

She had to admit he was immaculately turned out, his arms felt strong even if his feet were all over the shop, his fingertips probing the small of her back as if searching for something. Looked like he had money, too, even if something about him made her wonder *for how long?*

If I'm honest, she probably just wanted a way out of there. That was what he was.

"Don't worry," she said. "You'll get better with practice."

⟨○⟩

A Diamond ring and a trip to Gretna Green later and she was the lady of the mock-Tudor manor with the wax fruit on the table. Not exactly Eltham Palace but an improvement on the pebble-dash poverty she was used to.

But the garage was his castle.

It didn't matter to her. The grounds were extensive, dominated by gigantic twin conical conifers, a sundial in between. At least, I remember them as gigantic from when I was a child.

I also remember how frightened I was of that upper-crust ventriloquist doll on the TV variety show.

But I can't remember why.

It will come back to me, I'm sure.

That's why I'm writing it down. Turning it into a story helps me make sense of it. When you're young, the grown-ups are always telling you stories. If it isn't fairy tales at bedtime, it's their own personal stories. 'How I met your father/mother.' After a while, they get all mixed up in your head, and you can't imagine your mother ever having a life before your father, before . . .

⟨○⟩

"Dance with me," I said.

I didn't expect her to say "yes," thought she'd slap me for being forward, phrasing it as a command like that. But I soon saw that wasn't the way of things up here. You dancing? You asking? *All very rough and ready in this Scotch provincial hall, the girls around her whispering to her and giggling when they caught me looking.*

I knew she was a free spirit, but I also knew I was going to make her my princess.

Bit like me, Daddy?

Bit like you, sweetheart. But different.

She was such a free spirit. I thought of her as an untamed lass, dancing barefoot among the smoke and coal dust of these streets full of granite houses under granite skies. Would I be able to tame her? Did I even want to? But I didn't worry about that for now. I just let her do the talking. Danced with her on my two left feet.

And did you, Daddy?

Did I what, sweetheart?

Tame her?

No sweetheart. I never did. You know your mother. No one ever could.

◄○►

Fast forward twenty-five years or so to my own marriage. I didn't meet my husband at a tea dance or ceilidh, but somewhere between my work station and the water cooler. Things always look more romantic through the filter of the past. There's barely an old film or TV clip from my dimly-remembered youth but makes my tear-ducts swell with an ache of longing and nostalgia these days. And I've no doubt, if we have children of our own, we'll spin our meeting into a fairy tale for them.

Our eyes met over the fake potted plant . . .

Maybe we could tell them about the time I screamed my head off when he suggested we watch a film about Ray Charles. Eventually he managed to calm me down and we finally established I'd got the blind soul singer mixed up with the Seventies variety act Ray Allen and Lord Charles, the very duo that gave me the screaming ab-dabs back when I was seven. Of course, they weren't your usual TV double act. For starters, one of them was made of wood.

But that was part of the trouble.

◄○►

"There, there, sweetheart, don't take on so. He's not real! He's just a vent's doll . . . a ventriloquist's doll, like the ones in the warehouse. Look, the man's doing the talking for both of them, see? His mouth isn't moving, but the doll's is, so it looks like His Lordship's doing the talking."

My father had switched the TV off by now, and was trying to tickle me while poking fun at the puppet's airs and graces. I could still see it in my mind's eye: the hinged jaw snapping open and shut like a gamekeeper's trap, allowing clipped, aristocratic one-liners to escape, the lips always fixed in the same wide grin; the glass eyes rolling, one knowingly monocled, the eyelids lowering slyly, then rising again to reveal the fixed stare that so terrified me. The manikin sat on the man's knee like a child, but its dapper tweed jacket and silk cravat and barbed insults suggested an urbane man-about-town. If this was a child, it was a creepily precocious one.

Father sat by my bed until I went to sleep that night, reassuring me the dummy wasn't a real person, couldn't really talk.

"So the man was . . . letting the doll do the talking?"

This was the only time he got angry with me that evening, stiffening at the way my words echoed his tale of the Wooing of Mary, glaring at me with the same hard, blue ice-chip eyes he'd worn when he told me never, but never, to go in the garage.

◄◦►

Yes, that would be a funny story to tell the kids, if we ever have them.

Well, not the last bit.

Just the bit about me getting into a lather over Ray Charles. Ben would tell the tale without all the creepy stuff about the dummy or the garage, as a way of enabling them to laugh at how kooky their old mum is!

◄◦►

My father should have known I'd react like that to the dummy on the telly.

Because that's the thing I've remembered that I previously forgot: the time he took me to see his toy warehouse.

It's odd he was so tight-lipped about it when he first wooed Mary. I mean, toy-wholesaler! It's not as if he was an arms dealer or something.

He never took me again after that first time.

Maybe if it had just been one of them.

But rows and rows and rows of them lined up on the shelves, glass eyes staring at me from the shadows, a dust-specked finger of sunlight poking through a small window, picking out a pair of them.

Maybe if the eyes hadn't moved.

It could have been an employee of Fox Bros. lurking behind the shelves, playing a practical joke.

On a four year-old girl?

That's almost more frightening than the thought of one of those wooden things taking on a grinning, unnatural life!

But that's too awful to contemplate, so let's go with the idea that Barry Giles or Beryl Mott or one of the others thought, *I know! Let's scare the boss's daughter into screaming hysterics! That'd be a great idea!*

Maybe the eyes didn't move at all. Eyes can follow you without moving, can't they? That's what they say about portraits, right?

So let's consider the scenario again: an impressionable, rather highly-strung child, a dimly lit warehouse full of vents' dolls, a father busy with his work, child foisted upon him by a mother at her wit's end.

You'll be all right here, princess. Lots of toys for you to play with. Keep half an eye on her, would you, Beryl? I've got a meeting with my accountant.

Beryl's eye wasn't on me, not even half of it. I later heard she had her eye on Barry Giles.

But dozens and dozens of other eyes *were* on me.

‹o›

Fast forward ten years or so to my Troubled Teenage Years, the years of rebellion. Derek and Mary having delayed parenthood for a decade after their nineteen fifties wedding out of the deeply-ingrained prudence they both shared, this was bound to be a fractious time.

And when I came home from university sporting a 'Support the Miners' badge, it was "Don't get me started on that Scargill beggar" from him.

And Maggie? Wouldn't hear a word said against her. She'd helped hard-working strivers like him, unlike those ruddy socialists on the other side. And as for the ne'er-do-wells like that brother of his, who'd never aspired to much, there was opportunity for them too, if they'd but take it. "Take

Sidney," he went on, and those blue ice-chips flashed in his eyes. "I offered him a share in the business, but he wasn't having none of it. I still call it Fox Brothers, in hope he might have a change of heart and come on board, but he'd rather wallow in drink and self-pity over in Sidcup.

"Wouldn't he Mary?" he called through the serving hatch.

I wasn't sure what I was expecting from Mary. She was usually full of blunt, pithy Caledonian wisdom, but not this time. I willed her to throw me a lifeline, perhaps invoke her father, buried under tons of rubble and fossil fuel, but she remained tight-lipped, fussing around her kitchen domain in her lilac twinset while the father-daughter row took place, cleaning every pot and pan and surface to within an inch of its life, until each one reflected a face as rigid as wood or wax, mouth shut like a trap.

⟡

Derek Fox went to his grave not knowing what really happened.

There were rumors it was an insurance job, that warehouse inferno. In the end, they arrested Uncle Sidney for the crime. He protested his innocence, but the judge and jury were convinced by the prosecution argument that he'd always resented his brother's success and burned the place down to get his own back.

I know better.

Years later, I visited him in prison, and he told me he never wanted anything to do with Derek's business, or any of the other vile, unnatural things his brother got up to. He pleaded with me to help him get out of jail. I just told him to stop saying those things about my dear father and left with his cries for help ringing in my ears.

There were other rumors too about the fire, wild talk of screams coming from inside, but that's just nonsense. The place was empty of the living. I made certain before I scattered petrol around like holy water, trying not to look at those accusing eyes on the shelves. After I let myself in with the key I borrowed from Derek's study, avoiding their glazed gaze was the first thing on my mind, after disabling the alarm of course.

Don't look in their eyes.

Don't look in *her* eyes.

It was for her sake I did it. It was the only way I could think of to free her. Because that was what *really* terrified me all those years ago.

Not just the glassy eyes staring at me.

But her staring at me out of one pair of them in particular.

Now I'm no longer four years old, it seems odd to say the least to have a dummy so closely resembling my mother in looks and dress, even down to the lilac twinset it wore, sitting there on that shelf in the shadows at the back of the warehouse.

But there she was.

And throughout the rest of my childhood, I could never shake the conviction that the resemblance was more than just superficial, that she herself, or at least some vital part of her, had been staring panic-stricken from those eyes, pleading for release. It was only when I reached my adolescent years that unformed unease about the world and my place in it changed into a certainty about the source of my alienation and its remedy.

It was only then that I knew what to do.

The argument about the miners' strike and her reaction to it confirmed the suspicions I'd harbored since I was old enough to entertain such thoughts: that the woman I'd always thought so feisty and indomitable was in fact well and truly under the thumb. Her sharp tongue was a sham concealing a lack, a sliver of something missing from her, cut out of her and hidden somewhere dark and musty.

She must have entered that forbidden garage. She must have seen what was in there.

After breaching that inner sanctum, he had to silence her, and she never spoke of it until after the fire. Everyone thought the trauma of this catastrophe had brought on her illness, but that wasn't what she raved about during the delirium of what my father would only call "brain fever," shooting me accusing looks, as if it were me responsible for her condition.

Which I suppose I was.

She was burning up, a reaction to the drastic measures I'd taken to bring her back to herself, as it were. The high fever she was running might explain her ravings about "the woman in the garage . . . the limbs rotting in the apple drawers . . . the hand neatly cut off at the wrist."

What was Mr. Fox doing in there? Making her, or unmaking her?

I call him Mr. Fox to make a story out of it of course, because it enables me to make sense of it.

My lovely, kind, gentle daddy, who soothed my night terrors, even if he was arguably responsible for them, cutting up women, cutting out part of my mother and putting it into a ventriloquist's doll! When you put it like that, it seems unthinkable.

But if you call him Mr. Fox and her Mary, that's a different matter.

It's like when he told us his war stories. My mother would scoff at some of the more far-fetched ones, purse her lips at the risqué ones about furtive encounters with girls who spoke but a few words of English. Yes, how she'd turn her face away from his apologetically kissing lips after some of those!

But when spinning yarns about storming the beaches of Normandy he edited out the worst of it, the bodies or bits of bodies floating around in the churning waters, just telling us about tearing up onto the shore dodging bullets. There he was, fantastic Mr. Fox, surviving a massacre by the skin of his teeth, getting out with maybe a singed brush, the rascal.

But to Mary's ain folk he was something more than that. They all came down when they heard, a small army of uncles crammed into a battered transit van, all built like the outdoor privies in their backyards. Men in black donkey jackets with coal-dust ingrained in the very pores of their skin that made their faces into brooding scowls, they crowded into that antiseptic room, mob-handed.

My father cowered outside as if they were more frightening than the Nazis strafing the beach as he put his head down and ran for it through the surf. When one of them came out to report on her condition—"there's been an improvement," was all he said—Mr. Fox tried to sit me on his knee like a shield, his arms grabbing at me, his mouth pleading "Come on, princess, sit on Daddy's knee!" Fully grown, I shook him off as the miner stood and stared at the scuffle, but then Mr. Fox muttered some words that came jibing out of my mouth even though he was not close enough to manipulate invisible wires in my back.

"Why-couldn't-you-help-my-grandmother-when-she-walked-barefoot-to-Carluke?" The words came streaming out like vomit, though I tried to hold them back with my teeth, gritting them in a dummy's grimace. *Gottle o' gear, gottle o' gear!*

"Princess!" said Mr. Fox, in a tone of scolding indulgence, laughing it off desperately. "What a thing to say! She's got a sharp tongue this one, just like her mother! Still, nothing like a child's simple, cruel logic, eh . . . ?" he added pointedly, still apparently convinced I was one.

My eyes pleaded with my great uncle to see these were not my words, but he just shook his head at the whole contemptible display my father and I were staging. He turned his sooty face away, saying "She was too proud to accept our help." Then he walked back into the private hospital room.

He didn't want to leave Mary there with her uncles. But one of them came out and said, "Best if you went home and got some rest, Mr. Fox," and he didn't argue.

◂◦▸

We never saw her again. They took her back to Lanark. She must have improved enough to travel.

He went downhill after that, visibly shriveling in her absence, whatever magic he might have possessed fading from his eyes, their blue ice-chip glint dissolving to a watery shimmer. Sitting there those last few months, he looked no more alive than when he was laid out in his suit one overcast morning in April. Trying to make me sit on his knee, as if I were a child or a dummy, must have been the first sign of the decline that later saw him asking who I was and where Mary was. "Has she gone out to the shops?" he kept asking.

SCREAM QUEEN

NATHAN BALLINGRUD

Can you shift your chair a little bit . . . no. Here. Let me—"

She stood while Alan adjusted the angle of her chair an inch. When she sat down again, he saw immediately that the lighting was better. He was hoping to get at least part of the interview using the natural light coming in through the picture window in her living room. It highlighted the contours of her face brilliantly. She was old—magnificently, regally old—and he wanted to play it up.

She let him angle her shoulders the way he liked; a natural pro, he thought. God bless her for that. Standing back a few feet, he gave her a quick critical appraisal.

She was eighty-two years old, she wore her hair long, and she was dressed in jeans and a red flannel shirt with the sleeves fastidiously buttoned at her wrists—too hot for Texas, Alan would have thought, but then he wasn't on the far side of eighty. Her face resembled a weathered rock. She looked goddamn beautiful, and it was hard for him not to smile like a stricken fool. "How's it look, Mark?"

Mark was standing behind the camera. When he didn't answer, Alan turned to look at him. Mark was staring at the screen, giving him a thumbs up.

"I can't see you when my back is turned," Alan said. "You have to speak out loud."

"Sorry."

Jennifer Drummond smiled, careful not to alter her position. "Are you a student, Mark?" she asked. Her voice sounded strong, and she articulated well. This was going to be so good.

"Yup. I'm in my last semester at USC."

Alan waited for Mark to brag about the fancy new job waiting for him after graduation, but surprisingly he managed to restrain himself.

"How nice! That's where Lionel went," she said.

"Yes ma'am, I know. John Carpenter, Lionel Teller, Dan O'Bannon—a lot of the old school horror guys went there. I feel like I'm part of a tradition."

Her smile faded a little, turning private. "Well. I didn't know those other gentlemen. I only knew Lionel."

Alan didn't want this conversation to happen yet. Better to wait until they started filming. He wanted her answers spontaneous and fresh. She might look robust, but he didn't want her telling the story once off camera and then deciding it was time for a nap. "We'll get to all that," he said. "I'm going to get in close for a sec, okay? I don't want you to think I'm getting fresh."

He loomed over her, fixing the microphone to the collar of her shirt. He half expected her to make some joke about not having been this close to a man since the Nixon Administration—she was a famous recluse—but she remained still and quiet. He caught the scent of perfume as he leaned in, and wondered if he should feel flattered.

Stupid to feel this giddy about a woman over thirty years his senior, but he couldn't help it. He'd been in love with her since he first watched her movie on a VHS tape when was a kid.

Alan's dream was making his own movies, but he was in his mid-fifties now, and his middle-of-the-night thoughts told him he'd missed his chance. He hadn't given up, though. Not yet. And in the meantime he made his living hustling work like this—producing featurettes and press kit material for feature films, both new and old, for release on disc. It was a precarious life, made more so as the advent of streaming services eroded the audience for physical copies of films, but it kept him in the business he loved. He picked up ad hoc work as a waiter or a barista to fill in the gaps. Somehow it all worked out. So far, anyway.

This one was going to strain the wallet. He and Mark had driven from Los Angeles to north Texas for this interview, hauling their equipment with them in Alan's 2005 Camry, and the cost in time and gas was going to be more than the small sum they'd make for the finished product. They were staying in a hotel in nearby Templeton, making the fifteen-mile drive to her isolated ranch house this morning. If the interview were with anyone else, they wouldn't have been able to justify it.

But this was Jennifer Drummond. He'd take the goddamn hit. Mark, to his credit, felt the same.

Drummond had only one film to her credit. Written and directed by Lionel Teller in 1970, *Blood Savage* crackled across the grindhouse circuit like chain lightning, where it was received with great enthusiasm by gore-hounds and lovers of sleazy exploitation, before being ushered off screen by the next tide of cheap thrills. It should have faded into obscurity, like most films of its kind—there was no arguing its low quality made it tough to watch—but people kept talking about this one. *Blood Savage* had a vitality that overcame its tiny budget, its bad script, and its terrible actors. Most people credited Lionel Teller for this: somehow he tapped into the ugly zeitgeist, as the optimism and the righteousness of the Flower Power generation wilted under all the assassinations, the Vietnam War, the Manson cult—Teller channeled all that infected energy and poured it into this nasty little film, which spat directly into the eye of an audience which had learned to crave abuse.

Some, though, credited the extraordinary performance of Jennifer Drummond, the lanky Southern girl with the long blond hair and the corn-flower eyes. She'd come from nowhere, like every other actor in the movie, but unlike the others she seemed to possess a natural talent for the job. Where the others moved woodenly, conscious of the camera, she was indifferent to its presence; while others looked as though they were waiting tensely for their cues before lurching into awkward speech, she seemed in easy conversation with the world. As the movie accrued its cult following over the years, she was sometimes compared to Mia Farrow in *Rosemary's Baby*, or Isabelle Adjani in *Possession*. She was the kind of person you fell in love with on sight.

Her defining moment was the midnight scene in the barn. The lights were placed outside so she was lit only by hard white beams sliding in through the wood slats. The horses huffed and whinnied in their stalls. As the scene progressed they reared and panicked, slamming their back hooves into the wood. Drummond's jittery depiction of a woman inhabited by the Devil mesmerized, even terrified. Naked, she shuddered and spat, undulated like something underwater. And then that godawful, howling, throat-ripping scream. Alan felt a happy thrill thinking about it. The scene displayed none of the obvious special effects enhancing Linda Blair's more famous performance a few years later; but there was a sense of taboo about it, leaving the audience feeling as though it had witnessed something it shouldn't have. Something genuinely evil. The scene wasn't the climax of the movie—just a throwaway scare, the second-act demise of a supporting character—but the rest of the movie dragged on in a predictable series of ridiculous plot points. Drummond's performance in the barn became the foundation for the movie's cult status. You could find echoes of it in the bigger, better films that followed, and it was still referenced by horror movie junkies as the possession scene yet to be topped. Naturally, rumors circulated that the possession was genuine. A fun bit of urban legend which only heightened the movie's appeal.

Despite its flaws, *Blood Savage* could have made Jennifer Drummond into a star—a bona fide scream queen—if she'd been at all interested.

"How's that, Miss Drummond? Are you comfortable?"

"I'm just fine, thank you."

Alan went back to the camera and checked the positioning. He came around once more and tugged gently on the bottom of her shirt, straightening a wrinkle near her shoulder. He didn't know why he was fussing with this part so much. Inevitably, she would move and shift as she spoke; but the process was a kind of ritual, and it helped him settle into his role.

He positioned himself in the stiff-backed chair which had been arranged opposite her, taken from its place in front of the hearth. He hunched forward. It didn't matter what he looked like; he wouldn't be in the shot. They'd try to edit her answers so they wouldn't even need his questions in the finished cut, but he'd be careful to articulate anyway, just in case.

He fixed his own mic to his collar. "I figure we can get a good twenty-five or thirty minutes to start, and then we'll break for lunch. Does that sound okay?"

"It sounds fine." She didn't seem nervous or impatient.

"Mark, how's the sound?"

"You're both coming through loud and clear," Mark said.

"Well, Miss Drummond? Shall we begin?"

She smiled and sat up a little straighter in her chair. "I'm ready," she said.

"So, I'm going to start kind of generally, hit the basics, and then as we go we'll focus on particular topics. There are some points I definitely want to touch on—Lionel Teller, the barn scene, your life afterwards—but really I just want to see where the conversation takes us. I think these things always turn out better when there's an organic quality to them. Okay?"

"Sure."

"Okay. So. What were you doing before you were cast in *Blood Savage*? Did you have any acting experience at all?"

"Christ, no." She laughed. "Have you *seen* the movie? None of us did!"

Alan smiled encouragement.

"I wanted to be a painter. I'd dropped out of college years before and was just kind of drifting. I was apolitical, which sounds terrible, but it's true. No protests for me. I had this idea I was going to have a show in Dallas and get discovered by some fancy New York art dealer. Me and some friends were renting out this big house, sharing all the costs. None of us ever had a real job, we were always late on rent. It was a miracle we didn't get evicted."

"So, how did you get involved with *Blood Savage*?"

"Lionel was over at the house one night. He was dating one of my roommates. It was the usual stupid thing. We were all stoned, he and I hit it off. We spent the whole night talking about art. I wanted to talk about Warhol and Picasso. He was into the Surrealists and Grand Guignol theater."

"Did he talk about Satanism?"

"Not right away. That came later."

"Okay. I interrupted you. Please continue."

"Well there isn't much more. He started in about the movie he was going to shoot, and all his high talk about art went right out the window. It was just a cheap horror flick. A chance to show naked girls and a lot of blood."

"What did you think about that?"

"Well I thought it was all very silly and childish, but I was hoping he'd ask me to be in it."

"Really? Even though you thought it was childish?"

Drummond smiled. "I was silly and childish myself. Why wouldn't I be interested? Besides, it was a movie. Everybody wanted to be in the movies."

"Did he ask you that night?"

"Yes he did. And I said yes right away. I thought I was going to be a movie star."

"What about your dreams of being a painter?"

"Why couldn't I be both?" She didn't seem wistful or sad. She spoke about those old feelings as if they belonged to someone else, someone she'd been assigned to observe, and she was making a field report.

"A lot of people think you could have *been* a movie star, if you'd wanted to be. Me, for example. I mean . . . I'm sure you get this all the time, but a lot of us think you gave one of the all-time great performances in horror cinema. You could have been up there with icons like Barbara Crampton and Jamie Lee Curtis." He realized he'd phrased that tactlessly, and he felt himself blush. "I mean, I think you already are, but . . ."

"I don't know who those women are," she said. "I don't keep up with the movies. But I'm sure it's a flattering comparison."

"It is!"

"Well, thank you. But I think you're full of shit." She smiled when she said it, but it was clear she meant it. "I didn't invite you here to blow smoke up my ass."

Despite the rebuke, Alan was thrilled. She was no washed up relic. She had a sharp tongue and she wasn't afraid to flash a little steel. The classic Texas no-bullshit personality. He began to wonder if there might be more to this interview than simply press kit material. Maybe he could turn this into a book, or a documentary even. Maybe this was the beginning of something.

"You're not talking about my acting," she said. "My acting was terrible. We were all terrible. None of us had a future in the movies, including Lionel. You're talking about the barn scene."

He cast a glance at Mark, who looked up from his place at the sound board. This was what they'd come for.

"Yes," Alan said. "I guess I'm talking about the barn scene."

She looked out the window. The day had just crossed noon. The rolling hills and the brush were bathed in light. There was nothing around them but open land for as far as he could see. Nevertheless, the black energy of that scene intruded into the room. Goosebumps rippled over his skin.

When she didn't speak, Alan pressed her. "The rest of the movie has plenty of charm, but that scene seems like something spliced in from another project altogether. There's a rawness to it, a realness, the rest of the movie doesn't have. And I've tried to figure out what it is. It's not like there's anything inexplicable happening onscreen. No rotating heads or impossible contortions. It's just, I guess you'd say an *eeriness*. A sense of transgression."

She watched him while he fumbled through his thoughts. It made him nervous, which surprised him; he'd done a million of these things, sometimes with big stars. What should he be nervous about?

"And like, it's iconic for so many people of my generation." He said *like*. He was talking like a fucking teenager.

"So many men, you mean," she said.

He paused. He cast another glance at Mark, but Mark was now focused solely on the sound board. "That's true. It's a very sexual scene."

"Why do you think so?"

Nothing in her inflection had changed; her expression was neutral, not hostile. And yet Alan felt as though the balance had shifted, and his footing was unsteady. He tried to get it back. "Were you uncomfortable performing the scene naked?"

"Of course. Who wouldn't be? But there was nothing squalid about it. Everyone was very respectful. What I think is interesting is how uncomfortable *you* seem."

She watched him for another moment, and then reached over to an end table and fished a pack of cigarettes from a drawer. She leaned back in her seat and lit one up. All his careful compositional arrangements came undone, but there was no stopping that, and he didn't care. He was on the verge of getting something good.

Fuck it, he thought. *Be candid.* He could always edit this later. "You were a sexual fantasy for a lot of boys my age," he said. "Maybe that's why I'm uncomfortable talking about it." Heat crawled up the back of his neck.

He feared he'd crossed a line. Some people like to ambush their interview subjects with sensitive or intrusive questions, making them uncomfortable in hopes of getting at some emotional payoff. They didn't care if it upset the person or embarrassed them. If it was for an in-depth feature, that was one thing; but for press kit material like this, he'd always considered it a cheap move. Alan did not consider himself one of those guys. And he *liked* Jennifer Drummond; he respected her. The thought of putting her in a bad position appalled him.

And yet.

"Of course," she said. "A lot of teenage boys like to look at naked girls. There's nothing wrong with adolescent libido. Girls have libidos too, it might surprise you to know."

He accepted the chastisement with a smile and a shrug. "I know, but—"

"Fantasies are normal, and as long as they're kept in context they're usually healthy, too. You can let them go too far, though." She paused and took a pull from her cigarette. He noticed nicotine stains on her fingers. "It never occurred to me to think people might find the barn scene charged in that way, but it wouldn't have bothered me very much. We filmed it in 1969. It was a wild time."

"It never occurred to you? Forgive me, but that seems a little hard to believe."

"You can believe what you like."

He paused to regroup. "Let's talk about Lionel Teller and his obsession with Satanism. Obviously, at this point, he'd already started talking about it openly. Can you tell me about that?"

She looked down at her hands, fidgeting in her lap. The cigarette burned between her fingers, untouched. "What you have to know about Lionel is that he was an egomaniac. He had to have the first and last word on everything. He was obsessed with black magic—reading everything he could get his hands on about Anton LaVey, Aleister Crowley, who knows what else. We all thought it was a bunch of nonsense, but God forbid he heard you say such a thing. He'd fly into one of his tantrums, and it could last a long time. He could hold a grudge like you wouldn't believe. He'd host rituals and séances at his house, and he'd expect the cast and crew to come. He'd feel personally slighted if someone didn't attend. I made that mistake once—he didn't talk to me for a week."

"What were those sessions like? Does anything stand out?" He glanced over at Mark, who was watching her intently. Seeing Alan's glance, he flashed him a thumbs up.

"They were boring, mostly. Lionel was impossible. We got stoned, we drank. But there wasn't much fun to be had. A few of the others took it seriously, I suppose. Jake McDonell, the leading man, was so scared one night he drove away in the middle of it. Lionel had to meet him the next day and convince him not to quit. But most of us just did it to go along."

"I've never heard that story," Alan said. "Have you, Mark?"

"Nope. New to me."

"McDonell was going to quit the movie?"

"He did quit it. For a night, anyway. Lionel was very persuasive, though. That man could talk anyone into anything he wanted." She paused, thinking. "Jake was convinced something had come to the house. Even after Lionel talked him into coming back, he asked us all, at one time or another, if we'd heard it."

"Heard it doing what?"

"Walking. Breathing."

"Did you believe it?"

"No. Not then."

"But . . . later?" Alan felt his excitement ramping up. Was she going to cop to believing in black magic? On *his* featurette?

"When it came time to shoot the scene, Lionel believed filming a real ceremony would give it—and the whole production, really—a sense of legitimacy. Something genuine the audience would respond to, even if it was just—you know, subconsciously."

"Did anybody object? Jake?"

"By that time, no. We knew what he was like. And Jake, well. Despite his tough guy attitude, he was meek in his heart. He always did what he was told." She seemed to remember she had the cigarette in her hand and brought it up for a deep draw.

"Do you know the rumors circulating around the movie?"

Silence stretched between them. She took another pull before she said, "No."

Alan had the strong sense she was lying. But if she'd been as reclusive as she claimed, he guessed it was possible. "An urban legend has grown up around the movie, specifically around the barn scene. You were so good, and the scene is so creepy, some people say you were actually possessed."

"Oh. Well, yes. I was."

Alan and Mark exchanged a glance. "You're saying Lionel used actual summoning rites to film the scene?"

The question irritated her. "Lionel didn't *do* anything, except give us the script and stand behind the camera. *We* did it. We said the words and made the motions. And I opened my heart to it. Please don't give him credit he doesn't deserve."

"I'm sorry." He took a breath, watching the sunlight move across her face as she turned her head. "But I want to be clear. You're saying you actually summoned a real demon onto the set."

"I'm saying more than that. I'm saying I was physically possessed by a demonic entity, and that same entity has not left my body in almost fifty years."

Alan was stunned. How to respond? His new ambitions for a book about her shifted; she was either a crank after all, or she was exhibiting some late-life William Castle-style showmanship. Either would be a compelling subject.

"Are you um—are you possessed right now?"

"We can talk more about it after lunch," Miss Drummond said. "I'm feeling a little tired. I could use a break." Her enthusiasm seemed reduced from its former high; she looked distracted, almost sad.

Alarmed, Alan said, "Maybe we can push a little further? We're just getting into the good stuff." If they stopped now, she might never come back to this subject. Or she might be more circumspect about it.

"I don't know . . ."

"Another few minutes. I don't want to lose momentum—"

Mark spoke up. "Alan. Let's get some lunch. I'm starving anyway."

Alan kept his mouth clamped shut; it was everything he could do not to tell his partner to shut his goddamn mouth. This was *his* interview. Mark was just the fucking tech support.

Jennifer Drummond smiled at him, arching one eyebrow. "You wouldn't push an old lady when she's tired, would you, Alan?"

He flushed. "Of course not, Miss Drummond. I'm sorry. I didn't mean to be rude." Recognizing the interview was at an intermission whether he liked it or not, he removed the microphone from his collar.

She patted his hand. "Call me Jennifer," she said. "I don't stand on ceremony. Now look, you boys go into town and get yourselves something to eat. I recommend Paco's. I would have prepared something for you myself, but frankly I wasn't up to it. I'm sorry to be such a poor host. I'm out of practice, you know."

He leaned over, unclipping her mic, too. "Please don't say that. You've been more than gracious. I wish you'd join us. My treat."

"Heavens, no. I'm going to have myself a little siesta. I don't believe I've talked this much in one sitting in ten years. If I'm asleep when you get back, just knock on the door. I'm a light sleeper."

"If you're sure."

"Don't ever ask an old Texas lady if she's sure. If she said it, then that's how it is."

Alan smiled. "Yes ma'am."

"Good. Well that's it then. Go fill your bellies and come on back in a couple hours. Say three or four?" When they agreed, she headed back to her bedroom, leaving them by themselves. Alan and Mark stepped out into the heat. The sun burned in a thin blue sky. Wind billowed over the land, smelling of sagebrush. They regarded one another quietly for a moment. Then, despite his irritation with him, Alan broke out into a smile. "Holy shit, dude."

Mark headed to the car. "Come on, man. We need to talk."

⟨⟩

They skipped Paco's and headed straight for the bar, a dingy little hole called The Canteen. The place was dark, cool, and empty, the bartender a threadbare soul who seemed stunned by the way they manifested into his world from the glare of daylight. They ordered a couple burgers and some beers. He served them and retreated into a shadowy recess.

They hadn't talked much in the car. Alan was fit to burst, but Mark was clearly troubled by something and put him off with a brusque, "I need to think." Now that they were settled in and had a few sips of beer in them, he loosened up. "I think she needs help, man."

"What do you mean?"

"I mean she's not well."

The irritation Alan had felt back at the house bubbled back up. "Come on. You have nothing to base that on."

"Are you kidding me?"

"You don't know her story. She's been living in this godforsaken town for half a century, she's probably grateful for the attention. She's feeding the legend."

Mark shook his head. "I don't know, man. I think that's wishful thinking."

Alan took a pull from his beer. "You shouldn't make judgments about the person you're interviewing until you've let them speak their mind, and even then you should probably try to refrain. We need to remain objective."

"Oh, here we go."

"What the fuck is that supposed to mean?"

"You talk to me like I'm a child. You do it all the time. I don't need a lecture on what to think. And don't talk to me about being objective."

"You *are* a child!" He tried to say it like he was kidding, but he didn't sell it very well.

"Look, this woman was taken advantage of," Mark said. "She was forced to attend these stupid rituals by some alpha-male douchebag, made to perform this fucked up scene in the nude, which she admitted made her uncomfortable—surrounded by god knows how many of them lighting their fucking candles and doing their stupid devil chants!—and she ended up becoming the wet dream of half the maladjusted teenage boys across America. And she was probably mentally ill already. Undiagnosed and untreated. And now here she is, thinking she has some actual demon roosting in her head. And we're putting her on camera. Exploiting her all over again. No wonder she ran away."

Alan stared at his plate, reeling from this little speech. "I'm surprised to hear you say that," he said. "If that's what you think, what are you even doing here? You seemed thrilled about it on the way out."

Mark pushed his empty mug away and called for another one. "I'm doing this because I love horror movies. Just like you. And because it's going to be great material, and that's what we're here to get. You know, Alan: *professionalism*. That doesn't mean I have to pretend I don't know what we're really doing."

The bartender put another beer in front of Mark.

"That's the last one," Alan said. "We're not done today."

"You're a piece of work," Mark said, turning to face him. "You just have to make your little power plays. Christ, I'll be glad to move on from this."

There it was. Alan knew Mark wouldn't be able to resist throwing his new gig in his face. A few more months and he'd be on set with a big studio production, making some real money. Not hustling anymore. Making the leap Alan never could manage. A young man with a future.

They'd been working on and off as a team for two years. They'd developed a good rapport. Mark had listened to Alan talk about the movie he was going to make someday, how he was going to get the funding, the strings he would pull to get some surprise stunt casting. "I've been in this business for a while," Alan had said, often. "I'm owed a lot of favors." He'd promised Mark he'd give him a job too, they'd climb up the ladder together. Mark had always been encouraging.

And then Mark got the call. A USC buddy had done all right by herself, landed a good job at Lucasfilm, and when a position opened up in her department, she called in her old friend.

He knew he shouldn't take out his frustrations on Mark. It wasn't the kid's fault he had somehow managed to waste the best working years of his own life. He should be happy for the guy.

But he felt like a goddamned idiot. He felt ashamed of his whole life.

"Well," he said. "You'll be out of here soon enough. Then you can go suck Hollywood's big dick."

"Okay, I'm done." Mark stood, leaving his beer unfinished. He threw down a few bills. "Hey bartender, you got cabs in this town?"

The bartender nodded.

"Call me one please." To Alan, he said, "I'll meet you back at her place."

"Fine."

Mark walked out the door, and Alan finished his lunch, taking his time about it. She'd asked for a few hours, and he was enjoying the cool and the quiet. He only hoped the dumb kid didn't wake her when he got back to the house.

Finished, he pushed his plate away and ordered another beer. He went over the argument in his mind, searching for justifications and weaknesses. He already regretted shitting on Mark's opportunity—the kid was good at his job, and he deserved it—but then he considered that little speech about taking advantage of Jennifer and got angry all over again. Who was Mark to decide she was crazy? Why not clever and playful? The self-righteous prick.

Glancing up, he was surprised to find the bartender standing right there, staring at him. "Um . . . you need me to pay my tab or something? Are you closing already?"

"No, no." The guy seemed nervous. Alan couldn't get a read on his age. Late forties? Early sixties? He seemed gray and indistinct; his whole presence was like an apology. "I was wondering if you fellas were here for Miss Drummond."

Hang on now. "What makes you say that?"

"Well, it ain't hard to figure out. You were talking kind of loud."

"I guess that's fair. Okay, yeah, we're here to interview her. You know she was in the movies, right?"

The knowledge seemed to surprise the bartender. "No, I did not."

"Yeah, man. She's a big deal." He smiled, feeling a little buzzed. He picked up his mug and offered an imaginary toast to him. "At least, to the discerning cinephile, she is."

"Well, isn't that something. I was hoping you all were here 'cause she was starting up her service again, but I guess that's not it."

Alan, about to drain his beer and fashion his exit, paused. He kept smiling, but it was a curious smile now. "What's your name, man?"

"Tom."

"Tom, how about another one of these? I want to hear about this service."

"I guess I probably better not talk about it."

"Why not?"

He seemed to take the question seriously and mulled it over for a minute. "Miss Drummond is a private person. That's probably pretty clear to you, since you had to come all this way to find her. It's not my place to tell her story. Not anyone's, really." He put a little emphasis on the last, making it clear what he thought of Alan's purpose here.

"Look. Tom. I don't know Miss Drummond very well personally, but I've been an admirer my whole life. I would not do anything to put her in a bad light. Just the reverse, actually. You heard my colleague. He thinks she's mentally unsound. Do you think so?"

"No I do not."

"Neither do I. I want the world to fall back in love with her. If she was holding church services or something along those lines, it could go a long way to helping me make that happen."

Tom ruminated. It was clear to Alan that he didn't do much of anything before giving it considerable thought. He supposed that was a virtue, but it made him impatient.

"She deserves that," the bartender said. "She deserves to be loved."

"We're on the same page, Tom. How about that beer?"

Pouring another draft, Tom said, "She used to hold it up at her house. This was a whole lot of years ago. I was just a kid myself." He produced an old ghost of a grin. "Not too young to fall in love, though."

"But this *was* like a church service, right?"

"I guess you could call it that." He became cautious again, as though he'd startled himself with his little flare of enthusiasm. "I don't really remember the specifics."

"What *do* you remember?"

"This was way back in the '70s. Like I say, I was young. She was in the same house she's at now. I don't remember how she came to be there, but I know she was a fairly recent addition to the scenery. My dad kept on calling them 'the city-slickers,' even when they'd been here for years."

"Wait. 'Them'?"

"Her and her boyfriend."

Alan sat up, tried to clear his head. "She had a boyfriend? What was his name?"

"Can't remember his last name, but his first name was Lionel. I remember 'cause it was the same name as the model trains. You remember those?"

"Lionel Teller?"

"Maybe."

"Holy shit." He rubbed his eyes. "So he was here with her. And he was what, hosting these services with her? What were they like?"

Tom's memory turned out to be ill-defined. He had a roundabout way of speaking, once he got going, so it took longer than it should have for Alan to get an impressionistic notion of these "services." It seemed everyone in town attended them, and there was little rhyme or reason dictating when they were held. From time to time an urge would come into their heads, and they'd go. Little Tom's parents would take his hands into theirs, and together they'd walk with others from Templeton in a loose procession to the Drummond house. People congregated outside until she and Teller came out.

"I remember she had a silver light, real powerful but not really shining beyond her own skin. Almost too bright to look at. But I couldn't not look. None of us could bear to look at anything else. Sometimes it was Miss Drummond in the middle of the light, sometimes it was something else."

"Something else?"

"Something holy. Something with a lot of limbs and a lot of faces. Its head spun like a carousel, showing them all to us. Or showing us to them."

He couldn't remember what would occur next. He believed it was possible that nothing happened at all, that the observance was the whole point; each side watching the other, the very act of looking fulfilling some unarticulated need.

After each service, Tom said, there were one or two fewer people making the walk home. No one wondered too much what happened to the missing people, not even later, when the services stopped. It was sort of understood that they were gone, and it was natural that they should be.

"You weren't scared?"

Tom thought about it. "'Scared' seems like too easy a word for what it was. We loved her, and as anyone who's lived a while knows, love and fear aren't strangers to each other. We felt like she was ours. She belonged to us, whatever that meant."

It meant quite a lot, it turned out. Lionel Teller became the object of some jealousy from people in town. Each time they were sent home—"or maybe 'released' is a better word," Tom said—Teller retreated into the house with her. His exposure to that magnificent light, and to the presence inside it, was ongoing. Why did he deserve it, and not they?

Well, that all stopped, eventually.

"What do you mean? What happened?"

"Somebody killed him."

"Killed Lionel Teller? How?"

"Hard, that's how. A mob of folks tore him to pieces."

" . . . What year was this?"

"'75, '76? Difficult to say for sure."

"Jesus Christ. How is it possible this has never gotten out? Doesn't anybody from this town ever gossip? Ever go online, even?"

Tom shrugged. He slid him another beer; Alan realized with some surprise that he'd downed three or four. There was no window in the bar to measure the sunlight. He checked his phone: He was late.

"It's just not something we think about, I guess."

"Do you know how crazy that sounds?"

Tom wasn't pleased by the question. "You weren't here for it. You don't understand. Hell, I wouldn't have thought of it at all if you two hadn't come into town and started shouting at each other."

Alan had to go. He stood, felt his head swim. He didn't want to leave this guy on a bad note, though. Fuck the featurette; he was definitely going to come back here and make a documentary. Lionel Teller murdered! This was what was going to save him. What a godsend. But what would it do to *her*? Was he really prepared to throw her to the wolves? He paid his bill and left a generous tip. His brain scrambled to process what he'd heard, to figure out how he was going to proceed. Maybe Mark was right: maybe she was crazy, and it was contagious. Maybe everybody in this town was batshit.

His scalp prickled. He'd seen enough horror movies to know what was supposed to come next. He imagined the people of Templeton arrayed outside the bar, staring at the door with dead eyes, waiting for him to come out. "I'm curious," he said. "If no one's said anything all these years, why now? Why are you telling me? Makes me kind of nervous."

Tom didn't smile. He said, "Nobody's set foot in that house since that Lionel son of a bitch got hisself killed. And she's been quiet as the grave since then. If she's invited you fellas in, I figure she's getting ready to start back up again. I miss it. I miss her. I still dream about her, and that silver light." He paused. "Tell you the truth? I'm not worried about you telling anybody. Nobody who sees that light ever chooses to leave this place."

Alan had nothing to say to that. He nodded noncommittally and headed out the door, where the late afternoon was still warm and the parking lot was empty of angry townsfolk, where his car waited right where he'd left it and started easily when he turned his key. He turned onto the road and drove the fifteen miles toward Jennifer Drummond's house, the sky a gorgeous rose hue above him.

⟶⟨○⟩⟶

He drove slowly. He was closer to drunk than he liked, and he was already very late; he didn't want to compound his problems by getting pulled over by a Texas cop. By the time he pulled up to the ranch house, daylight had receded to a ghostly echo in the sky. Night with all its distant stars loomed behind it. Getting out of his car, he paused to stare up into it. He rarely left LA anymore, and when he did, it was usually for another metropolis like New York or Toronto, so it had been a long time since he'd been intimidated by the sky. Like any student of the genre, he knew the decreed reaction to this kind of display: a feeling of smallness, of inconsequence. But as he progressed further into middle age, he no longer needed an empty sky to feel cosmic horror; the deep, formless awareness of a wasted life engulfed him every night. It was the impetus for many 2 a.m. breakdowns. He always felt afraid.

Light shone from the living room window, warm and welcoming. He crunched a few Altoids to mask the smell of beer and climbed the steps, bracing himself for Mark's withering look. He rapped once on the door and then walked in. "Sorry I'm late. I was interviewing some of the local wildlife."

He was struck by a sudden gust of rot-stench, a rolling wave of it which made his eyes water. Involuntarily he brought his hand over his mouth. It passed in seconds, replaced by the scent of sandalwood incense. He noticed a stick of it smoking in a corner.

Jennifer Drummond was sitting in the same chair she'd used for the interview. Mark sat across from her, in the chair Alan had used. Alan paused. The room was gravid with moment, as though he'd intruded upon some delicate transaction. Jennifer looked at him and smiled in a way that seemed wounded and hesitant. Mark lowered his head and wiped a hand over his eyes.

"Uh, is everything okay?"

"Who were you talking to?" Jennifer asked.

"The bartender at the Canteen. Tom. I lost track of time."

"Alan," Mark said. "I think we need to go."

Jennifer looked startled. "Nonsense."

"Yeah, really. It's late. We can come back and finish in the morning." Saying this, he looked up at Alan. His eyes were red and swollen. He'd been crying.

"Mark? What the hell happened?"

Jennifer put a hand on Mark's wrist. He flinched. "Mark thinks I'm crazy," she said.

"God damn it."

"That's not how I put it," Mark said.

"He was trying to protect me." She looked away from Alan and back at Mark. "But you were being presumptuous. Weren't you, Mark."

He nodded, his face lowered. Alan could see the backs of his ears turn red. Mark was trying to hold back tears. He felt deeply unsettled. Something was badly wrong. "Miss Drummond—Jennifer—I think Mark is right. It *is* late, and he looks like he might be feeling sick. It's probably best to come back and finish in the morning."

She ignored him. "Go sit on the couch, Mark."

Mark did what he was told, avoiding Alan's eyes as he brushed past him. Jennifer gestured to the vacated chair. After a moment, he sat across from her. "What's going on here?"

"I had to show him," she said. "I didn't like his insinuations."

Alan sought for something to say, some way of defending Mark without risking her trust. There wasn't any. Instead he just stared at Mark, who sat on the couch like some chastened little boy, struggling to keep his composure.

"What did you show him?"

For a moment she seemed to be on the verge of tears herself. "I didn't want to." Her hands were clutched tightly in her lap, knuckles white with tension. Then she closed her eyes and he could see a resolve settle over her like a garment. When she spoke again, all trace of weakness was gone, "I won't be told who I am anymore."

"Then tell me yourself. Who *are* you, Jennifer?"

She smiled politely and settled back into her chair. "Sit down, and I'll tell you. Turn the camera on. Let's finish."

Alan did as she asked. The light had all but gone from the world outside, and he drew shut the curtains. He gestured for Mark to resume his place at the sound board. In a couple of minutes they were ready to record. He resumed his seat and took a deep breath.

"Tell me what you want to tell me," he said.

"Lionel was a monster. He was charming and funny when he needed to be, but once you got right down to it, he only cared about what he wanted. Power. Over the people in his life, over his actors, and over me. Especially over me." As she continued to speak—describing Lionel's exacting direction, his rages, the way he eroded her will over a period of several days before the barn scene, insulting her abilities and criticizing her appearance when she disrobed for the night's shoot, leaving her vulnerable and defenseless—that rancid odor intruded into the room once more: first an unpleasant tickle in the nose, swelling quickly into the brute stink of decay.

Alan ignored it for as long as he could bear to; then he pulled his shirt up over his mouth, squeezing shut his watering eyes. Jennifer continued talking for a few seconds, then trailed to a stop. She made no effort to cover her nose, nor did she seem offended by the smell. She only seemed sad.

"Jesus," Alan said. "What *is* that?"

She continued as if he hadn't said anything. "When I realized what had happened—what had moved into me—I came out here. I wanted to be far away from people, so it couldn't hurt anyone. I wanted to isolate it. Lionel didn't care. He followed me, and I was too weak to refuse him. He wanted to feed it and see what happened. He wanted to make a documentary—the film that would make him a star. The two of them together overwhelmed me for a while. But Lionel didn't last long. The people loved me." She stopped. "Well. It was really the demon they loved. But they thought it was me. Maybe that's the same thing. They did what I wanted them to do."

Somebody killed him . . . a mob of folks tore him to pieces.

"So Lionel was filming when he was here? Where are the reels?"

"Under the house."

"Buried? They might be ruined."

"Not buried. In the nest."

"What are you talking about, Jennifer?"

"After Lionel was gone, it was just the two of us. It was strong, but I was stronger. I locked myself in this house, cut myself off from everyone. I killed it, finally. I starved it. It took years. So many years." She put her hands on her chest, her belly. "It's rotting inside me now ."

Alan fought back a wave of nausea. His head swam. "What do you mean? What do you mean it's rotting inside you?" He stood up, for what purpose he wasn't sure. He was confused. He needed fresh air. The stink had grown even worse. It was like something physical in his throat. "What did you show Mark?" he said. "What was it?"

From the corner, Mark started weeping. He didn't try to stifle it; he sounded like a child who had lost something, or was lost himself.

"I didn't mean to." Jennifer's voice trembled, her resolve crumbling. "When he told me I was crazy, I just—I got so angry. I lost control for a minute. I didn't mean to hurt him."

"Jennifer. Please let me see."

"Not here," she said. She rose from her chair and headed down the hallway to her bedroom. The stink of decay followed her. She left a tarry sediment on the floor with each footstep. Alan put the camera onto his shoulder and followed.

Her bedroom was unlit, the bed itself upturned and leaning against the wall, its underside covered in a heavy layer of dust. A great hole had been excavated in the floor, rough steps descending in a steep gradient. Darkness pulsed from inside it.

Jennifer began to change. Her clothes fell from her body in rotten tatters, like the wrappings of a mummy. The skin shifted on her body, turning a pallid gray, covered with black patches of mold. It glistened with some kind of interior light—a luminous rot. She seemed taller, stronger, more beautiful. She was naked, but her body was androgynous: gorgeous, magnetic, dead. Through her failing flesh he saw an equine skull bearing too many pale, sightless eyes. She was at once regal and putrid, her body wavering between her own elderly form and the holy beauty of the Corpse, as though seen beneath rippling water.

The light on his camera surged and went out.

Alan fell to his knees, his cognition crumbling beneath the weight of this like rotten wood. Something primordial in his brain shrieked and danced. His clasped his hands together under his chin, his lips seeking a prayer he'd never learned.

"Don't you pray to it," Jennifer said, her voice leaking from that cracked skull like a gas. "Don't you dare."

Alan couldn't fathom the strength of resolution it would have taken to do what she had done. To endure a contest of wills that spanned decades, to tame a hunger that had crossed the gulf between this world and whatever aching hole it had crawled from—it beggared the mind. It cast into harsh relief the meandering path of his own life: the passive hoping, the cowardly wait.

Even in death the Corpse exerted its influence. Alan felt the snapped-bone shock of a fundamental reordering in his brain. He peered through its eyes. He saw that Mark was dead, despite the heart beating the blood through his body. Like Tom and the people of Templeton he had borne witness to a beauty so terrible that it would ruin everything that followed it. Mark felt his body rotting around him and would long for an escape from it for whatever years remained to him. Alan saw a small handful of people making their way along the empty road from Templeton, the bartender and a few others, not pulled by the mysterious impulse of decades ago but by a doomed hope that she remembered them, that she called them back to her. They would wait outside her house as they had before, shivering in the dark, though this time no light would come. And he saw Jennifer Drummond, her whole life thwarted by the desperate war she'd fought for her own body and her own mind, lonely now in her victory.

She descended into the hole, and he trailed behind her. The stuttering, decayed light from her body illuminated the walls in brief flashes. It was a nest, walled in human faces, scores of them peering out from battlements of melded flesh, their mouths blackly gaping, their eyes cataracted and blind. It was like walking through an abandoned wasps' nest. Once, it rang with screams and hosannas.

Their silence now was obscene. The demon was dead, but this woman still lived. She was still sweetly beautiful, she still yearned to fill her heart's need. "Is it too late?" she asked.

She started to dance, a gorgeous rotted thing, undulating in the way she had done so long ago. Tears spilled down Alan's face. He fixed the camera on her, recording it all. He was making terrible sounds. They echoed in the nest and soon it seemed the faces joined his effort, like a choir in a cathedral.

WE DO LIKE TO BE BESIDE

PETE W. SUTTON

And the doors open and we are out and we are running. The dog, Tyr, streaks far ahead. I couldn't keep up with him if I tried. Little God, mother calls him. My sister, older, longer legs, is next, her yellow blouse like the Tour de France jersey; then me. I look back to see my parents getting the things from the car—a brand-new beige Austin Allegro—windbreaks, blue plastic picnic cold box, foldable chairs. And then my feet on are on sand and I put my head down and pump my arms and fly as fast as I can to try and catch up with my sister. And there's the sea, the open, blue, glittering sea. The dunes bump against it, and running in sand is hard and climbing the dune is hard and I'm panting.

The dog is barking and my sister has stopped and I'm catching up and that's when I see, when I crest the top of the dune. Our dune. There's someone else there; that family—father, massive, glistening in the sun; the mother small, Irish hair; the children, excessive amounts of them. How I hate that family.

The father lies, his bulk in stasis, his hump of a belly proud of the sand. The wife looks up to where my sister holds the dog, straining at its collar, barking. The children don't cease in their tumult but I sense they've seen us. They know us. We live so very near them after all.

"She's a witch," my sister says. Has said a thousand times before. Almost proud of the fact.

And still the mammoth father does not move. They have our spot in the sand and I look back at my own parents trudging across the beach towards us. I glance at my sister. At the line of her mouth.

"This is our place," she spits out.

"It's public," I say.

"Go and tell the olds they have to set up somewhere else," she says, narrowing her eyes. I've seen that look far too many times. I take one last look at the family below, the children shrieking, their mother staring at us in open curiosity, the father unmoving. I shudder, they have brought their clutter with them. The sand littered with the same sort of crap they fill their front yard with. Bamboo poles with woven wool dreamcatchers, brightly coloured cloth bags full of God-knows-what, and stacks of curling paper. Do they not want a break from what Dad calls "the detritus of their failed lives?"

"Go on," she growls, her voice blending with the dogs. Tyr's upset too. I spin on my heel and run to where my parents are slowly, too slowly, walking to where we always set up when we come to the beach.

As I get closer I hear them arguing.

"She's your daughter," Mum is saying.

"I'd like to think that by now you'd consider her yours as well," Dad answers back.

Then she spots me and says, "Toby."

"What is it, Toby?" Dad asks.

"There's someone in our spot. It's that family from the corner," I tell them. They know immediately which family of course.

"Then we'll just have to choose another spot," Mum says.

Dad sighs.

"Can you go and look for another sheltered area please, Toby?" she asks me.

I nod and look back to where my sister still waits at the top of the dune; the yellow of her blouse standing out against the pure blue of the sky. The dog now sits quietly beside her.

"Amy is angry," I tell my parents. They share a look. I put my fingers in my mouth and whistle and see the dog jump up and turn to face me. I whistle again and he races towards me. My sister glances back at us once then walks down into the bowl of the foot of the dune. That's brave of her.

I race off knowing Tyr will catch up. I know that the flat part of the beach will be packed so I have to run up and down the dunes. It occurs to me that another family may get anywhere I find by the time I get my own family back there and wonder what to do about that. I can't think of one thing.

I immediately find another nook with shade for Dad and close enough to the sea for me and out of the wind for Mum and with an area to sunbathe for Amy. It's perfect. It's the next dune to where we usually plonk ourselves anyway. I climb to the top to signal to my sister and parents but they're not there.

Above, I notice that the seagulls are flying in a circle. Their raucous cries suddenly loud, as if the lee of the dune I had been in had blocked their noise. Even better. We all hate seagulls. Last year, on this beach, we'd bought chips from the chip van parked by the concrete toilet block and were mobbed as soon as we brought them on the beach. Mum said that next time we need to eat them near to the van where they had bird scarers. But next to the van smelt like toilets and I wanted to eat mine this year on the beach again but with no seagulls.

I take off my t-shirt and hop-jump down the dune to where I've chosen for us and then place it down on the ground and find a few stones to weigh it down. Just to show that someone has chosen this spot.

"Watcha doin'?"

I spin from where I was assessing my handiwork to come face to face with one of the ragged tribe of children from that family. Well, his face is around my chest-height really but chest to face doesn't sound right. Close up my nose wrinkles to the sour milk and biscuit smell of unwashed body. The child smiles a gap-toothed smile. Younger than me, stick legs and baggy shorts, looking like Micky Mouse. Looking like me at that age but dirtier and with hair that needs cutting.

"Making sure no one takes our spot," I reply. I think a second and take out a lollipop I was saving and give it to him. He smiles shyly and squirrels it away in his filthy shorts.

He puts a finger up his nose and has a good root about. Ignoring the grimace on my face he pulls it out with a slimy green globule at the end which he immediately puts in his mouth. He cocks his head and taking his finger out points behind me. "He sick?"

I frown, and look to where he's pointing. The dog had come back without me hearing, tail between his legs and, as I watch, he heaves, once, twice and then a thick stream of purplish vomit comes out. What the hell has he been eating? A stench of rotten fish rolls over me, my stomach contracts, and I taste acid.

"Are you okay, Tyr?" I ask and walk towards him. He whines and pants. I need to get him some water. Where are my parents? Amy?

"Can you stay here and make sure he doesn't run off?" I ask the boy and when he nods I run up the dune again. Like before, the seagulls wheel through the bright blue sky, screaming to each other. I still can't see my sister, or my parents.

I jump-skip down the dune. "Does your family have any water?" I ask the child. Again he nods. "Come on, boy!" I call to the dog but he just whines. I have to pick him up. Gosh, he's heavy; a good sheep-chaser Dad had called him when we first got him.

"Come on," I say to the boy and lead him around the front of the dune, past the cleft between their dune and the one I'd staked out. The dog's rancid breath wafting up, his heart racing fast, squirming a little in my arms. I look up the small valley between dunes and still don't spot my parents.

The kid remains silent, keeps turning to see if I'm following, his eyes wide. We round the corner, the squealing of the gulls our intro music, and his family aren't there. No, mostly aren't there. No mother, no horde of children, but there, in the centre of the clearing, the patriarch, unmoved and unmoving, a hillock of pink.

The kid scoots over to a plastic bag and takes out a sand-encrusted bottle and holds it out to me. I lay the dog down, my legs and arms screaming from the weight, and grab the bottle. I don't bother asking for a bowl, whatever this family has is covered in grime anyway. I pour a small amount of water into my hand and hold it out for the dog to lick, which he does enthusiastically.

Last year he'd drank seawater and gotten sick too. This year he must have eaten something bad. After a few handfuls of water he starts to look a bit perkier. And I scan around. In among the dirt and jumble there's an intricate display of sandcastles and trenches surrounding the man where he lies. I watch the sand flies hover and a glossy black beetle wend its way across the sand.

"Thanks for the water," I say loudly. The kid grins. The bulk in the middle of the maze doesn't move. "Is your dad okay?" I ask and the kid nods vigorously.

"He's dreaming," the kid says.

I stroke the dog's head and he wags his tail a bit. "Ready to get up?" I ask him and he sits up.

"Well . . . I'd best go find my family," I say. I stand and wipe my hand on my shorts. "Can I take this?" I ask giving the water bottle a shake to slosh the water inside a bit. The kid nods again. Not much of a talker.

"Thanks." I turn. "Thanks mister!" I say.

I take a step in the direction of the man and stop, he's asleep, must be to be so still. Best not disturb him.

I scan the top of the dune and only spot a circle of gulls. Time to go.

Back to where my shirt is staked out on the sand. The dog looks done in. "Stay!" I order him and he flops down on the t-shirt and rolls to his side. I give Tyr another cupped hand of warm water and then close the bottle and put it next to him. "Guard!" I order. He lifts his head but then lets it fall back on the sand.

I go to find my family. It feels like a long time since I've seen them—but I don't have a watch, the strap broke and it's at home on my bedside table. I stride to the top of the dune—three steps forward, one slide back—and stand at the top blowing. Carrying the dog took a lot out of me. There's no one in sight. I march down the side of the dune and up the side of the one we usually camp out, disturbing the seagulls that all leap to the air screeching like witches, calling to each other like drunken sailors.

Below: the dome of the man's belly, solid, stately, still. The kid is off at the side of the dune, poking at something with a twig. I try to see the man's features but his bald head is partly covered, his face obscured with a scrap of brightly coloured cloth.

I retrace my path back to the car, which is burning hot in the midday sun, so hot it scalds my hand when I try the door handle. There's no one inside anyway.

I stand on the wall separating road from beach and turn in a circle. I can't see Dad's red t-shirt or Mum's blue beach dress or my sister's yellow blouse anywhere. I run down the road to the concrete toilet block, ash-black and shaped a bit like a shoebox with a too-large lid. My family aren't here either, nor by the ice cream van. I wander onto the beach and decide that they must have got fed up waiting for me and found somewhere else, maybe even on the flat bit.

I'm a bit worried about Tyr. Maybe I should go back and get him before going for another look? But that would take too much time. So I walk up and down the beach, the flat bit, searching. I walk past families and couples, kids and adults, other families with dogs, and people listening to the radio, a bunch of friends on lilos, and a couple of guys throwing a Frisbee. But not my family.

I'm starting to get real worried now. Where could they be? I know they haven't left because the car is still there. I go to where the sea sucks obsessively at the shore. I like the sea, usually I'm the only one who goes paddling, or swimming, on a day as hot as today. I think the rest of them are mad not to have a cold dip. I shade my eyes and try to spot who's in the water. Dad never goes swimming; Mum says he's afraid of the water but he says he's not afraid of water, he's afraid of drowning, which is different. My sister says he saw someone say that in a film once. I think it's sensible to be afraid of drowning but that it shouldn't stop you swimming.

Dad doesn't like the family down the road, avoids them as much as possible. It was him who first said their mum was a witch, something my sister repeats often. My mum says that he should know, but I don't know why.

I can't decide what to do. I should go back to the dune and find the dog and then go sit by the car. They'll find me at the car. Eventually. As I walk back, the buzz of music and people talking, playing, laughing, surrounds me but something a teenager says to his friend catches me up.

"What did you say?" I ask.

The young man, first moustache trembling atop flaky lips, gazes up at me. "Huh?"

"Just now. You said someone's been arrested?"

"Uh-huh,"

"When? Was it here?"

The dude smooths his 'tache and nods. "Just over there." He's pointing to the dunes. To where I've left the dog. To where the family from down the close were. To where I'd last seen my parents, and sister.

"What happened?"

"I don't know, man, they dragged them away, there was a bit of a crowd. Something about it not being natural?" The two youths exchange a glance.

"What's it to you?" The other one asks.

"Oh nothing," I say. "Nothing." I nod a thanks and walk away. Arrested? I'd best get Tyr and then . . . And then? Do something—surely Mum and Dad would have said something about me. Nah, it can't have been them arrested. Unnatural? What did Mum mean earlier that Amy was Dad's daughter? What did Dad mean by she should have accepted her by now? My mind races as I run down the beach, back to the dunes.

The dog's gone when I return. The t-shirt I took off too. There is a gull eating the dog's vomit. That makes me gag. I need help. I go to the where the man from the corner house is, maybe the family has come back.

Around the corner the girth of the man remains unyielding. I edge closer. There is no child here now. The maze is deeper, the mounds I'd taken to be sandcastles now apparent as just heaps of unburied sand. I edge closer—the bulk does not move. The trenches, narrow and deep, wind around the flat foot of the dune. I edge closer and venture a "hello" and still no movement. A squirt of seagull poo lands on my foot and soon I'm kicking sand as I try to wipe it off my trainer. I kick a mound of sand over and into the dug-out labyrinth.

There is a sound behind me like air leaking from a tyre. I turn and the wife is there, her children tucked in behind her like kittens. She beckons urgently. I give my shoe one last scrape across the sand and walk gingerly to her. She places a finger, blackened by who knows what, to her wrinkled lips. I frown but keep quiet and when I reach her she places a hand on my shoulder and grips me hard. It hurts a little and I start to struggle.

"Your sister is waiting for you," she hisses.

"Where is she?" I ask and stop struggling.

"Come with me and find out." Her grip does not lessen as she marches me away from the dune. The kids skip in and out and around us. I'm scared, but also really want to see my sister. I hope the woman isn't lying to me.

"What have you done with my sister?"

The woman turns piggy eyes upon me. "Done? Nothing, she wants you to come too. Prevailed upon my better nature, she did."

"What do you mean?" I ask.

"You don't belong. She does. But she convinced me that we can make you belong too. Once the Dreaming is complete."

The boy I gave the lollipop to skips ahead and looks back at me smiling. His siblings keep their distance.

"Dreaming? The man, your husband, he—"

"We like living near you, you know," she says.

"What?"

"We do like to be beside you."

"Thanks . . .?" I wonder why she feels like telling me this. I try to shrug out of her grasp but her hand is like an iron claw. We are heading back to the carpark.

"There's only one problem," she continues. "Your mum's innocent, we don't see that much of you but—"

"But what?"

"Your father." She glances at me and I see disgust in her eyes.

"What about him?" We are getting nearer the cars. She's not turning to go towards our car though. I spot their campervan, dirty-white, battered, leaking oil no doubt, like it does on our road.

"He's . . . Well, he's always staring. At us."

"Is he?" I'm flustered, the lady from down the road has been walking me at a quick pace, and we are now nearing the camper. I can hear the dog whining and scratching.

"It's not polite. It's not nice. You're his blood too, that's how she convinced me. Your sister." We come to the van and she pulls a set of keys from the pocket of her tatty dress. The keyring is unidentifiable, a purple blob that might once have been furry. She fits a key to the lock and pulls the door slightly open. Without letting go of me. With her foot she shoves the dog further inside and then opens the door enough to push me in. Tyr, ready to go for her, jumps ecstatically at me instead.

"Wait—" I say but she's slammed the door behind me and locked it. I try the handle but it won't open, and the van's interior—stinking of old chip fat, soiled, sweaty linen and an underlying rusty, oily odour—has no method of getting into the van's cab.

"Hey!" I shout and bang on the door, giving it a good few kicks. "Hey!"

But nothing doing. She's gone and locked me in here, with the dog, but not with my mum or dad. Or sister. How dare she say Dad wasn't nice.

There isn't much room inside—a soot-blackened kitchen, some pots and pans, a couple of bunkbeds and several cupboards locked with padlocks. There is a door to the small chemical toilet, and the windows are high up and thin. I sit on the edge of the bed and wonder what to do next, absent-mindedly stroking the dog.

After a while of kicking the door and shouting I realise that no one is going to come and rescue me. I grab a saucepan as a makeshift weapon—I can find no knives or other cutlery—I sit on the bed to wait. My gaze wanders and alights on an old cardboard suitcase with an advert for laundry on it. Held closed with leather straps. I grab it. Maybe there'll be something useful inside? I struggle to open it. Inside are hundreds of photographs. Photographs of our street, of our house, of our family, of us on the beach, of our car, our dog, of my sister. Many of my sister. In each one with my parents in, Dad's face is erased. Scratched out. That's horrible. I spend a long time looking at the photographs.

After a while I lie down, just to rest my eyes. I've no idea how long I've been asleep but I leap up having heard the van's cabin door open then someone climbs aboard. My hand searches the bed until it lands on the saucepan handle. "Ready, boy?" I ask Tyr. He's sat up too, ears pricked.

The door opens a crack and a child eels inside—I leap to the door and try to push it open as the engine starts. The door springs open and I leap out, past a startled dirty child. The whole horde is there but the parents are in the cab. The child I'd talked to earlier gestures from the door and the horde disappears inside. At his command they leave me alone. He raises the lollipop I gave him to his mouth.

I don't wait around. I run, the dog with me. No one raises the alarm. I glance back and all the children have climbed inside. The child who gave me the water bottle waves from the open door which swings shut as the van lumbers away. As the van turns the corner I glimpse yellow in the passenger seat. Amy! I need to tell my parents they've taken Amy.

It's almost night-time. The light slowly fading into the summer evening. I stop and watch the van pull away. Have I escaped? Now what?

I run over to our car. It's still there. It's still empty. I again go to the chip van. I wish I had some money because I'm starving. At least I can get a drink at the water fountain outside the toilet block. No sign of my parents here either. I ask the chip-van man if he's seen them, describe them to him, but no. He's also not seen the police arrest anyone. Said that was a rumour passed around by stoners.

The beach is emptying of families. Young couples will turn up soon and walk up and down because it's "romantic." I need to find my family. I hurry back to the dunes and there's no one at the place I'd staked out for us. I climb the hill and look down to where we usually stay and the man has gone and all that's left is the weird maze-pattern in the sand. I sit down and put my head in my hands. I'm going to have to ask a grown-up for help, to call the police.

The dog barks and gallops down the hill. Where the man had lain all day was a smooth circle of clear sand. The dog races across the bottom of the dune to this circle, barks again and runs towards the sea. I watch for a second then start down the side of the dune and I realise something. The weird pattern? It's the street plan of the estate I live on. The central bit being where our house would be—and theirs is blank. Where the man had lain dreaming all day.

I hurry down the dune and see the dog racing towards a figure dressed in blue. The sweat I'd worked up running now cools unpleasantly on my skin. It's Mum! I race to her and grab her in a hug. I've started crying but I'm not embarrassed like I'd usually be.

"Toby. Where have you been, I've been worried sick!" She strokes my head.

"The family from the corner have Amy!" I blurt out. Mum frowns. "Where's Dad?" I ask through the tears.

"What's got into you? Who's Amy? And your dad . . . your dad is in our hearts, where he'll always be. He did used to love it here though, didn't he? Beside the sea." She gazes at the sea.

"Amy is . . . is . . . what do you mean? Dad is dead?" I'm frowning, it's hard to think, my mind feels foggy, what's happening?

She ruffles my hair. "Wake up sleepy head."

I shake my head. I had something important to tell her. What was it? I can feel my mind being rewritten, settling into a new groove, history and memory reconfiguring, I try to keep hold of it. Amy is my sister. Dad isn't dead. Amy is . . . Dad . . .

The dog barks and runs at the waves and I look up and the sun is sinking into the sea and I wish that Dad hadn't died, a heart attack at forty, and that we'd not buried him last year. I shake my head, falling asleep in the sun has meant I've awoke confused, that's all. "Amy was just a girl in my dream. She wore yellow." I give Mum a quick hug, dry my eyes and run to play with the dog.

CONTRITION (1998)

J. A. W. McCARTHY

His wallet caught my eye, a bulging leather square that sailed across two lanes of traffic before hitting a parked car right in front of the theater. I remember how the two halves seemed to flap through the air like a fat brown bird, sprinkling business cards and grocery receipts and ticket stubs in its wake. I saw a teenage girl pick up a twenty then hurry down the sidewalk while everyone else was staring in shocked fascination at the broken man in the street.

One of his receipts stuck to my shoe; I didn't notice it until I went back inside. It was from the Italian place down the block, date stamped just two hours before: *1 red wine, 1 pasta special.*

That's what I told the cops when they questioned us later, after Tori called 911 and the owner Ed shuttered the theater before the last showing. The older cop stopped writing in his notepad and rolled his eyes two sentences into my effusive observations. *What do you expect?* I wanted to ask him. I had been an English major, last year before I dropped out.

After taking our statements, the cops asked to see the reels for the film we had just shown. Ed, grumbling the whole time, brought the metal canisters downstairs for the two officers to examine. I was already imagining being stuck there late that night, running popcorn and sodas out to the two cops while they watched the film in the dark theater, but that didn't happen. They handed the canisters back to Ed and never asked to see the film.

◄◦►

"He was a widower, don't you think? One last night out . . . That suit, Alex!" Tori mused the next afternoon, pouring the orange oil into the popcorn kettle. Both she and her girlfriend Emily often complained that the smell made them nauseous, but I was still new enough to enjoy it. "It's like those little old ladies you see in the grocery store, all dressed up with the gloves and the pantyhose and the red lipstick. People back then, they cared how they presented themselves to the world."

I looked down at the receipt tucked under the loose corner of the ticket printer. *1 red wine, 1 pasta special.* My wet footprint had smeared the big looping *L* in Lombardi's. "Why this movie, though? People were leaving all dead-eyed and in tears last night," I said, reaching across the counter to pluck a program from the stack. "'Two days only, exclusive screening of A. Todesfurchten's *Contrition.*' Is that really the last thing you want to see before you die?"

Tori shrugged. "Maybe he needed something like that to seal the deal."

David slid behind the concessions counter and helped himself to the first kernels of popcorn that tumbled from the kettle. "I can't believe we're still showing this shit. We should be closed out of respect for the poor guy."

"It's not like he killed himself in here," I said.

"Yeah, but I mean, what is Ed thinking showing *Contrition*? The title alone, Christ . . . We should be showing *The Big Lebowski*. No one's gonna kill themselves after *The Big Lebowski*."

I turned to Tori as she started filling the second concessions cash drawer. "Where is Emily anyway?"

"She's finally getting that tattoo. After last night . . ." She paused, eyes sunk into the thick wad of ones in her fist. "Anyway, she should be here soon."

Though I hadn't actually seen him get hit, I had thought about the man all last night and upon waking this morning. I remembered selling him the ticket before the show, how he had called me "miss" and smiled like he was excited, like he was having a good day. Emily had sold him popcorn, and though I couldn't hear what he said to her as she was handing him his change, it was something that made her laugh. His age was probably the only thing he had in common with my grandfather—who had been anything but dapper, and so angry at the end, calling me selfish and ungrateful—but I, of course, thought of him. I thought of my grandfather every time I waited for morning, his voice in my head singing the lullaby he used to sing to me when I couldn't sleep after my parents died. I had curled so tightly in my bed last night that my limbs still ached, covers pulled over my head as if I could keep the guilt from finding somewhere to hook into me.

Emily finally showed up just as David was opening the doors. I had sold one ticket so far, to a middle-aged man who was now sitting on the sidewalk below my window holding an umbrella over his bald head.

"Shit, sorry guys," she sang, still fixing her tie as she hurried behind the counter. She gave Tori a quick kiss. "Thanks for covering, babe."

"How'd it go?"

Emily appeared to think for a moment before a tentative smile surfaced on her lips. "Good. It was good."

We gathered on both sides of the counter and watched as Emily rolled her sleeve all the way up to her shoulder. On her left bicep, glistening under a thin layer of lotion, was *Andrew 6.18.1973 - 10.22.1997.* The black script was a stark contrast to the colorful mermaids and pinup girls that covered the rest of her arm.

"It's awesome. I'm glad you did it," Tori said, drawing her arm around Emily's waist.

Only five more people showed up before David closed the theater's heavy double doors and turned off the lights. While Tori and Emily bickered over where they were going for spring break, and David worked on his philosophy paper on the worn lobby carpet, I stared out the ticket window at the street, watching the cars roll right over the spot where the man had died last night. The cops had blocked traffic while people in navy windbreakers walked around taking photos long after the coroner van pulled away. Now it was like nothing had ever happened. Like last winter. *Nothing,* my aunt Kath had said at the time. *It's like it's nothing to you.* I'd told her I had finals, but what I really meant was *I have a boyfriend.* Sex with a hot guy who might lose interest if I was gone too long had sounded more appealing than hospital hallways and an old man who couldn't remember my name anymore.

Halfway through the film, a woman came out of the theater with her fists balled at her sides as she marched across the lobby towards us. Her face was the kind of bright red that usually preceded a rant about the filth theaters were showing these days. "There's a woman crying in there," she announced, slapping her palms on the concessions counter. Emily and Tori looked at each other and I could see the start of a giggle flare Tori's nostrils. "Did you hear me?" the woman continued. "She's *crying. Loudly.* It's very distracting."

"Well, we can't kick her out for crying," Tori said.

"Which one of you's the usher? Isn't the usher supposed to do something?"

David scooted behind a planter, sweeping his books with him.

"I'll go check on her," Emily volunteered.

Once Emily and the woman disappeared back into the theater, the rest of us burst out laughing until we saw Ed coming down the stairs.

"What's going on down here?"

Kara, our manager, was trailing several steps behind him. As they crossed the lobby Ed stepped on David's notebook, stopping only long enough to glare down at him and nudge his leg with a scuffed loafer.

"Some woman's crying in the theater," I said. "Emily went to go check on her."

Ed grunted, turned his attention to Tori who was already pouring him a coffee. "Didn't I tell you to put a hat on that thing? You're going to scare away the customers."

Rolling her eyes, Tori scooted the paper cup across the counter, sloshing hot coffee onto the glass. I thought her shaved head was cool, just this little bit of black fuzz that Emily was always running her hands over.

"Listen, Ed—"

"You know what's scaring away the customers? This movie," David cut in, rising to his feet with a messy armload of books and papers. He dumped everything onto the counter then grabbed a couple of napkins and blotted at the spilled coffee. "Why are you playing this thing? There's six people in there. *Six.* Some woman's crying, a guy killed himself last night . . . You know, I was just at the Cinerama. They're playing *The Big Lebowski* and people were lined up around—"

"The toilet in the men's room is clogged," Ed muttered, taking a big swig of coffee. He didn't even glance at David before turning around and heading back upstairs.

Kara braced both hands on the edge on the counter, arching her back in a feline stretch. She was a ghost, long white-blonde hair and translucent skin punctuated by a bright red mouth; even her all black wardrobe looked weightless as she glided around the theater. I liked to imagine she lived in the attic-like office above the projectionist booth, only coming out at night to smoke cigarettes and conduct vodka tasting parties with her Dame Darcy doll collection.

"He doesn't watch any of the movies, you know," she said, inverting her stretch so that it looked like she was trying to push the concessions counter into the popcorn maker. "He doesn't care what we play as long as it makes money."

"Then why's he playing this bomb?" David asked.

Kara glanced back at the stairs, then gathered the three of us in her gaze. "It's a pay-to-play. I don't know how much, or who this guy is, but I know the distributor is paying us a shit-ton to screen this movie. This theater's one bad weekend away from shutting down. The rest of us can get new jobs, but this place is Ed's life. I mean, look at him. He's fifty-eight years old and he hates everyone. Who would hire him?"

David had stopped listening, abruptly rushing to lock the doors while Kara was talking. A group of frat boys was crossing the street towards us. I recognized the largest one, the one who approached the door first—he'd been coming around for the last month or so, usually drunk and making lewd remarks to the female employees. Emily once got into it with him, calling him a misogynist pig, and now he made oinking noises whenever he saw her. Last week he shook my ladder while I was up there changing the marquee. I threw my shoe at him, but it didn't have quite the impact I'd intended.

Frat Trash, as we'd taken to calling him, tried the locked door then cupped his eyes with his hands to stare in at us. His grin widened as he focused on Kara.

"Hey, it's *Goth*feratu!" he hollered, banging on the glass to get her attention. His three buddies nodded approvingly behind him. "What are you doing out before dark, Gothferatu? Aren't you gonna turn into a bat or some shit?"

Not even bothering to look his way, Kara gave him the finger.

Frat Trash turned his attention to me and reached around to tap the ticket window. "How about you then, ticket girl? When you gettin' off?" He paused to show me his sneer. "Would you like to get off?"

"Go fuck yourself," I sighed, staring down at the Lombardi's receipt.

The other three frat boys laughed as their leader made a show of kissing and tonguing the glass in front of me. I focused on *1 red wine, 1 pasta special.* As they started to walk away, the smaller blonde frat boy stopped to grind his finger into the door closest to the usher's stand, as if he had seen David slip behind the adjacent wall. "We're coming for you, son!" he whooped before they were out of sight.

"They're just bored assholes," Kara said to no one in particular. "If they had to face what they've done . . ."

Kara was already upstairs when Emily emerged with the puffy-eyed weeper. Usually there was a gush of dramatic music or gunfire whenever the double doors opened in the middle of a film, but this time there was only an eerie silence behind the woman's ragged sniffles. Emily offered her a handful of napkins as she walked her to the door, but the woman seemed to push her away before stopping then folding in half at the waist. Hands braced on her khaki thighs, she proceeded to vomit what looked like yellow oatmeal all over the carpet in front of the usher stand.

David gagged into his fist then ran to the bathroom. The woman started crying rather violently again, and I watched as Emily made a motion to put an arm around her then retracted, a strange emptiness sliding over her face as if she was only performing for us. David came back with a wad of paper towels and tossed them down on top of the puke.

"So now people are vomiting?" I said to Emily once she'd tucked the woman into a cab.

She nodded, still staring out the glass doors at the rainy street where the cab had just been, where the old man had been last night.

"Did you see any of the movie?" I asked.

She placed her left palm on the glass, just hard enough to push the door open a couple of inches. I could see a brownish-yellow splatter on her shirt cuff.

"Emily?"

"Nothing," she finally answered, the end of the word dragging as if it had a heavy weight tied to it. She stepped away from the door, and when she turned towards me her eyes were glassy and her lips were pressed so tightly together that they were turning white. I thought she must be trying to block out the smell of the vomit, a sickly-sweet odor that was already making its way behind the counter. "It wasn't much," she added as Tori approached her.

"Maybe you should go take a break, babe."

Nodding, Emily started across the lobby towards the bathrooms.

No one wanted to touch the puke, so we left it there, piling more paper towels on top while Tori and I tried to cajole David into cleaning it up. He finally grabbed an empty box from the back and arranged it over the pile right as the first couple of people came out at the end of the film. I noticed the bald man with the umbrella stopped to look at the overturned candy box as he was leaving, a purple and yellow tragedy on the lobby floor.

◄◦►

The film was still running. That was what stopped me in the aisle as I scanned the dark theater for David's curly brown head. Just a flash of textured black against dirty white against what looked like summer-burnt grass, then the screen faded to an almost fuzzy black with the thinnest white fractures jolting in and out like lightning strikes. There were no words, no credits, no sound. It was kind of like when an old film runs out at the very end of the reel, but I knew that wasn't what was happening. The black screen throbbed, seemed to be leaching out onto the red curtains all around it, then outwards, towards me. For just a moment I wanted to plunge my hand into it, fully expecting to feel velvet or animal fur.

"Alex."

I turned to my right and saw David sitting in a seat on the other aisle, still facing the screen so that I suddenly wasn't sure that he'd called my name. His garbage bag sat abandoned on the orange and red carpet several rows behind.

"There weren't any credits," he said.

I walked through a long row of seats until I was standing behind him. Emily had told me that Ed had sent him in here to investigate a complaint once—a bunch of guys talking and giggling through *Boogie Nights*—and David had ended up with gum in his hair and half a soda down the back of his pants. She'd made me promise never to let on that I knew.

"Are you okay?" I asked, touching David's shoulder when he didn't turn around. I could see little white streaks reflected in his glasses. "Did you see something?"

He nodded, a slow stripped movement that made it look like his head was coming loose from his neck. "I'm fine. I'm okay."

I had to take David by the hand to get him out of there. I dragged him back into the lobby along with his empty garbage bag, causing Tori to remark that we should close up concessions for the night because no one in their right mind would be downing Milk Duds while watching *Contrition*. As I was stuffing the garbage bag back into the box behind the counter, I noticed what looked like tufts of black animal fur coating my palms and the front of my white button down shirt.

"David . . ." I started, thinking of how clammy his hand had felt as I'd pulled him up. "Hold up your hands."

"What?" He was sitting on the carpet, staring out the glass doors.

"Just hold your hands up."

He showed me both palms, clean and slightly glistening under the low lobby lights.

I looked down at my own palms again, still covered in little clumps of longish black fur, then turned them over and saw some of the same black hairs imbedded under my nails. I could feel some on my shirt collar too, tickling my neck.

"You okay?" Tori asked, brows pulling together as she watched me pick at the little tufts of hair.

I brushed some of the fur off my chest, saw it float across the space between Tori and me until it landed on her cheek. She didn't flinch, didn't seem to notice.

"I gotta go wash my hands," I said.

All the way across the lobby I picked black fur off myself, watching it swirl in the air then dodging it as if the little hairs were magnetized to me. Chasing me. I felt a hollowness in my stomach, a delayed sense of familiarity that I couldn't quite parse though it was making me anxious. Around the corner, behind the stairs and out of sight, I rubbed my hands together until I felt the fur ball between my palms into something I could flick away. My skin was itching—my hands, my neck, the v-shaped peek of flesh where my shirt was unbuttoned—and I was afraid I'd caught some kind of infection from David. Clawing at my neck, I barreled into the women's room, stopping only when I saw Emily.

She was standing at the sink farthest from the door. Her back was to me, but I could see that she was hunched towards her left side, her right arm bent and shifting in small, tight movements. She let out a whimper, then a sort of squashed scream that sounded like it was grinding through her teeth. Her legs were shaking violently.

"Emily! What's going on?" I called, running to her.

She had a pocketknife in her hand. Her left sleeve was rolled all the way up to her shoulder and she was dragging the blade of the knife in a jagged rectangle around the tattoo she had shown us just a couple of hours earlier. The *A* in *Andrew* bobbed loose on the drooping flap of skin she had created.

"Oh my god, Emily, stop, stop!"

I wanted to take the knife from her, but I didn't know how to without cutting myself. Blood speckled the basin of the sink and even her pink and blonde hair. Red snaked down her arm, dripping from her left elbow and pooling on the white tile floor.

"I didn't do anything," Emily sobbed, still digging the blade into her bicep. "He needed me and I pretended like I didn't know and I did nothing. I let him go. I did nothing and I let it happen."

I tried grabbing her left arm, pulling it away from the knife. "Emily, please . . ."

"No!" she screamed, then jabbed the knife back into her flesh and screamed again. I pulled her arms apart, causing the blade to tear a line through the *1997*. "I don't deserve this," she cried, the knife shaking in her fist. "A tattoo—like that's going to make up for what I did. He was my brother—he loved me and he needed me and I treated him like he was an inconvenience!"

I backed away from her, watching as the blade hovered over her bicep again, but her hand was shaking too hard and she ended up doubled over, heaving and gasping for breath through her tears. It wasn't until she dropped the knife into the sink that I approached her again. As she leaned against the wall and cried, I pressed paper towels to her bicep, tried to hold her up. I could see the little tufts of black fur from my hands everywhere I touched her, all up and down her arm, sticking to her blood.

◄◦►

Ed said we would stay and work if we wanted to keep our jobs. Even after Tori took Emily to the ER and David threw up in the alley and I had to toss my bloodied shirt in the dumpster, we still had to get ready for the last showing of *Contrition*. Ed hung an OUT OF ORDER sign on the women's room door, so it was in the men's room, where I finally got to wash up, that I saw there was no longer any fur on my hands and neck, only Emily's blood.

Kara gave me a T-shirt of hers to wear: The Cure from their Swing tour, supporting my theory that she was living upstairs. While I sat in the ticket window staring through the cars and thinking about Emily and still smelling her blood, David made more popcorn. We didn't need it—the case was still three-quarters full—but the noise was a relief, the popping kernels filling the huge space that continued to expand all around us.

The popcorn was so loud that I almost didn't hear the customer, didn't even see the smudged black street turn to black leather even though she was standing just inches from me on the other side of the glass.

"Alex, right? Professor Harding's class?"

My eyes travelled up to the Lisa Simpson pin on her lapel. I used to stare at that pin during critiques because I couldn't meet her eyes, but I didn't want her to see me staring down at my hands either.

"Yeah, and you're, uh . . ."

"Callie. Callie Cutler," she said quickly, still smiling, not at all defeated.

I wanted to see that defeat, that fleeting sting that would make her blink hard and her mouth seize. I'd wanted that even after I finished Harding's creative writing class and left school all together. Just once I'd longed to lob the same words at her that she'd used during my critiques—*cliched, mawkish, pedestrian, "I mean, we've seen that imagery a hundred times before, haven't we, Alex?"*—but no matter how much she'd humiliated me under the guise of constructive criticism, I could never justify it. She could eye-fuck Professor Harding all she wanted and the rest of us still couldn't question those *As* because she really was that good, because she was already where the rest of us wanted to be.

"So, wow, I didn't know you work here."

There was no obvious judgement in her voice, but I could feel my whole body bracing anyway, already flinching, the immediate shame I'd felt back then turning over in my gut. "Yeah, so one for *Contrition*?" I replied briskly.

Callie slid a five and two quarters into the metal tray, exactly the amount Ed insisted would somehow keep this failing theater afloat. As she started to turn away, she paused and stared down at the ticket I'd just handed her. The sense of trepidation that had been lurking this whole time crept from my stomach to my chest and into my throat. I thought of her crying that day in class—not over the pain but over who would do such a thing—and how what little satisfaction I'd finally gained deflated as quickly as it had burgeoned.

"So, Alex," she started, and the apologies were already thickening on my tongue. "You know, I hope you're still writing. I really liked that story, the one about the house that was the little girl's mother. Maybe we could catch up, get coffee sometime?"

What I wanted to say was, *If you liked it so much, then why did you call it maudlin? Why did you say that my metaphor was unoriginal? Why did you tear me down so hard that you made everyone giggle in discomfort?* Instead, I just said, "Sure."

Callie proceeded to write her number on one of the programs. I stared at it as if I intended to call, then looked back up at her and forced an awkward smile that was supposed to be a polite goodbye. She didn't walk away, though. She just stood there staring at me, then met my smile with one that bloomed so wide on her face that I could see all of her teeth. All of her teeth that were no longer teeth but now shiny metal tacks sunk into her gums, the sharp points gnashing against each other as she opened and closed her mouth again and again.

—◇—

The rusty brown of Emily's blood on the worn blue and orange lobby carpet was real, real enough to squish under my shoes in front of the bathrooms and leave faded tracks criss-crossing the lobby. The crying, puking woman had been real too; the candy box David had thrown over her vomit was failing to contain the smell. Callie's teeth had definitely been a hallucination, though, especially considering David's lack of reaction when he took her ticket. I knew the black fur I'd started seeing in the popcorn case also wasn't real, but I still couldn't dismiss the fur that had been all over me.

I looked at David who was behind the concessions counter with me now. Even though we hadn't sold anything for the final show and I was pretty sure the three patrons in the theater weren't going to come out in the middle of the film and tearfully request Red Vines and a 52 oz Coke, I didn't bother asking Ed if I could leave early. It wasn't just that I needed this job; a part of me was scared to go home alone.

"Hey, David, what did you see in there?"

He didn't look up from the notebook page where his pen had landed and retreated countless times over the last half hour. "In the theater? I just went in to clean up," he said.

"Yeah, but the movie was still going. When I went in you were sitting there, watching it. What did you see?"

He shrugged. "I don't know. It didn't look like anything."

"I've been seeing things," I started, weighing just how much I wanted to tell him. "I don't know what I saw in the theater either, but there was black fur all over me. And you know that girl, the one with the leather jacket? Her teeth were fucked up. They were tacks."

David brought his pen down to the paper again, and drew what looked like a little tack between two blue college ruled lines. I could see an intricately sketched pocketknife and a cascade of *A*s spilling down the left margin.

"So you're telling me you haven't been seeing anything strange?" I prompted.

"Hey, ticket girl!"

It was Frat Trash again, banging on the doors to make sure David and I were looking at him. I was still irritated that I had to see Callie today and now him twice, interrupting yet another conversation. At least he didn't linger this time, pausing to rub his lips all over the glass before continuing down the sidewalk, his takeout bag swinging heavily against his legs.

"I'm gonna get a burrito," David announced, staring out at the gutter punks and students who were now walking where Frat Trash had been. "You want anything?"

I let him go. Any other time I would have been afraid for David with his kicked-puppy hunch and pretentious film-related ramblings, but after the old man last night and Emily today, I knew everything was different. I knew he felt that searing shame and rage that tears across your chest and finally breaks you, burns you up inside so that you're forced to create an outlet. I didn't try to stop him as he darted out the back door. I didn't go out there when I heard glass breaking in the alley, and I didn't follow when I saw him march down the sidewalk with a broken beer bottle in each fist.

It didn't take long, what he did. The movie was still going when David came back through the alley door, blood speckling his face and white button-down, beer bottles crushed to dust if his hands were any indication. My heart was pounding just from imagining what broken glass could do to Frat Trash, but David didn't seem as harried as I expected. He swept past me, grabbed his books from the counter, then headed back to the door.

"You okay?" I asked, surveying the sweat dotted along his forehead, the way his glasses sat crooked halfway down his nose. I knew none of the blood was his. "Seriously, are you . . . ?"

Smiling a little, he nodded. "See you around, Alex."

◂◦▸

I wanted to leave too after that, but I couldn't bear the thought of going back to my cold, empty apartment where I knew I would hear my grandfather's lullaby bounce along the walls as I had last night. I didn't want to go home where I would see Callie's teeth when I closed my eyes. I didn't want to be alone, picking black fur from my skin in the dark.

Last employee standing. Maybe Ed would reward my loyalty with another ten cents an hour.

"Where's David?" Kara asked when she came downstairs carrying the empty bank bags. We usually didn't count out the drawers with half an hour of the movie left, but I wasn't about to question this small mercy.

"He wasn't feeling well," I answered.

She started to open her mouth, but became distracted by the bloody smear David had left on the counter. I threw a bunch of napkins on top of it and she went back to unzipping the bank bags. I was glad she hadn't said anything about the candy box over the vomit and the blood still on the carpet either.

"Do you think it's worth it, the money we got for this movie?" I asked as we stood elbow to elbow behind the counter, emptying the concessions drawers.

"It'll keep us afloat for a long time, maybe the next year."

"Yeah, but what about what's happening to people? The old man who killed himself last night, and Emily—she was in there for, like, ten minutes and she comes out and . . . I saw her—she cut off a chunk of her own arm!

David was in there for five minutes and I think he—" I stopped myself, not quite sure that I could trust Kara. "I only saw the last few seconds and things are weird . . . it's not right."

"It's just a movie, Alex." She continued stuffing cash into the bank bag, pale eyes focused on each anemic stack as if it was worth much more than the $60 I had calculated. "A really bad, sad movie that's attracting people who are already depressed and messed up."

Aunt Kath's words slithered around in my head again: *What kind of person are you Alex? It's like it's nothing to you.*

"I want to go in there," I announced, surprising myself. "I need to see what's causing all this."

Kara stopped to focus on me, seemed to wait for me to take it back as a joke. "Aren't you afraid of what it might make you do?"

"I don't think a movie can make you do anything you don't already want to do."

"Then go in." She shrugged. "Unless you've been thinking about murdering me."

"Come with me. If it's just a movie, then it's no big deal."

She looked down at the bank bags, then at her hand now resting on the counter next to David's napkin-covered blood smear. "Okay, fuck it."

We left the money on the counter and walked together into a theater so dark I couldn't even find the screen at first. I felt Kara stop next to me in the aisle, the string of weak lights along the carpet's edges revealing her pointy black boots lined up next to my own worn Converse. The only other light came from the three movie-goers scattered around the theater, their silhouettes outlined with a silvery glow that came from the projectionist window above and behind us. Despite the solid black screen, the cavernous room was crackling with an intentional moment of anticipation and uncertainty. The sour odor of sweat rose above years of stale popcorn and spilled soda. Near the front, as little threads of white lightning began to appear on the screen, I heard the sound of muffled sobbing.

The first clear image was of me, age eight, in the front yard of my house just before I went to live with my grandfather. Sharper than a home movie, and as vivid as the early spring sunshine I'd walked in on my way here this afternoon, there I was on the screen, pushing the neighbor girl down the hill. She had been pestering me to be her friend, but I thought she was too weird and needy. When her parents found her, arm broken and crying in the driveway, she told them she had tripped. Later, she asked me to sign her cast.

The next image materialized as dirty white against summer-burnt grass against fuzzy black: me at age twelve, standing on the sidewalk staring down at my friend Amanda's Scottish terrier. He had gone missing the night before, as she had tearfully told me in the cafeteria that afternoon. Even after she spent weeks papering our town with missing dog fliers and calling the animal shelter every day, I didn't tell her or anyone that her dog was decomposing in a ditch just three blocks from my house.

Next was me in high school, sophomore year, in a darkened bedroom at a party. I was kissing Stef Rockwell as my friend surreptitiously took photos, all for $20 and the respect of some popular girls hell-bent on proving the shy, awkward junior was a lesbian. After the photos were posted all over school, my identifying features scratched out as promised, Stef was bullied relentlessly. I never told anyone that I liked kissing her; I couldn't end up like her, forced to change schools a month later.

The following image was from just last year in Professor Harding's creative writing class. I was still smarting from an especially brutal critique the previous Wednesday, when Callie Cutler had called my story about my grandfather overwrought and contrived. Callie always sat across from Harding, so I knew on which seat to place the tacks. Four of them in a perfect square, pointed ends up, the brushed metal blending into the dirty grey upholstery. I sat in giddy anticipation as everyone poured in, taking their usual seats. I hated myself even before Callie sat down.

The final image was from last December, right after my aunt Kath called to tell me my grandfather wasn't going to make it. I was lying in bed with a boyfriend who would cheat on me a week later, near tears over how she had chastised me for not making time for the man who had raised me. I hadn't seen the point—the last time I'd visited, he was delirious on morphine and hurling insults when he wasn't calling me by my mother's name. I'd told Aunt Kath I didn't want to remember him that way, but it was as if she could smell the sex through the phone. That night, in my dreams, I heard my grandfather calling for me, asking Kath where I was.

There was more, of course, but these were the memories that had been lingering in my mind and now on the screen; they were the memories that played inside my head on those sleepless nights when I had all the time in the world to tally the proof of what a weak, spiteful person I was. How this was even possible didn't matter. Though the feelings of shame and self-loathing had risen to the surface, I didn't feel an overwhelming urge to walk into traffic or mutilate myself or kill someone who had humiliated me. I could only imagine what Emily, David, the old man, and all of the others had seen.

Or what kind of person that made me.

I turned to Kara, still afraid that she was seeing me and all of my sins projected in front of us, but the diluted mascara running down her face proved that she was seeing her own life on the screen.

"Are you . . . ?" I started.

A man brushed between us in the aisle, long strides that couldn't carry him out fast enough. The far end of the theater lit up when another man opened the exit door to the alley. The last person to leave, Callie Cutler, stopped in front of me.

"I'm sorry, Alex," she said, her voice blurry, her wet face glowing from the indiscernible shapes and colors smeared across the screen.

I could feel my breath seize in my chest. It wasn't nothing. "I'm sorry too," I said.

Clutching her arms in front of her chest, Callie hurried out of the theater.

Kara continued to stare at a screen that had gone to crackling black for me. "You know what we have to do," she said.

◀◆▶

As Kara had expected, the distributor let us keep the reels. We put ads in the free alternative weekly and the student paper, all of the places Ed would never look: *Free Midnight Screening of The Big Lebowski*. Next month we would change it to *Wild Things*, then *Fear and Loathing in Las Vegas*. We figured between the nearby campus and the people who read the weekly, we could get maybe two hundred people per screening. Four screenings per week and we could cover half our city in a year. If Ed ever caught on, all we had to do was make him watch a few minutes of the film.

Not a single person walked out, not even when it became clear that they'd shown up for a midnight screening of *Contrition*. For the first few shows Kara and I blocked the doors just in case, but those doors didn't so much as shift in the breeze until the theater lights came on. We had to put out extra napkin dispensers in the lobby.

There were two suicides after those first few shows, but people mostly cried and huddled in the phone booth outside, pouring tearful apologies into the dirty receiver. I liked to imagine what they were seeing when they left: the woman who abruptly sat down on the lobby floor and attempted to open her wrist with a ballpoint pen; the man who collapsed on the sidewalk, knees drawn to his chin and hands up his pant legs as he seemed to be pulling out his own leg hair; the group of teenage boys who took turns throwing each other up against the wall outside, yelling something about "that girl behind the school." Kara was worried that the sociopaths were the only ones leaving unaffected, so I told her about David. I told her there had to be more victims like him gaining the strength to take those people out.

Frat Trash was found dead in the alley between the dry cleaner's and the pizza place two blocks over, face ribboned like ground beef and his jugular severed. Emily never came back to the theater, and Tori quit a week later only because she didn't want to leave without giving notice. Though we never heard from David again, I sometimes hoped to see him at one of our midnight screenings; I wondered what he would see in the film now, after what he had done.

As for me, I never saw Callie Cutler's tack teeth again, though the black fur would still appear at times, especially after Kara and I started taking the film from town to town. There were places where I would look down into the crowd from the projectionist's booth, searching the dark for the familiarity of Stef Rockwell or Amanda or someone who could be the little neighbor girl grown up, and I would practice my apologies in my head, ready and hoping for a relief that might come even if the forgiveness didn't. Though those sins could be checked off a list, they still weighed on me, but not as heavily as the one that continued to loom over even my most recent transgressions. It was my grandfather's voice I still heard almost every night—a voice that I knew I would continue to hear—singing his lullaby and asking where I was.

TETHERED DOGS

GARY McMAHON

It was always quiet on weeknights in The Gut Punch, when the wild weekend crowds gave way to sombre men and women winding down with a drink after a hard day at work, lonely singletons or divorcees who didn't want to sit at home alone watching the TV soaps, and the other ones—the people who were committing a slow suicide by alcohol.

It was my night off but for some reason I couldn't stay away. If I'm honest, that seedy little bar is the only place that feels like home. Living alone doesn't make you lonely but only lonely people tend to live alone.

I smiled at the relief barman, Ledley, as I walked in and he nodded slowly. There was a look in his eyes that I couldn't read. I took off my coat and hung it on a hook at the end of the bar and slipped onto one of the tall wooden stools.

"The usual?"

"Thanks."

Ledley flicked a switch on the ancient coffee machine and it started to grumble. I had no idea how old that thing was, or how it still worked after all this time, but the coffee was always good.

"Slow night?"

He shrugged. "It's a Monday. They're always slow." He glanced over my shoulder, briefly but long enough for me to notice.

"Any trouble this evening?"

"No . . .no trouble. Just a vibe. A bad one." He nodded at someone in the bar behind me and turned back to the coffee machine. His shaved head glistened as it caught the light from a nearby wall lamp.

Slowly, I slid around on the stool and surveyed the room. There were approximately a dozen drinkers in there: two small groups and three solitary figures. A woman sat reading a paperback and nursing a glass of wine. A young kid who looked somewhere between nineteen and twenty-three was staring at his half-filled pint glass. A heavy-set man whose face I recognised sat alone in a booth slowly turning a cardboard beer mat over and over in his hands.

"Him," said Ledley, nodding at the beermat-fiddler as he placed a steaming coffee cup in front of me. There was a little red Ironman tattoo on the inside of his left forearm. He liked to keep fit; he was always training for some road race or triathlon. I just thought he was trying to outrun himself.

I took a sip of the coffee and then stood, walked across the room. Halfway there I remembered the guy's name, and where it was I knew him from. He was a heavy guy, into all kinds of stuff, but he'd never given me any trouble.

"All right, Joel?"

He looked up at me. His face was grey. Not pale, but actually grey, as if he were on the verge of death.

"Jesus, mate, you look a bit rough."

He smiled but it made me feel uncomfortable. There was no humour in that smile, or anything even approaching human emotion. There was just a deep hole into which light could disappear.

"Are you okay?"

"I . . . I'm not sure."

"If you want to be alone, I'll fuck off."

"No. No, I don't want to be alone. That's why I'm here. I needed to be around people, part of a familiar scene."

I sat down in a chair opposite him without being asked. "Can I get you a drink?"

He looked at his empty glass, a confused expression on his face. "I can't even remember drinking that."

I turned to Ledley, motioned for him to pour Joel another pint, and then took a mouthful of wonderfully hot, bitter coffee. Waited for him to tell me what was on his mind.

"We've known each other in passing for a few years, right?"

"Yeah. That's right."

"I don't think we've ever had a conversation that lasted longer than a quick hello before now, have we?"

I shook my head. "Not that I recall, no. I suppose that would make us what they call 'nodding acquaintances.'"

He smiled again. I wished he'd stop doing that. It was making me feel nauseous.

"I don't have a lot of close friends. Not real ones. You know something of what I do for a living, yeah?"

"It's none of my business what you do."

"But you do know . . . you know I'm a bad man."

"We're all bad men in some way. I don't believe in white hats and good guys. That shit's for kids."

I think he'd already decided he was going to tell me his story. Nothing I said could have altered that.

He clenched his fists on the table and then eased off the pressure, slowly opening his hands. "Something weird happened tonight. I'm going to tell you about it so I don't have to keep it inside my head. This is something I need to share, if only for my own sanity."

"Give me a second." I got up and collected his drink from the bar. Ledley didn't say anything, just stared at me as he pretended to clean glasses. When I returned to the booth it looked like Joel had been trying not to cry. His eyes were red but there were no tears."

"Here." I pushed the pint of ale towards him.

"Thanks, man." Joel drank half the contents in one swallow and then put down the glass.

"You know me, Joel. I'm not going to judge you. I've done a lot of bad things myself, so I can claim no moral high ground. We're just two blokes sitting in a pub and having a chat."

He blinked once, slowly, as if he was trying to clear his vision, and then continued. "One of my girls tried to kill herself tonight. She climbed onto the roof behind my place and jumped. I saw her do it. Her neck snapped when she hit the ground. Sounded like a gunshot."

"Who was it?"

"Jenny Dope."

"The little junkie girl from Marsh Street? I know her. She's the one whose kid died in that road accident, isn't she?"

"Yeah. Six months ago, now. But it was no accident. A hit and run. Nobody ever found the guy who did it." He stared at me and I knew that, contrary to popular belief, someone *had* found him, but nobody else would ever know where the body was buried.

"Okay. Say no more."

"Jenny couldn't deal with the loss. She'd gone rapidly downhill, taking more drugs, stronger ones, and treating herself badly."

"Yeah, I heard a bit about that. Someone told me recently that she was selling herself for a hit from a dirty needle in some squat in East Leeds."

"I was trying to wean her off that shit. I took her out of that hovel and gave her a room. Thought I was actually getting somewhere. Until tonight."

"So, she's dead?"

"Kind of."

His answer hit me right under the ribs, almost winding me. I didn't know how to respond, so I said nothing. I wished that I hadn't sat down with him in the first place but by then it was too late to get up and go.

"Her neck snapped. Head was twisted all the way around—literally all the way—so that she was staring backwards. She wasn't breathing. I checked. Her heart wasn't beating. I checked that too. She should've been a goner. Should've but wasn't. Not quite."

In the depths of the brief silence that followed, when he stopped speaking and simply stared at me, I sensed so many things that should remain unknown. I smelled the hint of decay, heard a silent scream on the wind, felt the presence of someone or something I knew I'd meet again, face to face, on my death bed.

"She was dead, but she was still speaking. I don't know how, or why. With her head turned back-to-front, she was gabbling, talking a lot of shit. Me and one of the boys carried her back inside and put her on a bed in one of the back rooms, the ones we don't let the customers use. The rooms where the girls can go for a rest and grab a bit of privacy. Clean sheets, new carpets, painted nice and bright. We had to lay her down on her front so that she was face-up. Her eyes were open, but you could tell she couldn't see us. I have no idea what she was looking at . . ."

The jukebox in the corner started playing an old song but I couldn't focus clearly enough to make out the words. All I could think of was this young girl with her head facing the wrong way, dead but still managing to speak.

"The thing is, she kept on talking. Couldn't stop. She kept up this strange monologue, reciting names and dates and causes of death. It took us a little while to realise that she was giving us the death dates of everyone she knew. Then she moved onto other things—predictions. She told us that ten years from now there'll be a terrorist attack on the houses of parliament. Next week a family of six will be killed in a house fire in Sheffield. Stuff like that . . . and some things I can't even bring myself to repeat."

"Then what happened?"

"I had to get the hell out of there, so I came here. I needed a drink, and to be in the company of real people. We didn't call the police or the ambulance service—I mean, what the fuck was I meant to tell them? How do you explain a dead woman with her head twisted a hundred and eighty degrees on her neck predicting death and destruction? It's crazy. They'd think I was insane."

"So she's still there?"

He nodded. "We locked her in the room. You can still hear her droning on behind the door in that flat, lifeless voice. I don't know what to do."

Neither did I. None of us ever knows what to do in times of great duress, but something always comes up. And round here I'm usually the one who comes up with it.

"Show me, "I said, and I have no idea why. It was none of my business. I didn't want to get involved. Yet I stood and followed him out of The Gut Punch, walked half a mile to his place on a quiet street that backs onto fields grown wild with neglect. The night was warm, the air was clear. I could see every star in the firmament; if I'd wanted to, I could have counted each one of them and given them names.

"Come on. This way." He opened the door and we walked along a short corridor, bedrooms branching off it, doors shut tight in their frames. I don't think there were customers behind any of those doors. Joel must have shut up shop after the last one left, his balls and wallet emptied.

We went into the kitchen of the converted house. A middle-aged woman sat in her underwear at the dining table drinking tea. She didn't look up at us as we passed through; her mind was on other matters. A thin young man with a bad complexion stood at her side, staring at the top of her head as if he could find the secret of existence within her greasy blonde curls.

I don't think either of them was even aware of us being there.

We left them behind. For a moment it felt like I was leaving everything behind. Those people, this house, my life . . . all of it.

Joel stopped outside a door at the end of a second narrow corridor. He stood and stared at the door, as if he were trying to wish it away or convince himself that it wasn't really there; that a solid wall had appeared in its place. "She's in here," he said, reaching out a hand and placing his palm against the painted timber. "We didn't know what else to do."

As I watched, he took a set of keys from his jacket pocket. Examining them, he selected one and used it to unlock the door. I could hear mumbling from inside the room. When he opened the door, the voice became clearer. It sounded like chanting, or a repeated prayer.

Joel stepped through the door and then to one side, giving me a view of the room. The walls were painted bright yellow; the carpet was clean and white. Pretty curtains hung at the small window. Flowers in a vase on the windowsill. I could smell lavender air-freshener. There was a wardrobe, a small chest of drawers, a neat double bed.

On the bed was a woman. She was small and thin and wearing a pair of tight black jeans and a faded Motorhead tour t-shirt. No shoes or socks. She had tiny feet, small nubs of toes. Her arms were bruised. Her neck was twisted in a kind of fleshy spiral and she lay on her belly, but face-up, talking non-stop. Her voice was quiet, but she wasn't quite whispering. It sounded like an old recording: flat, distant, lacking tone and timbre.

I didn't want to hear what she was saying. Names, dates, numbers, causes of death. It sounded like she was reading from a list.

"She hasn't stopped. She won't. She just keeps on talking and telling us these things . . . and we don't know what to do."

I remembered this girl from before, when she used to push a pram through the park and pick wild flowers to put in her baby's hair. She'd been as happy as anyone I'd ever seen, but even then, she'd been using and working occasionally in Joel's grotty little suburban whorehouse. The shadows were already gathering; darkness had never been far from her side.

I'd walked into a trap. Joel was relinquishing all responsibility for this girl by bringing me here. He knew enough about me to be certain I'd do the right thing, the thing that he couldn't bring himself to do.

It was always the same. People dragged me into their business and expected me to sort it out. I've spent my life cleaning up other people's messes and don't expect things to change any time soon. They seek me out. It's like a mark upon my skin, a stain on my flesh. They can see it when they look at me—they know I can never turn them down when they come to me for help.

We all have our roles to play, and this, it appears, is mine.

I felt like punching Joel in the face, but I knew that if I got started on that I might not stop until I'd killed him. He looked pathetic, standing in the corner with his eyes shining and his shoulders stooped. He was already a beaten man; anything that I could have done would have added little to his current sense of defeat.

It was then that I realised what he must have been told by the girl on the bed: the date of his own death, and how it would come about. I wondered if she'd told him he would be murdered, or if he would go quietly in his sleep. Would he die young or old? If he was to be murdered, had she named his killer?

These are the things that we can never know for it will break our minds; the secret knowledge we must not be told. We dance through life unaware of the date of our own extinction. It's the only thing that stops us from losing our sanity. To know that—to be informed of it with such unwavering certainty—is surely the definition of hell on earth.

I turned my attention back to the girl on the bed. Did she know that I was here? I didn't want her to tell me anything about myself. A bell, once struck, can't be unrung. A scream cannot be unheard.

Quickly, quietly, I stepped forward and stood by the bed, staring down at Jenny Dope. Her eyes were wide open, but she couldn't see a thing. She wouldn't even know it was happening. Her shoulder blades were sharp beneath the thin material of her t-shirt; her spine was prominent. She looked used up, wasted.

I reached down and clasped her head, a hand on each side of her small, sweaty skull, and twisted hard, turning her head back the right way. The bones grated, blood spurted from her mouth as she coughed involuntarily, staining the pillow red. She stopped speaking mid-sentence. I was glad she hadn't yet said my name.

I left her lying face-down on the bed, silent at last.

Joel tried to follow me out of the room as I left, but I turned and pushed him away. He was smart enough to stay where he was. The couple in the kitchen were standing, locked in a loose embrace, as I walked through the room, and towards the front door. It looked like they were slow dancing to a tune only they could hear.

Outside, everything was the same as it always had been. Nothing had changed. The sky was still above me, the earth remained solid beneath my feet. My life was a mess, my job was pointless, and my children were still on the other side of the world, growing up without me in their lives.

I heard a song comprising of distant sirens and the barking of tethered dogs as I headed back to The Gut Punch, not knowing where else to go. It was the best home I had, the only one I knew. When I got there, I stood outside the building and stared up at the roof, wondering how long it would take me to climb up to its highest level, and how far I might see when I got there.

The journey would be much quicker on the way back down.

Jenny Dope had known that better than anyone, even at the end.

I stayed there for a long time until finally, feeling tired and useless and sick of myself, I stalked away into the muggy northern night, looking for something I would never find. Searching for something—anything—that I could pretend was better than this.

BLOODY RHAPSODY

ALESSANDRO MANZETTI

Deep Red, Deep East End
smell of men and women
of misery, sweat and then the rainbow
of blood right after the knives' storms
and all shades of red, see,
violet, purple, amaranth and vermilion
splashed on the sidewalk
by the Titian of Whitechapel
who knows well all colors
flowing inside people
arteries, veins, ventricles, secret boxes
odalisques with white, warm skin
porcelain trained from life
in the universities of the alley
between cold kisses and whistles of policemen
wearing stiffened mustaches
with their heart always scared.

Deep Red, Deep East End
the ghost with the razor, Death
with a black and white face
and a necklace of sharp oyster shells
reading Shakespeare's sonnets
around every dark corner
blowing storms of hanging clothes
and the first five symphonies
of the spectre that everyone calls
The Ripper, tall and thin, short and fat
alive and dead, Jesus Christ and Lucifer
an angel with a blue tongue
or a demon with a long, coiled tail
lit like a fuse and ready to detonate
grenades of shouts, prayers
waking pimps in underwear and braces
who're sleeping under the sharp roofs
of London slowly dying, bled out.

IN THE ENGLISH RAIN

STEVE DUFFY

So what's it like living next door to a Beatle?"

Sally Holden asked me the question, with her usual mixture of mischief and amusement. Sally had come to our school at the start of the lower sixth, after her mother got divorced and left her town house in Highgate for a Surrey maisonette. My dad and I had made a similar journey three years earlier, except in our case it was from Hampstead to a big four-bedroomed house at the end of an affluent cul-de-sac. I'd yet to make any friends either in or out of school.

It would never have occurred to me to seek out Sally's friendship. She was startlingly beautiful—or so I thought, anyway—and I was far too shy to approach her. It was only thanks to Miss Aston's seating plan in English that we were thrown together, and only then because she made us read the parts of *Antony and Cleopatra* in lessons that we actually exchanged words, even if they were all Shakespeare's at first. I was taken aback at how much of herself she seemed to put into the reading. Everyone else in the class was grunting their way through Charmian and Enobarbus and the rest as if they were reading a bus timetable, but Sally was actually emoting: she was giving it her throaty, husky all, and giving it in my direction, which I found both disconcerting and amazing.

Walking home from school one autumn afternoon, after I had done my hoarse and red-faced best to respond in kind to the serpent of old Nile, Sally had fallen in step with me on the tree-lined pavement. Despite having vowed not half an hour earlier to be treble-sinew'd, hearted, breathed, and fight maliciously, it was all I could do to look up from the toes of my shoes as she buttonholed me. "Which is the best record shop in town?" she asked me. "I want to buy the new Blondie album with my birthday tokens." The album in question being *Eat To The Beat*, which pins the encounter nicely to October 1979, not that I was ever likely to forget the occasion.

"I like SpinDisc," I said to the drifts of dead leaves through which I was kicking.

"Ooh, I don't know that one," Sally said. "Where is it?"

"I'll show you," I said, not quite believing the turn of events.

"All right," she said simply, as if we did this sort of thing every day. And to SpinDisc we went; and to the Lite-a-Bite for coffee afterwards. It turned out we both liked cappuccino: what were the odds? Over the next half-an-hour or so we worked out that we both liked Blondie, we both liked Kate Bush (even though nobody else in the school did), and we both identified as New Wave, but were still secret fans of the Beatles. This was the point at which Sally brought up the matter of my legendary neighbour.

"I mean, somebody told me you were supposed to live next door to a house that belonged to one of the Beatles? Something like that?"

I sighed, and inwardly wished for the cracked leather Chesterfield to swallow me. I'd originally shared this tidbit in one of my ham-fisted attempts to acquire friends when I first came to the school. It had been met with a mixture of indifference and ridicule, and seemed to have impressed nobody. "Yeah, it's not . . . I mean, apparently, it's only half true. One of them's supposed to have bought the house in the Sixties, but I don't think anybody ever moved in there. Nobody lives there now."

"It's still pretty good, though," Sally said. "We've got a taxi driver in the flat next door to ours, and he tries to look down my top when he talks to me. I think you win."

It was just as well I didn't have a mouthful of cappuccino.

◄◦►

After that, it was all surprisingly easy. We found ourselves in an easy routine of walking into town after school, meeting up on Saturday mornings. It fell short of actual boy-girl going-out stuff, but for me at least there was a sort of intimacy in it, as unfamiliar to me as it was intoxicating. Our friendship remained steady all through the school year, never more than the best of friends, never any less. When Sally's mother took her to visit relatives over the summer, my holidays lost all their sense of potential, became nothing but a less humiliating version of what school had been like before Sally. For the first time ever, I was anxious for the new term. And on that first day back in September, there she was, with a tan and a new haircut, swinging from the school gate. In Miss Ashton's English class, we moved on from *Antony & Cleopatra* to *The Tempest*, a text with less erotic charge but with a weirdness we both found appealing.

Come the October half-term, I had the house to myself. My father, a widower with an unfussy attitude towards child care and a busy professional schedule, was away on a business trip to Leeds, and would not be back till late on Friday night. So it happened that I was ambling downstairs unusually late on the Tuesday morning when the front doorbell rang. The cleaning woman, I remembered, wasn't due until Thursday. I quickly pulled my sweater on, and craned over the banisters to look who was there. Through the rippled glass I saw Sally's silhouette.

For a second I just didn't know what to do, not in the least. For a year we'd been in each other's company almost every day, but on neutral ground: the school, the cafe, the streets of town, and the grassy spaces of the park. The thought of Sally actually here, in my home, was at the same time exhilarating and a little bit scary. It would, I thought, be the same as having a proper girlfriend, or at least what I assumed having a proper girlfriend might be like. This thought was almost too much for me to cope with, and only when the bell rang again did I snap out of it and hurry down to the door.

"You *are* in!" she said, and I blushed. "I thought you were still in kip, you lazy pig. Am I coming in, then?" Apparently she was.

In the kitchen I made us coffee, surreptitiously checking my eyes for gunk and my hair for flattening from the pillow. She perched on her stool at the breakfast bar, keeping up a stream of chat while inside me my heart bounced around like bingo balls in the blower. My dad was away, remember: we had the place to ourselves till Thursday, at least Thursday.

We took our drinks through to the back room, where I put the latest Kate Bush album—*Never For Ever*, which I knew Sally loved—on the stereo. She sat cross-legged on the sofa singing along, and squinted through the French windows at the garden. All morning it had been drizzling on and off, and the trickle of rain on the windowpanes blurred the leaf-strewn lawn.

"Is that it, then?" she asked, pointing to the high chimneys just visible behind the stone wall at the end of our property. "Is that the Beatles house?"

"That's it." In truth, I hardly ever noticed it, unless prompted. It was just a feature in the middle distance, like trees or hills.

"Bloody hell! Brilliant! Which Beatle is it, do we know?"

I'd asked my dad about it, on the off chance it came up again. "Lennon, apparently. He was looking for a new place in 1968, about the time he was moving out of Kenwood, his house in Weybridge. He sent one of the Beatles roadies round viewing properties—Mal Evans, I think it was. He saw this place, thought John might like it, and the word is that Apple Corps bought it, sight unseen."

"No!" Sally was entranced. "So did he move in?"

"Well, no," I admitted. "I mean, he still owns it, or Apple do, whoever, but the story goes that he only ever spent a long weekend here, and either he didn't like it or Yoko didn't, or they both didn't, and he ended up buying Tittenhurst Park the year after. And that was it; nobody ever moved in, and it's been empty ever since."

"Wow!" Sally got up, crossed to the window, and peeked through the net curtains. The sun was coming back out after the rain, and now whenever the weather turns that way I often remember her standing there silhouetted against the nets, her figure edged with golden light. "I asked my mum about it, you know. She said she thought there'd been a big scandal about it at the time. Apparently there was a rhyme that the kids used to sing, to the tune of *Yellow Submarine*: 'We all live in a Quentin Bascombe dream.' No idea who Quentin Bascombe was, but she said it had something to do with that house. Have you ever been over there?"

"No," I admitted. "Our place and the place next door are the only two houses that actually back on to Shelgrave—that's the name of it. This end of the cul-de-sac is Shelgrave's western edge, there's woodland to the south and the east, and the golf course to the north, with a stream that marks the boundary. We're the only neighbours."

Sally was still peering through the windowglass. "I'd have been over that wall so fast," she said. She looked round at me, and her eyes were bright with monkey business. "Come on," she said, and unlatched the French windows. Before I knew it, we were out on the patio.

The raindrops made tiny prisms on the lawn as we ran across the soaked garden, breaking up the soft October sunlight into its constituent colours. There was a wooden compost bin against the biscuit brick wall, and Sally swarmed up it easily. "Get that," she directed me, gesturing at the tall ladder we kept around the side of the house. "We'll need it to get down the other side." I manhandled it to where she sat waiting, and together we hoisted it up and over, letting it rest on the other side. Joining her on the wall, I looked where she was pointing; across the mossy red ridge tiles on top of the wall into the long-abandoned grounds of Shelgrave.

There were lawns, as shaggy as country meadows, descending from the wall to a reed-filled duck pond. The pond lay at the bottom of a natural bowl, and the ground rose on the far side in a series of overgrown formal terraces to the house. Oh, the house. It took our breath away. A large half-timbered villa in the stockbroker Tudor style, it was all gables and turrets and odd angles. There was no way of guessing how many rooms it might contain, or what you might find inside them. Pine trees clustered up close behind it, hiding any view of what might lie beyond. It looked like a solitary homestead in some magical wilderness land like Narnia, instead of a des. res. surrounded on all sides by the decorous Surrey suburbia.

"Oh, wow," breathed Sally. "It's . . . it's unbelievable." And looking at it, slightly dizzy from the suddenness of it all, I thought, *yes, yes you're right, I don't believe it.* Sitting in the shadows of the tall trees, dense leaden rainclouds above that turning the sky into a baleful backdrop, wasn't there something weirdly stagey about it all?

The thought struck me that it looked more like some insanely detailed diorama than an actual view; the inside of somebody's head, reconstructed in scale model form. However, I had no time to get to the bottom of this curious feeling.

"Sally, hang on—!" But she'd already scrambled down the ladder and had both arms raised, beckoning me to follow. What choice did I have?

She took my hand and led me down through the overgrown meadow towards the pond. The grass came up over our knees in places, wet and slippery, and the bottoms of our jeans were soon soaking. Sally leaned close to me and whispered, "This is a real adventure." I don't know why she whispered: our cul-de-sac was never noisy at the best of times, but here beyond the wall we might have been in the middle of the countryside, it was so quiet. No jets overhead, no sound of distant traffic. No birds, even.

The house was confusing; you might almost say devious. It looked different from every aspect, a function, I supposed, of its mismatched angles, those multiple gables and randomly pitched roofs. To this day I doubt if I could draw you a floorplan of Shelgrave, but I only need to close my eyes to summon up an image of it that's as vivid and improbable as the view through a camera obscura. Its blind windows caught the sunshine, one after the other, the nearer we got to the house, then as we climbed from terrace to terrace, they surrendered it, and showed nothing but streaky grime.

The terraces were wildly overgrown, and in some places the brick retaining walls had given way, spilling soil and rubble that had grown thick with weeds. Still holding hands, we picked our way up the levels, till we came out on a broad patio area with monkey-puzzle trees to right and left. The builders had banked the structure half into, half projecting from the slope. If we'd looked back we'd have seen the whole of the landscaped vista across the pond and the lawns, the redbrick wall beyond with the tops of the houses peeking over it. Our world, the world where we belonged; not this place, where we didn't know the rules, or even if there were any. Away off in the distance, thunder rumbled.

Sally had let go of my hand and was peering through the windows on the ground floor. Some were curtained, thick dusty drapes hanging heavy from runners that were giving way under their own weight, while others were bare and let on to bare interiors.

All of a sudden, she started back with a gasp, and I almost fell over the low patio wall in fright. *"What?"*

"Look! In there!" she breathed, and then, as I raced to her side, "Got you." Just an empty room. She snorted with laughter, and it is a measure of my devotion that I couldn't even manage to be annoyed with her for tricking me.

There was a large front door with a stained-glass fanlight above. Sally tried the handle, and of course it was locked. I was all for leaving it there, to be honest, but not her.

Around the corner of the building stone steps led up to a conservatory on the side elevation. Sally ran up them in a shot and put her weight to the sliding glass door. It came open, screeching on rusted metal runners. "Ta-daaa," she announced in triumph, beckoning me to hurry up and join her.

Inside the conservatory it was airless, muggy. There were wooden trays of potted plants, or the withered brown remains of plants. The greenhouse glass had gone unwashed for years, and a few of the panes were cracked or shattered. Sally poked at one of the trays, and a brood of fat little short-legged spiders scuttled out and ran up the filthy glass. She exclaimed in disgust and started back so that she bumped into me. I patted her on the shoulders, for all the world as if I was in a position to hand out reassurance.

There was a door giving entrance to the house, with three long panels of frosted glass. Somehow, I knew it wouldn't be locked, which in fact it wasn't; Sally opened it. We stood there and looked at each other for a second, and then she grasped my hand once more and led me inside.

The room was a kitchen, bare and grimy, stripped of all but the basic things: a Belfast sink, an old gas stove, a sturdy little table with wooden drawers, and sea-green cupboards of porcelain steel with their doors ajar, nothing inside except cobwebs. There was a smell in the house that was familiar from the conservatory: the smell of things long dead and thoroughly desiccated, not even the taint of decay lingering about them. "Ugh," breathed Sally. There was really not a lot else to be said. She pulled me after her, and we tiptoed through to the inner part of the house.

There was a corridor tiled like a chessboard in black and white diagonals. The walls were panelled in dark stained wood, with empty hooks where pictures had once hung. One painting alone remained: a portrait of a fat, jowly man dressed in a pinstripe suit, perched on an armchair like Humpty Dumpty on his wall. On his face was a smile that was presumably meant to look benevolent, but succeeded only in looking irretrievably sinister, or so I thought. Sally and I exchanged a glance, and I saw in her face that she'd come to the same conclusion. She wrinkled her nose in revulsion, and we pushed on towards the end of the corridor.

Here the way widened into a large vestibule. There was the locked front door, the actual sun picking out the stained-glass rays of the fanlight, and there on the far side was the main staircase, winding around the walls to the first floor. Again, what fixtures there had been were all gone now; here and there, the ghosts of the old furniture could still be seen, lighter silhouettes against the discoloured plaster. Above our heads was a Tiffany stained-glass skylight dome, littered with the needles of pine trees that had built up in drifts over many years. There were birds' nests, and in one place a cracked pane that had let in the weather: a little bed of lichen had formed on the tiled floor below.

"This is wrong," I whispered to Sally—we were both still whispering, for some reason. "There shouldn't be a skylight there, it was all gable end from outside . . ."

"I know," she said, looking up at it with something like wonder. "This place is *amazing*. Which way should we go?"

"You choose," I said, hoping that she'd opt for the door that led outside, where the thunder seemed to be getting nearer. I wouldn't have minded the oncoming storm. Instead, she made a pantomime of eeny-meeny-miney-mo, alighting on the door to the side of the entrance vestibule.

The room was empty, dilapidated. Bare floorboards littered with scraps of old newspaper, cobwebs thick in the corners. The only feature of interest, if you could call it that, was a set of step-ladders standing in the exact centre of the room, below a ragged hole in the plaster ceiling where once, I assumed, there had been the rose of a light fixture.

"Look," said Sally, pointing, but I was already looking. Around the hole, in brightly coloured poster-paint letters, ran the exhortation:

CLIMB THE STEPS—TAKE A TRIP

Of course, I knew what Sally would do. Up she went, till she was balancing on the top step, invisible from the waist up. "Oh my God . . ." She was whispering still. "Come here, you've got to see this."

I clambered awkwardly up the back of the ladder, balancing on slanted props instead of steps, until I had to squeeze my head and shoulders through the hole. There was barely enough space for the two of us to fit, and we were pressed closer together than ever before.

"*Look*," said Sally, but I didn't need telling.

It was as if the rest of our adventure had been in black-and-white, and the set had suddenly been switched over to colour transmissions. Across every bit of wall-space in that bare upstairs room snaked a maze of illustrations in the childlike Sixties psychedelic style; flowers and rainbows and dancing Paisley people. There were blues and reds and yellows and purples and greens, all as vibrant as the day they were first mixed, or so it seemed.

We might have been on a trip in a time machine, only somehow it seemed we were going back far further than the decade or so since that paint had still been fresh. In these surroundings, the decoration was more than just incongruous. It felt—this is the best way I can describe it—it felt like an image of a time when everything had been young, apart from a few very old things that had always been there, and always been old, a time when the distinction between the two had never been plainer or more jarring than it now appeared.

"Is this our man at last, do you think?" I asked Sally.

"Oh yes," she said, her voice filled with wonder. "This is him."

"Look," I said, as the realisation struck me, "there aren't any doors or windows, only skylights. How did anybody get in there?" I looked again, to make sure I hadn't missed anything. No doors; not even a crack in the painted images. Sally shook her head, as if the magic of it all outweighed the practicality.

In places the illustrations swirled down to cover the bare floorboards, and in others they spilled across the ceiling. I turned from side to side as best I could, pressed tight up against Sally, and tried to make some sense of them. I soon decided that this was not a place that would ever make sense. In the flow of motifs, I saw bicycles and caterpillars, peace signs and guitars, flowers and long-haired maidens, melting letters that spelled out E-G-O and L-U-V, all the kitschy trappings of high psychedelia. In amongst them were some characters I recognised from Lewis Carroll: Alice, the mad hatter, the walrus and the carpenter.

"Look over there," I said. "Lennon wrote 'I Am The Walrus,' you know? They say he only knew the names; he didn't realise that the walrus was a baddie . . ."

"Well," Sally said, so close to me that I could feel her breathing, "they were both very unpleasant characters." Which sounded for all the world like a thing I'd heard her say before, in some other room, or maybe it was somebody just like her. She stopped peering around for a moment, and held her forehead against mine. In her eyes I saw wonderment, and maybe something else. "This is amazing," she said, "this is magic."

She slipped her arms around me. Hesitantly at first, I followed suit, and we teetered on the top of the ladder, balancing against each other, keeping each other from tumbling down through the hole. It felt like the most natural thing in the world, suddenly not playing a game, or maybe a special game for grown-ups. And yes, we kissed; for the very first time, and as it turned out also for the last. Timidly at first, hesitantly on my part, then slower, longer, deeper. L-U-V.

Was it L-U-V for Sally too? I can't say. Part of me wonders if the whole thing might not have been purely situational, so to speak: what a girl like her might have felt obliged to do in circumstances such as this. Was it her first time? Probably back in Highgate she'd kissed lots of boys; how could she not have? Maybe it was no big thing. But equally, ever since I'd known her, there had only been me. She liked me, I know; did she know how I felt about her? Could she have known? I didn't tell her my side of it, and so she never had a chance to say, or to reciprocate, or perhaps even to make up her mind. Perhaps it was just a kiss in the dream house.

When we broke, I was still breathless. "You took your time," Sally said, and kissed me again, first on my lips, then in the hollow of my neck. Abruptly she stiffened, and broke away, looking over my shoulder and behind me. "Oh my God—" Terror in her voice. I gasped in fright, and twisted to see what she'd seen; the step-ladder rocked and almost fell from under us.

There was, of course, nothing there.

"You are *so easy*," she said, and burst into a fit of the giggles. "Every time. Come on," and she boosted herself up into the room. The stepladder lurched again and this time it actually went over; I was just able to brace myself on the edge of the hole as it clattered to the floor below.

"Oh my God, are you OK? Hang on—" Sally went to grab me, but I could feel myself slipping.

"Let me go, it's OK—" A portion of the lath and plaster gave way, and I fell ignominiously to the bare floorboards.

"Oh no! Are you all right?" Sally was looking down anxiously.

"I'm fine," I said, brushing the debris off myself. "Just let me get my breath."

"I'm such an idiot," she said contritely.

"No, I'm fine," I said. "Give me a minute." I struggled to a sitting position, and Sally's head vanished from the hole. I sat there for a while, trying to gauge if I'd actually done myself any harm, and I happened to glance at the crumpled newspaper that had been no help whatsoever in breaking my fall.

"BEATLE JOHN BUYS HOUSE OF HORROR," ran a headline in thick tabloid caps, and beneath it was a photograph of a large house in its own grounds, a scene I recognised instantly. This house; the house we'd broken into.

I've looked up the article since then: it was from the *News of the World* on the 25th August, 1968, and the lede ran thus:

BEATLE JOHN LENNON has shocked local homeowners in Surrey with his plans to buy the house at the centre of a notorious 1963 sex scandal. This reporter has gained exclusive confirmation from sources close to the troubled Beatle that Shelgrave, the luxury home in . . .

Here the page was partly torn away. I picked it up again where the body text read:

Lennon, currently said to be undergoing marital problems, said: "You people will write what you always write, and I can't do anything about that. I haven't even seen the house, and I probably won't be moving in to it, so all those stockbrokers can stop worrying, you know? It's entirely a business deal, done through our business arm which as you know is Apple Corps, our new thing, and I don't know what'll happen there just yet. It won't be like anything that might have happened there before, I'll tell you that." When asked about the house's former owner, Lennon said: "Look, this guy did what he did, and that's his bag, alright. I'm not going to carry that—I've got my own bag, that's all the luggage I can carry, you know? You can look backwards, or you can look forwards, that's what I'm saying—"

Sally's voice came from above: "What are you doing? Are you OK?"

"Yeah, I'm just—there's a bit of paper here, hang on," I called back. A sidebar caught my eye:

PERVERT WHO PREYED ON CHILDREN

It is ten years since the News of the World first broke the story of Quentin Bascombe, the sex monster of suburbia. Since then, he has been convicted of his crimes, sentenced to indefinite detainment in a mental institution, and scandalously released, despite our campaign to make sure he remained locked away for life. His current whereabouts are unknown, and it is our understanding that his estate has been transferred into the hands of relatives, who refused to comment on the purchase of Shelgrave by Beatle John Lennon. The disappearance of several children in the Surrey stockbroker belt has often been linked to Bascombe, but no evidence was brought at his trial . . .

And there the text was torn away again. I've read the whole of it since, and done my own research, and learned about—learned too much about—what Quentin Bascombe got up to in his house of horrors. It was a notorious case of the day back in 1963. Bascombe, independently wealthy since the death of his parents, would drive his Rolls-Royce around the streets of suburban Surrey, parking outside playgrounds with the window rolled down. He'd invite children to come for a ride, tell them there was a tea-party in the grounds of his big house, then lead them inside on the pretext of a game of hide-and-seek. What happened to them in there was not the sort of thing a family newspaper could print, not in 1968, maybe not even today. But even if I'd known all the facts back then in 1980, it would already have been too late.

I called up through the hole in the ceiling, "Sally?"

An upside-down head lowered itself. "What?"

"You remember that song you were singing before? The one your mum told you about?"

"What, back in your house?" She sang it again. "We all live in a Quentin Bascombe dream, a Quentin Bascombe dream, a Quentin Bascombe dream . . ."

"I've found out who Quentin Bascombe was."

The upside-down head registered surprise. "No way! Was there really a Quentin Bascombe?"

I held up the newspaper. "This is his house. Lennon only bought it afterwards." I read her the gist of the story. For a while after she didn't say anything. "They say he was still on the loose," I said—I don't really know why. Perhaps it was just for the sake of saying something; to break the silence, which was becoming oppressive.

"Then if that's true . . ." She paused, as if unwilling to make the connection. "If that's true, then this is really Quentin Bascombe's dream, and we're in it."

I was trying to frame an answer when Sally gave a little gasp. Her head jerked up and out of sight, as if someone had tapped her on the shoulder.

"Oh give it a rest, Sally," I said. "You must think I was born yesterday. You're not getting me again with that routine."

No answer from above. No sign of Sally.

"Ha-ha, very funny," I said, loud enough for her to hear. Still no answer.

And then there came a scream, so different to the breathless playacting that had gone before that I had no doubt it was real. I knew that this wasn't Sally fooling me for a third time. All the apprehension I'd felt but could not articulate since we'd climbed over the garden wall and entered Shelgrave found a voice in that scream. It pushed me into full-on panic.

"Sally!" I scrambled to my feet, tried to see into the room above. All I could see was movement; I couldn't even tell of what. A thumping on the floor above dislodged more fragments of plaster from the hole in the ceiling. A stifled noise that I thought might have been Sally.

I grabbed the stepladder and tried to set it up below the hole again. One of the hinges was broken and I couldn't get it to stand straight; when I put my weight on the first step the whole thing gave way again. The thumps and muffled cries from above continued. Desperately, I jumped for the gap, pulled away another lump of plaster, fell to the floor again. The next time, I managed to hang on to one of the beams in the ceiling that bore my weight, and I pulled myself up on it.

The room was absolutely empty. I looked this way and that, but there was nothing. No sign of Sally; no sign of any other living thing; no sign of a door to open or to close. Only those insane paintings on the wall, and the sound of my own ragged breathing.

I tried to pull myself up all the way, but there was something about that impossible chamber that repelled me. I wonder now what would have happened if I had entered it, whether whatever happened to Sally might have happened to me too. Instead, I dropped to the floor again, and tried to overcome for a moment the bursting, toppling terror I felt. I knew I had to do something. But what?

I ran out of the ground floor room back into the vestibule, heading for the staircase. My thought was that there *must* be a door to the room—perhaps it was obscured by the painting or whatever, but there had to be a door. I turned right at the head of the stairs, tried all the rooms on that side of the landing. Nothing. Only empty spaces filled with dust and decay and the shadows of where things once had been. Rooms that existed in the real world, rooms with windows and doors. No paintings on the wall; no sign of Sally.

I went from room to room, kicking open the doors so that they raised little puffs of dust before rebounding against the jamb and slamming back in my face. I shouted her name, and no answer came to me. Once I thought I heard movement, away off in the depths of the house, somewhere I couldn't see and perhaps was never meant to. "Sally!" I screamed, one last time, and as if to mock me the lightning came, and the thunder right on top of it, and the storm broke.

I looked out of the nearest window. In retrospect what I saw made no sense, because when I try to recreate it now the view was the view I ought to have seen if I'd been looking out from that room with the hole in the floor. The view I should have seen, had there only been a window. There were the terraces, and the grounds spread out beyond, barely visible through the rain. But none of that incongruity registered with me, because I had eyes for one thing only: Sally.

She was lying face down on the patio as if she'd fallen out of the front door, or perhaps been pushed. I shouted her name again and hammered on the windowpane so hard that the glass splintered. She didn't respond.

I half scrambled, half fell down the stairs, threw myself at the front door, which now seemed to be unlocked, on the inside at least. Out on the patio, I knelt in the rain at Sally's side and turned her face up, saying her name over and over again.

She was breathing; she was conscious, or at least her eyes were open. She tried to say something, but it was aimed at the space beyond me, and she couldn't get it out in any case.

"Can you get up?" She didn't answer, but she did her best when I tried to lift her to her feet. "Come on, we've got to get away." She managed a step before swaying and almost falling over. I wrapped an arm around her and placed her arm around my own shoulders. "Try now," I urged her, and she broke into a sort of lurching gait. Like contestants in some dreadful parody of a three-legged race, we crossed the patio and began to negotiate the steps down to the pond. I threw a look over my shoulder.

What I saw has stayed with me since that day, and I'm a middle-aged man now, all too willing to brush away the irreconcilable in any experience. It was what it was, the thing I saw when I glanced back over my shoulder. I only looked for a second, and the rain was in my eyes, and I was filled with a dread that simultaneously made it impossible to move a muscle, and impossible not to run, but I saw it, and I can't rationalise it away, no matter how much I'd like to, no matter how hard I've tried.

There in the open doorway was a figure, half obscured by the dark inside the house, a darkness that was absolute, without any dimensions, just a total absence of light. As I watched, the figure grasped the door with one hand—with one paw, I ought to say—and began to close it. It paused for a moment, no more: just long enough to lean through the aperture, to raise its other paw and wave at us, almost mockingly: *bye-bye*. Then the door slammed shut, and I no longer had to believe the evidence of my eyes, or to cope with the notion that a figure in an animal suit, the costume of the Walrus from the old Beatles' *Magical Mystery Tour*, had manifested in the doorway of Shelgrave for a second, just to wave goodbye.

-◇-

I managed to get Sally down the terraces and around the water feature. All the while, the storm threw its worst at us, soaking us to the skin while it whipped the surface of the pond into a boil. It was more a case of me carrying her as we struggled across the field, and I practically had to push her up the ladder back into the garden of my house. For a second I was afraid she'd fall over the other side and do herself more damage, but she seemed to realise the danger and clutched at the stonework as I clambered up after her. I tried to take as much of her weight as I could in letting her down the other side, but our hands were slippery in the rain and she dropped heavily—to the grass, thank God. In all this flight I hadn't looked back, not once, after that glance over my shoulder on the terrace. Now I bundled her inside through the French windows, still open from our impulsive exit, and deposited her on the sofa while I tried to work out what to do next. I was in the kitchen, with the stupidly conventional thought of making her a cup of tea, when I heard a muffled crash from next door. I ran back in to find her fallen on the rug. As I looked, I could see a spreading patch of deep red soaking through the sopping material of her jeans.

After the ambulance came and I accompanied her to the hospital, there was a spell in which I sat in the corridor, conscious only of the rainwater dripping from my clothes in three separate puddles on to the linoleum floor. A doctor came to speak to me, asked me what had happened. I told him that Sally had fallen from the top of a ladder. He looked at me, at first impatiently, then with greater attention. He bent to stare into my eyes, pulled out a flashlight and shone it, and when the policeman arrived I was in a hospital bed of my own.

Late that evening, though the passage of time was by this point lost on me, my father came on to the ward. He had a long conversation with both the doctor and the policeman, who I remembered had been asking me questions, though I don't know what they were, and I don't know what I told him. Nor do I know what was said that evening, in the light of the nurses' station, between my father and the police. Eventually, Dad came to the side of my bed and asked me whether I thought I could get up and come home with him. I considered this proposition for a while. Apparently, I could not.

I was released from the psychiatric ward around the beginning of November. My father hired a nurse, who stayed with me the first week back home, and then it was just me and him, alone in the house, me not talking, him not asking. In all this, Sally's name was never mentioned. I remember when I started to come off the medication my nights were bad, and it was after one particularly bad episode that my father came and sat on the bed, and I finally told him what had happened in Shelgrave that October afternoon.

He listened, with a grave attention that I couldn't have expected. He asked a few questions, and received my answers in silence. The matter of the figure in the doorway seemed to startle him, but again he said nothing. He stayed with me until the pills he gave me took effect, and what he did then I can only recreate in my head, for he never told me about it. As long as he lived he kept his secret, but it seems clear to me what happened.

In our garden shed was a two-gallon jerrycan of petrol for the lawnmower. I believe Dad must have lugged this over the wall and down the ladder into the Shelgrave estate that night, all the way up to the big house. Did he have a torch, I wonder? The moon was the frailest crescent that night, what little of it showed through the wind-driven clouds, so I think he must have lighted his way somehow. I hope so, at any rate. The thought of him in the total darkness I'd glimpsed through the closing front door fills me with disquiet. He had at least a lighter with him, anyway, or matches, because when I woke it was to the sound of fire engines, the rise and fall of their sirens. They were coming from across the garden wall, where the firemen were trying in vain to put out the last of the flames in the wreckage of Shelgrave, now just a charred and broken ruin.

The police came to the house, but my father refused to let them speak with me. I could hear little snatches of the conversation from downstairs; the policemen asking polite if loaded questions, my father poking away every delicately framed suggestion with the straightest of bats. Later I remembered that my father played golf with the Chief Constable, which may have had a bearing on many things. We'd gone to bed early, he told them; neither of us had heard a thing, we'd both taken sleeping tablets. After a while the police went away, and my father came upstairs. "Do you want a cup of tea?" he asked, and I said I'd come down for it. We exchanged a smile, tentative on my part, all but imperceptible on his.

In the kitchen, waiting for the kettle to boil, my father switched on the radio. The disk jockey was in the middle of telling his listeners the news; that last night in New York City, December 8, 1980, Beatle John Lennon had been shot.

I did not go back to school: it was arranged that I should take my A-levels come the summer, that was all. As I left the exam hall after the last of these (English Lit, discuss the dramatic function of the storm in *The Tempest* by William Shakespeare), one of my former classmates came up to me. "Where the hell have you been? Is it right that you got Sally Holden up the stick?"

I shook my head; as usual, the merest mention of Sally's name shut me up like a clenched fist. "That's what everybody's saying," he said, scornfully. "She left school when you did, and Fishy says he saw her about six months gone coming out of the doctor's surgery. None of us thought it could have been you, you're such a virgin."

I don't remember what I said to him, if anything. I don't remember the bus journey I must have taken to the top of Sally's street—I had a ticket in my hand afterwards, but all the ink had rubbed off it with the sweat of my palm. I suppose I rang the bell, which I suppose went unanswered. I only remember standing on the grass slope outside the block of maisonettes, looking up to the second floor picture window that I knew was Sally's. Behind the blank opacity of the net curtains, ceiling to floor, there was a figure that might have been her, or perhaps I only wanted it to be her. I stared up for a long minute, and then it turned away and there was nothing.

A TREAT FOR YOUR LAST DAY

SIMON BESTWICK

O n our last family holiday, it rained all week and blew a gale. We couldn't even go to the beach; we were usually stuck in our rented house or in the car, en route to a nearby village. There wasn't much to do in any of those, either: there were cafes, charity shops, and sometimes a 'museum' (an upstairs room with a few cased artefacts.) Basically, it was a succession of confined spaces.

I was thirteen—neither quite a child any longer, nor an adult—and I knew I ached for *something*, but couldn't have said what: I was too old to believe in magic or buried treasure, not quite old enough for chasing girls or getting drunk. Whatever it was, I wanted to go running off in search of it, since I *did* know, by the end of that week, that it wasn't to be found in my parents' company.

Having said that, I'm sure my presence made things between them equally uncomfortable. For years I wondered whether, if I hadn't been there, they might have managed to talk honestly, one last time. I know they wouldn't have fallen in love again, I wasn't that silly or naive—but things might, at least, have ended differently. I wanted to believe that, except that it would mean the events of that day were my fault.

I know now that everything that happened had been planned well in advance, but that meant accepting that so many things I'd believed in were a lie. In which case, what was true? Pull one thread, and the whole weave unravels.

Here's what *is* true: on the morning of our last day there, the rain finally stopped, and my parents let me choose how we spent our one sunny afternoon. A treat for your last day, Dad said. I told him I wanted to go up the hill overlooking the town. So we did.

The clouds had cleared and the sky was blue; the earth was still sodden and there were pools of water everywhere, but the sun was bright and hot. My parents walked together, talking quietly, as we came up the steps to the old slate quarry, and I ran ahead, laughing.

Mum called after me, but I pretended I didn't hear. I wasn't an athletic boy by any standards, but I didn't like being physically inactive anyway. Being stuck inside all day had made me sullen and lethargic, which hadn't helped the atmosphere in the family, but within seconds my head felt clear, and I felt both happy and full of energy, striding up the hill towards some ill-defined but essential goal and leaving my parents far behind.

Another reason for quickening my pace was that I could hear them starting to bicker again. I couldn't tell the specifics or make out the words, but the tone was enough: it was one of the low, muttered arguments they so often had, barely audible but hanging like a black cloud over the dining-table or the car or wherever we happened to be when it took place.

I can remember our being happy, or at least I think I can; maybe those undercurrents were always there, and I just didn't pick up on them till I was older. My parents did, after all, try their best to hide their mutual animosity from their friends, work colleagues, and even family members—which included me.

The specifics? That's taken more piecing together, because nothing they let slip in front of me was meaningful, except much later, in retrospect. Dad had seemed a promising young man when they met, full of ideas. But after two hoped-for promotions at work had failed to materialise and he realised that he'd spent the better part of a decade stuck in the same role while other, newer employees were promoted over him, he quit and tried to start his own business. That failed, around the time we moved house. I'm not sure—I was very small at the time—but it's possible we either had to sell quickly for the money, or even that they defaulted on the mortgage.

Not long after that, he got a new job—very like his old one, but for considerably less money. He found his knowledge of his field out of date and struggled to catch up, and was now competing with younger men and women, who were once more promoted while he, try as he might, remained stuck in the same job. I know from my aunt that this was an increasingly painful and frustrating time for he'd once been considered to have a glittering career ahead of him, and at some point he couldn't identify, for no reason he could ascertain, his day had come and gone without his knowing, and now he was yesterday's man, a failure—not even a has-been, as he wrote to her, but a never-was.

And Mum? She supported him, at least to begin with. I don't know when her faith in him broke down, or why. My aunt talked about the rage that began to show through in my father's letters—not at Mum, at least not then, but at the world in general. Maybe that rage and bitterness alienated her. Or did he do something? Strike her? Have an affair? I have no idea, as the pair of them managed to hide the state of their marriage from me. But as I got older that changed. I became better at noticing things, they got tired of keeping up the act, and they didn't think I needed protecting any more. I suppose those were the reasons.

My grandmother didn't have any letters, and had had far less idea than my aunt that anything was wrong until very late in the game. There were a couple of phone calls from Mum that she would never discuss in detail with me. I got the impression Mum was finally contemplating leaving Dad, and taking me with her. I've no idea if he knew or not; although I know a lot more than I did that day, there are still things I'm unclear about that I'll probably never learn the details of now.

I know now, for instance, that Dad had recently lost his job, but I still haven't been able to determine why. He might have been made redundant, or caught with his hand in the till, or drinking on the job. That was why we'd gone to the coast that summer, rather than the planned trip to France. Why we went on holiday at all, when surely we should be cutting back, I don't know either—whether it was Mum's idea, or Dad's, or whether both of them had actually agreed on something for a change.

But on the day I knew none of that, only that I had an hour or two of freedom, and could use it to do what I'd so often done before on holidays here: make it to the summit so that I could take in the view, which stretched for miles around. I think I might even have made a sort of bargain with God—the way children do, and sometimes adults as well—that if I got to the summit everything would be all right. The cloud would lift, and everything between my parents—whose voices had risen higher—would be well again.

We'd taken the easiest route to climb the hill. Stone steps led from the coast road to the lower bank of the slate quarry. The quarry was roughly wedge-shaped, but the upper bank was only about fifty feet from the summit, while the lower bank was much further down. The upper bank was a sheer stone face that loomed at least a hundred feet above the lower bank, where we'd emerged, and which I was running up. The lower bank sloped gently and was easy going even for the least fit or experienced climbers; at the top, a footpath led past the end of the quarry over the upper bank and on to the hilltop.

The quarry path became steeper over the last twenty yards, so I stopped to catch my breath before pressing on. My breathing was a little ragged, but when I had it under control I noticed how quiet everything was. I could hear a few gulls calling and a sheep bleating, and that was it. I couldn't even hear Mum and Dad bickering, and I remember thinking that maybe my wish was already being granted.

Then—as if I'd tempted fate by thinking that—Dad called my name. If it had been Mum, I'd probably have ignored it, because she always seemed determined to prevent my having fun of any kind—stop doing that, sit up straight, elbows off the table, eat what's put in front of you—and it had become impossible to miss the barbed comments she'd taken to aiming at Dad. But Dad was different—he was funny, and he was fun. So when he called me, I paid attention.

I turned—by this point I was a good way up the quarry path, and could see out to sea. Dad waved up at me from the slope below. Come back down, he called.

Why? I asked.

We're going to have our picnic, he answered.

I thought we were going to eat on the summit?

Your Mum's not feeling at her best, love, so it might just be the two of us going to the top.

I didn't mind that. As I said, Dad was the fun parent and Mum was the killjoy, or that was how it seemed to me. It would be a while yet before I saw things differently.

Okay, I said, and started back down the slope. As long as I could finish my climb. I was still thinking of the bargain that I'd made: whatever happened, I had to reach the top.

Dad had spread out a plastic sheet. He'd clipped fishing weights to the metal rings at the corner so that it didn't blow away, and he was unpacking cold chicken and pork pies from his rucksack. Where's Mum? I asked.

Just over there. He pointed, not looking at me. Just go and look in on her, love. Make sure she's all right. She really wasn't feeling too well.

By the old mine?

Yeah, that's right, love.

I turned and went. I even remember thinking that this might even work out for the best. Dad had sounded worried about her. Perhaps they'd be nice to one another again, instead of arguing.

As well as quarrying for slate, there'd been manganese mining on the mountain. Not much; I only knew of three shafts. They were short, horizontal tunnels, bored into the mountainside, not branching off or sinking underground—dead-end caves with dripping ceilings and thin streams of water running along their rocky floors. The deepest one was about twenty feet. Two of them were on the other side of the quarry, but one of them was cut into a shelf of rock next to the quarry path. The approach to it was overgrown with thick, spiky gorse, and a small stand of trees, not much more than saplings, screened the entrance. I could see Mum wanting to sit under those, in the shade. She wasn't, though; when I brushed the drooping branches aside, I realised she was in the cave.

Mum? I said. I could see the blue Wellingtons she wore, but that was all. They stuck far enough out of the shadows to be in plain view, and appeared to be resting on the stone floor, as though she was lying down rather than sitting up. And of course that didn't make any sense, because Mum was very neat and tidy, and it didn't make sense that she'd be lying down on the wet, dirty floor under that dripping water—not unless she *really* wasn't well.

I shouted Dad, because I thought he must not realise how ill she was, and I heard his footsteps coming through the bushes. As that happened, I stepped closer to the cave entrance, and that was when I got a better look at my mother. I saw how still she was. And I noticed, too, that her upper body was covered by a blue plastic sheet, exactly like the one Dad had been spreading out beside the quarry path.

I remember saying Mum? again, but I think I knew. I'm sure I already knew. I just didn't want to believe it. And then I heard Dad's footsteps coming up behind and I turned around, because surely he'd have an explanation for this.

But he didn't. What he did have was that plastic sheet in one hand, and he threw it at me. The idea was, I suppose, that it would cover my head and shoulders as the other sheet had Mum's, so he wouldn't get blood everywhere. Or so that he wouldn't have to look at my face when he did it. But it caught on one of the branches and didn't go over me, which meant I could see what he was doing (which was probably another reason for the sheet.) He was holding what looked like a small pickaxe in his other hand—I've since found out that it was what they call a chipping hammer—which he had raised ready to bring down. The worst thing about it was the look on his face. He didn't even look angry, or hateful. He didn't, really, look like anything. Just blank.

As I said, he must have planned it all some way in advance. I don't know how far. So all the kindnesses, all the jokes—everything, really, that made Dad *Dad* to me—had just been an act. Something he'd switched off at that moment. Which is why thinking about something this is like pulling on a thread—you end up looking back over all the years you spent with someone, going over every interaction the two of you ever had, and trying to decide if any of it was ever real.

I couldn't make sense of it at the time, of course. Not then. And if I'd spent even a split-second longer trying to, then I'd probably have been killed. Luckily I was pretty good at dodging blows, because I was a comparatively small boy at a school where things could get fairly rough. So I jumped aside just in time for the chipping hammer to miss, and it tore into the sheet instead and plunged through it. The sheet got wrapped around Dad's arm. He cursed, looking angry again, and pulled it off. By then I was already moving away, through the trees. When he threw down the sheet and looked back towards me, his face was blank again. And then he came after me, and I ran.

I went down the quarry path, making for the steps, but Dad was faster, and moved to cut me off. We stood there, facing one another. As we did, the warm, bright day seemed to become cold and dark. When the first spots of rain began to fall, I realised it hadn't been my imagination.

Dad reached up with his free hand to wipe spots of rain from his glasses. His face was blank, calm—at most, he looked slightly irritated at things not having gone to plan. He was looking right into my eyes and inching up the path towards me, his free hand now extended, as though to pacify an animal.

Dad, I said. Dad. I wanted him to tell me that I'd got it wrong, that he hadn't done what he so obviously had, and wasn't trying to do what he so clearly was. He didn't answer, but instead kept sidling slowly up as the rain intensified, until I took a step back. Then he ran at me, at which point I turned and ran as well.

The quarry path became steeper as I reached the final stretch, and my legs began to ache. The rain was now a downpour, and within seconds my jeans and t-shirt were soaked through. I could hardly see for the rain in my eyes, either, and my boots skidded a couple of times on the muddy path. I could feel the vibration of Dad's boots, thumping on the ground behind me.

For all that, when I reached the end of the quarry and risked looking back I could see that I'd opened a substantial lead over Dad. He wasn't unfit, but he was older than me. That lead wouldn't last though: he was running hard after me, his face still blank but with a hard, determined look to it, and his lips were a thin, angry line I'd learned to be afraid of on the two or three occasions I'd seen it on before. He'd given me a hiding once or twice when I was younger—it was common practice for parents in those days—and I remembered seeing him coming towards me to do so, wanting to get away but knowing I couldn't, because he was my father and couldn't be avoided.

I felt the same way now, except that I *had* to avoid him. The normal rules of parent-child relations no longer applied; if he caught up with me he would kill me, and I could no longer afford to think of him as my father. I had to escape or fight him, although I couldn't see any physical confrontation ending with anything other than my death.

I rounded the end of the quarry and ran upwards, along the path that led to the summit. There wasn't anywhere else to go. I only knew one other way back to the town from here—the long, steep trail that wove and zigzagged down across the unquarried side of the mountain. It was a picturesque route, perfect for a long, leisurely walk in good weather. Neither of which would describe today's journey.

Still, having no alternative, I pressed on. It's hard to be sure, at this remove, but I think that on some level I was still clinging to the idea that if I could reach the top, everything would be all right again. As if it would wipe out Mum's death, and return Dad to being Dad. I knew that wasn't going to happen, though.

The route to the summit led through a shallow, wooded combe. The trees were covered in green moss. I clutched at them to steady myself, but when I looked back, there was no sign of my father. I heard movement among the trees, but couldn't tell what sounds were caused by the rain and what by something else.

The rain quickened; it dripped heavily through the trees. The air became a grey haze. I couldn't see more than a few feet in any direction, and I was shaking—more from shock, I think, than the cold. I could see shadowy movements in that fog of rain, but nothing I could be certain of. Through a gap in the trees, the rocky peak of the summit was visible, and the last few yards of path, but for all I knew he'd made his way up ahead of me and was waiting.

I remember very little after that. The rain went on for some time, through most of that day, in fact. At some point I remember sitting down, huddled against the nearest tree, almost blind with rain. Mossy tree-trunks, rain-puddles in the thin soil, the cold. I also have a sort of blurred image of warmth and sunlight, of the earth and my clothes steaming. I discovered later that the rain stopped a couple of hours before night fell, which might have saved my life.

The following morning, a farmer whose sheep grazed on the hillside went out to check on his flock, to see how they'd fared during the storm. He sighted a couple near the combe, and went into the trees. He didn't find any, but he did stumble—literally—over me.

I was half-dead from hypothermia by that point. Those few dry, warm hours before dusk might have made all the difference. If we'd gone there in autumn or winter, the weather would have done Dad's job for him. I was still conscious enough to scream in panic, though, because when he tumbled over me I thought he was Dad. He said later that I'd nearly given him a heart attack.

I was able to stammer out my story, or enough of it to be understood. I was able to be very specific, of course, about Mum; the police went straight to the manganese mine by the old quarry and found her there. But my father was long gone by then. He'd gone back to the house, dropped the keys through the landlady's door, packed all our belongings and driven off, keeping up the appearance of normality as much as he could.

He'd planned, I'm guessing, to disappear and resurface elsewhere—with a new name, another life, where he would no longer be a failure. He just had to erase his old life first, his mistakes. In other words, his wife and child.

Presumably, he'd have hidden both our bodies in the cave, which would have given him a few days where no-one would have known anything was amiss. Or perhaps he'd meant, once he'd killed us both, to dump the bodies somewhere they'd never be found.

Why did he spare me? Remorse? I'd like to believe that, but I think the real reason's far simpler and more practical—he'd lost me in the woods and rain and had no clue where to find me. For all he knew, I'd cleared the summit and was running back down towards the town to raise the alarm. And so he panicked, and within twenty-four hours of the murder the police were looking for him.

Not that it did any good. He'd vanished. They never found him, or even the car. Not until—but I'll come to that. Be warned, though, that I can't offer you much in the way of an ending.

My aunt took me in. My grandmother helped her take care of me, financially, and I'd occasionally stay with her, but she could never bear to have any contact with my aunt that wasn't absolutely necessary, and even that unwillingly. There wasn't much of a family resemblance, but what do you say to someone whose brother killed your only child? My grandmother wasn't even particularly comfortable with my presence as I grew up; I'm told I take after my father. I don't see a resemblance myself; perhaps I simply don't wish to.

For years I thought he would come back. Every scratch against the bedroom window of a night, every creak made by the house settling, was my father coming back to finish the job. It never was, of course.

My grandmother and my aunt are both dead now, my aunt almost ten years ago. They were my only family, and I never added to it. My counsellor says that I have trust issues. I've never been sure if I'm more afraid of what any potential partner might be hiding, or what I might. My father wasn't a monster, or at least he wasn't born one. My aunt had no idea what had gone wrong, that he'd do what he did. And my mother was a kind woman. I know I haven't done justice to her here, because by the time of the murder she'd become embittered and angry. But she wasn't responsible for my father. So I can only guess that it was something in the two of them together, a flaw that became something pernicious and terrible. In which case, how can I be sure the same flaw isn't in me? What I might carry from my father is one of my greatest fears; better, then, that it becomes extinct with me.

It's made for a lonely life, but not entirely an unhappy one. The nightmares are more or less gone, all these years later, and if I'm detached—cold, even, according to some—I'm content. Like anyone else, I am the sum of my experiences, both good and bad, so to wish I had a different history would be, in a way, to will my own destruction. Which casts further doubt on my present course of action, but I'm going to do it anyway.

Seven years ago, some human remains were discovered in woodland seventeen miles to the south-east of the town we'd spent our last holiday in. They'd been there for decades and were almost completely skeletonised, but were identified as those of an adult white male aged between thirty-five and forty-five years. There was no identification on the body, but last year some enterprising officer in the relevant cold case unit connected the estimated year of decease to the date of the murder and contacted me. They were able to extract usable DNA from the remains and compare it with my own.

Nobody could be sure of the cause of death, but from rope fibres found on the remains, my father was assumed to have hanged himself from a convenient tree branch. More than likely, he'd done so within forty-eight hours of leaving the seaside town.

I'd never had anything to be afraid of.

I suppose his suicide could have been out of remorse, but once again, I doubt it. Whatever plans he'd made for his new life, they'd have involved leaving the country, and by then they'd have been watching for him at every air- or seaport. He'd never have made it through. So it had all been for nothing, and there was only one way out.

Four months after he was identified, hikers in the woods found what was left of a car about a hundred yards from where his bones had been discovered; it had been half-buried in silt washed down a nearby stream over the years, overgrown with creepers and wasn't much more than a very thin shell of solid rust, but it was identified as our family car. The luggage he'd packed was still in the boot.

As I said before, I don't have much of an ending for you. And I know you want an ending. So do I. Who doesn't? We want our lives to make some sort of sense, because none of us want to believe that bad things can happen to good people for no real reason at all other than, at best, bad luck. Life is basically a field full of hidden landmines, and nothing you can do protects you against treading on one: I believe that's the truth, but I also believe nobody wants to believe that if any other explanation's available.

My family trod on a landmine; so could you, or yours. As simple as that. And, one day—sooner or later, one way or the other, life being what it is—you will.

But that isn't an ending anybody wants to read, so instead, I'll offer you this one.

At this moment, I'm sitting at a little cafe overlooking the beach in that seaside town. It's the first time I've gone back there since that day. If I turn my head, I can see the mountain from here, with the slate quarry gouged out in the side of it. It's a nice day, clear and warm; I have a cup of tea in front of me, of which I've drunk about half.

When I've finished the cup, I'm going to go up the steps and make my way along the quarry path. I may or may not stop at the manganese mine, if I can convince myself it retains any echo of what happened there, which I probably won't. But what I will do is go on to the summit, because I never did get that far. If nothing else, it's a beautiful view. I can enjoy that.

At least I'll have finally kept the deal I made that day, although I don't know how everything can be made all right. Perhaps I'll be able to fool myself, if only briefly, that some kind god might wind back time and straighten whatever was crooked. Give me a different past. Another life.

TRICK OF THE LIGHT

ANDREW HUMPHREY

It was November and the trees were bare as we drove through Henstead and Wrentham and South Cove and pulled into the drive of our hired cottage on the outskirts of Southwold.

"No Satnav required," I said as I extracted myself from our ageing Toyota.

"Smartarse," Gayle said. She'd fretted the whole drive, convinced we were lost. Actually, at times we had been, and the drive took longer than it should have, but I wasn't going to admit that. She stretched and leant against the passenger door. "Let's check out the digs. We can unload in a bit."

"We could go for a walk," I said. "Before it gets dark. Check out the locals."

"What locals?" Gayle said. She had a point. The cottage was more isolated than I had imagined. We were renting from a friend of Gayle's, Janice. We'd picked up the keys from her early that morning. She was blurry-eyed and chilly on her doorstep as she handed them over. "The village is a mile away. Give or take," she said. "Easy walk. There's a pub, a church. What more does one need?"

I wasn't sure about the easy walk. The road was narrow and pathless. The cottage itself was compact and pretty with whitewashed walls and dark wooden window frames and a thatched roof that needed attention. The drive was gravelled and a short path led to the front door. There was a small garden at the back of the building. Enveloping all was a patchwork of fields, dun-coloured, mostly empty, but some dotted with pigsties and the tiny, pink smudges of the pigs themselves. To the east, past a copse of trees and the hint of a church spire, was the sea, or a trace of it at least. The silence was all encompassing. The light, as the sun dipped, was the colour of weak whisky.

"It's beautiful," I said. "You could get your camera out, take a picture of that sunset."

"Nah," she said, pulling the door keys from her coat pocket. "It's a bit of cliché." She wrinkled her nose at me in that way she did. Sometimes it was cute, sometimes not so much.

⟨○⟩

Janice said that the cottage was well equipped, and she was right. All mod cons. Too many, perhaps. Some of the building's character had leached away, drained by the flat-screen TV, the sound system, the vast pink Smeg fridge, the sparkling, stainless-steel coffee maker. But there was still the stone floor in the kitchen, the beamed ceilings, the unadorned bare-brick walls in the living room and study.

"I love it," Gayle said. She was in the study, setting up her laptop and unpacking her cameras and accessories. "Can you sort out the heating, Dan? It's a bit chilly."

I did as I was told, with the help of Janice's laminated instructions. I checked upstairs. One large room dominated by an enormous bed dressed in pristine white linen. The en-suite bathroom was white too, tiled and gleaming.

I heard Gayle make her way carefully up the steep, narrow stairs.

"That bed is massive," she said from the doorway. She had the sleeves of her cardigan pulled over her hands and her arms were wrapped around themselves.

"You'll need a map," I said. Gayle was tiny. Waif-like, I said. Fine-boned, she said.

"Funny man."

"You still cold? Give the shower a try. That'll warm you up. Or we both could."

She wrinkled her nose again. "Let's unpack. I'm hungry."

◄○►

We could drive to the pub, I said, for food, but she didn't want to do that either. We'd brought some soup with us, so we ate that with warm baguettes. I opened a bottle of wine. Gayle shook her head when I fetched her a glass. She was reviewing the photos on her digital camera. After we ate she took her Pentax into the study to download her pictures. When I went through she had Light Room loaded up and was selecting shots for editing. I put my hand on her shoulder. Her cardigan was thin and the flesh beneath close to the bone. She touched my fingers briefly. "I'm working, hon."

Back in the living room I drank wine and read whilst the darkness gathered outside. It was utterly silent.

◄○►

The thing is, I cheated. A couple of years ago, more or less. I didn't tell Gayle; she found out on her own. I was careless with some texts, a couple of emails. I tried to manufacture some outrage because Gayle had gone through my phone and computer but it didn't take. I thought she would leave but she didn't. She wasn't angry either, not outwardly, at least. She retreated into hurt, disappointed silences that I was unable to penetrate. I kept trying though, because I loved her. Yes, I know. But after an affair you justify and deflect. You attempt to rewrite history. It meant nothing. It was a terrible mistake. You hide behind a second-person narrative to distance yourself from your behaviour. But at some point you have to face it. You did these things. I did these things. I enjoyed them. At the time. It seems absurd now, something abstract, of little substance. I don't mention her name, the other woman, not even in my head. I don't want to make it real again.

I'm not sure why Gayle didn't leave. We shared six good years and a mortgage. Perhaps that's enough.

◄○►

It's not work for Gayle, the photography. Not really. She's employed by the local tax office. But she is good and getting better. She takes pictures of the mundane and ordinary, all digital, and uses filters and software to twist them into something other. None of this is particularly original, I gather, but Gayle has an eye, a sensibility for odd, angled, fractured beauty that is starting to garner approval and attention. She had a small exhibition a couple of months ago and sells her work online and through a few independent shops and cafes.

Actually, her photos leave me cold. I prefer sunsets, seascapes, beauty unadorned. The kind of work that Gayle quietly despises. I enthuse about her stuff, of course, tell her I love it, but I've noticed that she is asking my opinion less and less. And why should she? I'm no expert. I'm an accountant. I like reading ghost stories and watching cricket. I like drinking red wine until the edges of the world blur and my thoughts stop tangling and turning in on themselves.

‹o›

Gayle was awake before me and when I came downstairs she was drinking coffee from a cafetière for one and nibbling at an apple segment. I made myself some tea and sat at the dark wood table. "Sleep well?" I said.

"Like a log. You?"

"It's too quiet. I thought we'd hear animals. Or birds. Or something."

"That would be better, would it? A badger or a fox snuffling around outside."

"Yeah. A sign of life, at least."

She put a hand to her ear and tilted her head. "Hark? What's that I hear? Birdsong? And a distant tractor perhaps?"

"Well, it's daylight now, isn't it? It's after dark that the world switches off."

"You just need to get used to it. I love it. After the city, it's bliss." She glanced at the empty wine bottle next to the kettle. "How's your head?"

"Sore."

"Serves you right. Looks like I'm driving this morning, then?"

"I can drive."

She had a map in front of her on the table and she smoothed it with a sweep of her right hand. "I want to do a recce this morning. We can park at the church and walk to the beach at North Hale from there. Then I want to catch the church and the beach at dusk. We need to watch the tides though."

"Yes, sir."

"Sorry," she said, her voice softening through a half smile. "Am I being bossy again?"

"Little bit." I raised a hand. "It's fine. I do love a controlling woman."

Her gaze dropped. "I did say I'd come on my own."

"I know. But it's all good. You'll get some great shots, we'll both recharge our batteries. What's not to like?"

Gayle's smile was thin and her eyes didn't leave the map.

—◇—

The weekend was ostensibly for Gayle's benefit. She had an exhibition planned and needed new material. The beach at North Hale was particularly isolated and striking and had a reputation for a kind of leftfield otherness. Gayle felt she could harness this, distort it. Her work had become stale, she said, she needed inspiration. It wasn't only her work that had become stale; our relationship was calcifying around us. This was my fault, I know, but the knowledge didn't help me to break the ever-tightening spiral of our conversations, our routines. A weekend away would be something different at least and if Gayle could break her creative logjam perhaps things could shift between us as well. It seemed worth a try. Anyway, I loved the stories of MR James, adored the thought of a creepy beach, imagining I was Michael Hordern, crouched beneath an East Anglian sky, raising an ancient, Latin-inscripted whistle to my lips.

—◇—

It was a fifteen-minute drive through quiet, narrow roads. We encountered no other traffic. The throbbing in my head was like a relentless bass line. The day was hushed, chilled; an indolent mist lay over the flat fields. We parked across from the church.

"Weird," I said, zipping my jacket up to my throat.

"They built the new church inside the ruins of the old one," Gayle said. "Seventeenth century." There was a tower to the west, almost intact, abutted by ruined walls with window openings framing the thin blue sky. "That dates back to the fourteenth century. It was too big for the parish so they used some of the original materials when they built the new one."

"Who needs a guidebook?"

"It's interesting."

"I didn't say it wasn't." The graveyard was overgrown, the headstones worn, mostly unreadable. We approached the new church. "Is this still in use?"

"Apparently," Gayle said. "They're a pretty conservative bunch. Very traditional Anglican. No ordination of women here."

"Who would have thought it? But who are 'they' exactly?" We'd passed a handful of attractive, detached houses on the way to the church, but seen no sign of human habitation. There were a few pigs, at least, scattered prettily in the near distance.

Inside, the church was immaculate and austere. The high-vaulted ceiling was white-washed between dark beams. The pews and the carved wooden font were fifteenth century, Gayle told me. I could see no sign of contemporary life although the interior was clearly cared for.

Gayle unpacked her camera and took pictures of the pulpit and diamond-leaded windows. I wandered outside again, leaving her to it. From the inside the ruins of the old church were skeletal and looming. I walked along the outside, running my fingers against the old flint. I tried to appreciate the age of it, to feel something other than the grainy tedium of my hangover, but it was no use. I wanted a coffee. I wanted something stronger, which alarmed me a little.

I cut through the graveyard towards the entrance of the new church. The day had been completely still but a sudden breeze snickered through the headstones and the long grass, tugging at my jacket and my trouser legs. Then it dropped again and the sunlight grew stronger. The mist had gone.

◄◦►

The walk to the beach took half an hour. We meandered through flat fields, past knots of pigs and one enormous, irritable boar. Its vast head turned towards us, baleful, obsidian eyes crackling with dull light. The soil grew sandy and there were scrubby tufts of marram grass as the cliffs tapered down to the beach. We were wordless as we walked. Gayle led the way, her canvas bag, the strap angled across her right shoulder, bouncing against her hip. The air was still and becoming unseasonably warm.

◄◦►

We're on the beach. It's narrow but widens towards the horizon as the cliffs rise. From here, in the gauzy sunlight, the cliffs appear buttery and soft. They seem to have the consistency of fudge. As though reading my thoughts, Gayle says, "They're being eaten away. Coastal erosion. This will all disappear in time."

"If we stand still too long perhaps it will take us as well."

She gives me a cold look as she shrugs her bag to the ground and kneels next to it. For the first time, as I breathe in, I notice the clarity of the air. My headache eases and I wonder if the air has magical properties.

There are trees dotted along the horizon. They are bleached white, as though from shock. They are twisted, distorted. They appear to be flinching against the relentless sea, the salt, the wind that so often drives in from the east.

Gayle has her camera around her neck now. She takes a number of shots but she seems listless, not even framing them properly. "It's too bright. I didn't expect this, not in November."

"Bloody weather," I say. "Still, we can come back later."

"Yeah." She has her hands on her hips. She looks oddly crestfallen. The strap of the camera has pulled the top of her blouse open. Her skin is milky, translucent. Sprays of freckles adorn her throat and the bridge of her small nose.

"We may as well walk," I say.

She gazes at the caramel cliffs, a hand shielding her eyes against the flat glare of the beach and the sea. "It's a bit 'Whistle and I'll Come to You', isn't it?" she says.

The reference pleases me, even though, as always, she misses the "Oh" from the start and the "My Lad" from the end of the story's title. "Not bleak enough," I say.

"You think?"

I come to her side and share her view. The ancient coast is laid before us, stark and unapologetic, its architecture stripped bare. I feel giddy suddenly. The landscape is vast, unknowable and yet, at the same time, immensely claustrophobic. A half breeze appears from somewhere and tugs at my shoulder. I turn, expecting something, someone, but there is merely more emptiness. "You may have a point," I say.

"I'm talking about the John Hurt one, of course."

"Of course."

"I know you prefer Michael Hordern. Corny old thing that it is."

"Sacrilege." It's an old argument, if a mild one.

"Still, I might try and get some of that atmosphere into my pictures."

"Quis est iste qui venit."

"Who is this who is coming?"

"Indeed." I think of MR James' quiet, unsparing prose. The words crawl across the flesh on my hands, my arms and up to the base of my neck. "Should be good," I say.

We walk and as we walk the beach widens and the tide recedes. As we get closer to the twisted trees they appear less tortured. They are merely odd, a little embarrassed perhaps, caught in the wrong place at the wrong time. Gayle takes some shots, despite the light. She stands, stretches, then pauses and points into the distance. "What's that?"

The horizon is hazy but as I peer at it a figure forms. It's too far away to be sure but it seems curved, petite, although in reality it's merely a smudge, a dash of charcoal. "It's a woman, isn't it?"

"I'm pretty sure it's a man," Gayle says, squinting hard. "He's tall. He has an arm raised."

"I can't see an arm. They seem short to me. And female."

"Naturally," Gayle says.

"I can't help what I see. Are they getting closer?" I shield my eyes with my right hand. It doesn't help. "I can't quite make out . . . it's not just one, is it? There are many. Rows of them."

And there were. Just like that. Many figures, blurred and indistinct.

"Too many to count," Gayle says. That breeze again. I see it tousle the curls in Gayle's fair hair, feel its fingers brush my cheek.

"My name is Legion, for we are many."

"What?"

My face is close to hers suddenly, although I'm not sure how. My left hand grips her shoulder too tightly.

"You're hurting me."

"They're coming for us." I don't recognise my voice. Gayle's eyes are wide. I feel her breath on my cheek.

"What did you say?"

I release her arm, take a step back. "I don't know."

She rubs her shoulder. "You do." Her head, her whole body, is angled away from me. "You frightened me." When I don't reply she says, "What is wrong with you?"

"I'm sorry." I say, although I'm not sure that I am. When we look back into the distance the figures have gone.

◄O►

As we retrace our steps Gayle walks ahead. The sea leaves debris as the tide ebbs. Some wood, a green glass bottle. Something glints in the sunlight and I approach it. "I don't believe this," I say.

Reluctantly, Gayle turns. "What?"

I pick the object up and hold it out. It's a referee's whistle. Silver, worn. "What are the odds?"

"You shouldn't touch it."

"I'm not . . ."

"Don't blow it, Dan." Her voice is high pitched, not quite her own.

"I wasn't going to." I toss the whistle back into the sea. "Jesus."

She seems close to tears. At her feet, abandoned by the tide, is a child's shoe. She picks it up.

"Looks old," I say, approaching her. It's a right shoe, pink with purple stitching. She brushes the wet sand from it and places it carefully in her canvas bag.

She walks ahead again without speaking. The sunshine is stronger than ever but there is little heat to it, little substance. I watch Gayle as she walks. She appears soaked in light. It's as though she's drowning in it.

◄O►

We took a different route back to the cottage, cutting through a tiny hamlet and stopping at a pub in the next village.

"They've got some decent beers by the look of it," I said, as though the quality of the alcohol made the slightest difference to me.

"Have a pint," Gayle said. "I'll drive."

"I can still drive."

"Have a couple. It's fine." Her voice was stiff and odd.

I ordered drinks and food at the bar. It felt strange, speaking to someone other than Gayle. The barman was gruff, borderline rude. Two locals stood at the bar, father and son, by the looks of them. They spared us a single curt glance, nothing more.

Back at our table, in an alcove, I said quietly, "Still no sign of intelligent life then."

Gayle shushed me, frowning. After a moment she said, "Why did you say what you said? On the beach?"

"I don't know."

"You were . . ." She struggled for the correct word. "You weren't you."

"I'm sorry I hurt you."

"It's not even that. Not really. Jesus . . . your voice . . ."

"It was nothing. Honestly."

She extracted the knife and fork from her napkin. Her features were crimped. Still pretty though. Nothing she could do about that. A woman appeared from a door next to the bar and dumped two plates in front of us.

"Thanks," I said to her back.

"You and your ghost stories," Gayle said, picking at her skinny fries.

I ate some of my chilli. It was surprisingly good. "I wonder what it was we saw."

"Trick of the light," Gayle said.

"You should have taken a picture."

That made her pause. "I didn't think. I have a telephoto lens."

"It doesn't matter. We don't have to go back."

"Of course we do. I want to."

"Well, if you want to," I said, "I guess we will."

◄◦►

Back at the cottage I made coffee for us both. Gayle sat cross-legged on the sofa, examining her camera. I turned the radio on. "That's the Fall, isn't it?"

"Probably," Gayle said, shrugging. "Not really my thing."

"I don't recognise the song."

I switched it off and joined Gayle on the sofa.

"We don't have to go back," I said again.

"Yes we do."

"Janice said . . ."

"I know what Janice said."

"Stay away from the beach. There are stories."

"And you do love your stories."

"People have . . ." I hesitated.

She turned towards me. "Yes. Foolish people, taken by the tides. I know the tides. I am not foolish."

"They've never been found."

"It's a big sea, Dan."

"And old. Like the beach, the cliffs. Ancient, in fact." Hungry, I nearly said, but didn't. "I saw something. We both did. I'm not sure that it's a story at all."

"You didn't blow the whistle. You haven't summoned anything."

"I don't think I need to. I think it's already there."

She sighed heavily. Then she surprised me. She shifted so that her thigh touched mine. "Look, we've got a couple of hours. We could go upstairs for a bit."

So we did.

⤙⚬⤚

It was the last time we made love. Gayle's kisses were distant and she kept her eyes closed throughout. But it was something. Afterwards we lay on our backs in the vast bed. I breathed heavily. Somewhere above a gull screamed, a sound like a woman's cry. After a moment another answered.

⤙⚬⤚

We showered separately and packed our respective bags. When we went out to the car it had gone.

"Seriously?" I said. I looked around as though it would suddenly appear.

"I didn't hear anything."

"Jesus." I headed back indoors. "I'll make some calls."

"Tomorrow," Gayle said. "We can walk."

"We need to sort this out. Anyway, it's pointless. It will be dark by the time we get there."

"Not if we hurry. We'll skip the church, go straight to the beach."

I started to challenge her but she was already walking. I hesitated, but only for a moment, then I followed.

◄◦►

I was glad not to linger at the church. It was predictably Gothic in the half light. Gayle barely spared it a glance as she continued her route march to the beach. The sky was an ink-wash, flat against the land. We passed the boar again. It ignored us this time. Negotiating the scrubby, crumbling earth we hit the beach.

◄◦►

It's different here as the dusk closes in. The cliffs seem steeper, vertiginous, much more substantial. I do not believe that they are yielding to the sea at all. Perhaps it's the other way around.

And now the beach appears narrower and there are no trees.

"Is the tide coming in?"

"Not possible," Gayle says. "I checked."

"We should go back."

Gayle ignores me as I knew she would. Distantly, without much concern, I think, it's already too late.

The driftwood is there, where water and beach overlap. Some of it has been fashioned into a cross and driven into the wet sand. At the base of the cross are items, offerings. We approach them. Gayle gives a little gasp as she picks up a camera. "It's a Pentax. Exactly the same as mine." She tries to peer at the serial number but it is getting darker now and it is hard to see. There is also a dead cat, the whistle again, and a child's shoe. It's a left shoe, I see as I get closer, pink with purple stitching.

The horizon is endless, the sky violet, febrile, darkening. The skin of the world seems thin here and stretched to breaking point. I squint into the distance and the figures are there. I knew they would be. They are vague but seem to be beckoning. They are miles away and almost upon us.

"You see?"

"Yes." Gayle takes the telephoto lens from her bag and fixes it to her camera. She then raises it to her eyes. She drops it instantly, yanking the lens free again. "I don't understand."

Turning to face her, I say, "Sunt venire." I don't recognise my voice. "They are coming."

Gayle does not reply. Her eyes are on the horizon.

She pulls the camera free from her neck and hurls it in the direction of the figures. She extends her arms in front of her, palms outwards. Behind me a noise gathers. A voice of sorts. It punches through dead air. I do not turn. Gayle stares past my shoulder. I reach for her as a shadow engulfs us. Her mouth is open, her eyes wide.

I want to hold her but it's too late now.

TWO TRUTHS AND A LIE

SARAH PINSKER

n his last years, Marco's older brother Denny had become one of those people whose possessions swallowed them entirely. The kind they made documentaries about, the kind people staged interventions for, the kind people made excuses not to visit, and who stopped going out, and who were spoken of in sighs and silences. Those were the things Stella thought about after Denny died, and those were the reasons why, after eyeing the four other people at the funeral, she offered to help Marco clean out the house.

"Are you sure?" Marco asked. "You barely even knew him. It's been thirty years since you saw him last."

Marco's husband, Justin, elbowed Marco in the ribs. "Take her up on it. I've got to get home tomorrow and you could use help."

"I don't mind. Denny was nice to me," Stella said, and then added, "But I'd be doing it to help you."

The first part was a lie, the second part true. Denny had been the weird older brother who was always there when their friends hung out at Marco's back in high school, always lurking with a notebook and a furtive expression. She remembered Marco going out of his way to try to include Denny, Marco's admiration wrapped in disappointment, his slow slide into embarrassment.

She and Marco had been good friends then, but she hadn't kept up with anyone from high school. She had no excuse; social media could reconnect just about anyone at any time. She wasn't sure what it said about her or them that nobody had tried to communicate.

On the first night of her visit with her parents, her mother had said, "Your friend Marco's brother died this week," and Stella had suddenly been overwhelmed with remorse for having let that particular friendship lapse. Even more so when she read the obituary her mother had clipped, and she realized Marco's parents had died a few years before. That was why she went to the funeral and that was why she volunteered. "I'd like to help," she said.

Two days later, she arrived at the house wearing clothes from a bag her mother had never gotten around to donating: jeans decades out of style and dappled with paint, treadworn gym shoes, and a baggy, age-stretched T-shirt from the Tim Burton *Batman*. She wasn't self-conscious about the clothes—they made sense for deep cleaning—but there was something surreal about the combination of these particular clothes and this particular door.

"I can't believe you still have that T-shirt," Marco said when he stepped out onto the stoop. "Mine disintegrated. Do you remember we all skipped school to go to the first showing?"

"Yeah. I didn't even know my mom still had it. I thought she'd thrown it out years ago."

"Cool—and thanks for doing this. I told myself I wouldn't ask anybody, but if someone offered I'd take them up on it. Promise me you won't think less of me for the way this looks? Our parents gave him the house. I tried to help him when I visited, but he didn't really let me, and he made it clear if I pushed too hard I wouldn't be welcome anymore."

Stella nodded. "I promise."

He handed her a pair of latex gloves and a paper mask to cover her mouth and nose; she considered for the first time how bad it might be. She hadn't even really registered that he had squeezed through a cracked door and greeted her outside. The lawn was manicured, the flower beds mulched and weeded and ready for the spring that promised to erupt at any moment, if winter ever agreed to depart. The shutters sported fresh white paint.

Which was why she was surprised when Marco cracked the door again to enter, leaving only enough room for her to squeeze through as she followed. Something was piled behind the door. Also beside the door, in front of the door, and in every available space in the entranceway. A narrow path led forward to the kitchen, another into the living room, another upstairs.

"Oh," she said.

He glanced back at her. "It's not too late to back out. You didn't know what you were signing up for."

"I didn't," she admitted. "But it's okay. Do you have a game plan?"

"Dining room, living room, rec room, bedrooms, in that order. I have no clue how long any room will take, so whatever we get done is fine. Most of what you'll find is garbage, which can go into bags I'll take to the dumpster in the yard. Let me know if you see anything you think I might care about. We should probably work in the same room, anyhow, since I don't want either of us dying under a pile. That was all I thought about while I cleaned a path through the kitchen to get to the dumpster: If I get buried working in here alone, nobody will ever find me."

"Dining room it is, then." She tried to inject enthusiasm into her voice, or at least moral support.

It was strange seeing a house where she had spent so much time reduced to such a fallen state. She didn't think she'd have been able to say where a side table or a bookcase had stood, but there they were, in the deepest strata, and she remembered.

They'd met here to go to prom, ten of them. Marco's father had photographed the whole group together, only saying once, "In my day, people went to prom with dates," and promptly getting shushed by Marco's mother. Denny had sat on the stairs and watched them, omnipresent notebook in his hands. It hadn't felt weird until Marco told him to go upstairs, and then suddenly it had gone from just another family member watching the festivities to something more unsettling.

She and Marco went through the living room to the dining room. A massive table still dominated the room, though it was covered with glue sticks and paintbrushes and other art supplies. Every other surface in the room held towering piles, but the section demarcated by paint-smeared newspaper suggested Denny had actually used the table.

She smelled the kitchen from ten feet away. Her face must have shown it, because Marco said, "I'm serious. Don't go in there unless you have to. I've got all the windows open and three fans blowing but it's not enough. I thought we could start in here because it might actually be easiest. You can do the sideboard and the china cabinets and I'll work on clearing the table. Two categories: garbage and maybe-not-garbage, which includes personal stuff and anything you think might be valuable. Dying is shockingly expensive."

Stella didn't know if that referred to Denny's death—she didn't know how he'd died—or to the funeral, and she didn't want to ask. She wondered why Marco had chosen the impersonal job with no decisions involved, but when she came to one of his grandmother's porcelain teacups, broken by the weight of everything layered on top of it, she thought she understood. He didn't necessarily remember what was under here, but seeing it damaged would be harder than if Stella just threw it in a big black bag. The items would jog memories; their absence would not.

She also came to understand the purpose of the latex gloves. The piles held surprises. Papers layered on papers layered on toys and antiques, then, suddenly, mouse turds or a cat's hairball or the flattened tendril of some once-green plant or something moldering and indefinable. Denny had apparently smoked, too; every few layers, a full ashtray made an appearance. The papers were for the most part easy discards: the news and obituary sections of the local weekly newspaper, going back ten, fifteen, thirty-five years, some with articles cut out.

Here and there, she came across something that had survived: a silver platter, a resilient teapot, a framed photo. She placed those on the table in the space Marco had cleared. For a while it felt like she was just shifting the mess sideways, but eventually she began to recognize progress in the form of the furniture under the piles. When Marco finished, he dragged her garbage bags through the kitchen and out to the dumpster, then started sifting through the stuff she'd set aside. He labeled three boxes: "keep," "donate," and "sell." Some items took him longer than others; she decided not to ask how he made the choices. If he wanted to talk, he'd talk.

"Stop for lunch?" Marco asked when the table at last held only filled boxes.

Stella's stomach had started grumbling an hour before; she was more than happy to take a break. She reached instinctively for her phone to check the time, then stopped herself and peeled the gloves off the way she'd learned in first aid in high school, avoiding contamination. "I need to wash my hands."

"Do it at the deli on the corner. You don't want to get near any of these sinks."

The deli on the corner hadn't been there when they were kids. What *had* been? A real estate office or something else that hadn't registered in her teenage mind. Now it was a hipster re-creation of a deli, really, complete with order numbers from a wall dispenser. A butcher with a waxed mustache took their order.

"Did he go to school with us?" Stella whispered to Marco, watching the butcher.

He nodded. "Chris Bethel. He was in the class between us and Denny, except he had a different name back then."

"In that moment, she remembered Chris Bethel, pre-transition, playing Viola in *Twelfth Night* like a person who knew what it was to be shipwrecked on a strange shore. Good for him.

"While they waited, she ducked into the bathroom to scrub her hands. She smelled like the house now, and hoped nobody else noticed.

Marco had already claimed their sandwiches, in plastic baskets and waxed paper, and chosen a corner table away from the other customers. They took their first few bites without speaking. Marco hadn't said much all morning, and Stella had managed not to give in to her usual need to fill silences, but now she couldn't help it.

"Where do you live? And how long have you and Justin been together?"

"Outside Boston," he said. "And fifteen years. How about you?"

"Chicago. Divorced. One son, Cooper. I travel a lot. I work sales for a coffee distributor."

Even as she spoke, she hated that she'd said it. None of it was true. She had always done that, inventing things when she had no reason to lie, just because they sounded interesting, or because it gave her a thrill. If he had asked to see pictures of her nonexistent son Cooper, she'd have nothing to show. Not to mention she had no idea what a coffee distributor did.

Marco didn't seem to notice, or else he knew it wasn't true and filed it away as proof they had drifted apart for a reason. They finished their sandwiches in silence.

"Tackle the living room next?" Marco asked. "Or the rec room?"

"Rec room," she said. It was farther from the kitchen.

Farther from the kitchen, but the basement litter pans lent a different odor and trapped it in the windowless space. She sighed and tugged the mask up.

Marco did the same. "The weird thing is I haven't found a cat. I'm hoping maybe it was indoor-outdoor or something . . ."

Stella didn't know how to respond, so she said, "Hmm," and resolved to be extra careful when sticking her hands into anything.

The built-in bookshelves on the back wall held tubs and tubs of what looked like holiday decorations.

"What do you want to do with holiday stuff?" Stella pulled the nearest box forward on the shelf and peered inside. Halloween and Christmas, mostly, but all mixed together, so reindeer ornaments and spider lights negotiated a fragile peace.

"I'd love to say toss it, but I think we need to take everything out, in case."

"In case?"

He tossed her a sealed package to inspect. It held two droid ornaments, like R2-D2 but different colors. "Collector's item, mint condition. I found it a minute ago, under a big ball of tinsel and plastic reindeer. It's like this all over the house: valuable stuff hidden with the crap. A prize in every fucking box."

The size of the undertaking was slowly dawning on her. "How long are you here for?"

"I've got a good boss. She said I could work from here until I had all Denny's stuff in order. I was thinking a week, but it might be more like a month, given everything . . ."

"A month! We made good progress today, though . . ."

"You haven't seen upstairs. Or the garage. There's a lot, Stella. The dining room was probably the easiest other than the kitchen, which will be one hundred percent garbage."

"That's if he didn't stash more collectibles in the flour."

Marco blanched. "Oh god. How did I not think of that?"

Part of her wanted to offer to help again, but she didn't think she could stomach the stench for two days in a row, and she was supposed to be spending time with her parents, who already said she didn't come home enough. She wanted to offer, but she didn't want him to take her up on it. "I'll come back if I can."

He didn't respond, since that was obviously a lie. They returned to the task at hand: the ornaments, the decorations, the toys, the games, the stacks of DVDs and VHS tapes and records and CDs and cassettes, the prizes hidden not in every box, but in enough to make the effort worthwhile. Marco was right that the dining room had been easier. He'd decided to donate all the cassettes, DVDs, and videotapes, but said the vinyl might actually be worth something. She didn't know anything about records, so she categorized them as playable and not, removing each from its sleeve to examine for warp and scratches. It was tedious work.

It took two hours for her to find actual equipment Denny might have played any of the media on: a small television on an Ikea TV stand, a stereo and turntable on the floor, then another television behind the first.

It was an old set, built into a wooden cabinet that dwarfed the actual screen. She hadn't seen one like this in years; it reminded her of her grandparents. She tried to remember if it had been down here when they were kids.

Something about it—the wooden cabinet, or maybe the dial—made her ask, "Do you remember *The Uncle Bob Show*?"

Which of course he didn't, nobody did, she had made it up on the spot, like she often did.

Which was why it was so weird that Marco said, "Yeah! And the way he looked straight into the camera. It was like he saw me, specifically me. Scared me to death, but he said, 'Come back next week,' and I always did because I felt like he'd get upset otherwise."

As he said it, Stella remembered too. The way Uncle Bob looked straight into the camera, and not in a friendly Mr. Rogers way. Uncle Bob was the anti-Mr. Rogers. A cautionary uncle, not predatory, but not kind.

"It was a local show," she said aloud, testing for truth.

Marco nodded. "Filmed at the public broadcast station. Denny was in the audience a few times."

Stella pictured Denny as she had known him, a hulking older teen. Marco must have realized the disconnect, because he added, "I mean when he was little. Seven or eight, maybe? The first season? That would make us five.

Yeah, that makes sense, since I was really jealous, but my mom said you had to be seven to go on it."

Stella resized the giant to a large boy. *Audience* didn't feel like exactly the right word, but she couldn't remember why.

Marco crossed the room to dig through the VHS tapes they'd discarded. "Here."

It took him a few minutes to connect the VCR to the newer television. The screen popped and crackled as he hit play.

The show started with an oddly familiar instrumental theme song. *The Uncle Bob Show* appeared in block letters, then the logo faded and the screen went black. A door opened, and Stella realized it wasn't dead-screen black but a matte black room. The studio was painted black, with no furniture except a single black wooden chair.

Children spilled through the door, running straight for the camera—no, running straight for the secret compartments in the floor, all filled with toys. In that environment, the colors of the toys and the children's clothes were shocking, delicious, welcoming, warm. Blocks, train sets, plastic animals. That was why *audience* had bothered her. They weren't an audience; they were half the show, half the camera's focus. After a chaotic moment where they sorted who got possession of what, they settled in to play.

Uncle Bob entered a few minutes later. He was younger than Stella expected, his hair dark and full, his long face unlined. He walked with a ramrod spine and a slight lean at the hips, his arms clasped behind him giving him the look of a flightless bird. He made his way to the chair, somehow avoiding the children at his feet even though he was already looking straight into the camera.

He sat. Stella had the eeriest feeling, even now, that his eyes focused on her. "How on earth did this guy get a TV show?"

"Right? That's Denny there." Marco paused the tape and pointed at a boy behind and to the right of the chair. Her mental image hadn't been far off; Denny was bigger than all the other kids. He had a train car in each hand, and was holding the left one out to a little girl. The image of him playing well with others surprised Stella; she'd figured he'd always been a loner. She opened her mouth to say that, then closed it again. It was fine for Marco to say whatever he wanted about his brother, but it might not be appropriate for her to bring it up.

Marco pressed play again. The girl took the train from Denny and smiled. In the foreground, Uncle Bob started telling a story. Stella had forgotten the storytelling, too. That was the whole show: children doing their thing, and Uncle Bob telling completely unrelated stories. He paid little attention to the kids, though they sometimes stopped playing to listen to him.

The story was weird. Something about a boy buried alive in a hillside—"planted," in his words—who took over the entire hillside, like a weed, and spread for miles around.

Stella shook her head. "That's fucked up. If I had a kid I wouldn't let them watch this. Nightmare city."

Marco gave her a look. "I thought you said you had a kid?"

"I mean if I'd had a kid back when this was on." She was usually more careful with the lying game. Why had she said she had a son, anyway? She'd be found out the second Marco ran into her parents.

It was a dumb game, really. She didn't even remember when she'd started playing it. College, maybe. The first chance she'd had to reinvent herself, so why not do it wholesale? The rules were simple: Never lie about something anyone could verify independently; never lose track of the lies; keep them consistent and believable. That was why in college she'd claimed she'd made the varsity volleyball team in high school, but injured her knee so spectacularly in practice she'd never been able to play any sport again, and she'd once flashed an AP physics class, and she'd auditioned for the *Jeopardy!* Teen Tournament but been cut when she accidentally said "fuck" to Alex Trebek. Then she just had to live up to her reputation as someone who'd lived so much by eighteen that she could coast on her former cool.

Uncle Bob's story was still going. "They dug me out of the hillside on my thirteenth birthday. It's good to divide rhizomes to give them room to grow."

"Did he say 'me?'"

"A lot of his stories went like that, Stella. They started out like fairy tales, but somewhere in the middle he shifted into first person. I don't know if he had a bad writer or what."

"And did he say 'rhizome'? Who says 'rhizome' to seven-year-olds?" Stella hit the stop button. "Okay. Back to work. I remember now. That's plenty."

Marco frowned. "We can keep working, but I'd like to keep this on in the background now that we've found it. It's nice to see Denny. That Denny, especially."

That Denny: Denny frozen in time, before he got weird.

Stella started on the boxes in the back, leaving the stuff near the television to Marco. Snippets of story drifted her way, about the boy's family, but much, much older than when they'd buried him. His brothers were fathers now, their children the nieces and nephews of the teenager they'd dug from the hillside. Then the oddly upbeat theme song twice in a row—that episode's end and another's beginning.

"Marco?" she asked. "How long did this run?"

"I dunno. A few years, at least."

"Did you ever go on it? Like Denny?"

"No. I . . . hmm. I guess by the time I'd have been old enough, Denny had started acting strange, and my parents liked putting us into activities we could both do at the same time."

They kept working. The next Uncle Bob story that drifted her way centered on a child who got lost. Stella kept waiting for it to turn into a familiar children's story, but it didn't. Just a kid who got lost and when she found her way home she realized she'd arrived back without her body, and her parents didn't even notice the difference.

"Enough," Stella said from across the room. "That was enough to give me nightmares, and I'm an adult. Fuck. Watch more after I leave if you want."

"Okay. Time to call it quits, anyway. You've been here like nine hours."

She didn't argue. She waited until they got out the front door to peel off the mask and gloves.

"It was good to hang out with you," she said.

"You, too. Look me up if you ever get to Boston."

She couldn't tell him to do the same with Chicago, so she said, "Will do." She realized she'd never asked what he did for a living, but it seemed like an awkward time. It wasn't until after she'd walked away that she realized he'd said goodbye as if she wasn't returning the next day. She definitely wasn't, especially if he kept binging that creepy show.

When she returned to her parents' house she made a beeline for the shower. After twenty minutes' scrubbing, she still couldn't shake the smell.

She dumped the clothes in the garbage instead of the laundry and took the bag to the outside bin, where it could stink as much as it needed to stink.

Her parents were sitting on the screened porch out front, as they often did once the evenings got warm enough, both with glasses of iced tea on the wrought iron table between them as if it were already summer. Her mother had a magazine open on her lap—she still subscribed to all her scientific journals, though she'd retired years before—and her father was solving a math puzzle on his tablet, which Stella could tell by his intense concentration.

"That bad?" Her mother lifted an eyebrow at her as she returned from the garbage.

"That bad."

She went into the house and poured herself a glass to match her parents'. Something was roasting in the oven, and the kitchen was hot and smelled like onions and butter. She closed her eyes and pressed the glass against her forehead, letting the oven and the ice battle over her body temperature, then returned to sit on the much cooler porch, picking the empty chair with the better view of the dormant garden.

"Grab the cushion from the other chair if you're going to sit in that one," her father said.

She did as he suggested. "I don't see why you don't have cushions for both chairs. What if you have a couple over? Do they have to fight over who gets the comfortable seat versus who gets the view?"

He shrugged. "Nobody's complained."

They generally operated on a complaint system. Maybe that was where she'd gotten the habit of lies and exaggeration: She'd realized early that only extremes elicited a response.

"How did dinner look?" he asked.

"I didn't check. It smelled great, if that counts for anything."

He grunted, the sound both a denial and the effort of getting up, and went inside. Stella debated taking his chair, but it wasn't worth the scene. A wasp hovered near the screen and she watched it for a moment, glad it was on the other side.

"Hey, Ma, do you remember *The Uncle Bob Show*?"

"Of course." She closed her magazine and hummed something that sounded half like Uncle Bob's theme song and half like *The Partridge Family* theme. Stella hadn't noticed the similarity between the two tunes; it was a ridiculously cheery theme song for such a dark show.

"Who was that guy? Why did they give him a kids' show?"

"The public television station had funding trouble and dumped all the shows they had to pay for—we had to get cable for you to watch *Sesame Street* and *Mister Rogers' Neighborhood*. They had all these gaps to fill in their schedule, so anybody with a low budget idea could get on. That one lasted longer than most—four or five years, I think."

"And nobody said, 'That's some seriously weird shit?'"

"Oh, we all did, but someone at the station argued there were plenty of peace-and-love shows around, and some people like to be scared, and it's not like it was full of violence or sex, and just because a show had kids in it didn't mean it was a kids' show."

"They expected adults to watch? That's even weirder. What time was it on?"

"Oh, I don't remember. Saturday night? Saturday morning?"

Huh. Maybe he was more like those old monster movie hosts. "That's deeply strange, even for the eighties. And who was the guy playing Uncle Bob? I tried looking it up on IMDb, but there's no page. Not on Wikipedia either. Our entire world is fueled by nostalgia, but there's nothing on this show. Where's the online fan club, the community of collectors? Anything."

Her mother frowned, clearly still stuck on trying to dredge up a name. She shook her head. "Definitely Bob, a real Bob, but I can't remember his last name. He must've lived somewhere nearby, because I ran into him at the drugstore and the hardware store a few times while the show was on the air."

Stella tried to picture that strange man in a drugstore, looming behind her in line, telling her stories about the time he picked up photos from a vacation but when he looked at them, he was screaming in every photo. If he were telling that story on the show, he'd end it with, "and then you got home from the drugstore with your photos, but when you looked at them, you were screaming in every photo too." Great. Now she'd creeped herself out without his help.

"How did I not have nightmares?"

"We talked about that possibility—all the mothers—but you weren't disturbed. None of you kids ever complained. It was a nice break, to chat with the other moms while you all played in such a contained space."

There was a vast difference between "never complained" and "weren't disturbed" that Stella would have liked to unpack, but she fixated on a different detail. "Contained space—you mean while we watched TV, right?"

"No, dear. The studio. It looked much larger on television, but the cameras formed this nice ring around three sides, and you all understood you weren't supposed to leave during that half hour except for a bathroom emergency. You all played and we sat around and had coffee. It was the only time in my week when I didn't feel like I was supposed to be doing something else."

It took Stella a few seconds to realize the buzzing noise in her head wasn't the wasp on the screen. "What are you talking about? I was on the show?"

"Nearly every kid in town was on it at some point. Everyone except Marco, because his brother was acting up by the time you two were old enough, and Celeste pulled Denny and enrolled both boys in karate instead."

"But me? Ma, I don't remember that at all." The idea that she didn't know something about herself that others knew bothered her more than she could express. "You aren't making this up?"

"Why would I lie? I'm sure there are other things you don't remember. Getting lice in third grade?"

"You shaved my head. Of course I remember. The whole class got it, but I was the only one whose mother shaved her head."

"I didn't have time to comb through it, honey. Something more benign? Playing at Tamar Siegel's house?"

"Who's Tamar Siegel?"

"See? The Siegels moved to town for a year when you were in second grade. They had a jungle gym that you loved. You didn't think much of the kid, but you liked her yard and her dog. We got on well with her parents; I was sad when they left."

Stella flashed on a tall backyard slide and a golden retriever barking at her when she climbed the ladder and left it below. A memory she'd never have dredged up unprompted. Nothing special about it: a person whose face she couldn't recall, a backyard slide, an experience supplanted by other experiences. Generic kid, generic fun. A placeholder memory.

"Okay, I get that there are things that didn't stick with me, and things that I think I remember once you remind me, but it doesn't explain why I don't remember a blacked-out TV studio or giant cameras or a creepy host.

You forget the things that don't stand out, sure, but this seems, I don't know, formative."

Her mother shrugged. "You're making a big deal of nothing."

"Nothing? Did you listen to his stories?"

"Fairy tales."

"Now I know you didn't listen. He was telling horror stories to seven-year-olds."

"Fairy tales *are* horror stories, and like I said, you didn't complain. You mostly played with the toys."

"What about the kids at home watching? The stories were the focus if you weren't in the studio."

"If they were as bad as you say, hopefully parents paid attention and watched with their children and whatever else the experts these days say comprises good parenting. You're looking through a prism of now, baby. Have you ever seen early *Sesame Street*? I remember a sketch where a puppet with no facial features goes to a human for 'little girl eyes.' You and your friends watched shows, and if they scared you, you turned them off. You played outside. You cut your Halloween candy in half to make sure there were no razor blades inside. If you want to tell me I'm a terrible parent for putting you on that show with your friends, feel free, but since it took you thirty-five years to bring this up, I'm going to assume it didn't wreck your life."

Her father rang the dinner gong inside the house, a custom her parents found charming and Stella had always considered overkill in a family as small as theirs. She and her mother stood. Their glasses were still mostly full, the melting ice having replaced what they'd sipped.

She continued thinking over dinner, while she related everything she and Marco had unearthed to her mildly curious parents, and after, while scrubbing the casserole dish. What her mother said was true: She hadn't been driven to therapy by the show. She didn't remember any nightmares. It just felt strange to be missing something so completely, not to mention the questions that arose about what else she could be missing if she could be missing that. It was an unpleasant feeling.

After dinner, while her parents watched some reality show, she pulled out a photo album from the early eighties. Her family hadn't been much for photographic documentation, so there was just the one, chronological and well labeled, commemorating Stella at the old school playground before they pulled it out and replaced it with safer equipment, at a zoo, at the Independence Day parade. It was true, she didn't recall those particular moments, but she believed she'd been there. *The Uncle Bob Show* felt different. The first time she'd uttered the show's name, she'd thought she'd made it up.

She texted Marco: "Did Denny have all the Uncle Bob episodes on tape or only the ones he was in? Thanks!" She added a smiley face then erased it before she hit send. It felt falsely cheery instead of appreciative. His brother had just died.

She settled on the couch beside her parents. While they watched TV, she surfed the web looking for information about *The Uncle Bob Show*, but found nothing. In the era of kittens with Twitter accounts and sandwiches with their own Instagrams and fandoms for every conceivable property, it seemed impossible for something to be so utterly missing.

Not that it deserved a fandom; she just figured everything had one. Where were the ironic logo T-shirts? Where was the episode wiki explaining what happened in every Uncle Bob story? Where were the "Whatever happened to?" articles? The tell-alls by the kids or the director or the camera operator? The easy answer was that it was such a terrible show, or such a small show, that nobody cared. She didn't care either; she just needed to know. Not the same thing.

◄◊►

The next morning, she drove out to the public television station on the south end of town. She'd passed it so many times, but until now she wouldn't have said she'd ever been inside. Nothing about the interior rang a bell either, though it looked like it had been redone fairly recently, with an airy design that managed to say both modern and trapped in time.

"Can I help you?" The receptionist's trifocals reflected her computer's spreadsheet back at Stella. A phone log by her right hand was covered with sketched faces; the sketches were excellent. Grace Hernandez, according to her name plaque.

Stella smiled. "I probably should have called, but I wondered if you have archives of shows produced here a long time ago? My mother wants a video of a show I was on as a kid and I didn't want her to have to come over here for nothing."

Even while she said it, she wondered why she had to lie. Wouldn't it have been just as easy to say she wanted to see it herself? She'd noticed an older receptionist and decided to play on her sympathies, but there was no reason to assume her own story wasn't compelling.

"Normally we'd have you fill out a request form, but it's a slow day. I can see if someone is here to help you." Grace picked up a phone and called one number, then disconnected and tried another. Someone answered, because she repeated Stella's story, then turned back to her. "He'll be out in a sec."

She gestured to a glass-and-wood waiting area, and Stella sat. A flat screen overhead played what Stella assumed was their station, on mute, and a few issues of a public media trade magazine called *Current* were piled neatly on the low table.

A small man—a little person? Was that the right term?—came around the corner into reception. He was probably around her age, but she would have remembered him if he'd gone to school with her.

"Hi," he said. "I'm Jeff Stills. Grace says you're looking for a show?"

"Yes, my mother—"

"Grace said. Let's see what we can do."

He handed her a laminated guest pass on a lanyard and waited while she put it on, then led her through a security door and down a long, low-ceilinged corridor, punctuated by framed stills from various shows. No Uncle Bob. "Have you been here before?"

"When I was a kid."

"Hmm. I'll bet it looks pretty different. This whole back area was redone around 2005, after the roof damage. Then the lobby about five years ago."

She hadn't had any twinges of familiarity, but at least that explained some of it. She'd forgotten about the blizzard that wrecked the roof; she'd been long gone by then.

"Hopefully whatever you're looking for wasn't among the stuff that got damaged by the storm. What *are* you looking for?"

"*The Uncle Bob Show.* Do you know it?"

"Only by name. I've seen the tapes on the shelf, but in the ten years I've been here, nobody has ever asked for a clip. Any good?"

"No." Stella didn't hesitate. "It's like those late-night horror hosts, Vampira or Elvira or whatever, except they forgot to run a movie and instead let the host blather on."

They came to a nondescript door. The low-ceilinged hallway had led her to expect low-ceilinged rooms, but the space they entered was more of a warehouse. A long desk cluttered with computers and various machinery occupied the front, and then the space opened into row upon row of metal shelving units. The aisles were wide enough to accommodate rolling ladders.

"We've been working on digitizing, but we have fifty years of material in here, and some stuff has priority."

"Is that what you do? Digitize?"

"Nah. We have interns for that. I catalogue new material as it comes in, and find stuff for people when they need clips. Mostly staff, but sometimes for networks, local news, researchers, that kind of thing."

"Sounds fun," Stella said. "How did you get into the field?"

"I majored in history, but never committed enough to any one topic for academic research. Ended up at library school, and eventually moved here. It is fun! I get a little bit of everything. Like today: a mystery show."

"Total mystery."

She followed him down the main aisle, then several aisles over, almost to the back wall. He pointed at some boxes above her head.

"Wow," she said. "Do you know where everything is without looking it up?"

"Well, it's alphabetical, so yeah, but also they're next to *Underground*, which I get a lot of requests for. Do you know what year you need?"

"1982? My mother couldn't remember exactly, but that's the year I turned seven."

Jeff disappeared and returned pushing a squeaking ladder along its track. He climbed up for the "*Uncle Bob Show* 1982" box. It looked like there were five years' worth, 1980 to 1985. She followed him back toward the door, where he pointed her to an office chair.

"We have strict protocols for handling media that hasn't been backed up yet. If you tell me which tapes you want to watch, I'll queue them up for you."

"Hmm. Well, my birthday is in July, so let's pick one in the last quarter of the year first, to see if I'm in there."

"You don't know if you are?"

She didn't want to admit she didn't remember. "I just don't know when."

He handed her a pair of padded headphones and rummaged in the box. She'd been expecting VHS tapes, but these looked like something else— Betamax, she guessed.

The show's format was such that she didn't have to watch much to figure out if she was in it or not. The title card came on, then the episode's children rushed in. She didn't see herself. She wondered again if this was a joke on her mother's part.

"Wait—what was the date on this one?"

Jeff studied the label on the box. "October ninth."

"I'm sorry. That's my mother's birthday. There's no way she stood around in a television studio that day. Maybe the next week?"

He ejected the tape and put it back in its box and put in another, but that one obviously had some kind of damage, all static.

"Third time's the charm," he said, going for the next tape. He seemed to believe it himself, because he dragged another chair over and plugged in a second pair of headphones. "Do you mind?"

She shook her head and rolled her chair slightly to the right to give him a better angle. The title card appeared.

"It's a good thing nobody knows about this show or they'd have been sued over this theme song," he said.

Stella didn't answer. She was busy watching the children. She recognized the first few kids: Lee Pool first, a blond beanpole; poor Dan Heller; Addie Chapel, whose mother had been everyone's pediatrician.

And then there she was, little Stella Gardiner, one of the last through the door. She wasn't used to competing for toys, so maybe she didn't know she needed to get in early, or maybe they were assigned an order behind the scenes. She'd thought seeing herself on screen would jog her memory, give her the studio or the stories or the backstage snacks, but she still had no recollection. She pointed at herself on the monitor for Jeff's benefit, to show they'd found her. He gave her a thumbs-up.

Little Stella seemed to know where she was going, even if she wasn't first to get there. Lee Pool already had the T. rex, but she wouldn't have cared. She'd liked the big dinosaurs, the bigger the better. She emerged from the toy pit with a matched pair. Brontosaurus, apatosaurus, whatever they called them these days. She could never wrap her head around something that large having existed. So yeah, the dinosaurs made sense—it was her, even if she still didn't remember it.

She carried the two dinosaurs toward the set's edge, where she collected some wooden trees and sat down. She was an only child, used to playing alone, and this clearly wasn't her first time in this space.

The camera lost her. The focus, of course, was on Uncle Bob. She had been watching herself and missed his entrance. He sat in his chair, children playing around him. Dan Heller zoomed around the set like a satellite in orbit, a model airplane in hand.

"Once upon a time there was a little boy who wanted to go fast." Uncle Bob started a story without waiting for anyone to pay attention.

"He liked everything fast. Cars, motorcycles, boats, airplanes. Bicycles were okay, but not the same thrill. When he rode in his father's car, he pretended they were racing the cars beside them. Sometimes they won, but mostly somebody quit the race. His father was not a fast driver. The little boy knew that if he drove, he'd win all the races. He wouldn't stop when he won, either. He'd keep going.

"He liked the sound of motors. He liked the way they rumbled deep enough to rattle his teeth in his head, and his bones beneath his skin; he liked the way they shut all the thinking out. He liked the smell of gasoline and the way it burned his nostrils. His family's neighbors had motorcycles they rode on weekends, and if he played in the front yard they'd sometimes let him sit on one with them before they roared away, leaving too much quiet behind. When they drove off, he tried to recreate the sound, making as much noise as possible until his father told him to be quiet, then to shut up, then 'For goodness sake, what does a man have to do to get some peace and quiet around here on a Saturday morning?'"

Dan paused his orbit and turned to face the storyteller. Two other kids had stopped to pay attention as well; Stella and the others continued playing on the periphery.

"The boy got his learner's permit on the very first day he was allowed. He skipped school for it rather than wait another second. He had saved his paper route money for driving lessons and a used motorbike. As soon as he had his full license, he did what he had always wanted to do: He drove as fast as he could down the highway, past all the cars, and then he kept driving forever. The end."

Uncle Bob shifted back in his chair as he finished. Dan watched him for a little longer, then launched himself again, circling the scattered toys and children faster than before.

Jeff sat back as well. "What kind of story was that?"

Stella frowned. "A deeply messed up one. That kid with the airplane—Dan Heller—drove off the interstate the summer after junior year. He was racing someone in the middle of the night and missed a curve."

"Oof. Quite the coincidence."

"Yeah . . ."

Uncle Bob started telling another story, this one about a vole living in a hole on a grassy hillside that started a conversation with the child sleeping in the hole next door.

"Do you want to watch the whole episode? Is this the one you need?"

"I think I need to look at a couple more?" She didn't know what she was looking for. "Sorry for putting you out. I don't mean to take up so much time."

"It's fine! This is interesting. The show is terrible, from any standpoint. The story was terrible, the production is terrible. I can't even decide if this whole shtick is campy bad or bad bad. Leaning toward the latter."

"I don't think there's anything redeeming," Stella said, her mind still on Dan Heller. Did his parents remember this story? "Can we look at the next one? October 30th?"

"Coming up." Jeff appeared to have forgotten she'd said she was looking for something specific, and she didn't remind him, since she still couldn't think of an appropriate detail.

Little Stella was second through the door this time, behind Tina, whose last name she didn't remember. She paused and looked out past a camera, probably looking for her mother, then kept moving when she realized more kids were coming through behind her. Head for the toys. Claim what's yours. Brontosaurus and T. rex and a blue whale. Whales were almost as cool as dinosaurs.

Tina had claimed a triceratops and looked like she wanted the bronto-saurus. They sat down on the edge of the toy pit to negotiate. Uncle Bob watched them play, which gave Stella the eeriest feeling of being watched, even though she still felt like the kid on the screen wasn't her.

"So what was it like?" Jeff asked, but Stella didn't answer. Uncle Bob had started a story. He looked straight into the camera. This time it felt like he was truly looking straight at her. This was the one. She knew it.

"Once upon a time, there was a little girl who didn't know who she was. Many children don't know who they will be, and that's not unusual, but what was unusual in this case was that the girl was willing to trade who she was for who she could be, so she began to do just that. Little by little, she replaced herself with parts of other people she liked better. Parts of stories she wanted to live. Nobody lied like this girl. She believed her own stories so completely, she forgot which ones were true and which were false.

"If you've ever heard of a cuckoo bird, they lay their eggs in other birds' nests, so those birds are forced to raise them for their own. This girl was her own cuckoo, laying stories in her own head, and the heads of those around her, until even she couldn't remember which ones were true, or if there was anything left of her."

Uncle Bob went silent, watching the children play. After a minute, he started telling another story about the boy in the hill, and how happy he was whenever he had friends over to visit. That story ended, and a graphic appeared on the screen with an address for fan mail. Stella pulled a pen from her purse and wrote it down as the theme music played out.

"Are you sending him a letter?" The archivist had dropped his headphones and was watching her.

She shrugged. "Just curious."

"Is this the one, then?"

"The one?"

He frowned. "You said you wanted a copy for your mother."

"Yes! That would be lovely. This is the one she mentioned."

He pulled a DVD off a bulk spindle and rewound the tape. "You didn't say what it was like. Was he weird off camera too?"

"Yes," she said, though she didn't remember. "But he kept to himself. Just stayed in his dressing room until it was time to go on."

Jeff didn't reply, and something subtle changed about the way he interacted with her. What if there hadn't been a dressing room? He might know. When had she gotten so sloppy with her stories? Maybe it was because she was distracted. Her mother had told the truth: She'd been on a creepy TV show of which she had no memory. And what was it? Performance art? Storytelling? Fairy tales or horror? All of the above? She thanked Jeff and left.

She had just walked into her parents' house when Marco called. "Can you come back? There's something I need to show you."

She headed out to Denny's house. She paused on the step, realizing she was in nicer clothes this time. Hopefully she wouldn't be there long.

"Hey," she said when Marco answered the door. Even though she braced for the odor, it hit her hard.

He waved her in, talking as he navigated the narrow path he'd cleared up the stairs. "I thought I'd work on Denny's bedroom today, and, well . . ."

He held out an arm in the universal gesture of "go ahead," so she entered. The room had precarious ceiling-high stacks on every surface, including the floor and bed, piles everywhere except a path to an open walk-in closet. She stepped forward.

"What is that?"

"The word I came up with was 'shrine,' but I don't think that's right."

It was the sparest space in the house. She'd expected a dowel crammed end to end with clothes, straining under the weight, but the closet was empty except for—"shrine" was indeed the wrong word. This wasn't worship.

The most eye-catching piece, the thing she saw first, was a hand-painted Uncle Bob doll propped in the back corner. It looked like it had been someone else first—Vincent Price, maybe. Next to it stood a bobblehead and an action figure, both mutated from other characters, and one made of clay and plant matter, seemingly from scratch. Beside those, a black leather notebook, a pile of VHS tapes, and a single DVD. Tacked to the wall behind them, portraits of Uncle Bob in paint, in colored pencil, macaroni, photo collage, in, oh god, was that cat hair? And beside those, stills from the show printed on copier paper: Uncle Bob telling a story; Uncle Bob staring straight into the camera, an assortment of children. Her own still was toward the bottom right. Marco wasn't in any of them.

"That's the thing that guts me."

Stella turned, expecting to see Marco pointing to the art or the dolls, but she'd been too busy looking at those to notice the filthy pillow and blanket in the opposite corner. "He slept here?"

"It's the only place he could have." Marco's voice was strangled, like he was trying not to cry.

She didn't know what to say to make him feel better about his brother having lived liked this. She picked up the notebook and paged through it. Each page had a name block-printed on top, then a dense scrawl in black, then, in a different pen, something else. Not impossible to read, but difficult, writing crammed into every available inch, no space between words even. She remembered this notebook; it was the one teenage Denny always had on him.

"Take it," Marco said. "Take whatever you want. I can't do this anymore. I'm going home."

She took the notebook and the DVD, and squeezed Marco's arm, unsure whether he would want or accept a hug.

Her parents were out when she got back to their house, so she slipped the DVD into their machine. It didn't work. She took it upstairs and tried it in her mother's old desktop computer instead. The computer made a sound like a jet plane taking off, and opened a menu with one episode listed: March 13, 1980.

It started the same way all the other episodes had started. The kids, Uncle Bob. Denny was in this one; Stella had an easier time spotting him now that she knew who to look for. He went for the train set again, laying out wooden tracks alongside a kid Stella didn't recognize.

Uncle Bob started a story. "Once upon a time, there was a boy who grew very big very quickly. He felt like a giant when he stood next to his classmates. People stopped him in hallways and told him he was going to the wrong grade's room. His mother complained that she had to buy him new clothes constantly, and even though she did it with affection, he was too young to realize she didn't blame him. He felt terrible about it. Tried to hide that his shoes squeezed his toes or his pants were too short again.

"His parents' friends said, 'Somebody's going to be quite an athlete,' but he didn't feel like an athlete. More than that, he felt like he had grown so fast his head had been pushed out of his body, so he was constantly watching it from someplace just above. Messages he sent to his arms and legs took ages to get there. Everything felt small and breakable in his hands, so that when his best friend's dog had puppies he refused to hold them, though he loved when they climbed all over him.

"The boy had a little brother. His brother was everything he wasn't. Small, lithe, fearless. His mother told him to protect his brother, and he took that responsibility seriously. That was something that didn't take finesse. He could do that.

"Both boys got older, but their roles didn't change. The older brother watched his younger brother. When the smaller boy was bullied, his brother pummeled the bullies. When the younger brother made the high school varsity basketball team as a point guard his freshman year, his older brother made the team as center, even though he hated sports.

"Time passed. The older brother realized something strange. Every time he thought he had something of his own, it turned out it was his brother's. He blinked one day and lost two entire years. How was he the older brother, the one who got new clothes, who reached new grades first, and yet still always following? Even his own story had spun out to describe him in relation to his sibling.

"And then, one day, the boy realized he had nothing at all. He was his brother's giant shadow. He was a forward echo, a void. Nothing was his. All he could do was watch the world try to catch up with him, but he was always looking backward at it. All he could do—"

"No," said Denny.

Stella had forgotten the kids were there, even though they were on camera the entire time. Denny had stood and walked over to where Uncle Bob was telling the story. With Uncle Bob sitting, Denny was tall enough to look him in the eye.

For the first time, Uncle Bob turned away from the camera. He assessed Denny with an unsettling smile.

"No," Denny said again.

Now Uncle Bob glanced around as if he was no longer amused, as if someone needed to pull this child off his set. It wasn't a tantrum, though. Denny wasn't misbehaving, unless interrupting a story violated the rules.

Uncle Bob turned back to him. "How would you tell it?"

Denny looked less sure now.

"I didn't think so," said the host. "But maybe that's enough of that story. Unless you want to tell me how you think it ends?"

Denny shook his head.

"But you know?"

Denny didn't move.

"Maybe that's enough. We'll see. In any case, I have other stories to tell. We haven't checked in on my hill today."

Uncle Bob began to catch his audience up on the continuing adventure of the boy who'd been dug out of the hillside. The other children kept playing, and Denny? Denny looked straight into the camera, then walked off the set. He never came back. Stella didn't have any proof, but she was pretty sure this must have been the last episode Denny took part in. He looked like a kid who was done. His expression was remarkably similar to the one she'd just seen on Marco's face.

And what was that story? Unlike Dan Heller's driving story, unlike the one she'd started thinking of as her own, this one wasn't close to true. Sure, Denny had been a big kid, but neither he nor Marco played basketball. He never protected Marco from bullies. "Nothing was his" hardly fit the man whose house she'd cleaned.

Except that night, falling asleep, Stella couldn't help but think that when she compared what she knew of Denny with that story, it seemed like Denny had set out to prove the story untrue. What would a person do if told as a child that nothing was his? Collect all the things. Leave his little brother to fend for himself. Fight it on every level possible.

Was it a freak occurrence that Denny happened to be listening when Uncle Bob told that story? Why was she assuming the story was about him at all? Maybe it was coincidence. There was nothing connecting the children to the stories except her own sense that they were connected, and Denny's reaction on the day he quit.

She hadn't heard hers when Uncle Bob told it, but she'd internalized it nonetheless. How much was true? She wasn't a cuckoo bird. Her reinventions had never hurt anyone.

Marco called that night to ask if she wanted to grab one more meal before she left town, but she said she had too much to do before her flight. That was true, as was the fact that she didn't want to see him again. Didn't want to ask him if he'd watched the March 13 show. Didn't want to tell him his brother had consciously refused him protection.

-◇-

She should have gone straight to the airport in the morning, but the fan mail address she'd written down was in the same direction, if she took the back way instead of the highway. Why a show like that might get fan mail was a question for another time. This was strictly a trip to satisfy her curiosity. She drove through town, then a couple of miles past, into the network of county roads.

The mailbox stood full, overflowing, a mat of moldering envelopes around its cement base. A weather-worn FOR SALE sign had sunk into the soft ground closer to the drainage ditch. Stella turned onto the long driveway, and only after she'd almost reached the house did it occur to her that if she'd looked at the mail, she might have found his surname.

The fields on either side of the lane were tangled with weeds that didn't look like they cared what season it was. The house, a tiny stone cottage, was equally weed-choked, but strangely familiar. If she owned this house, she'd never let it get like this, but it didn't look like it belonged to anyone anymore. She tried a story on for size: "While I was visiting my parents, I went for a drive in the country, and I found the most darling cottage. My parents are getting older, and I had the thought that I should move closer to them. The place needed a little work, so I got it for a song."

She liked that one.

Nobody answered when she knocked. The door was locked, and the windows were too dirty to see through, and she couldn't shake the feeling that if she looked through he'd be sitting there, staring straight at her, waiting.

She walked around back and found the hill.

It was a funny little hill, not entirely natural looking, but what did she know? The land behind the house sloped gently upward, then steeper, hard beneath the grass but not rocky. From the slope, the cottage looked even smaller, the fields wilder, tangled, like something from a fairy tale. The view, too, felt strangely familiar.

She knew nothing more about the man who called himself Uncle Bob, but as she walked into the grass she realized this must be the hill from his stories, the stories he told when he wasn't telling stories about the children. How did they go? She thought back to that first episode she'd watched in Denny's basement.

Once upon a time, there was a boy whose family planted him in a hillside, so that he took over the entire hillside, like a weed. They dug me out of the hillside on my thirteenth birthday. It's good to divide rhizomes to give them room to grow.

That story made her remember the notebook she'd taken from Denny's house, and she rummaged for it in her purse. The notebook was alphabetical, printed in a nearly microscopic hand other than the page headings, dense. She found one for Dan Heller. She couldn't decipher the whole story, but the first line was obviously *Once upon a time, there was a little boy who wanted to go fast.* She knew the rest. In blue pen, it said what she had said to Jeff the archivist: motorcycle wreck, alongside the date. That one was easy since she knew enough to fill in the parts she struggled to read. The others were trickier. There was no page for Marco, but Denny had made one for himself. It had Uncle Bob's shadow-brother story but no update at the bottom. Nothing at all for the years between.

Who else had been on the show? Lee Pool had a page. So did Addie Chapel, who as far as Stella knew had followed in her mother's footsteps and become a doctor. Chris Bethel, and beside him, Tina Bevins, the other dinosaur lover. If she spent enough time staring, maybe Denny's handwriting would decipher itself.

She was afraid to turn to her own page. She knew it had to be there, on the page before Dan Heller, but she couldn't bring herself to look, until she did. She expected this one, like Dan's, like Denny's own, to be easier to decipher because she knew how it would go.

October 30, 1982. Once upon a time, there was a little girl who didn't know who she was. Many children don't know who they will be, and that's not unusual, but what was unusual in this case was that the girl was willing to trade who she was for who she could be, so she began to do just that. Little by little, she replaced herself with parts of other people she liked better. Parts of stories she wanted to live. Nobody lied like this girl. She believed her own stories so completely, she forgot which ones were true and which were false.

If you've ever heard of a cuckoo bird, they lay their eggs in other birds' nests, so those birds are forced to raise them for their own. This girl was her own cuckoo, laying stories in her own head, and the heads of those around her, until even she couldn't remember which ones were true, or if there was anything left of her.

There was more. Another episode, maybe? She had no idea how many she'd been on, and her research had been shoddy. Maybe every story was serialized like the boy in the hill. It took her a while to make out the next bit.

November 20, 1982. Our cuckoo girl left the nest one day to spread her wings. When she returned, she didn't notice that nobody had missed her. She named a place where she had been, and they accepted it as truth. She made herself up, as she had always done, convincing even herself in the process. Everything was true, or true enough.

Below that, in blue pen, a strange assortment of updates from her life, as observed by Denny. Marco's eleventh birthday party, when she'd given him juggling balls. Graduation from middle school. The summer they'd both worked at the pool, and Marco'd gotten heatstroke and thrown up all the Kool-Aid they tried to put in him, Kool-Aid red, straight into the pool like a shark attack. The time she and Marco had tried making out on his bed, only he had started giggling, and she had gotten offended, and when she stood she tripped over a juggling ball and broke her toe. All the games their friends had played in Marco's basement: I've Never, even though they all knew what everyone else had done; Two Truths and a Lie, though they had all grown up together and knew everything about each other; Truth or Dare, though everyone was tired of truth, truth was terrifying, everyone chose dare, always. The *Batman* premiere. The prom amoeba, the friends who went together, all of whom she'd lost touch with. High school graduation. Concrete memories, things she knew were as real as anything that had ever happened in her life. Denny shouldn't have known about some of these things, but now she pictured him there, somewhere, holding this notebook, watching them, taking notes, always looking like he had something to say but he couldn't say it.

Below those stories he'd written: *Once there was a girl who got lost and when she found her way home she realized she'd arrived back without herself, and her parents didn't even notice the difference.* Which couldn't be her story at all; she hadn't been on the episodes he'd been on.

After graduation, he had no more updates on her. She paged forward, looking at the blue ink. Everyone had updates within the last year, everyone except for Denny, everyone who was still alive; the ones who weren't had death dates. Everyone except her. She tried to imagine what from her adult life she would have added, given the chance, or what an internet search on her name would provide, or what her parents would tell someone who asked what she was doing. Surely there was something. Parents were supposed to be your built-in hype machines.

She pulled out her phone to call Marco, but the battery was dead. Just as well, since she was suddenly afraid to try talking to anyone at all. She returned to the notebook and flipped toward the back. *U* for *Uncle Bob.*

Once upon a time, there was a boy whose family planted him in a hillside, so that he took over the entire hillside, like a weed. They dug me out of the hillside on my thirteenth birthday. It's good to divide rhizomes to give them room to grow.

This story was long, eight full pages in tiny script, with episode dates interspersed. At the end, in red ink, this address. She pictured Denny driving out here, exploring the cottage, looking up at the hill. If she ever talked to Marco again, she'd tell him that what he'd found in Denny's closet wasn't a shrine; it was Denny's attempt to conjure answers to something unanswerable.

She put the notebook back in her purse and kept walking. Three quarters of the way up the hill she came to a large patch where the grass had been churned up. She put her hand in the soil and it felt like the soil grasped her hand back.

Her parents said she didn't visit often enough, but now she couldn't remember ever having visited them before, or them visiting her. She couldn't remember if she'd ever left this town at all. She lived in Chicago, or did she? She'd told Marco as much, told him other things she knew not to be true, but what was true, then? What did she do for a living? If she left this hill and went to the airport, would she even have a reservation? If she caught her plane, would she find she had anything or anyone there at all? Where was there? She pulled her hand free and put it to her mouth: The soil tasted familiar.

"I walked down to the cottage that would be mine someday"—that felt nice, even if she wasn't sure she believed it—"and then past the cottage, through the town, and into my parents' house. They believed me when I said where I'd been. They fit me into their lives and only occasionally looked at me like they didn't quite know how I'd gotten there." That felt good. True. She sat in the dirt and leaned back on her hands, and felt the hill pressing back on them.

She could still leave: walk back to her rental car, drive to the airport, take the plane to the place where she surely had a career, a life, even if she couldn't quite recall it. She thought that until she looked back at where the rental car should have been and realized it wasn't there. She had no shoes on, and her feet were black with dirt, pebbled, scratched. She dug them into the soil, rooting with her toes.

How had Denny broken his story? He'd refused it. Whether his life was better or worse for it remained a different question. To break her story, she'd have to walk back down the hill and reconstruct herself the right way round. She thought of the cuckoo girl, the lost girl, the cuckoo girl, so many stories to keep straight.

The soil reached her forearms now, her calves. The top layer was sun-warmed, and underneath, a busy cool stillness made up of millions of insects, of the roots of the grass, of the rhizomes of the boy who had called this hillside home before she had. She'd walk back to town when she was ready, someday, maybe, but she was in no hurry. She'd heard worse stories than hers, and anyway, if she didn't like it she'd make a new one, a better one, a true one.

THE WHISPER OF STARS

THANA NIVEAU

don't trust that guy.

Those had been Alison's first words to her brother Sean after meeting their guide, Eric. It was nothing she could put into words. He just seemed twitchy, over-eager. Sean was an easy mark, always eager to believe what he wanted to believe, and his partner Jeff was even more naive. But they were all here now, at the mercy of Eric's expertise, assuming he had some. Alison was determined to enjoy the adventure no matter what.

It was hard work trekking through the snow. They'd set off at an ungodly hour to make the most of the short window of daylight. Fortunately, they had Olga and the dogsled to carry their equipment.

The team of huskies—eight in all—had boundless energy, pulling ahead to vanish over the white horizon. Alison felt anxious each time they moved out of sight. All their supplies were on the sled with Olga. But soon enough the team would return, cutting tight corners as they circled the walking party, showering them with an arcing spray of snow.

"Showoff," Sean muttered.

Alison thought that was a bit rich, considering his unwavering faith in Eric's grand claims.

"The dogs have to run or they get bored," Alison said. At Sean's look she added, "Olga told me."

"She's right."

The defence came from Jeff.

"They're super intelligent so you have to keep them busy."

"Whatever," Sean said, and quickened his pace to get ahead of both of them. Jeff shook his head indulgently.

"Why do you put up with him?" Alison asked.

"Why do *you*?"

She shrugged. Why *did* she? Because he was her brother? Because they'd always done things like this together? Even once he'd met Jeff, the three of them went on holidays together, exploring places off the beaten track. Sean could be selfish and stubborn, but she'd always been tolerant of his idiosyncrasies. After all, it wasn't like she was a saint herself.

Alison looked up to see Jeff watching her, smiling.

"Is your mind burning?" she asked.

The smile melted, leaving behind a puzzled, uneasy expression.

Alison blushed. "Sorry. Joke fail. I couldn't say are your ears burning because I wasn't talking, not out loud. So instead I . . .Oh, never mind." God, why did she always have to embarrass herself?

Jeff humoured her with a laugh, but it was forced. He rescued her from the awkward moment by quickening his pace to catch up with Sean. He patted Alison's shoulder as he moved past, but through her layers of silk thermals, wool sweater and down parka, she felt nothing. It was like being touched by a ghost. A little shudder coursed through her and she directed her gaze to her feet, focusing on the crunch of her boots in the snow, a peaceful, soothing sound.

The tundra was a strange, alien landscape. Here the light was weird, fragile, and tentative. The pale pinks and yellows of the Siberian sky offered a teasing glimpse of dawn, although the sun barely got above the treeline.

The original plan had been to come here in spring, when their quarry would be easier to find. But the wise, all-knowing Eric had suggested the tail end of winter instead. Climate change had brought unpredictable weather, including mid-winter thaws. They might get lucky.

The original plan had also been to go with a professional—and legal—tour group, one led by indigenous mammoth tusk hunters from Yakutsk, to well-known sites along the Lena River. However, once Eric joined the party, that idea got scrapped.

"Everyone goes there," he'd scoffed, christening it with the kiss of death: "tourist trap."

Alison doubted whether any place in the Arctic Circle could truly be called a tourist trap, and she resented the mansplaining. But she'd allowed herself to be persuaded by his and Sean's other arguments. They wouldn't be able to keep anything they found, or profit from any tusks or fossils unearthed by the tour group. Eric probably wasn't above stealing, but Alison had no desire to fall foul of the Russian police. And so Middle of Nowhere, Eastern Siberia, had become the new destination. It was here, Eric claimed, that the melting permafrost gave up its *real* treasures.

The sled returned. The dogs were huffing and panting hard, and Alison wondered if they'd keep running until they dropped. Dogs didn't sweat, so overexertion wasn't a problem for them. Not so the humans who'd been advised to keep a measured pace. They had to avoid perspiration, which could freeze on their skin. It was potentially lethal.

Olga pulled alongside the hikers and slowed the dogs. Even though their tongues were lolling almost to the ground, the huskies seemed incapable of moving at a leisurely pace. Their slowest gait was a light trot. And they were always, always alert, constantly looking around, sniffing and investigating.

Alison had been frightened of them at first. They looked so much like wolves, their eyes keen and piercing. And their 'talking' was extremely unnerving. The little yips and half-howls sometimes sounded like human words. Before setting off, Olga had reassured her in broken English that there was nothing to fear.

One dog seemed particularly interested in Alison. It was a rusty red colour mixed with white. The others had mostly black or grey markings, with one dog that was solid white. The red husky's name was Zarya. Alison's attempts to pronounce it seemed to amuse the dog, who cocked her head and stared at her with gleaming amber eyes.

Olga had coaxed the nervous Alison into crouching down in the snow with her, and the grown dogs immediately transformed into a pack of enormous puppies, rolling around, licking and chewing on each other and the two humans in their midst.

"See?" Olga had said, grinning. "Now you are friends."

Alison had liked the woman immediately. More importantly, she trusted her. She'd wished then that they could ditch Eric and let Olga guide them into the wilderness instead. Olga at least had come via a proper tour company's recommendation rather than a chance meeting in a pub, swapping drunken stories with her brother.

Olga was easily a full head taller than Alison, and the furs hid an athletic physique. She moved gracefully, with none of the stoop often found in tall people, who were accustomed to hitting their heads on doorways not designed for those of their stature. There was a quiet confidence about her, as if she had grown up in the wild and knew its ways instinctively. To watch her drive the sled, one could easily imagine she had a telepathic link with the dogs.

"There is forest," Olga said, nodding in the direction she'd come from. "Good for camping."

Alison felt a wave of relief at the thought of stopping for the night. She was no novice hiker, but she'd never have imagined that simply walking across snow could be so exhausting.

Eric and Olga began talking heatedly in Russian, a conversation that involved a lot of pointing and gesturing at the horizon. Clearly Eric wanted to keep going and Olga was advising him not to. Great. Their supposed 'leader' was squabbling with the dog driver and the person who probably knew this place best. It was also obvious that Eric's Russian wasn't as fluent as he'd let on, as Olga had to ask him to repeat himself several times, which he did in slower, louder tones. Olga made no secret of her annoyance, and Alison didn't fancy Eric's chances if it came to blows.

Finally, Sean stepped in. "Hey, cool it. What's the problem?"

Eric spoke up first. "We can easily go another couple of miles, but she—" he pointed at Olga "—is worried about the darkness. We have lights, for God's sake!"

Alison looked at the huskies, who were finally starting to show signs of fatigue. It was as though stopping for a few minutes had made them realise that they weren't perpetual motion machines after all.

"I'm happy to stop now," Alison said. "I'm tired and the dogs are tired."

Eric's eyes flashed, a momentary slip of the mask.

Alison frowned. Why the hell was he so impatient?

Sean looked from one to the other, presumably gauging which of them it was safer to disappoint. "Jeff? What do you think?"

But Jeff was standing apart from the group. He had one glove off and was playing with his phone. He shook his head without looking up. "No way. I'm not gonna be the tiebreaker. You guys work it out."

Sean rolled his eyes. He turned in a slow circle, scanning the area, and Alison could hear him grinding his teeth. Someone had to play diplomat.

She cleared her throat. "Compromise: one more mile and then we stop?"

Olga agreed immediately. Jeff raised a hand without looking up from his phone.

Sean nodded. "That's fair."

"Fine," Eric said. He didn't sound delighted, but he didn't argue. He sighed and the group trudged on into the fading winter sunset.

⟶

The little stand of snow-covered conifers didn't look like much of a forest, but Alison could see denser clusters of trees further ahead, eerie blue outlines in the moonlight. Eric and Sean began putting the tents together while Alison and Jeff gathered wood for a fire.

The huskies ran free, newly energised by the excitement of stopping to make camp. Zarya followed Alison, sniffing at her legs and murmuring in husky-speak. All of that seemed normal, but then she began whimpering and barking whenever Alison moved towards the forest.

Alison turned to ask Jeff why the dog was acting weird, but he was already on his way back to the campsite with an armful of sticks.

"Come on," she told Zarya, "I won't get lost."

But the anxiety was contagious, and Alison began to feel uneasy too, as if being watched. A sound from the shadows made her jump and she kept to the outer edge of the trees.

She found an enormous pine, its trunk blackened and split by lightning. The bark was peeling, and Alison could see something beneath it. She tore the bark away and shone her torch against the exposed wood, frowning at the strange symbols. It didn't look like Cyrillic letters. It could be Japanese.

Or Arabic. Or any other language she didn't speak or read. It was most likely the universal "X loves Y" formula that teenagers the world over carved into trees. Odd that it was *beneath* the bark, though.

Zarya interrupted her thoughts by yipping and nudging her. Then the dog tore the bark from her hands and ran off with it. Alison laughed. "Okay, okay, I'm coming!"

Soon a campfire was burning, crackling, and sending firefly sparks up into the darkening sky. Two small domed tents stood facing each other across the fire. Sean was crouched in front of one, unpacking.

"Is this one ours?" Alison asked.

Sean looked puzzled for a moment, then jerked his chin towards where Eric was hammering in the final stake for his tent. "Two and two," he said, as if it was obvious.

Understanding dawned like a clammy hand on bare skin. "Oh, no way. You're not serious."

Sean got to his feet, rolling his eyes. "Don't be such a baby. Campers do this all the time. If we were in a hostel you wouldn't think twice about it."

"In a hostel I'd be in my own bed, not cheek to cheek with a total stranger!"

"We're all in ten layers of clothes."

"Uh-uh. Deal-breaker. This tent is mine. I'll bunk with you or Jeff, but I'm not sharing a tent with *him*." She didn't even want to say Eric's name.

Sean sighed, a world-weary sound that reminded her of when they were little. He'd always had a way of making her feel guilty when he didn't get his way. Not this time.

"Look, this isn't your honeymoon," she said, keeping her voice low. "You're the one who decided to bring that grifter when it was just supposed to be you, me and Jeff. So you're the one who has to compromise."

"Pretty sure Eric heard you," he said, barely modulating his voice.

Sure enough, Eric was standing with his arms crossed, watching them across the campfire, glaring.

"Great," she grumbled. "Thanks a lot." She resented Jeff for not being around to back her up like he had before, but she imagined he didn't want to share with Eric either. Or let his boyfriend.

The dogs were milling around as Olga spread a pallet of furs beside the sled. Sean called over to her. "Olga, don't you have a tent?"

She shook her head. "I sleep with dogs," she said simply. She had obviously overheard the argument, though, and after a moment she beckoned Alison over. "Come. It is warm."

Olga knelt on the furs. Several of the dogs took the cue and snuggled close to her in a cosy bundle.

Alison dared a glance at Eric, but he had disappeared inside his tent. There was the sharp sound of the zipper as he sealed himself in and Alison couldn't help but think of body bags. She pushed away the intrusive mental image and instead imagined forcing herself between Sean and Jeff, their three bodies packed like sardines in the two-person tent. She was just pissed off enough to do it, mostly to annoy Sean. But it wouldn't be worth the misery the next day.

She looked up at the sky. There were more stars than she had ever seen, and the Milky Way was also visible, a glorious spray of light. She had never in her life slept under the open sky, although she'd always wanted to. Now, as she watched, the heavens began unfurling the ethereal green ribbons of the aurora borealis. They performed a seductive dance against the backdrop of stars, like luminous snakes, teasing and tantalising.

One of the dogs made a little *roo-roo* sound. Alison smiled. She guessed it was husky-speak for "wow."

The pack made room for her as she spread her sleeping bag on the furs and lay back, enveloped in the musky scent. Zarya curled beside her, resting her head on Alison's leg. Alison watched the light show until it faded, leaving her to gaze at the unimaginable vastness of the universe. So many stars, so many galaxies, so many worlds. How different must the sky have looked when mammoths still roamed? Or dinosaurs? What might be out there, on planets orbiting those stars?

For the first time on the journey, she felt truly at peace. She fell asleep to the lullaby of doggy snores.

In the dark, something shifted beneath the snow.

-◦-

The temperature had dropped several degrees in the night and Alison woke shivering. Her face burned with the cold and when she exhaled, her breath made a sound like the tinkling of tiny bells. Seeing her startled expression, Olga smiled.

"Whisper of stars," she said. "That is what we call it." She demonstrated and Alison watched as a plume of breath crystallised before Olga's face.

It was a fascinating phenomenon, but the novelty soon wore off. The air was so cold it burned her throat. She hadn't imagined she'd actually need a balaclava, but she was relieved to have packed one. Even the soft wool burned as she pulled it down over her face.

Sean and Jeff were already up, dismantling their tent. Eric's tent was still zipped.

"Good morning," Alison said.

They laughed at her balaclava, even as their own breath turned to ice in the air.

"Yeah, yeah," she said, "at least my nose won't turn black from frostbite."

Sean shifted his feet in the snow before finally speaking. "Sorry about last night. You can have the tent tonight if—"

"No, it's fine, really. I had an amazing night. Every time I woke up I saw stars and northern lights. I felt like I was floating up there with them!"

Jeff shuddered. "That sounds like my kind of hell," he said.

"Agoraphobia?"

"No, I just like layers between me and the creepy-crawlies."

"Well, the only crawlies were the dogs and they were anything but creepy."

Sean moved close to her and made an exaggerated show of sniffing and then grimacing.

Alison laughed and aimed a mock punch at his face. "You're the real creepy-crawly!"

"Oh? I thought that was Eric."

And just like that, the playful mood was spoiled. Alison frowned and looked over at the still-sealed tent.

"Someone had better wake him up so we can get moving," she said. "And it's not going to be me."

"Fair enough," Sean said.

Alison and Jeff melted snow to make coffee and instant noodles for breakfast. Olga had her own food, which she ate after feeding the dogs. The animals ate greedily and noisily, then ran off into the trees, kicking up snow. Alison could hear them talking to each other as they explored. Their howls shattered the pristine stillness of the morning.

"Christ, are you all right?"

Alison jumped, but Jeff's question hadn't been aimed at her. Eric stood by the fire, and he looked awful.

"Yeah," he said with irritation. He hunched over the fire to pour some coffee, then drank it like a shot of tequila. "Didn't sleep much."

Alison had to restrain a smile, thinking of her magical night under the stars. She huffed out a breath to hear their whisper once more. The fragile tinkling had lessened as the morning sky brightened. It was hard to believe that the pale lemony sun was actually putting out heat, but her breath didn't lie. By the time breakfast was over, the stars were no longer whispering.

The cold was bone-chilling, but the snow was indeed melting. There were several places where Alison could see straight through to the ground. She closed her eyes for a few moments as she walked, trusting the crunch of snow to guide her. She imagined how the area must have looked millions of years ago, when dinosaurs ruled the earth. How many feet had stepped exactly where she was stepping now?

The trees grew denser as the group made their way into the forest. The tall pines were sheathed in snow, and they grew so tall and straight it was dizzying to peer up into them, like looking up from the bottom of a well. The dogsled was forced to slow, and the huskies strained against their harnesses, working harder without the momentum they generated on the open snow field.

"Are we there yet?" Sean asked.

His voice startled Alison out of her thoughts and she looked at her watch, surprised to see that the day was almost gone. Their trail of footprints seemed to go on forever. It was as if she'd slipped into a trance and sleepwalked here.

Eric stopped and checked their surroundings, presumably looking for landmarks. There were none that Alison could see, nothing to distinguish this area from any other bit of the snowy forest they'd come through.

"Yeah, this is it," Eric said.

"*What's* it?" Alison asked. "There's nothing here but trees and snow."

His eyes narrowed slightly. "This *forest* is it."

"This is where we dig?" Sean asked.

"Yeah."

"And you've found stuff here before?"

"Yeah."

Alison exchanged a glance with her brother. She could see that he was concerned too. Eric was acting very weird. Jeff was some distance away, taking pictures with his phone.

"Okay," Sean said, "what do we do now?"

"Now we dig."

"Now? It's already getting dark."

Eric turned away, mumbling as he went, something that sounded like "already serious."

Sean called after him. "Sorry—didn't catch that!"

But Eric didn't respond. He just continued on, eventually vanishing into the trees.

Sean looked at Alison and shrugged. She returned the gesture and went to help Olga unload the dogsled.

The huskies ran free once more, bounding through the snow. Zarya yipped at Alison, but when Alison went to pet her she darted away. The dog yipped again and looked off into the trees, then stared at the uncomprehending human.

"I don't know what you want," Alison said, "but if you're trying to tell me Eric's a dick, you're too late."

The light was fading fast. All Alison wanted to do was collapse on the furs and watch the northern lights again.

Sean and Jeff worked together to put up their tent, but Eric was struggling by himself, crouched in the snow and wrestling with tangled ropes. Alison decided to try and make peace. She still wasn't about to share the tent with him, but maybe she could lessen his hostility towards her by helping him set it up.

"Hey," she said. "Need a hand?"

He gave a little cry and lost his balance, but he caught himself before he could fall over. He glared up at her.

Baffled by his reaction, Alison took a step back. "Sorry. I didn't mean to startle you."

"You didn't," he spat, returning his attention to the ropes.

She took a deep breath. "I just thought you might need some help."

He seemed to consider her offer before looking over at Olga, scowling like a petulant child. "Aren't you sleeping with Brienne of Tarth?"

Alison glanced towards the dogsled, but if Olga had heard, she gave no sign. "You do realise," Alison said, "that's not exactly an insult."

"Whatever."

She shook her head in disbelief. "Fine," she said. "I tried. Good luck with the tent."

When she told Sean and Jeff about the encounter, they both looked disturbed. But they didn't want to risk his wrath either. An hour later, Eric still hadn't erected his tent, and he seemed to have given up. He didn't join them for dinner; he just burrowed inside the loose canvas.

"Something's wrong with him," Sean said. "He's been weird all day."

Jeff nodded. "We passed this tree where someone had carved their initials or something and when I tried to take a picture he practically knocked my phone out of my hands."

"I saw some carving last night too," Alison said.

"What if we're on someone's turf?" Jeff asked. "Like—other fossil hunters?" He glanced sheepishly at Alison. "Ali said she didn't trust him."

Yes, she thought, eyeing Sean pointedly, *I did*.

Sean jabbed a stick into the fire, stirring it and sending sparks spiralling up into the sky. He sighed. "We're here now. We don't need Eric to dig for fossils, and Olga can lead us home if . . ."

Jeff looked up as Sean trailed off. Alison waited, but the follow-up question never came.

The dogs were milling around, doing their husky-talk and howling. Above them, the aurora borealis began to dance, and Alison was once more transfixed. From the forest all around them came answering howls, deeper, richer and more primal. The song of wolves.

Jeff's eyes went wide and he edged closer to Sean.

Alison was surprised by her own reaction. She felt simultaneously connected and detached, as though she *ought* to be frightened, but wasn't. The echoing howls were beautiful and strange. They silenced the huskies, who froze, their silhouetted heads lifted high, ears pricked. Two of them chuffed softly and another issued sharp answering barks. A warning? An invitation?

Alison looked for Zarya, but she couldn't make out the red husky in the dark. Moonlight revealed the white one but the others seemed to blur into a single creature with multiple heads and myriad gleaming eyes. Olga murmured to them in Russian, but the dogs stayed alert, watchful and curious.

"Olga doesn't seem worried. And she'd let us know if we were in danger." She got to her feet and stretched. "Well, goodnight."

"You sure you're okay out in the open again?" Sean asked. "I still feel bad about last night."

"I'm fine. I want to watch the aurora again."

Sean and Jeff both looked up at the sky. "Yeah, it's cool, isn't it?"

Alison wasn't sure which one of them had spoken, but she felt the sudden urge to get away. Earlier she'd seen Jeff trying to take a selfie with the northern lights behind him, and—truth be told—no, she hadn't forgiven Sean for the previous night. They were here for the same reason as Eric—to find something ancient and magnificent, and make money off it. But no one else seemed to appreciate the wonder of their surroundings. An overwhelming feeling of disgust made her lip curl and she turned her back on them and went to join Olga on the furs.

Zarya found Alison in the darkness, licking her balaclava-covered face and then curling up against her, whining softly.

She peeled off her gloves to stroke the dog's thick fur, marvelling that the animals had ever made her nervous. Above them the sky surged and rippled, an ocean of light and colour. Howling emanated from the forest in all directions, and sometimes the huskies answered back. Zarya stayed silent, but Alison could feel her restlessness. The only sound from her was the tinkle of her breath in the deepening cold.

Alison drifted to sleep and her dreams took a visionary turn. The green ribbons flickered above, branching like lightning, filling the sky. At times they seemed to form words, but the characters were from an unknown language. Still, she felt an urge to understand. Her mind ached with the desire to know.

The light continued to dance and tease, waving like the fingers of a beckoning hand. The giant hand descended to the ground, lying open and inviting. Alison padded through the snow to reach it, only to realise that it had moved farther away. She closed the distance again, but the hand was once more out of reach. Zarya peered up at her with an inquisitive expression, her breath pluming in the air with a brittle sound. The whisper of stars. Alison reached out to capture the dog's breath. A scattering of crystals lay on her palm.

From all around her came other voices, howls and whispers, the song of eternity. She was part of it, but such a tiny part as to be insignificant. None of what she did here mattered. Nature didn't care how she felt, whether she was adoring or irreverent. Her existence would never even be noticed, never remembered. Only the stars mattered.

She could feel those stars now, pressing into her eyes. The cold jagged shards tore at her lids, forcing them open. They gouged channels down her face, and the streaming blood burned like acid. Tears, she realised. The dream had made her cry and the pain had made her lucid. She knew she was dreaming and she could control what was happening. All she had to do was wake up.

She opened her eyes, expecting to see the aurora. Instead there was only blackness. Profound, endless blackness. With a jolt she sat up, clawing at her face. But she could feel nothing, nothing at all. Where was her face?

Calm down, she told herself. *Don't panic.*

She'd been crying in her sleep and tears had frozen on her face, sealing her eyes behind ice.

"Zarya?" There was no answer to her call, and when she reached out into the darkness, she couldn't feel the presence of another living thing. Even so, she was sure she wasn't alone. Something else was out there.

Her heart was racing, but she forced herself to breathe slowly. It was the layers. She couldn't feel anything through them. She hadn't even been able to pet the dog without taking off her gloves.

Gloves. The realisation made her stomach plunge. Had she fallen asleep without them? Her hands were completely numb. Despite her attempts to stay calm, her breath came in short, quick bursts. The whisper now sounded like something else. It sounded like laughter.

With a cry she stumbled to her feet, waving her arms like a drowning swimmer. "Hey! Sean, Jeff, I need help! Olga?"

No answer came.

"Wake up! Someone help me!"

She dropped to her knees and reached out in the darkness, hoping Zarya at least would respond to her distress. But when she couldn't find the dog, she realised she was alone. Utterly alone, and utterly helpless. She pictured herself stranded at the top of a narrow peak, the threat of a bottomless plunge surrounding her on all sides.

Think.

She needed to see. That was the most important thing. Panic and terror were like wolves chasing the rabbit of her mind, but she finally managed to focus. Unless she had walked through the snow in her sleep, she should still be on the fur pallet. She touched the ground beneath her. While there was no sensation in her hands, she met clear resistance. She pressed against it as she inched away. Finally, the resistance gave way and she heard the crunch of snow. Relief flooded her whole body and she edged back, feeling her way across the furs.

"Olga? Wake up!"

It was easier to concentrate in silence, so she stopped calling out. Soon she met more resistance, a hard shape lying on the furs. She pushed against it repeatedly, willing it to be Olga, fast asleep. But the shape did not respond.

Alison visualised herself grabbing Olga and shaking her awake, and she hoped her hands were doing just that. There was no movement, only a thick, wet squelching sound. It was then that she noticed the smell. Hot, ripe. Unmistakable.

Alison gave a little cry, but she swallowed her revulsion as she lowered her head to the source of heat. She couldn't help but be drawn to it and without even thinking, she plunged her face and hands into the wetness. The horror wasn't enough to distract her from the most disturbing fact—that if the blood was still warm . . .

Stop it!

She forced herself to focus on the single goal of melting the ice that was blinding her. Once she could see, she could solve the next problem.

Her hands began to tingle and burn, and flexing her fingers was agony. But at least she could feel. The pain was welcome after the numbness. She reached up to her eyes, picking at the ice there. She peeled away the blood-soaked balaclava, dislodging the frozen crust that had formed over her face.

Her eyes felt scalded, and at first all she could see were blurs. But the vicious red smear before her was not something she wanted to see in perfect clarity. Tears distorted her vision further and she blinked them away. No grief, not now. Survival was everything.

At last her hands swam into focus before her, covered in scarlet gore. She cleaned them in the snow and gasped when she saw her blackened fingertips. She found her gloves and pulled them back on, for all the good they would do her now.

She got unsteadily to her feet. The lights were still dancing in the sky, and the moonlight revealed even more. All around her lay the bodies of dogs, with trails of blood leading off into the forest. Tufts of rusty red fur were scattered nearby. Zarya.

Alison scrubbed away icy tears that threatened to turn her eyes to glass. Nearby, Olga's body was in pieces. Alison bit back a scream as she ran to her brother's tent, only to stop short when she saw it. The tent had been ripped apart, and her mind recoiled at the initial thought that what lay scattered around it were lumps of hamburger meat. A head lay on its side, but the eyes that might have stared at her had been torn out. Other parts lay strewn in the snow, too many to belong to a single person. She stumbled away, fighting the urge to be sick.

At the edge of the trees lay another body. Eric. And somehow Alison knew that the dark lump staining the snow beside him was a heart.

The wolves were no longer howling. They had had their fill.

Long moments passed as Alison tried to process the horror, and failed. Numbness consumed her and she stood staring around her at the mutilation. She knew she had to get away, but she couldn't seem to make herself move. She had no idea where they even were, let alone how to get back.

She thought of Zarya, how she'd been acting in the forest. Had the dog known what was out there? Had she been trying to get Alison away? Worst of all, had Zarya died protecting her?

Fury blazed in her mind, shocking her with its vehemence. This was all Sean's fault. Reckless Sean, who believed nothing bad could ever happen to him. She had been so disgusted with him the night before, with both him and Jeff, vacuously posing in front of the awe-inspiring beauty of the arctic night sky. Oh, Eric had found the perfect pair to tempt out here with his ideas of finding buried treasure and getting rich off the bones of creatures even the native Siberians couldn't find. Such arrogance.

The sky was just beginning to lighten, and her breath chimed in the icy air, like a voice whispering secrets to her. Everyone else was dead, and yet she didn't feel alone. There was something oppressive in the air, the sense of a presence. A chill came over her as she peered into the depths of the forest. She felt watched.

Suddenly it came to her—what Eric had said the night before: *They can already see us.*

He'd known something was out here and he'd deliberately led them to it. But he must have disappointed his masters because now he was just meat like the others.

Alison batted away the crystalline cloud of her breath as the whispers grew insidious.

Daylight was breaking through the wispy clouds, turning the black bloodstains into gleaming pools of scarlet ice. The trees surrounded the scene, silent sentinels. Watchful, impassive.

Alison's skin burned and her breath came in quick, sharp bursts, each exhalation like shattered glass. She was soaked to the skin with blood, drowning in it. No, she realised, not blood. Sweat. She was burning up.

Frantically, she tore at her clothing, stripping off layer after layer. Her feet blazed as if she'd stood in a fire and she jabbed at the laces with a tent peg, carving her way down to her bare feet. When she had torn or cut away every stitch of clothing, she stumbled off naked into the snow, trailing her own blood as she went.

She felt slick mud against her feet. The ground was rising beneath her, pushing up through the blanket of snow. It was hard to walk on the slimy, viscous surface. It bulged and stretched around her, a spheroid lake of glutinous white. Thin red tributaries spread out in all directions from a central dark circle. Alison felt not just watched, but *seen*.

The ground cracked and rumbled and far off in the distance she saw what looked like a huge eye peering up through the snow. Impossible. Sean's eyes had been torn out. Or Jeff's. She hadn't been able to identify what was left. But it was their own fault. Eric may have led them here, but she was the one who was wanted. She was the one who understood the sky. The stars and the lights and the whispers. They saw her now. They had kept her because she heard their voice. She had answered their call.

From the top of the domed surface she could see other orbs. One by one they blinked open in the snow, incomprehensibly huge. The pupil of each one swivelled, searching. When they were all staring at her, the eyes within her flesh began to open.

HONORABLE MENTIONS

Addison, Linda D. "Mud," *Don't Turn Out the Lights.*

Bailey, Dale "Das Gesicht," *Final Cuts.*

Barrett, E. C. "We Aren't Violent People," Bourbon Penn #20.

Barron, Laird "Ode to Joad the Toad," *Miscreations.*

Burke, Kealan Patrick "I Used to Live Here," *A Winter's Tale.*

Day, Victoria "The Mosaic Maze," *The Ghosts & Scholars Book of Mazes.*

Duffy, Steve "White Noise in a White Room," Weird Horror, Issue 1, Fall.

Evenson, Brian "The Cabin," Come Join Us By the Fire, Season 2.

Ferrell, Keith "Cronenberg Concerto," *It Came From the Multiplex.*

Files, Gemma "Carmagnole," *The Willows: Complete Anthology.*

Hand, Elizabeth "The Owl Count," Grendel's Kin, Conjunctions 74.

Ho, Millie "A Moonlit Savagery," Nightmare 91, April.

Hodge, Brian "Insanity Among the Penguins," *Final Cuts.*

Houser, Chip "Smilers," Bourbon Penn #20.

Howell, A. P. "5:37," Translunar Travelers Lounge Issue 3, August.

Iglesias, Gabino "The Song of the Lady Rose," Come Join Us By the Fire
Season 2.

Jennings, Kathleen *Flyaway*, (novella) Tor.com.

Jones, Stephen Graham "Wait for Night," Tor.com, September 2.

Jones, Stephen Graham *Night of the Mannequins* (novella), Tor.com.

Kadrey, Richard "Razor Pig," *Tales of Dark Fantasy 3.*

Kiernan, Caitlín R. "Cherry Street Tango, Sweatbox Waltz," *Tales of Dark Fantasy 3.*

Kilworth, Garry "Lirpaloof Island," *The Alchemy Book of Horrors #2*.

Kornher-Stace, Nicole "Getaway," Uncanny 33.

Langan, John "Altered Beast, Altered Me," (novella) *Final Cuts*.

Littlewood, Alison "Swanskin," *After Sundown*.

Malerman, Josh "One Last Transformation," *Miscreations*.

Malik, Usman T. "City of Red Midnight: A Hikayat" Tor.com, October 21.

Manzetti, Alessandro "From Hell," (poem) *Whitechapel Rhapsody*.

Marr, Melissa "Of Roses and Kings," Tor.com, April 27

Mason, Rena "To the Marrow," Weird Tales 364.

Mason, Rena "To the Marrow," Weird Tales 364.

Moraine, Sunny "If Living is Seeing I'm Holding My Breath," Come Join Us by the Fire Season 2.

Nix, Garth "Many Mouths to Make a Meal," *Final Cuts*.

Parenti, Dino "Blue Was Her Favorite Color," *Arterial Bloom*.

Parker, Michael "Las Llorasangres," Penumbra No.#1.

Rebecca, Parfitt "Sometimes They Come Late," New Gothic Review #2.

Richardson, Endria Isa "The Black Menagerie," Fiyah #15.

Rickert, M. "The Little Witch," Tor.com Tor.com October 28.

Rogers, Ian "Go Fish," Tor.com, April 15.

Van Samson, Steve "No God But Hunger," *Slay: Stories of the Vampire Noire*.

Volk, Stephen "The Naughty Step," *After Sundown*.

Wagner, Wendy N. "The Smell of Night in the Basement, PseudoPod 730.

Ward, C. E. "Real Estate," *The Ghosts & Scholars Book of Mazes*.

Watson, D. A. "Restless Natives," *Footsteps in the Dark*.

ABOUT THE AUTHORS

Nathan Ballingrud is the author of *North American Lake Monsters* (basis for the series *Monsterland*) and *Wounds: Six Stories from the Border of Hell*. His first novel, *The Strange*, will be published in 2022.

Simon Bestwick lives on the Wirral and dreams of moving to Wales and owning a dog. He is the author of six novels, four full-length short story collections and has been four times shortlisted for the British Fantasy Award. He is married to long-suffering fellow author Cate Gardner, and still hasn't kicked his addictions to Pepsi Max, semicolons, or Irn Bru Xtra. His latest books are the novellas *Roth-Steyr* and *A Different Kind of Light*, and the mini-collection *Nine Ghosts*, all published by Black Shuck Books, and he posts new fiction every month at www.patreon.com/SimonBestwick.

Steve Duffy lives and works in North Wales. He's a winner of the Shirley Jackson Award for Best Novelette of 2015, and of the International Horror Guild's award for Best Short Story, 2000. His most recent collection of weird fiction, *Finding Yourself in the Dark*, was published in 2021 by Sarob Press.

Gemma Files was born in England and raised in Toronto, Canada, and has been a journalist, teacher, film critic, and an award-winning horror author for almost thirty years. She has published four novels, a story-cycle, three collections of short fiction, and three collections of speculative poetry; her most recent novel, *Experimental Film*, won both the 2015 Shirley Jackson

Award for Best Novel and the 2016 Sunburst Award for Best Novel (Adult Category). Her fourth collection, *In That Endlessness, Our End*, has recently been published; her next, *Dark Is Better*, will be published by Trepidatio in 2022.

Richard Gavin's work explores the realm where horror and the sacred converge. To date, he has authored six volumes of nightmarish fiction, including *grotesquerie* from Undertow Publications and several books of Gothic esotericism. He lives in Ontario, Canada. You can find more information about him at www.richardgavin.net.

Elana Gomel was born in a country that no longer exists and has lived in several others that may, or may not, be on the road to extinction. She is an academic with a long list of publications, specializing in science fiction, Victorian literature, and serial killers. She is also a fiction writer who has published more than eighty short stories, several novellas, and three novels: *A Tale of Three Cities*, *The Hungry Ones*, and *The Cryptids*. Her story "Where the Streets Have No Name" was the winner of the 2020 Gravity Award.

Christopher Harman currently lives in Preston, Lancashire, in the UK. His work has been published in magazines including *Ghosts and Scholars*, *All Hallows*, and *Supernatural Tales*, and in the anthologies *Acquainted with the Night*, *Shades of Darkness*, *Strange Tales*, *Unfit for Eden*, *Rustblind and Silverbright*, *Shadows and Tall Trees*, the *Terror Tales* series edited by Paul Finch, and three previous *Ghosts and Scholars* books published by Sarob Press. Some of his fiction is collected in *The Heaven Tree and Other Stories*.

Maria Haskins is a Swedish-Canadian writer, reader, and reviewer of speculative fiction. She grew up in Sweden and debuted as a writer there, but currently lives outside Vancouver with a husband, two kids, a snake, several noisy birds, and a very large black dog. Her work has appeared in *Black Static*, *Fireside*, *Beneath Ceaseless Skies*, *Flash Fiction Online*, *Mythic Delirium*, *Shimmer*, *Cast of Wonders*, and elsewhere. Her short story collection *Six Dreams About the Train* is forthcoming in 2021. Find out more on her website, www.mariahaskins.com, or follow her on Twitter @mariahaskins.

Sam Hicks lives in Deptford, south east London. Her fiction has appeared in various anthologies, including *The Fiends in the Furrows, Nightscript, Dark Lane, Vastarien, and The Best Horror of the Year Volumes Eleven* and *Twelve*.

Andrew Humphrey is the author of two collections of short stories, both published by Elastic Press. *Open the Box* appeared in 2002 and *Other Voices*, which was one of the winners of the inaugural East Anglian Book Award, in 2008. His debut novel, *Alison*, was published in 2008. His stories have appeared in magazines such as *The Third Alternative, Black Static, Crimewave, Bare Bone*, and *Midnight Street*. He lives and works in Norwich and is currently working on a third short story collection.

Tom Johnstone is the author of the collection *Last Stop Wellsbourne*, and two novellas, *The Monsters are Due in Madison Square Garden* and *Star Spangled Knuckle Duster*. His stories have also appeared in such publications as *A Ghosts and Scholars Book of Folk Horror, Black Static, Best Horror of the Year Volume Eight, Terror Tales of the Home Counties, Nightscript VI*, and *Body Shocks*. More information at www.tomjohnstone.wordpress.com.

Stephen Graham Jones is the author of twenty-five or so novels and collections, and there's some novellas and comic books in there as well. Most recent are *The Only Good Indians* and *Night of the Mannequins*. His novel *My Heart is a Chainsaw* was published in August. Stephen lives and teaches in Boulder, Colorado.

Jack Lothian is a screenwriter for film and television and worked as showrunner on the HBO Cinemax series *Strike Back*. His short fiction has appeared in a number of publications, including *The Best Horror of the Year Volume Twelve, Weirdbook, The New Flesh: A Literary Tribute to David Cronenberg, The Fiends In The Furrows II*, and the Necronomicon Memorial Book. His graphic novel *Tomorrow*, illustrated by Garry Mac, was nominated for a 2018 British Fantasy Award.

Alessandro Manzetti is a two-time Bram Stoker Award-winning author of horror fiction and dark poetry whose work has been published extensively in

Italian and English, including novels, short and long fiction, poetry, graphic novels, and collections. Among his English publications are the novels *Shanti* and *Naraka*, the novella *The Keeper of Chernobyl*, the collections *The Radioactive Bride* and *The Garden of Delight*, the poetry collections *Whitechapel Rhapsody*, *The Place of Broken Things* (with Linda D. Addison), and *Eden Underground*. His stories and poems have appeared in Italian, USA, UK, Australian, Polish, and Russian magazines. www.battiago.com.

J. A. W. McCarthy is the author of the collection *Sometimes We're Cruel and Other Stories*, published August 2021 by Cemetery Gates Media. Her short fiction has appeared in numerous publications, including *Vastarien*, *LampLight*, *Apparition Lit*, *Places We Fear to Tread*, *Tales to Terrify*, and *Nightscript V*. She lives with her husband and assistant cats in the Pacific Northwest, where she gets most of her ideas late at night, while she's trying to sleep. You can call her Jen on Twitter and Instagram @JAWMcCarthy, and find out more at www.jawmccarthy.com.

Gary McMahon is the author of several novels, novellas, and short story collections. His latest books are the novella *Glorious Beasts* and the collection *Some Bruising May Occur*. His fiction is often regarded as bleak, but he likes to think that it also has a lot of heart. As well as writing, he trains in Shotokan karate, currently holding a first dan black belt. Gary lives in West Yorkshire with his wife, his teenage son, and two cats that are quite, quite mad.

Thana Niveau is a horror and science fiction writer. Originally from the United States, she now lives in the UK, in a Victorian seaside town between Bristol and Wales. She is the author of the short story collections *Octoberland*, *Unquiet Waters*, and *From Hell to Eternity*, as well as the novel *House of Frozen Screams*. She shares her life with fellow writer John Llewellyn Probert, in a crumbling gothic tower filled with arcane books and curiosities. And toy dinosaurs.

In 2020, **Sarah Pinsker**'s first novel, *A Song For A New Day*, won the Nebula Award, and her collection *Sooner or Later Everything Falls Into the Sea* won the Philip K. Dick Award. Her stories have won the Nebula and Sturgeon

Awards, and have been finalists for the Hugo, Locus, Eugie Foster, and World Fantasy Awards. Her second novel, *We Are Satellites*, was published in May 2021. She was born in New York and has lived all over the US and Canada, but currently lives with her wife and terrier in Baltimore. Find her @ sarahpinsker in most places hospitable to Sarah Pinskers.

Jason Sanford is a three-time finalist for the Nebula Award who has published dozens of stories in *Asimov's Science Fiction, Interzone, Beneath Ceaseless Skies*, and *Fireside Magazine* along with appearances in multiple "year's best" anthologies along with *The New Voices of Science Fiction*. His first novel *Plague Birds* will be published in late 2021 by Apex Books. Born and raised in the American South, Jason currently works in the media industry in the Midwestern United States. His previous experience includes work as an archaeologist and as a Peace Corps Volunteer. His website is www.jasonsanford.com.

Michael Marshall Smith is a novelist and screenwriter who has published nearly a hundred short stories, and five novels. He is the only author to have won the British Fantasy Award for Best Short Fiction four times, and 2020 saw a *Best Of Michael Marshall Smith* collection. Writing as Michael Marshall he has written seven internationally bestselling conspiracy thrillers. Now additionally writing as Michael Rutger, in 2018 he published the adventure thriller *The Anomaly* and its sequel, *The Possession*, in 2019. He is also Creative Consultant to Neil Gaiman's production company in Los Angeles. He lives in Santa Cruz, California, with his wife, son, and cats.
For more information, check out: www.michaelmarshallsmith.com.

David Surface lives and writes in the Hudson Highlands of New York. His stories have been published in *Shadows & Tall Trees, Supernatural Tales, Nightscript, Phantom Drift, The Tenth Black Book of Horror, Darkest Minds, Ghost Highways, Twisted Book of Shadows, Crooked Houses: Tales of Cursed and Haunted Dwellings*, and other venues. A novel co-authored with Julia Rust, *Angel Falls*, will be published by Haverhill House Publications in 2022. Some of his stories have been collected in *Terrible Things*. You can visit him at www.davidsurface.net.

Pete W. Sutton is a writer and editor. His first book—*A Tiding of Magpies*—was shortlisted for the British Fantasy Awards in 2017 for Best Collection. He is also the author of the novels *Sick City Syndrome* and *Seven Deadly Swords*. He has edited a number of anthologies, most recently *Forgotten Sidekicks*, in 2020. His next book, *The Museum for Forgetting*, will be published by Grimbold Books in 2021.

Stephen Volk created BBCTV's notorious "Halloween hoax" *Ghostwatch* and the paranormal drama series *Afterlife*. His many other screenplays include *The Awakening* (2011) and *Gothic* starring Natasha Richardson as Mary Shelley. He is a two-time British Fantasy Award winner, and the author of three collections: *Dark Corners, Monsters in the Heart*, and *The Parts We Play*. *The Dark Masters Trilogy* features Peter Cushing, Alfred Hitchcock and Dennis Wheatley, while his latest book, *Under a Raven's Wing*, sees Sherlock Holmes and Poe's detective Dupin investigating bizarre crimes in 1870s Paris. www.stephenvolk.net.

Catriona Ward was born in Washington, DC, and grew up in the US, Kenya, Madagascar, Yemen, and Morocco. She studied English at Oxford and took the University of East Anglia Creative Writing Masters. Her latest gothic thriller, *The Last House on Needless Street,* was recently published by Tor Nightfire. Ward's second novel *Little Eve* won the 2019 Shirley Jackson Award and the August Derleth Prize. Her debut *Rawblood* won the 2016 August Derleth, making her the only woman to have won the prize twice. She lives in London and Devon.

A. C. Wise's short fiction has appeared in *Uncanny, Clarkesworld*, and *Apex*, among other publications. Her work has won the Sunburst Award for Excellence in Canadian Literature of the Fantastic, as well as twice more being a finalist for the Sunburst, twice being a finalist for the Nebula Award, and being a finalist for the Lambda Literary Award. Her debut novel, *Wendy, Darling*, was published by Titan Books this past June, and a new short story collection, *The Ghost Sequences*, is forthcoming from Undertow Books in Fall 2021.

ACKNOWLEDGMENT OF COPYRIGHT

ABOUT THE EDITOR

Ellen Datlow has been editing science fiction, fantasy, and horror short fiction for forty years as fiction editor of *OMNI* magazine and editor of *Event Horizon* and SCIFICTION. She currently acquires short stories and novellas for Tor.com. In addition, she has edited about one hundred science fiction, fantasy, and horror anthologies, including the annual *The Best Horror of the Year* series, *The Doll Collection*, *Mad Hatters and March Hares*, *The Devil and the Deep: Horror Stories of the Sea*, *Echoes: The Saga Anthology of Ghost Stories*, *Final Cuts: New Tales of Hollywood Horror and Other Spectacles*, *Body Shocks: Extreme Tales of Body Horror*, and *When Things Get Dark: Stories Inspired by Shirley Jackson*.

She's won multiple World Fantasy Awards, Locus Awards, Hugo Awards, Bram Stoker Awards, International Horror Guild Awards, Shirley Jackson Awards, and the 2012 Il Posto Nero Black Spot Award for Excellence as Best Foreign Editor. Datlow was named recipient of the 2007 Karl Edward Wagner Award, given at the British Fantasy Convention for "outstanding contribution to the genre," was honored with the Life Achievement Award by the Horror Writers Association, in acknowledgment of superior achievement over an entire career, and honored with the World Fantasy Life Achievement Award at the 2014 World Fantasy Convention.

She lives in New York and co-hosts the monthly Fantastic Fiction Reading Series at KGB Bar. More information can be found at www.datlow.com, on Facebook, and on Twitter @EllenDatlow. She's owned by two cats.